TRAPPED

There was an instant in which Favian saw his enemy's strategy in all its cunning, cautious glory, and then he was turning forward and barking at the top of his lungs, "Everyone lie down! Pass the word to lie down right on deck!"

He saw the enemy guns in their ports, the white faces of gun captains peering over their pieces. *Tenedos* could stay there forever. If Favian turned to fight, he would no longer be running: *Endymion* would soon arrive, and that would be the end.

Tenedos's broadside exploded into smoke, flame, and iron; the shot came screaming overhead. . . .

Other books in the series

THE PRIVATEER
THE YANKEE
THE RAIDER

THE MACEDONIAN

Jon Williams

A DELL BOOK

Published by
Dell Publishing Co., Inc.
1 Dag Hammarskjold Plaza
New York, New York 10017

Copyright © 1984 by Jon Williams

All rights reserved. No part of this book may be reproduced
or transmitted in any form or by any means, electronic or
mechanical, including photocopying, recording, or by any
information storage and retrieval system, without the written
permission of the Publisher, except where permitted by law.

Dell ® TM 681510, Dell Publishing Co., Inc.

ISBN: 0-440-15411-1

Printed in the United States of America
First printing—February 1984

DD

1

The room's design was unmistakably nautical; there was not a straight line in it, from the perfect arching curve over the stern windows to the immaculate grace of the inward-leaning bulwark—even the commodore's table was curved, rounded on the ends, set up on rounded, flowingly carved legs. The gunports were triced up; the three stern windows were open, revealing the green Jersey shore on the horizon, and windsails were set up atop the open skylights. A fitful Atlantic breeze, drifting through these apertures, provided a thankful relief against the New York early summer, occasionally stirring the multitude of papers set up on the commodore's table and cooling the sweat of the assembled captains in their blue and gold. They, defying the heat in their full-dress coats and massive epaulets, proceeded with the business at hand—for the business was serious, the court-martial of a brother officer for the loss of his command.

The officer being judged was Captain Favian Markham, of Portsmouth, New Hampshire, and late of the *Experiment* brig—both man and brig famous for what had become known as Markham's Raid, a circumnavigation of the British isles in which forty-odd enemy ships were set ablaze, famous also for the destruction of the enemy brig *Teaser* in a yardarm-to-yardarm fight the summer before, and famous as well for the subject at hand, the wreck of the brig on a Maine sandbank last autumn, with a loss of her first lieutenant, her pilot, and all but twenty-three of the eighty-odd men who had been aboard.

It was June of 1814, and the nation was at war; assembling for the purposes of a court-martial the minimum number of five captains, each busy with his own wartime affairs, had taken months. During that time the accused Favian Markham had been fortunate not to have been removed entirely from duty; he'd spent the months in New London, under nominal arrest and unable to wear his sword, supervising the building of what—had the misfortune in Maine been avoided—would have certainly been his new command, the twenty-two gun ship-sloop *Shark*, due for completion by the first of the year. But the five captains had at length been assembled, and for the last hot, humid week had been assembled in the commodore's cabin of the frigate *President*, praying for a cool breeze and sifting the evidence.

The American service was small, and the accused captain knew most of the men who would decide his fate. The president of the court, Commodore John Rodgers, was a crusty veteran, at forty-three years of age something of an old man in this young service, the former captain of the *President*, unlucky (it seemed) in war and now en route to take command of the defenses of Baltimore. Favian had known him early in the war, when Favian had been first lieutenant on the *United States* and Rodgers, commanding a squadron that had included *United States*, *President*, *Congress*, and *Argus*, had groped his way across the Atlantic in search of a Jamaica convoy that had proved to have had too great a start on them; Rodgers had then turned around and come home, the voyage showing no profit. Rodgers, Favian knew, was a short-tempered, blustering man, vain and snappish. The heat and lengthy testimony had shortened his fuse, and he barked left and right, sending witnesses and clerks flying; but as to how this would affect his verdict Favian could form no conclusion.

Commodore Rodgers's decision to turn away from the English Channel, that first summer of the war, had precipitated an explosion on the part of the man sitting on Rodgers's immediate right: Commodore Stephen Decatur, new captain of the *President* and commander of the New York defenses, a man for whom the word *audacity* had surely been coined, the greatest hero of the young navy, and the model to every ambitious junior. Favian had reason to suppose Decatur would favor the accused: Favian had been considered a protégé of Decatur's ever since he had volunteered, back in '04, for the ketch *Intrepid* that had sailed into Tripoli harbor under Decatur's command and burned the captured *Philadelphia*. The two had been linked ever since. Favian had fought alongside Decatur in Preble's bombardments of Tripoli, leaping in hand-to-hand combat from boat to boat; he had served in Decatur's gunboat squadron on the Delaware between wars; he had been Decatur's first choice for executive officer of the *United States*, the ship that two years before had taken the *Macedonian*, turning her into a mastless hulk in the process, rerigged her in mid-Atlantic, and sailed her home to a jubilant American welcome.

Decatur had spent the trial leaning back in his chair, his black eyes half-closed, a grim smile often visible through the close-cropped, curly black beard. The beard, recently grown, gave Decatur a faintly piratical appearance, somehow subverting the clean-shaven, gold-laced dignity of the court, as he must have known it would—Stephen Decatur had always known how to stand out in a crowd.

Sitting on Decatur's right was another old shipmate, Captain Charles Stewart, another magic name connected with the Mediterranean and Tripoli, another of the generation of officers known as "Preble's boys." The red-haired Irishman was a friend, pressed onto the court-martial while traveling to Boston in order to take command of the *Constitution*. Stewart, oddly enough, had once commanded the vessel Favian had wrecked; back in the year 1800 he'd captured the *Deux Amis*, as well as the *Diana* commanded by Hyacinthe Rigaud, a Haitian pirate known as the King of the Picaroons. Favian knew that, despite the amused, somewhat impudent way in which Stewart chose to regard the world, he was unquestionably one of the most dangerous men in the navy, and possibly the most intelligent.

On Rodgers's immediate left was a man Favian did not know well, Captain Jacob Jones; even though Jones was currently stationed in New London, Favian had not seen him often, as Jones seemed to spend most of his time in transit from one place to another, inspecting the condition of the squadrons on the Great Lakes and on Champlain, writing memoranda to Washington on the construction of the steam battery in New York. . . . Jones, even though he had not been to sea in a year, was a very busy man.

Jones was a long-nosed man of forty-six, which made him older than anyone else on the court, older even than Rodgers; he had practiced medicine and law before entering the navy at the very advanced age of thirty-one. He had served in the Mediterranean but Favian had not known him there, for Jones had been on the *Philadelphia* when it was captured; he'd spent most of the war in a Moorish jail. At the opening of the current war he'd commanded the *Wasp* sloop in her celebrated action with the crack brig-sloop *Frolic*, which he had shot to pieces in about twenty minutes, killing or wounding ninety of her 107-man crew.

In one of the coincidences of which war is so fond, *Wasp* had that very afternoon been captured by the British *Poictiers*, a seventy-four-gun liner that could have turned her into driftwood with a single broadside, and which, due to battle damage, she could not escape.

Despite their lack of acquaintance, Favian was well aware of the ties that bound him to Jones: there was the *Philadelphia*, which Jones had helped to surrender and which Favian had helped to burn; there was the very neatness of the *Wasp-Frolic* action, imitated by Favian's own fight with the *Teaser*. More importantly there was the *Macedonian*, which Decatur and Favian had captured, and which Jones now commanded. *Macedonian* currently sat on the Thames river mud at New London, bereft of its crew, which had been transferred to Isaac Chauncey's command on Lake Ontario. *Macedonian* would not be sailing anywhere soon, and so Jones, with little to do but run errands for the secretary of the navy, had been pressed onto the court-martial board.

The only man on the board of captains with whom Favian was not acquainted at all sat on Jones's left; he was Commodore Lewis, a thin, beak-nosed Tartar of a man subject to temper and indigestion. He had spent the war in command of the New York flotilla of gunboats, which could scarcely have improved his disposition—while every other man present had been given his chance for glory and prize money, Lewis had spent his thankless hours rowing over the waters of New York harbor and Long Island Sound, hoping that a sudden calm might strand an enemy merchantman within reach. Apparently a few such merchantmen *had* been so stranded, and the prize money might have provided some comfort; a few months ago there had been a neat action with the frigate *Maidstone*, in which two score of American coasters, covered by the gunboats, had escaped capture; but if this feat had granted Lewis any relief from his discontent, it was impossible to tell. Lewis, like Rodgers, had continued to snap out at every witness, at the clerk, at the deputy judge advocate, at the marine guards. Favian could not help but conclude that the man would oppose acquittal; he was so obviously opposed to everything else.

Such were the men who were to judge Favian's conduct; such was the complex network of friendships, rivalries, envies, duties, scars, acquaintances, comradeships that bound them together in service to the navy. Six of the navy's twenty active captains—over one-quarter of the senior officers currently on service—were gathered in the commodore's cabin of the *President*, participating in the court-martial of one of their number. No wonder it had taken so long to assemble them. If the British somehow managed to enter New York harbor and cut out the *President*, it would be a crippling blow. The room glittered with gold lace, epaulets, and the decorated hilts of presentation swords, and every man on the court-martial but Jones and Stewart was wearing the silver stars of a commodore on his shoulder straps.

There was something odd that happened to men like these, Favian thought, when assembled in full uniform and in one another's presence, when they were made so aware of their own power and privilege. The loyalties and friendships somehow grew less clear; or perhaps they were submerged beneath the one crucial loyalty, to the navy. Considerations of friendship would have little place, Favian knew, once the navy and the navy's good demanded a sacrifice. Stephen Decatur and John Rodgers had been friends with James Barron, but they had voted against him after the affair with the *Leopard*, knowing the friendship would end in bitterness—and so it had.

When Favian faced these five in their gilt-edged lapels and epaulets, he knew he was not facing a board composed chiefly of old friends and acquaintances, but facing rather the navy incarnate. The loyalties here ran to the navy for which they had all risked their lives; though each would use his private knowledge of Favian to reach their judgments—it was unfair, he supposed, that all these interweaving webs of friendship should be so used, but unfair in what sense? It was unfair, Favian supposed, that each might be prejudiced by previous acquaintance; but Favian himself was inclined to think the other way, that it was manifestly unfair of the navy to use his friends and acquaintances' knowledge of his character for the navy's iron purposes. Yet he was himself a navy man, he supposed, by habit and training if not inclination, and he understood the necessity—but that did not end the resentment.

Despite having an understandable interest in the trial's outcome, Favian found his attention wandering frequently, and he suspected that of the men in the room only the clerk, who had to write everything down, was paying proper attention. Lord, this was a tedious business! First the paperwork—for a brig that had been lost with its log and every record it contained, there was an almighty great deal of it: a copy of the report of the surveyors who had found *Experiment* sound and seaworthy when it had been refloated in 1812, Favian's reports finding her ready for sea and pronouncing himself satisfied with her equipment, a copy of Favian's official report of Markham's Raid, together with an itemized list of the damage suffered during the fight with the *Teaser* ("Item: one carronade slide, 18lb, cracked by glancing roundshot, gun itself undamaged.") and Favian's official comment that, with some minor repairs, some knotting and splicing and patching of torn sails, *Experiment* would be ready for sea.

The deputy judge advocate—in effect the prosecutor—a short, pugnacious civilian attorney named Robinson, said to be a particular protégé of Aaron Burr, had tried to make the most of this. He had leaped to his feet, and with a flowery address that would have sent an entire roistering Irish wake to sleep, pointed out that the weight of the written evidence produced thus far showed that *Experiment* had not foundered from any fault in its construction, but rather from another cause. "Error on the part of its officers," Robinson had concluded, "ought not, by any means, to be excluded."

"This court is capable of making its own conclusions, God rot you," Commodore Rodgers had interrupted. "And this court will also be mighty obliged, you poxed bastard, if you deliver us no more speeches. Don't write that down." This last was addressed to the clerk.

Robinson's eyes almost leaped from his head, but he mastered himself well, considering that he was unused to the manners of the older generation of navy officers. "I shall endeavor, sir, to adopt the laconic mode," he said.

"Just be brief with it," Rodgers had said, muttering "you pompous little shit" under his breath.

The deputy judge advocate, from that hour, had kept almost entirely to question and reply, assuming it the way to the president's heart, and Rodgers's comments had been chiefly confined to directing the witnesses to speak up and telling the clerk not to write down his profane asides. Favian saw the way the wind was blowing and concluded that it was favorable. He had not hired an attorney to aid in the defense, and it seemed that Rodgers had a grudge of long standing against attorneys, dating, probably, from the month-long Barron court-martial five years before, on which

Rodgers had also sat as president. Favian, too, kept his remarks short and to the point.

Once the court had sifted through the written evidence, Favian called his witnesses: the quartermaster on duty at the time of the wreck; the acting bosun, Gable, a short-tempered man built like a prizefighter who demonstrated no discernible awe at the massive array of gold and braid; the corporal of marines (the sergeant having drowned); a master's mate; the two helmsmen; the two surviving midshipmen, Stanhope and Tolbert, the third mid—Dudley, little fifteen-year-old Dudley—having been drowned, lost with Hibbert, the lieutenant, and the two dozen men who had been clinging to the foremast when it had torn loose and gone on the rocks.

The evidence was clear and positive: *Experiment* had driven ashore the enemy privateer *Loyalist* during a rising gale, and then in attempting to escape the clutches of the coast had been driven by a backing wind toward a cape. With no room to wear around and no possibility of tacking, Favian had club-hauled her and got her off—an unprecedented maneuver, Midshipman Stanhope reported, club-hauling a brig off a lee shore and destroying a clipper-privateer in the same afternoon.

"God damn your scholarship, sir," Rodgers said. "Don't write that down."

Stanhope begged the commodore's pardon and continued, remarking that if the wind had not veered six points *Experiment* would have got off scot-free, and before Rodgers could damn his opinions Robinson leaped in to point out that Stanhope's remark assumed as true what the court-martial was assembled to discover and was therefore inadmissible—so Rodgers damned Robinson instead and ordered Stanhope's conclusions inserted in the record, remarking between curses that Stanhope was a fucking officer and perfectly capable of reaching an opinion regarding a fellow officer's seamanship.

Robinson was so cowed, or so amazed, by this performance that it was left to Captain Lewis to elicit the information that Midshipman Stanhope's tenure in the navy had been short; that he was a new-made midshipman when *Experiment* had first got to sea in late March of 1813, and so his entire sea experience had been during the few months before the brig had been wrecked. "We may judge, from Mr. Stanhope's experience, just how greatly to value his opinions," Lewis concluded blackly.

Questioning by the court brought from Stanhope a personal note: after the wreck, when *Experiment* was being pounded to bits on the mudbank, and he and the rest of the crew had been trying to save themselves, he had been saved from being swept overboard by none other than Captain Markham, at considerable cost—six of Favian's fingernails had been pulled out by the roots while trying to grasp Stanhope's slick oilskins. Favian saw the eyes of the court flickering, in sick fascination, to the doeskin gloves he now wore. His hands had not, actually, been incapacitated, but three of the fingernails had grown back black and malformed, and the other three had not grown back at all, their place taken by massive slabs of scar tissue; Favian wore gloves to avoid his hands' ugliness from distracting people, and so that he would not have to go through the entire tedious story every time he made a new acquaintance.

Midshipman Tolbert, the next witness, had fortunately been in the service a longer time than Stanhope, four years. Favian knew that he had just recently failed his examination for lieutenant, which should have cast some doubt on his knowledge of seamanship as well, but that fact, luckily, was not brought out by the court.

Tolbert could have passed for a son of Rodgers: they had the same damn-your-eyes stare, the same short temper, the same pugnacious manner. Tolbert confirmed the by now familiar story of *Experiment*'s last hours, confirming what the others had confirmed, that Favian had showed no sign of fear or panic, that his orders were clear and sensible, that he was, in Tolbert's opinion, a good seaman. "The best," Tolbert volunteered, "that I have served under. His escape from the British frigate in the Bristol Channel was prodigal."

Since Rodgers had not objected to this remark Favian asked Tolbert to describe the incident in question, and Tolbert gladly complied. The picture he painted was vivid: *Experiment*'s being pursued by a frigate sailing three feet to her two, night coming on, the launching of a boat with a lantern fitted at the masthead to lead the frigate astray, the boat's crew recovered by means of lifelines, the morning sun showing the horizon clear. Favian could see the story's effect on the assembled captains, the sudden dreaminess in their eyes—particularly the eyes of Decatur, Jones, and Stewart, who had all served in small craft like *Experiment*—as they viewed the scene Tolbert was painting: the heavy boat swaying out on the yardarms, threatening to smash against the brig's bilges as the sea rolled her, the frigate coming closer and closer, too close to trust to the cover of darkness in which to make an escape, the hours of tense night watch, men and officers alike straining their eyes for sight of the pursuit, the final exhalation of triumph as the morning revealed an empty sea.

Even Lewis could find no disparaging remark to make, and Tolbert was dismissed, to hold himself in readiness should the court require him further, et cetera; Tolbert stiffly saluted the court, then turned to salute Favian—a bold compliment, for it was not required by the regulations—before leaving the cabin. Rodgers, noting that it was past noon, dismissed the court for dinner. Even before Favian had left the room with his bluecoated marine escort the papers were being shuffled off the table along with Favian's sword, which the court was keeping in its possession until the verdict could be reached.

The court dined on the same table behind which they sat as judges, and the noon break for dinner was growing longer and longer. Favian, under arrest, could not eat with the captains, but had been saved the burden of dining alone by Archibald Hamilton, a new-made lieutenant, former midshipman on the *United States* and son of a former secretary of the navy, who had offered the hospitality of the wardroom. Favian would dine and sup with Hamilton and the other officers of the *President;* in so doing, he had found himself growing nostalgic for his own days as a lieutenant, when there was always company and a man was not forced, by the burden of his double epaulets, to dine in solitary magnificence.

Favian followed the marine officer down a companionway to the wardroom, watching the back of the man's swollen, reddened neck. The marine lieutenant was a newly appointed provost marshal, given the duty just this morning when it appeared that his captain had been conveniently indisposed. The new provost marshal scarcely seemed happy about the new duty; he clomped down the companion as if his boots had been surfaced with lead. Favian wondered if the marine was upset with him, having formed an opinion as to Favian's guilt, or whether it was the heat and boring duty; his question was answered as the marine entered the wardroom and skimmed his hat over the dinner table.

"Damn that Rodgers! Damn that fat old lady with commodore's stars!" the marine spat, venom in his every word, his voice pitched high enough so that the wardroom were compelled to notice it, but low enough so that it wouldn't carry to the deck above, where Rodgers was tucking in his napkin.

"Mr. Howell. Mr. Hamilton," Favian bowed—or bobbed, rather, since he was already bent far over to keep his six feet, four inches from encountering the deckhead.

"Favian, have some claret," Hamilton said, his pleasant features scarcely ruffled by the marine's bile. "I see you have met our Mr. Twiggs, your honorable escort."

"Bastard buggering trial is just the farce I knew it would be," Twiggs growled. "Trying a thorough seaman for doing his duty, and putting that shy, shy old grunter in charge."

"Careful now, Mr. Twiggs," said Hamilton. "I won't say you're wrong, but we must not speak so in front of our guests. We have buffalo steaks today, Favian, and fresh peas."

"The fellow is shy, for all his big talk and swearing," said Twiggs, sitting down to his wine glass. "What manner of prize money could we have got had we been captained by a proper hackum, and not by a gross, fat, blustering, vain, quarrelsome, niggling . . . Where's our prize money for the *Belvidere*, I ask you? The quarterdeck full of officers who knew their duty, ready for action at last; I with my marines, every man among 'em ready to let fly at the enemy—and what does that old woman do? Yaw to present the larboard bow guns, sirrah, and then yaw again to present the starboard bow guns—yaw one way, yaw t'other way, fill and back, back and fill, shilly and shally, and the end of it was the enemy making its escape. All that was needed was a real fire-eater in command, not scared to sail right up to pistol-shot range and fire off the whole broadside. That would have put an end to 'em—we could have been as famous as the *Constitution*, with money and promotions all around!"

"Twiggs," said Lieutenant Howell, "enough. Commodore Rodgers has been sent to the *Chesapeake*."

"God save Baltimore, then," Twiggs murmured. "I'm heartily glad to see a real man in command of *President*—this ship has always deserved better than she's got, and Decatur will bring us luck."

The claret brought even more color to Twiggs's reddened face. The buffalo steaks came in from the officers' galley, fried in onions, with the promised peas in a pewter bowl. The conversation was civil but, aside from Twiggs's outburst, not at all lively:

the officers avoided discussion of the trial occurring above their heads, and most of Favian's recent career, because his conduct was related to the trial, was also out of bounds. Several days ago the wardroom had exhausted the subjects of whether the Peace Commission would achieve its object any time soon; the course of nautical affairs; the British pillaging in the Chesapeake; the interesting way a confrontation was shaping up on Lake Champlain, where Favian's old *Constitution* messmate Thomas Macdonough was facing a British squadron much more powerful than his own, and on Lake Ontario, where Commodore Isaac Chauncey's strange lack of motion seemed to have resulted in distress to General Brown's Niagara army. Brown had either beaten the enemy or been defeated himself—the exact truth seemed to be open to interpretation, since it appeared that Brown had driven the British off the field of battle only to withdraw himself, with the British in pursuit. The wardroom had put it down to the rather inexplicable way the army in general seemed to have been behaving through the war, but at any rate it seemed Brown would have been better off had Commodore Chauncey's Lake Ontario squadron taken the bit properly in its teeth and attacked their British opposition under Commodore Yeo.

All this ground had been thoroughly covered in the first three days of the trial, with the officers being properly noncommittal on the subject of Commodore Chauncey and his persistent failure to engage the enemy decisively—no doubt he was in possession of intelligence that showed it unwise to attack, or perhaps he'd been ill; at any rate, there were few subjects open to conversation save politics and the weather. But politics was out: Favian was of that rare breed, a War Federalist, and his family had made their name in Federalist politics back in New Hampshire, whereas Archibald Hamilton was a died-in-the-wool Republican, his father having served as secretary of the navy under Madison. The other members of the wardroom were aware of this and kept off the subject. And the weather had remained hot and humid throughout the trial, with the barometer rising and promising worse, so conversation in general languished. This, for the most part, suited Favian well, at least today, for he would offer himself as a witness that very afternoon.

The fresh peas more than made up for the lack of conversation, however. Favian, though he had been ashore for close to a year, had been at sea often enough in his career to enjoy a proper delight in the sight of fresh vegetables, and he consumed his share of peas with great joy. The wine was adequate, the conventions of the wardroom informal enough so that he could open his coat and loosen his neckcloth against the heat, and the court-martial would be over, one way or another, fairly soon.

The last pea had been long devoured, Howell's watch had been called, and Favian was well into his second cigarillo before the single gun boomed to signal that the court-martial was to resume. Favian adjusted his uniform, squared his cravat, carefully touched the fashionable devil-may-care spit curls on his forehead and cheek to make sure they were in place, and then followed Twiggs's red neck back up the companion to the commodore's cabin.

The assembled captains appeared to have fed well; they were all leaning back in their chairs, seemingly convivial—all but Lewis, who was leaning his mean little body forward on the table, resting on his elbows, his pinched face looking forward with a malicious intensity. Favian was beginning not to like the man at all.

"Have you any further witnesses to call, Captain Markham?" Rodgers asked, having called the court to order.

"No, sir," Favian said. "I should like, however, to testify myself, if the members of the court should be willing to interrogate me."

There was something of a smile on Rodgers's face—a scowling sort of smile, but a smile. Favian had spent years serving under Decatur, and Decatur had conducted the inquiry on poor James Barron after the latter had surrendered the *Chesapeake* in peacetime; Decatur had also served, against his will, on the court-martial. One of the few comments Favian had ever heard Decatur make on the Barron trial was a criticism of Barron's manner of defense. Barron had never testified as a witness, which had been taken by some as an admission that he was afraid of cross-examination, and had instead chosen to give a closing plea running to eighteen thousand words, full of rhetorical flourishes inserted by his attorney, some of which managed to so twist the syntax that the point of the sentences was quite obscured. The patience of the court had been exhausted after the first eight thousand words or so, and the florid style had annoyed them. Favian would try to give the opposite impression; he would allow himself cross-examination as if he had nothing to fear, and he would keep his closing plea brief and his classical allusions to the minimum.

Decatur, leaning forward, occasionally mopping his brow with a handkerchief, undertook most of the interrogation. His questions led efficiently through the series of events: the dirty weather in the offing, Favian's decision to look into one last bay before beating up to get sea room, the appearance in the bay of the *Loyalist* privateer caught in the act of pursuing a local ketch, the chase in the rising gale that put *Loyalist* aground when she failed to stay, the wind backing and threatening to put *Experiment* onto a cape as she tried to beat out to sea. Favian had club-hauled her then, a desperate maneuver to avoid destruction, and had succeeded in getting *Experiment* onto the other tack, perfectly capable of beating out of the bay; but at the worst possible instant the wind had veered, heading them again. With no possibility of escape Favian had cut the masts away and thrown out two anchors, hoping to ride out the storm, but the cables had parted on the foul ground and the brig had smashed itself to pieces on the mudbanks.

"How many reefs had ye in yer tops'ls?" Lewis asked.

"Three reefs in the tops'ls, two in the main," Favian said.

"Ye did not find it necessary to close-reef yer fore-and-aft mains'l?"

"Not yet, sir."

"It was not, then, a raging hurricane, a giant storm? Ye had yer tops'ls set, yer main, yer jib?"

"A storm jib, sir."

"Answer my question, sir!" Lewis snapped. "Was it a great storm or not?"

"It was a sufficient storm, sir," Favian answered, far too quickly, "to drive the *Experiment* aground."

Damnation; he had been goaded into losing his temper. All too easy to do in this heat. Favian composed his features, feeling sweat trickling down his spine, seeing Lewis with a crabbed grin on his pinched face, the light in his eyes triumphant. A gust of wind whistled down the windsail, ruffling the clerk's papers.

"Have ye, Captain Markham, been in worse storms?" Lewis asked.

"I have, sir," Favian said. "I have endured worse storms on numerous occasions. But never on a lee shore, never on foul ground."

"Very well, Captain," Lewis said. He leaned back and took a breath while waiting for the clerk to catch up. "I should like to address the question," he said finally, "of how ye came to be in command of the *Experiment* brig during this storm in the first place, after ye were ordered by the secretary of the navy to relinquish command and report to New London."

The clerk held up his hand to hold Favian's answer until his shorthand had caught up with the question; Favian snatched a glance at Lieutenant Twiggs, the provost marshal, who was reddening, it seemed, to the point of apoplexy. It was pleasant, Favian thought, to have an unabashed partisan in the room, particularly as this was the line of questioning he'd been dreading. The circumstances in which he found himself aboard *Experiment* that day had been somewhat irregular, and his principal witness had been killed in the wreck. He had hoped this matter would have escaped the court's attention entirely.

"The order from the secretary was, I thought, provisional," Favian said. "It ordered me to proceed to New London 'as quickly as circumstances permitted,' or words to that effect."

"And in your view the circumstances did not permit?"

"No, sir."

Lewis put on his finest sneer, leaning forward, his inky eyes glittering. "Ye are aware, Captain Markham, of the particular regard with which the United States Navy is accustomed to view its orders?"

"Yes, sir."

"That perhaps there might be a reason for an order, a reason of which the recipient might be in ignorance?"

"I am aware of that possibility, sir."

"And yet you chose to disregard an order from the secretary of the navy, Mr. William Jones, that you report to New London?"

"The order, sir, was not written in imperative terms. I arrived in New London a month following the wreck, and discovered that work on the *Shark* had not commenced, and was not to begin for several weeks."

Lieutenant Twiggs was turning the color of a fresh-boiled lobster. The man will surely die of a stroke before he is forty, Favian thought.

"But you did not know this at the time of your decision to remain aboard *Experiment?*" Commodore Rodgers asked, his florid face showing some interest.

"I did not, sir."

Stephen Decatur leaped rapidly into the breach, ready to come to Favian's aid. "I think it might be useful to follow the chronology of *Experiment*'s last weeks," he said, "to discover the reasons Captain Markham had for remaining aboard."

Rodgers gave Decatur a gimlet-eyed look. "If the commodore feels it absolutely necessary," he said.

Decatur did not bother to reply, but sprang straight to the questioning. "*Experiment*, under your command, defeated *Teaser* on what date?"

"The third of August, 1813."

"Were any officers killed in the action?"

"Yes, sir. Sailing Master Bean, and Midshipman Dudley."

"And you returned to Portsmouth on what date?"

"To the best of my recollection, that would be the sixth."

"Was the *Enterprise* brig under Lieutenant Burrows present in Portsmouth at that time?"

"Yes, sir."

The deputy judge advocate was on his feet, apparently quite happy to maneuver himself onto Rodgers's good side with a plea to keep the trial brief. "All respects to Commodore Decatur, sir, but I fail to see the relevance of this line of questioning," he said.

"I am trying to ascertain the chain of command north of Boston during the late summer of last year," Decatur said smoothly, his white teeth flashing from amid his dark beard. "It may prove relevant, as it bears upon Captain Markham's decision to remain aboard *Experiment*."

Rodgers gave Decatur a resentful glare, but in the end huffed, "Very well, Commodore Decatur, if you think it's necessary. But keep it brief, for the love of God."

"Thank you, Commodore Rodgers," Decatur said, with his best deferential smile. He turned to Favian. "Do you recall why *Enterprise* was sent to the coast of northern Massachusetts?" he asked.

"I did not see Lieutenant Burrows's orders, but he confided to me that it was on account of the *Loyalist* privateer that had been raiding the coastal trade."

"Do you recall the date on which you heard the news of *Enterprise*'s encounter with the *Boxer*?"

"Yes, sir. That would have been September the eleventh."

"And what did that news contain?"

"It was reported that Lieutenant Burrows had been killed while the *Enterprise* was engaging and capturing an enemy brig."

"And what was your reaction?" The question brought a pang of grief to Favian's heart. William Burrows of the *Enterprise* had been his closest friend ever since their first acquaintance in Tripoli; they had shared much, including the knowledge that each was, in his own unique way, unsuited for the navy to which they had dedicated their lives. With Burrows buried in Portland, there was no real friend left in whom to confide, no one to whom Favian could speak his heart and be understood. The loss was a bitter one, even after all these months.

"I called in our liberty men," Favian said, answering Decatur's question with a fair disregard for the truth, though not for the facts, "and took *Experiment* to Portland, where I understood *Enterprise* had gone with its prize. We arrived the next morning."

"At this time, who was the senior naval officer north of Boston?"

"The commandant of the Portsmouth Navy Yard, sir."

"And did the commandant of the yard give his permission for this excursion?" Lewis interrupted, his face set in a malicious sneer.

"He was absent," Favian said.

"So ye chose to abandon Portsmouth when ye were the senior officer on station?"

Favian felt his fists clench as he tried to keep his temper. "The Portsmouth Navy Yard was not my responsibility; the commandant had his deputies," he said. "Permission was not strictly required; my orders of the previous March still applied."

"And the orders were to seek out enemy privateers off the American coast and in Canada?" Decatur asked, quickly jumping in to take command of the questioning.

"Yes, sir."

"What were your reasons for setting out for Portland?"

"If the rumor of Lieutenant Burrows's death was true, that would imply that his lieutenant, Mr. McCall, was in command of both the *Enterprise* and the captured *Boxer*. I did not know whether Mr. McCall was wounded, or how many of his officers had been killed or injured. Although I know Mr. McCall to be an efficient officer, I concluded that it might be a more efficient deployment of the officers available if an officer of command rank were to be in Portland, and another man-of-war present, both to render assistance to Mr. McCall, if he should require it, and to discourage any British prisoners from attempting to retake the *Boxer*. I believe my letter to the commandant of the Portsmouth yard, written while we were preparing to leave port, mentioned these reasons."

There: he had journeyed entirely into the realm of falsehood. Though he had in fact given these reasons in a note written that afternoon, they were merest sophistry; in truth he had run to sea in a fit of anxiety and grief that had so overwhelmed him as to give him little choice. There had been no alternative: he had run to Portland to find out if the rumor was true, whether his closest friend had been killed. His own men had been amazed at his driving; he had nearly torn the sticks out of *Experiment* as he piled on the canvas to run up the coast to Portland; he had come very close to running onto Cape Elizabeth as he shaved inches from his course.

"And were any of the *Enterprise*'s officers injured?" Decatur asked.

"Captain Burrows had been mortally wounded, dying some hours after the fight, and Midshipman Kervin Waters had been killed."

"So *Enterprise* was able to make use of the resources provided by *Experiment*?"

"I believe so, sir."

"And," Decatur added, making a sweeping gesture with one arm, "it is true, is it not, that as a result of *Enterprise*'s and *Experiment*'s victories over the *Boxer* and *Teaser*, the British made the decision to withdraw all their brigs of war from our coasts?"

"Irrelevant," droned Robinson, raising a finger, delighted, presumably, to be able to raise a point of order without crossing Commodore Rodgers's hawse.

"Commodore Decatur," Rodgers frowned, "I hope you recollect my instructions to keep things brief."

"Yes, sir," Decatur said.

"Captain Markham, upon what date did ye receive word of yer promotion to the rank of captain?" Lewis asked.

"That would have been the thirteenth of September, sir, though I did not receive word that the promotion had been confirmed by Congress until about a month later, immediately prior to my journey to New London."

"Are ye aware, Captain Markham, that a fourteen-gun brig is insufficient to support the dignity of a captain of the United States Navy?" Lewis demanded.

"So is a gunboat, you hypocritical wretch," Favian almost replied; but he bit it off short, containing the short-leashed temper that had been the terror of *United States*'s lower deck, and replied instead, "I know that it is so considered by some."

"Then what in blazes were ye doing aboard *Experiment* a week following news of yer promotion?" Lewis asked loudly. "I cannot for the life of me see what ye were doin' aboard at all!"

"I remained aboard at the express invitation of *Experiment*'s lieutenant, Mr. Hibbert," Favian said. He felt the rage inside him boiling still, as lobster red as Lieutenant Twiggs's neck. "He desired me to stay aboard until we had made up our losses in officers."

"If ye had not gone ashore, Mr. Hibbert would have been in command of *Experiment*, is that not true?" Lewis continued.

"He would, unless the secretary of the navy chose to put another captain aboard," Favian said.

"D'ye find it unusual, then," Lewis demanded acidly, "that a junior officer should turn down his first chance at independent command?"

"It is not the usual practice."

"It is a pity, is it not," Lewis continued, malevolent, "that this unusually modest Mr. Hibbert did not survive to confirm your statements."

That last goad was too much; Favian could no longer contain the explosion. "It is a greater pity, is it not," he roared, seeing the board of captains suddenly lean back away from him, as if shifted by a hurricane wind, "that this court sees fit to abuse the name and honor of a dead officer, in order to play at rhetoric!"

Red memories flashed in his memory: Hibbert seconding him in that duel in Norway; Hibbert defying the surgeon to come on deck after he'd been wounded in the fight with *Teaser;* the agony of composing the letter to Hibbert's family that announced his pointless death; the further agony of his visit to Hibbert's father back in Portsmouth, half-recovered from a series of strokes and unable to keep the tears from his eyes at the mention of his only son . . . Damned if Favian was going to let Lewis refer to Hibbert in that sneering tone!

Rodgers's eyes, for the first time since dinner, seemed to have opened fully. "The clerk will strike that last question and reply from the record," he said. "Captain Lewis, you will restrain your zeal."

"Aye, sir," Lewis said with a smug little smile, happy to have drawn Favian out; but before he could complete his work Decatur came smoothly to the rescue.

"Perhaps Captain Markham could explain how many of *Experiment*'s officers were absent," he said. "It might throw some light on Lieutenant Hibbert's decision."

"The bosun had been absent since April, detailed to take a prize to Boston," Favian said, breathing more easily now, his anger, always swift to rise and swift to vanish, ebbing now. "He had not yet rejoined. Mr. Bean, the master, had been killed in the fight with *Teaser,* as had Mr. Dudley, a promising midshipman. Of the three midshipmen remaining, Mr. Brook was only fifteen, too young to step into a lieutenant's part; Mr. Stanhope lacked experience; and Mr. Tolbert—" Here he hesitated; Tolbert had been a trial throughout *Experiment*'s cruise, a jut-jawed pig-headed pugnacious blundering glory-struck trial, fascinated with the *code duello,* exposing his life to every hazard whether the service required it or not, challenging Midshipman Dudley to combat with pistols; but on the other hand Tolbert had been a favorable witness, and it would not serve either courtesy or the interests of the service to publicly blot Tolbert's name in the official records of another officer's court-martial. It might even be, by Tolbert's lights, a challengeable offense; Favian was not going to weather a hurricane, a shipwreck, and a court-martial only to fall under the dueling pistol of a blockheaded midshipman.

"Mr. Tolbert," he concluded a bit lamely, "was at that time unpracticed in the navigation of a deep-sea vessel."

"Mr. Hibbert," said Captain Stewart, inserting himself into the line of questioning, "was reluctant to put to sea after the *Loyalist* without his proper complement of officers?"

This was redundant, betraying Stewart's friendship; but if it was going into the record, Favian thought, it might as well be laid on with a trowel. "Yes, sir," Favian said. "The *Loyalist* was known to have a large crew, experienced and practiced. For a privateer, that is," he added, not wanting to publicly suggest that a mere sea-going mercenary could possibly equal a man-of-war, although he knew damned well—his own family history was evidence enough—that a well-disciplined privateer's crew could prove the equal of many a naval vessel, and that privateers were usually faster and nimbler sailors as well.

"Just so," said Stewart, recognizing Favian's tact.

That proved to be the end of the court's questioning, and the deputy judge advocate's cross-examination was mercifully brief, trying to wring the last ounce of advantage out of the irregularity of Favian's remaining on board *Experiment* during the critical week, trying to imply "disobedience" without actually naming it, and edging toward the conclusion that, even if Favian were not actually disobedient, he had not done quite the gentlemanly thing by staying aboard a vessel considered below his dignity, and in denying his worthy subordinate his first command. Not being a naval man, the exact technicalities of *Experiment*'s going aground seemed a little beyond him, and he steered away from the subject, apparently considering Commodore Lewis's questioning to have done the job for him.

Favian then made his closing plea. It was a great deal shorter than Barron's famous eighteen-thousand-word address—he had actually gone so far as to count the words, and there were less than two thousand altogether, 1,572 to be exact. They summed up his position neatly enough, that he had stayed aboard *Experiment* at the request of her lieutenant and for the good of the service, that the brig's crew had performed faultlessly and with great heroism the afternoon of the wreck, and that it was only due to the infernal perversity of an autumn hurricane that the brig was destroyed at all.

As he spoke, Favian realized that his sword, which the court was supposed to keep in its possession until its decision was reached, had been cleared from the table at dinner and not returned; presumably it had been stowed somewhere in the after cabin or in the commodore's privy. This was quite irregular, and annoying because Favian had given the court the presentation sword given him by the town of Portsmouth following the *Teaser* victory; it was decorated with reminders of the battle, and Favian had intended the sword to remind the court of his past services and victories. But it would not do for Favian to mention it to the court; their little lapses should go unremarked.

His plea delivered, Favian gave a fair copy to the clerk, bowed to the court, and returned to his chair. Rodgers looked at his watch at the exact moment that six bells echoed down *President*'s windsail: another hour to supper.

"The court will consider its verdict," he said. "The provost marshal shall escort the prisoner to the wardroom. Everyone else will clear the court." Rodgers had now ended the public portion of the court-martial. Now would commence the second part, the secret deliberation of the five-man jury. Each captain would be under oath not to reveal the contents of any debate; there would be no record kept; the decision would be made by majority vote, the officers voting in reverse order of seniority, the most junior first. It was an odd system, at variance with American nonmilitary codes; it was based on Roman, rather than English, codes of justice, and had been borrowed wholesale from English naval law by John Adams, the author of the *Naval Regulations*.

"I hope," Rodgers said, eying his fellow captains, "that this business can be concluded quickly. We have two cowards, three cases of theft of navy stores, one card cheat, and a sodomite to try after this, and I'd like to end it all as soon as possible."

Favian smiled tightly at this; a quick verdict would almost certainly be in his favor. He detected little anxiety in himself; he knew that Stewart and Decatur, at least, were prejudiced in his favor, although Lewis worried him. Since Rodgers would only vote in case of a tie among the other four, Jones would cast the vote that would create the tie in the first place. Though Favian didn't know Jones well enough to be sure of his vote, he knew there was a factor working in his favor: Jones had lost his own *Wasp* to the enemy, had been tried and found innocent; for Jones to vote for Favian's condemnation was to cast doubt on the verdict of his own trial.

"By God, another week of this and I shall go mad!" cried Twiggs, loosening his cravat as soon as he had gained the safety of the wardroom. "No wonder Major Beekman faked sick! Would'ee like some ice punch? Here's to acquittal, and your next command!"

"You're too kind," Favian said, raising his glass. They found a deck of cards and played piquet for the length of more than a glass—it was just shy of eight bells, and Favian was four and a quarter dollars the richer, when a midshipman came down the companion to tell them they were wanted.

Absurdly, as Favian retied his neckcloth and cravat, he found his heart beating like a man-of-war's drum—sheer madness, considering he was to be acquitted. Yet Lewis had been so damnably persistent, harping on Favian's staying aboard *Experiment* following his promotion; and of course Favian did not know Jones well enough to be sure of his vote. Suppose Jones and Lewis had both voted against him, and Rodgers had been forced to cast the tie-breaking vote. Rodgers was notoriously short-tempered; suppose the crusty commodore had been so annoyed at having to be here at all, delaying the journey to his new command, that he had voted against Favian out of sheer spleen?

Favian took his hat from the table, followed Twiggs up the companion, waited while Twiggs beat on the great cabin door and announced the prisoner. Rodgers's voice answered, and Twiggs opened the door.

Favian's eyes instantly turned to his smallsword resting on the table before him, and before the court had spoken a word he knew it was over—he had been acquitted. The navy had adopted British customs in regard to courts-martial: if the accused was an officer his sword was taken from him and held in custody by the court athwart the table; if he was found guilty, the sword was turned with its point toward the accused; if innocent, the sword was returned to him hilt-first.

The hilt was toward him, and the court's members, even Lewis, bore pleased, relieved smiles. He barely heard the president reading the decision of the court, that the said Captain Favian Markham, USN, was not guilty of violation of Article XIX, to wit, that he, through intention, negligence, or any other fault, suffered a vessel of the navy to be stranded, run upon rocks or shoals, or hazarded in any way. Commodore John Rodgers then stood and picked up Favian's sword, holding it out to him. "I should like to shake the hand of a brave officer," he said, "and to wish him all joy and success in his new command."

Favian breathed out the required compliments—he hoped he had not been an awkward witness, he hoped the trial was not overlong, he thanked the court for their thoroughness and their verdict and hoped to do them honor with the *Shark*. He took the sword, shook the hand of each member of the court and of the deputy judge advocate, and clipped the sword to his belt.

"I hope you will sup with us," Decatur said with an easy smile, as the sound of eight bells came ringing down the skylight.

"Honored, sir," Favian said, shaking his hand again.

"Damme if I know why this case ever came to trial," Rodgers said. "I can't think what Brierly had in mind when he conducted the inquiry."

"Lieutenant Brierly is a most scrupulous officer," Favian said, willing at that moment to give anyone the benefit of the doubt.

"Scrupulous! In wartime! Ha!" Rodgers scorned, and then turned to Decatur. "Commodore Decatur, I wonder if my clerk might borrow your desk for a space of a moment—I have a brief order to dictate."

"Of course, sir," Decatur said.

There was a bustle to turn the court-martial's bench into a supper table, clerks clearing and servants setting six places. Favian received the congratulations of Lieutenant Twiggs, and turned to find Commodore Decatur standing by his side.

"I thought you should like to know, Favian," Decatur said in a low voice, "that the verdict was unanimous. No point in entertaining suspicions about who voted in favor and who voted against. I thought I'd relieve your mind."

And forestall a possible service feud, Favian thought, understanding Decatur's unstated motives without any need for prompting. Favian had served with Decatur for far too long not to know Decatur's motivations. The James Barron court-martial had created enough bad blood to poison the next three generations of sea officers, and Decatur had been splattered with more than his share—it was obvious why Decatur wanted to anticipate any resentment between Favian and Commodore Lewis, even at the expense of the oath taken not to reveal the vote.

"Thank you, sir," Favian said.

"I think," Decatur said, "that after all this time, Captain Markham, and considering our equivalence in rank, that you might call me Stephen."

Favian grinned. "I am honored," he said. "Stephen."

"Captain Markham." It was Commodore Rodgers, holding a freshly inked letter in his hand, with mischievous triumph in his eyes. "I hold in my hand your orders," he said. "You are to report aboard the United States ship *President,* there to replace Commodore John Rodgers on the court-martial proceedings being conducted thereon, in order that the latter might proceed to his new command in the Chesapeake. God give you joy, sir."

Favian, his heart sinking, looked down at the letter that Rodgers had just placed in his hand. Two cowards, three cases of theft of Navy stores . . . with all the formalities, his number one coat and cocked hat, the two heavy gold epaulets, *and in all this heat!* My God, Favian thought, the most dismal duty imaginable. He could almost wish himself back in the gunboat service.

"Well, Favian," Decatur said, thumping him on the shoulder, "at last you'll begin to earn that seventy-five dollars per month, eh?"

"I suppose I shall," Favian said weakly. The seventy-five per month was not enough, he thought, not nearly enough.

2

One coward was dismissed from the service; the other, the evidence conflicting, was given the benefit of the doubt. Two of the cases of theft were found justified, with the third producing a few surprises and a new indictment; the card cheat, who was being court-martialed at his own request in order to clear his name—a duel would have been the usual procedure, but the young man appeared to hold strong convictions against the practice—was found not guilty, there being no evidence against him other than the fact that he had been winning heavily and the biggest loser had been sodden with whiskey punch. The poor sodomite, an unhappy ship's corporal, had his charge reduced to gross indecency and was dismissed the service; his catamite, a powder monkey, had already fled, and if caught would be punished for desertion rather than what the indictment bluntly called "buggery."

The heat increased through the series of courts-martial, and the tempers of the court had grown similarly frayed: even the usually cheerful Decatur was reduced to grunting monosyllables, and Commodore Lewis turned positively savage. How much of Lewis's behavior was feigned, and how much the result of a naturally malicious temperament, was an interesting question; Favian had concluded, after a few days of watching the man work, that at least part of Lewis's personality was an affectation, but that his genuine disposition complemented the artificial one to such a great degree that the two were, for the most part, indistinguishable.

Lewis seemed to have taken it upon himself to ask all the awkward questions, to drag up any dirt or service gossip that might conceivably affect the outcome of the trial, and to twist any of the witness's words into the least favorable interpretation. He seemed to do it impartially, however; his acid comments were bestowed on any witness without discrimination between prosecution and defense. There was method in it, Favian concluded; the man seemed determined to get at the truth by means of terror.

The others were more moderate. Decatur proved as efficient as Rodgers at keeping the trial moving briskly and at—somewhat more tactfully—restraining the flowery prose of the deputy judge advocate. Favian generally confined himself to clarifying already-stated positions and pointing out possible contradictions, and Jones did much the same, also as a former attorney assisting with matters of legal procedure. But it was Charles Stewart who provided the only surprise of the session.

It was during the third of the trials for violation of Article XXIV, or "wasting, embezzling, or fraudulently buying, selling, or receiving any ammunitions, provisions, or other public stores," to use the language of the indictment. A master's mate had been accused of selling the *United States*'s spare cordage, canvas, and the boat's emergency supplies. The unscrupulous men ashore he'd dealt with seemed to have vanished, but the evidence seemed clear-cut enough, and Decatur, under whom the man had served for years, had reluctantly signed the order to bring about the court-martial. As both accuser and president of the court, he tried to maintain neutrality, keeping out of the examination altogether and announcing that, although he hoped the court's decision would be unanimous for guilt or acquittal, in the event of a tie between the other four he would vote for acquittal—a typically chivalrous remark, at which even the accused man's eyes shone with tears of gratitude. Stephen Decatur, Favian knew, was adept at producing such evidence of loyalty among his men; though Favian was more aware than the master's mate of Decatur's ruthless, ambitious side, and knew he would never have brought this to trial unless he had a certainty of obtaining a conviction, and a knowledge that his tie-breaking vote would never be necessary.

The master's mate did not help himself with his testimony; he was so confused and incoherent, and so obviously at a loss to offer an explanation for the missing stores, that he would have tried the patience of a court of saints, let alone five overdressed men sweating in the heat of a summer afternoon. Lewis's sarcasm alone almost reduced the man to tears. But Captain Charles Stewart took over the questioning, and slowly and with great effort, backtracking when necessary, produced a coherent narrative that seemed rather insubstantially to be pointing in a certain direction; and then with a flash of intuition Favian and Jacob Jones saw where Stewart was aiming and leaped into the questioning, almost stumbling over one another with eagerness. In the end the master's mate was acquitted and the finger of guilt seemed conclusively pointed toward *United States*'s bosun, who was shown not only to have taken money for the stores but cunningly arranged that, when the crime was discovered, the evidence should point to someone else entirely. Eyes blazing, Decatur signed an order for the man's arrest, and stood up to shake the acquitted man's hand and apologize personally for ordering his arrest. The poor man, overwhelmed, fainted dead away.

Afterwards Favian looked at Captain Stewart with greater respect. He had always known the man was talented, but to somehow penetrate the incomprehensible testimony of the poor, confused master's mate, to see the thread of truth interwoven with the rest, and to dexterously pluck it forth unaided—it had been an incredible performance, showing a mind far keener for this kind of work than was usually demonstrated by any board of captains.

Favian also became better acquainted with Jacob Jones, and during the supper that followed the last court-martial found himself invited by Jones for a tour of the new steam battery being built in Brown's shipyard on the East River, the steam battery designed by the celebrated Mr. Fulton and built at Jones's recommendation. Favian, who had heard a great deal about the battery, was happy to accept.

The last supper of the court's session was restrained; the mood was more of relief than of celebration. Favian and Stewart left early, taking a navy launch to Manhattan, where their ways parted. Stewart's lodgings were nearby, but Favian's were out of the city to the north; he'd wanted to avoid the recognition and celebrity that would inevitably have come with finding a place near the waterfront. He lodged north of the actual city limits in Greenwich Village, the Bossen Bouwerie that was, at a small farmhouse near the Minetta Water.

The actual farmland was in disuse now, but Favian's hostess still kept a few cattle and entertained lodgers. She was the widow of a Revolutionary deserter from Anhalt-Zerbst by the name of Fux, apparently a distant relation of the composer, and she bore this misfortune with a militant pugnacity that dared the world to offer comment, and which silenced in advance a helpful Favian, who would otherwise have suggested altering the spelling to Fuchs.

It was late by the time Favian crossed the stone bridge over the canal, had ridden north the length of the Greenwich Road, stopping to admire the sunset over the Hudson, and had stabled his roan mare—on loan from his father—a beautiful animal. There were several strange horses in the stable; evidently Frau Fux had other guests, presumably travelers heading south on the Greenwich Road who had decided to break their journey here rather than continuing the long ride to lower Manhattan in the dark.

The new guests had gone to bed, as had the widow, but there was half a peach pie, a jug of cream, and a bucket of beer waiting for him in the kitchen. Grateful—it had been a long ride since supper—Favian threw off the heavy, braided coat, happy to be rid of the weight of the bullion epaulets and all they represented, and filled a mug with the beer. Until he returned to New London and the *Shark*—and there was no obligation to hurry—he was free of the official navy, free to wear civilian rig, to go swordless, and to enjoy the world as a free man for a little space. He had prize money now, prize money for the *Teaser*, for his share of the *Macedonian*, money awarded by Congress for the British ships he'd burned in the Narrow Seas of England. There were other benefits as well: money and five hundred acres awarded by the state of New Hampshire, money and a house (now leased) granted by the citizens of Portland in gratitude for the destruction of the *Loyalist*.

Favian had now made the adjustment from an insolvent young officer, constantly on the brink of being thrown ashore on half pay, to affluent man of property. His money imposed new burdens that he had never anticipated. Most of it was in dollars that were losing their value with wartime inflation; the property in New Hampshire was uncleared and unsurveyed, but taxes still had to be paid on it; his only income was the seventy-five dollars per month navy salary, the (very low) interest being paid on his money by the banks, and the rent from the building in Portland.

Clearly something had to be done with the dollars, but what? His career had been a navy one; investments were not his line. And the traditional investments, commerce and merchant shipping, had first been crippled during the embargoes and then almost eliminated by the British blockade. In his home town of Portsmouth ships were moored three-deep alongside the wharves, awaiting times of peace.

These problems aside, he still had enough to call himself affluent, even if he weren't wealthy. Enough, he thought wryly, to be considered a serious prospect for son-in-law even by someone as conservative as Nicholas Greenhow. But the money had come too late, at least as far as Greenhow was concerned.

For years, the lean years for Favian and the navy following the war with Tripoli and before the declaration of war with Britain—the years in which Favian's service had been ashore or in leaky, dangerous gunboats, useless for defending the nation against its foreign enemies and used instead to enforce the embargoes that wrecked American commerce and kept almost every American sailor out of work for years—during those bleak years, Favian and Emma, old Greenhow's daughter, had an understanding. There was nothing formal, nothing spoken, but Favian and Emma had both been raised genteel and knew the genteel code and its unstated rules, and also how to manipulate them.

Greenhow had objected to Emma's attachment, chiefly on the grounds of Favian's profession—Favian was a naval lieutenant who belonged to a service that was being deliberately starved by President Jefferson, a service not likely to be at war and thus not likely to reward its heroes with prize money and promotion, but rather to cast them ashore on half pay or dismiss them from the service altogether at the least political change in Washington. No, not suitable for Emma at all. Nicholas Greenhow had paraded endless numbers of suitors before his daughter, but even though she would not marry without her father's permission—that too was a part of the genteel code—neither would she marry against her inclinations. Her inclinations had disposed her favorably toward Favian, and there they remained.

Yet her father's persistence had taken its toll; the years of Favian's absence had not helped. Favian's return to Portsmouth in the summer of 1813 with the success of Markham's Raid behind him and the *Teaser* gloriously sent to the bottom of the Atlantic, promotion assured and prize money on the way, would, Favian thought, be crowned by the announcement of an engagement.

Instead something had gone awry. There were misunderstandings, cross purposes, all complicated by the fact that the courtship was being conducted in semisecrecy, hidden from the Greenhow family. Emma Greenhow had been baffling, her behavior and attitude totally unexpected. She had instead engaged herself to Benjamin Stanhope, a talented shipbuilder and a pillar of the Federalist establishment; he was twenty-odd years her senior and a widower, the father of the Midshipman Stanhope who had testified at Favian's court-martial. The marriage had taken place the following February; Favian, for once quite happy to be out of Portsmouth on navy business, had written to his father asking that an appropriate gift be sent in his name. The latest news had Emma with child, her marriage an apparent success.

Her success was becoming a social one as well, not unmixed with politics. Her father and husband were antiwar Federalists, and that breed of politician, always strong in New England, had grown increasingly vocal since the British had extended their blockade north of New York in 1813. New Hampshire and Massachusetts had refused to place their militia under federal control; Connecticut and Rhode Island were growling ominously; the summer campaigns against Canada had once again gone nowhere; the navy was being forced to contend with a larger and more efficient blockade, and had almost had to give up the policy of deep-sea cruises.

For the war in Europe was over. Napoleon had abdicated in April—Favian remembered the celebrations, hundreds of Federalists dancing around bonfires to celebrate the exile of the Corsican Tyrant they had hated. Favian himself had joined the celebrations, delighted that France, a country he admired, was finally out from under the heel of the most ruthless dictator Europe had ever known, but even as he danced he had known the grim consequence. The hundreds of British warships that had been kept busy blockading France and her allies were free to cross the Atlantic, carrying with them the battle-hardened veterans of Wellington's undefeated peninsular army. The first such reinforcements, under General Sir George Gordon Drummond, had already reached the Niagara frontier, altering the balance of power.

The only disorder in Europe was created by the situation in

Norway, where Favian's old acquaintance Prince Christian Frederick was trying to form an independent state, a republic based on the American model. But the victorious European powers had decreed that Norway was to be a Swedish province, and free Norway was being blockaded by the European powers while Swedish armies prepared to invade. Favian and the *Experiment* had been in Norway in 1813, and from what Favian had seen there Christian Frederick had no chance at all: Norway was too poor, too divided, and too isolated to stand against the united might of all Europe. It was a pity; Favian had liked the prince royal and wished him success with his noble plans, but was morally certain the prince's effort was doomed.

So the sideshow in Norway would soon be over, Favian thought—perhaps it was already over—and that would release what little British strength had been diverted to the Skagerrak. The United States should be bracing for the assault and looking to its defenses; instead talk of New England secession was in the air, along with bluster concerning states' rights and a new constitutional convention.

And most of the talk was coming from Federalists of the stamp of Nicholas Greenhow and Benjamin Stanhope. Merchants with ties to the sea, they had been driven to hate and desperation by Jefferson's embargoes, and their hatred obscured their view of the war. They seemed to think the fighting no worse than the kind of bloodless newspaper skirmishing waged between the *Columbian Centinel* and the *National Intelligencer;* the incredible absurdity of calling a constitutional convention in the middle of a war was not apparent to them. Favian, with friends to mourn, bitterly aware of how real the battles had seemed with roundshot crashing into his bulwarks and cutting men in half on his decks, saw the war in a different way. He had fought the Tripolitans, who were bankrolled by British gold; he had served with men, born Americans, who had been pressed into the British service to have their backs torn open by the British cat. Yet all these radical Federalists could see were abstract political and constitutional questions—no wonder the nation was in such trouble.

The antiwar Federalists were being opposed, Favian knew. He was in regular correspondence with his brothers and his father, active men of affairs who had divided themselves from their Federalist friends by their support of the war. His father, who had retired from public life on New Year's Day, 1800, announcing his conviction that the new century required new public men, had even been moved to leave his estate and make speeches among his old Revolutionary comrades.

Favian's brother Lafayette had been even more active. Although he had almost left public life, disgusted, in 1813, he had lately been persuaded to return. He was not, Favian knew, a good politician; he was a cold man, perhaps even a repellent one, and he was not liked—but even his enemies admitted his brilliance, and his rhetorical broadsides were so weighty, so well delivered, and so cutting that few dared to oppose him on a public platform. Aware that he was not well liked even by those who agreed with him—this would not necessarily have been a handicap in a populous, more urbane place like Boston, where no one had liked John Adams much either, but it was fatal in a little world like Portsmouth—Lafayette had placed his considerable talents at the disposal of another, more popular figure, the young congressman Daniel Webster.

Favian was not acquainted personally with Webster; although a New Hampshireman, Webster had been raised on a farm inland and educated in Massachusetts: their paths had never crossed. He was apparently a true New England man and a Federalist; his opposition to the Madison administration and to Democratic-Republican policies in general was eloquently stated; but he was also a servant of the Constitution and opposed to New England secession.

The two men, Lafayette Markham and Daniel Webster, had formed an alliance against the faction represented by Benjamin Stanhope and Nicholas Greenhow. Lafayette had talent, money, an important name, and social position; Webster had his forum in Congress, considerable popularity, and great talents of his own. Lafayette's letters to Favian were full of acid musings on his enemies and unstinting praise for Webster; and praise by Lafayette of anyone at all was a rare thing. It was clear that Webster was the dominant partner in this alliance, and Favian had concluded that for Lafayette, who was older, more established in the community, and certainly wealthier, to cede precedence in this way spoke well of Mr. Webster's oratorical and political abilities.

It seemed, from Lafayette's letters, that Emma Greenhow Stanhope had entered the lists on the side of her father and husband; Lafayette's letters spoke bitterly of the political gatherings at which Emma had been hostess. Favian remembered Emma's curiosity on political questions, her resentment of old Greenhow's ranting, entirely self-centered political philosophies . . . She had surrendered, it seemed, to parental and conjugal authority. Surrendered to what, considering her marriage, was probably inevitable.

Favian finished his third mug of beer and contemplated the peach pie. He cut himself a generous slice, doused it with cream, ate it. He watched the candlelight glitter on the gaudy hilt of his presentation sword, on the American eagle, the thirteen stars, the date of the *Experiment-Teaser* fight graven on the burnished guard.

The sword had been returned to him. He was once again a member in full standing of the small society of American captains, the very few men that formed the cutting edge of United States power abroad. Theirs was a complex association, bound by its own rigid rules of conduct, and not to be understood by any outsider. Favian had fought three duels in his life, two of them to uphold the navy's idea of honor, and in the second he had killed his man. He knew that as long as he continued to wear the uniform he would have to be ready to draw that gaudy, keen-edged sword, not simply in defense of his life or honor, but in defense of those abstract ideals which the navy held dear, and that he should not be prepared merely to kill, but to die.

Favian's life had been at hazard many times, usually as the service required—only once had he been at risk for reasons of his own. That had been his third duel, the one fought in Norway. Certainly the navy and its requirements had played a part in that fight, for within the dueling ritual, the insult given and resented, the challenge given and accepted, there was a display of public courage, and Favian had used that for the navy's purposes. His crew had been unhappy and resentful, thinking him a coward for declining a British invitation to combat in the North Sea; Favian's duel had won them back from their disaffection, making possible the victory over *Teaser* that had happened later. The duel had, in that sense, been a tactic to win the hands' affection, and as a strategy it had succeeded.

But it was more complicated than that—a woman had been involved, for one thing, and Norwegian politics. Favian's opponent, a brutal man, had died; the fact that Favian had personally disliked him had made the killing easier. There was, however, a more disturbing element. The duel had been accepted easily, fought easily and without trepidation. The danger had not disturbed him; he had slept well the night before. Favian had wondered then, and wondered at greater length since, just how much he had desired the mortal danger for its own sake. Had he deliberately sought his own death in Norway, he wondered; was he a coward, not in the physical sense as his crew had supposed then, but in the sense that he was more afraid to face life—particularly life in the navy, with its burdens of isolation and command—than death?

He had known for years that he was not entirely suited for the navy. Decatur was more the sort that the service required, or Charles Stewart: the laughing cavalier, a romantic hero out of Walter Scott combined with the pragmatic man of science. Decatur was a dashing figure out of legend, inspiring devotion among his crew; but he was also a capable sailor, competent to make a myriad of practical and technical decisions when necessary. His victory over the *Macedonian* had been won with science and carefully studied tactics, not dash.

Yet dashing he certainly was, and thought himself to be; there was no greater a believer in Decatur's star than Decatur himself. The greatest weight on that board of captains that had just completed its work aboard *President*, greater even than the weight of the epaulets, greater than the weight of the collective power over life, death, and punishment, was the weight of vanity. Every man, the romantic Decatur, the vain and petulant Rodgers, the charmingly Irish Stewart, believed awesomely in himself, in his own talent and luck.

Favian was talented, as he himself knew; following the death of William Burrows, he was probably the best technical sailor in the service. He was a capable enough leader, he supposed; years of apprenticeship to Decatur had shown him tricks enough for inspiring allegiance among the ordinary sailors. But that resounding, trumpeting belief in one's own star, the belief so powerfully on display in that board of captains, was absent; he, like his friend Burrows, had been an outsider within the navy, feigning a submission to the code in which he did not truly believe, but which he was able to understand was necessary.

His feigning was certainly good enough. If he could not be a character from Walter Scott, he could at least imitate one. The decision had been made years ago; Favian was a navy man, and a navy man he would stay. But the burdens of command did not sit comfortably with him; the epaulets weighed more heavily on his shoulders than they ever would on Decatur's.

As he picked up his sword, uniform coat, and candle and headed upstairs to his room, Favian found his mind turning again to Emma. She had submitted to the inevitable; she had joined politically as well as matrimonially to her husband, accepting his judgment and guidance as her genteel code demanded. Was it any different from what he, Favian, had accepted? A life dictated not by his own inclinations, but by a code imposed from outside? And was it ever possible to do otherwise?

Favian pulled off his boots, peeled his tight trousers from his long, thin legs, and carefully hung his dress uniform in a closet. The questions, unanswerable really, flitted through his head. The closet doors were closed on his uniform; the captain had been put away. It was Favian Markham alone, whoever that was, who would turn into the bed, until the captain was roused again with the morning.

3

The next day Favian thankfully dressed as a civilian, a plain pair of gray cloth riding breeches with a leather seat, a pea-green clawhammer coat, a round hat, and boots. Because of the heat he'd go without a waistcoat and without the bulky neckcloth and cravat, leaving his collar open in the fashion set by Lord Byron.

Frau Fux's other guests were beginning their breakfast as Favian came down; they were not, as Favian had thought, travelers heading into the city, but inhabitants of the city itself, a graying surveyor and his apprentice. They'd been hired by the city to help plan a hypothetical expansion northwards; they were working long days and preferred to spend the night in the Village rather than returning to lower Manhattan each night. They were pleased to meet the celebrated Captain Markham, congratulated him on Markham's Raid and the outcome of his court-martial, and wished him all success with the *Shark*. They had been drinking Frau Fux's beer with their breakfast and were inclined to merriment.

"D'you think the city will really extend beyond Greenwich Village?" Favian asked, by way of politeness.

"Oh, aye," the surveyor replied, offhandedly. "There are only a few blocks separating New York from the Village as it is. The blocks would have inhabitants already if it weren't for the epidemic back in the year one, and for this damn—begging your pardon, Captain—for this damned war. Even with the war cutting off commerce the city is still growing. And there's only one way it can grow, and that's northward."

His apprentice, a gawky seventeen and not yet used to beer in the morning, broke into spluttering laughter. "Whether Henry Brevoort like it or no!" he said, and both he and his master broke into bawling laughter. As Favian looked at them questioningly, the man, between eruptions of laughter, explained the joke.

"Henry Brevoort keeps a tavern at Tenth Street and Broadway," he said. "And this tavern has a tree by it with a bench—haha! —and Brevoort likes to sit under the tree and gossip with his friends. When we tried to extend Broadway north of Tenth Street back in the year seven, Brevoort objected because"—he interrupted himself with a fit of red-faced laughter—"because we would have to cut down his *tree!*"

"His *tree!*" the apprentice echoed, banging on the table with his fist. Beer slopped foaming from the mugs.

"And damn if he didn't do it!" the surveyor laughed. "That's the joke of it! He went to City Hall to complain over a tree being cut down, and he won! That's why, when the city is built north, Broadway will be bent to the west at Tenth Street. Th' planners almost had apoplexy, an' the surveyors went mad. Some fine night I will sneak over to Brevoort's and cut that tree down. Or, as you navy men say—haha!—*cut it out!*"

The apprentice almost went into convulsions at this witticism. Favian laughed politely, and when Frau Fux brought him his breakfast of steak, fried potatoes, and eggs, Favian asked her for coffee.

"Dere ain't no coffee, my captain," the lady replied. "You had de last yesterday. Dis damn blockade is cuttin' off de supplies. I could give you Scotch coffee but I don't t'ink you gonna like it. No tea left eider, except herb tea."

"*Cut it out!*" giggled the apprentice, tears running down his face.

"Thank you anyway, Mrs. Fux," Favian said, making a mental note to buy coffee in the city later.

"I'm glad you ain't goin' in no uniform today, my captain," Frau Fux continued. "Dem Tories is meetin' in town and dere ain't no man in uniform gonna be safe."

"Really?" Favian was astounded. "Tories meeting here?"

The surveyor scowled. "Confound 'em!" he said. "I'm not an admirer of our Mr. Madison, but I'd rather have twenty Madisons than any one of those Tories. They fought against our country in the Rebellion, and now they parade in the city preachin' against the war. Before the blockade they wouldn't have dared, but now there are those who will listen."

"Let us hope there are not," Favian said, but he knew the surveyor was right. The antiwar Federalists would listen well to the Tories, he knew; to oppose Madison many would make an alliance with a faction that was opposed not only to Federalism, with its insistence on a strong, centralized American government, but to the very idea of American independence itself. Compared with some Federalists' outright hatred of Jefferson and Madison, their mild distaste of the British and their allies was of little account.

Following breakfast Favian rode to his cousin Micah's mansion at nearby Richmond Hill. Micah, the son of Favian's pious, fierce old privateer uncle Josiah, had married a New York heiress and become a banker. Because he'd forsaken his father's Congregational religion for his wife's Episcopalianism, his father and brothers had turned cool to him.

Favian himself had not spent a great deal of time at Richmond Hill, but it was not for religious reasons. The courts-martial had occupied a great deal of his time and energy, which supplied the excuse, but there was another reason entirely: Micah's household was so obviously an unhappy one. Micah seemed harassed and nervous in the company of his wife, and even though their manners in company were polished enough Favian had seen Angelica's glances at her husband when Micah was holding forth at table or speaking to any of their children, and he thought he'd detected in Angelica's eyes ungovernable resentment, hatred, and despite. What their private life must be like, Favian thought, did not bear thinking about.

Angelica, alone in the house save for the servants, received Favian cordially. Favian bowed, made his apologies for not enjoying their hospitality more frequently, and then was invited to supper the following evening. He accepted, exchanged civilities, and made an exit, pleading business at the navy yard.

On his way to the Brooklyn ferry Favian saw the Tories marching. There were only about a hundred of them, mostly elderly men with a few younger ones beside them—sons, probably, more than converts—a pitifully shrunken remnant of the thousands of Tories who had thronged New York during the war, when the British were in occupation and the city a haven for loyalists. They were hardly a threat to anyone in uniform, Favian thought. They were led by a sixtyish man on horseback dressed in rather old-fashioned knee breeches and an even more old-fashioned powdered wig; Favian, as he maneuvered his horse out of the way of the demonstration, heard the muttering of the crowd. There was no sympathy there for these old men; the Revolutionary scars had by no means healed over.

"Monarchy-loving bastards," he heard one man mutter. "I wonder that they'd dare show their faces."

"Aye," another answered. "They're brazen enough with an English squadron just off Sandy Hook. Look at that old St. John Delancey leadin' 'em, who fought with Howe and Arnold and butchered our men at Fort Griswold!"

"He's no less brazen with that Mrs. Markham on Richmond Hill," the first man said. "And at his age!" He spat. "They should all be hung."

Oho, Favian thought in surprise. Poor Micah. Left his family, changed his religion, and all to marry a woman who preferred the affections of an elderly Tory. If, he thought loyally, the slander was true. But it certainly had the ring of truth, and would serve to explain a few things.

The parade passed and Favian rode on. Before he'd ridden two blocks he came upon another parade. This was a martial one, the *President*'s marines marching under Lieutenant Twiggs, the man scowling and red-faced as usual, followed by two hundred of *President*'s shellbacks under Decatur himself. Decatur waved as he saw Favian's tall figure by the road, and Favian trotted over to him.

"Hello, Stephen," Favian said, saluting him with his short, coiled crop.

"Hello, Favian," Decatur said gaily. "We're marching to Fort Clinton and back. Will you join us?"

"I have an appointment with Jacob at Brown's shipyard."

"Ah, yes. I forgot. I'm sorry you cannot join us in confounding the Tories. They're marching today, you know."

"I saw them. Only about a hundred, and mostly old."

Decatur frowned, fanning himself with his round hat. "Those hundred are the ones who are foolish enough to declare themselves. There are a good many sympathizers who prefer to do their work indoors." He returned his hat to his head and grinned. "But it's a fine day for marching, and I thought it best to show the navy in force on the streets today lest the Tories grow too bold and think they can get away with breaking the peace."

"Was this your idea, Stephen?" Favian asked.

"Stewart's, actually," Decatur said. "I think the mayor and the local authorities will be thankful, though, don't you?"

"I should imagine they would be," Favian said. He'd thought he'd seen Charles Stewart's hand in this gesture; the idea hadn't seemed like one of Decatur's. "Good luck to you."

"Thankee," Decatur said, waving to someone on the street. Favian said his farewells and rode for the ferry.

It was a clear day and a hot one, but the sea breeze cooled him as Fulton's clattering steam ferry crossed the East River. The river was crowded with ships lying at their anchors, or two-deep along the wharves. Some had lain there for two years, since the declaration of war, lying with only an anchor watch aboard, their running rigging taken down, the standing rigging slowly wearing away, their masts marked at night by an anchor light that swung with the tide and wind. . . . For any seaman, a sad sight.

And on the southern horizon Favian saw the topsails of the British squadron off Sandy Hook. He recognized the big *Majestic*, Captain Hayes, a frigate the British claimed was the equal of any of the American forty-fours. It was a claim Favian doubted—*Majestic* might be equal in broadside armament, but *President*, a smart ship, could certainly outsail her. There was a smaller frigate accompanying *Majestic;* that would be either *Pomone* or *Tenedos*. Favian knew there was another British squadron to the north, in Long Island Sound; there Admiral Sir Thomas Masterman Hardy, the captain who had kissed Nelson farewell at Trafalgar, commanded *Ramillies* off New London, threatening at any moment to launch a force up the Thames to burn the *United States*,

Jacob Jones's *Macedonian*, or the half-completed *Shark*. The Federalist government of Connecticut had refused to adequately man the Thames batteries to prevent this, and so the American ships had been hauled for miles up the river to relative safety; it was only recently that Jones had established his own batteries, with navy gunners, that permitted *United States* and *Macedonian* to return to New London.

Favian knew all the names of his enemies: Hope of the *Endymion*, Henderson of the *Tigris*, Pearce of the *Rifleman*, Byron of the *Belvidera*, Townsend of the *Aeolus*, Bastard of the *Africa*, Burdett of the *Maidstone*. Farther north, off Boston, were Collier of the *Leander*, Stuart of the *Newcastle*, Kerr of the *Acasta*. The British had been there for months, the ships and the personalities of their captains growing familiar as the blockade wore on, as familiar as the dismal sight of all that shipping rotting slowly by the East River piers.

A year before Favian had seen what years of a British blockade had done to Norway: the useless shipping, the graying, once-gay city of Bergen, the half-starved inhabitants, the well-fed nobility and profiteers. . . . If the war went on a great deal longer, New York could go the way of Bergen, cut off from trade, from news of foreign lands, from the normal to-and-fro of populations, from all that a great city requires. Manhattan would be inhabited by apathetic ghosts and dogged by those distant, ever-present topsails. And it would happen not only to New York, but also Boston, Providence, Portsmouth, Charleston, Savannah, Washington, Norfolk, and New Orleans. The war was being lost.

Yet the British could still be hurt. England had been at war almost continually for twenty years. Could she stand those taxes, those incessant drafts on her population and resources for much longer? Markham's Raid had destroyed millions in commerce, had driven insurance rates skyrocketing. Porter in the Pacific had done as well, wiping out the British whaling fleet, removing that source of His Britannic Majesty's revenue. If the United States could somehow hang on, wearing Britain away by its simple refusal to lie down and die, its navy and privateers striking into the Channel, the Pacific, and perhaps even the Indian Ocean, then the war might yet be brought to a satisfactory conclusion.

But the likelihood of a good end to the war was waning. The Tories marching on the streets of New York made that clear enough, as did the unreasoning sedition of the antiwar Federalists.

The United States was under stress, and disunited. In another month Favian would turn thirty, which would allow him to vote in New Hampshire, the state where he owned property. He wondered if he would ever have the chance to vote for a President of the United States—if the talk of secession continued, he might find himself voting for the president of a British protectorate, New England having returned to the fold of the mother country.

Favian comforted his horse, made nervous by the clanking engine and gushing smokestack, as the ferry thudded against its pier, then rode to the shipyard. Captain Jacob Jones waited at the gate, dressed like Favian in civilian clothes. "We'll have an opportunity to view the steam battery in a few minutes, when the workers have their luncheon," Jones said, looking at his watch. "*Demologos* is being completed as quickly as possible, and I do not wish to impede the workers."

They spoke of the *Macedonian* as Favian stabled his horse; Jones was her captain, but had scarcely ever sailed in her, having only gone north from New York the year before in company with Decatur in the *United States*, before being forced into New London when *United States* was struck by lightning in a freak storm. He had then been promptly blockaded by the British and had never had another chance to take her to sea. Favian, as Decatur's first lieutenant, had commanded *Macedonian* after her capture, had rerigged her in mid-Atlantic to sail her to Rhode Island. Even though he had never been *Macedonian*'s captain he'd sailed her many more days than Jones ever had, and Jones was properly curious about her.

"Very fast off the wind," Favian said, "but close-hauled she's sluggish. I think with proper trimming you might get her five and a half points from the wind, but no closer."

Jones nodded sagely, a man who knew his craft; they went on to discuss the technical aspects of trimming *Macedonian*, and then Jones inquired about Markham's Recording Log.

Favian responded warmly; the recording log was one of his obsessions. When he'd captured *Macedonian* one of Massey's automatic recording logs had been captured with it. The device was a practical machine for measuring the speed of a ship, more efficient than the taffrail logs with their clumsy knotted lines that had been used since the days before Columbus, and Favian had written memoranda to the Navy Department recommending its investigation and use, but in the press of wartime affairs they'd been ignored. At first he'd accepted the department's judgment, but as he'd felt the boredom of the months ashore weighing on him he'd begun to occupy himself with the design of a recording log of his own.

It seemed to him that Massey's device could be improved. Massey's Recording Log was in two parts, an arrow-shaped head containing the actual recording device, which was connected to a finned "rotator" that turned as it passed through the water. It had seemed to Favian that the two elements could be combined, resulting in a simpler, more practical mechanism. His prototype designs, tested on the Thames at New London, had shown that the idea would work, but there had been no deep-sea tests, and there was a problem with the metallurgy.

"We can't use iron or steel, because it will rust," Favian explained. "Copper is too soft, and bronze too brittle. We'll be using an alloy of copper and zinc to produce brass, but we have to have the percentages right. Too much copper will make it too soft; too much zinc will make it too brittle. I've been working with a clockmaker, and he's carrying out experiments while I'm gone. I hope he may have the answer by the time I return."

"I hope you may," Jones said. There was the sound of a clattering noontime bell, and the distant bustle and clatter of the yard died away. Favian and Jones began their walk to the giant shed that housed the steam battery while it was building. Jones received the salute of the marine guard and threw open the door.

"Good God!" Favian murmured. He had never pictured the thing as quite this big. "She's a monster, Jacob!"

Jones smiled. "In the water she's going to look like an entire city block that has detached itself from Manhattan and swum out to fight the British."

"Two hulls, a what-d'ye-call it, a catamaran. I hadn't heard that."

"The battery has a beam of fifty-six feet and a length of a hundred forty," Jones said as they entered the shed, walking the length of the great hull, in the dim light sensed as much as seen, a thing like a slumbering giant, possessed of a latent, awesome power. "With those proportions on a sailing vessel, she'd have the handling of a floating brick. But with two hulls she rides higher, there is less water resistance, and the paddlewheel amidships will be protected."

"Protected by walls of wood," Favian said, walking up a

gangplank to peer into the starboard hull. The hulls were massive, enormous timbers providing cross-bracing that would absorb the shock of recoiling guns; there was a bulwark of a thickness greater than any Favian had seen.

"Fifty-eight inches of oak planking on the sides," Jones said proudly. "Even the largest men-of-war have only thirty. Over five feet of planking! That'll stop any cannon shot the British can throw at her, and in case a shot comes through one of the embrasures we'll have thirty inches protecting the paddlewheel.

"She'll have a battery of thirty heavy guns, with red-hot shot heated in boxes next to the boiler. Thirty guns ain't much, not compared to a British seventy-four, but when each of those thirty guns can fire a thirty-two pound shot hot enough to set a target alight, that's enough to make a holocaust of any blockading squadron."

Fire, Favian thought. Any sailor's greatest terror, greater than storms or sharks, greater than fear of decapitation in battle. Ships were made of wood, payed with tar, rigged with tarred lines, propelled by canvas sails—all of it flammable. Red-hot shot was a terror: even the British, bold as anyone, were careful to keep their blockading squadrons well outside the ranges of Forts Clinton, Totten, and Schuyler, the New York batteries that could incinerate their entire fleet if given the chance. Within a few short months *Demologos* would be launched, and later, on some calm day when the British could not maneuver or escape, the steam battery would set forth, a mobile fort that would bring the terror of red-hot shot out to sea. What could the British do to prevent it? All those celebrated names, Byron of the *Belvidera*, Hope of the *Endymion* . . . helpless. Jones had been right to use the word *holocaust*, meaning a flaming sacrifice to the gods. Even the old gods of war, Belial or Thor or Mars, might hesitate to accept a sacrifice of this dimension, all those frigates and liners going up like so many torches, flames licking up the tall pine masts, thousands of crewmen running in panicked frenzy over the decks, hot tar and ash dripping down on them as they tried to cast off the boats. . . .

"*Demologos*. Voice of the people," Favian whispered, translating, a little freely, the Greek. The American republic might be saved by such machines; *Demologos* might drive off the blockading squadrons and allow those hundreds of useless merchant ships access to the seas, preventing the despair and economic stagnation caused by the blockade.

But it was still horrible. Balanced on his plank, looking down into *Demologos*'s twin hulls, Favian knew he was seeing a new, double-edged creation, at once a thing of scarcely imaginable terror and the possible salvation of the United States of America, the first harbinger of a more deadly, more scientific, more destructive mode of warfare, as well as the instrument by which the voice of the American people might continue to be heard abroad. . . . Favian wondered if this duality had been considered in choosing the name: the Greek *logos* had many meanings, "voice" and "word" being only two. Others were "argument," "reason," or "debate." The steam battery was certainly an almighty argument, but was the argument, Favian wondered, also the voice of reason? It was doubtless in the service of reason that the American republic had been founded; but was the launching of this terrible mechanism a reasonable act? Was it the "reason of the people" that had declared this war, and now sent forth this machine to incinerate enemies by the hundreds? It was an unsettling question. Favian had heard that many were in favor of changing the name to *Fulton;* perhaps, he thought, they wanted to avoid the unsettling questions raised by her name.

Of course no one could picture *Demologos* venturing more than a few miles from shore; sailing vessels would still rule the high seas for at least another few generations, until the art of building steam engines rose to the challenge.

And while Favian stood wrapped in his thoughts, Jones prattled on about the steam battery, all the facts contained within his agile memory: the paddles would be fourteen feet wide, dipping four feet; the engine would be supported by one hull, the boiler by the other; there would be two short masts, used only for signaling, although there would be a bowsprit on each end to set jibs on, to aid in docking. There were twin rudders at each end; if one rudder was shot off, *Demologos* could reverse course and steam away; Fulton was promising six knots of speed. There would be pumps and hoses to discharge hot water and steam against any boarders; she would carry a crew of over two hundred.

"When will she be operational?" Favian asked.

"Fulton is building the engine and boiler at his own shipyard on the Hudson," Jones said. "After the hull's finished she'll be towed over to Fulton's to get her engine, and then she'll be ready for trials in the harbor, but she can't venture out of protected waters without her guns, and they're waiting in Philadelphia. They've got to be trucked overland, and each weighs two and a half tons—it'll take weeks."

"Aye. *Shark*'s guns aren't with her, either, and aren't likely to be," Favian said. Naval guns were scarce in the United States; guns for the first frigates were imported from Great Britain. Favian remembered well the royal monogram, GR, on the gun barrels of the *Constitution* and the *United States*. With the blockade all the guns were being moved overland rather than by sea, and the delays were enormous.

"We expect to be ready for trials in November," Jones said. "But there's no telling when she'll be ready to fight."

"Who's to command her?" Favian asked.

"Ah, the secretary has yet to decide," Jones said. "It might go to Lewis or Decatur, but Lewis has been against the project from the beginning and Decatur probably has ambitions elsewhere."

"Finding a captain might delay her more than the guns," Favian said.

"Yes. Do you wish to volunteer?" Jones was grinning. Favian looked down at the massive timbers of the half-completed machine and shook his head.

"I'll stay with the *Shark*," he said. "It will be completed earlier, probably, and I want to get to sea, not spend my time paddling up and down New York harbor."

Jones nodded. "I understand," he said. "For me, the temptation is greater. *Macedonian* may never sail—certainly she won't if the secretary keeps sending her crews to the Lakes. I'd take this steamboat rather than rot on the banks of the Thames for the rest of the war. And just think, Favian—*Demologos* would probably carry with it a commodore's pendant!"

A commodore's pendant! Jones was no more immune than most to the allure of that ridiculous honorary rank. The precedence and perquisites of a commodore, and who were rightfully entitled to them, were the cause of so much disgraceful wrangling and backstage maneuvering within the service that Favian wished the whole business dispensed with, either by creating the rank of rear admiral to regularize flag rank or by dispensing with the notion of "commodores" altogether.

"That would probably depend a great deal on who else is in harbor at the time," Favian said, diplomatic. "How many commodores will New York need? We have Decatur and Lewis here already."

"Stephen will probably try to run the blockade before long," Jones said. His tone was hopeful. "That'll mean one less commodore, at least. Would you like to meet Fulton? He's back from Philadelphia; I saw him going into this office this morning."

Favian had expected a burly, long-armed mechanic, a man at home amid the world of grease, coal, and iron represented by *Demologos* and Fulton's other designs, but instead Favian faced a large-framed, pale, long-fingered man, dressed in dramatic black and white, carrying a springy fruitwood cane like an English gentleman, a man more cut out to be a poet or painter than an engineer, the picture of a dandy and aesthete. His speech, like Favian's, echoed the accent of Britain; they had both been raised, perhaps, in the same genteel school.

Fulton bowed formally, declining to shake hands, and as Favian returned the bow he perceived the flushed spots on the pale cheeks, the unnaturally red lips, the slight effort Fulton was making to breathe normally. *Consumptive,* Favian thought.

"Sirs!" Fulton said. "I was about to have some coffee. Would you gentlemen join me?"

"Gladly, sir," Favian said. Fulton's movements, despite his illness, were vigorous and swift; he opened the door to an inner room where a coffee pot sat on a small iron stove. The walls of the room were covered with designs executed in a neat, clear hand: Favian recognized *Demologos*, but there were other plans for steamships, drafts for buildings, a few small oils, including a portrait of Fulton himself executed with a precise hand.

"Did you paint thèse, Mr. Fulton?" he asked.

"Oh, yes," Fulton said, looking up from pouring coffee into three battered tin cups. "Painting is my first love, of course, but there's no money to be made there. Would you like some, ah, nerve restorer with your coffee?" He opened a drawer in his desk and offered a bottle of whiskey.

"Thank you, no," Favian said. He took the coffee and sipped: the real thing, rare and costly in this blockaded city, and much appreciated.

"The trip to Philadelphia was a success!" Fulton told Jones delightedly. "The Defense Committee quite saw the point in my designs. They wanted another *Demologos*, but I'll give 'em something better!" He waved his hands as he spoke, sketching promiscuously in the air. "I've learned a great deal from *Demologos*, and I'll be able to apply it for the Philadelphia battery. Iron plating, that's the key! A few inches of iron will give the protection of several feet of oak—of course Philadelphia will have to establish an ironworks to make the plates, but I think I've convinced 'em the expenses will be justified by the results. Iron, sirs, iron! That's the key!

"And I'll prove it to 'em! In a few days my turtle boat will be completed. Twelve sailors peddling an armored paddlewheel, protected by an iron-plated pitched roof—don't need much iron there, y'see, because the shot cannot strike it head-on but will strike at an angle: glance off. She'll tow a mine—the blockade might be broke by July!"

Fulton paused, gasping for breath. The consumption seemed well advanced, and Favian wondered if phthisis had evolved. Apparently not; there was no coughing.

Jones asked a few polite questions about the turtle boat; it was apparent he was not an enthusiast. Favian could understand why: no boat, no matter how well armored, that was propelled by men peddling a paddle wheel would be able to catch a British vessel even in a light wind. It was steam power that could defeat the enemy frigates, not a dozen tars in a toy boat.

The conversation veered to the Philadelphia steam battery, and Favian asked whether the weight of the iron would not be a burden to the engine. Fulton replied that it would not, since weight would be saved by the subtraction of several feet of wood planking. Favian pictured to himself a rust-red iron battery the size of *Demologos*, belching smoke, steam, and hot shot; the thought was appalling. Favian had spent years with the Philadelphia gunboat squadron, the pathetic little cockleshells charged with the defense of the Delaware; he knew that the gunboats had spent the war trying, with no success at all, to discover some way to end the Delaware blockade. Fulton's iron battery could do the work in an afternoon. This pale aesthete would create a revolution in warfare, if only the Philadelphia Defense Committee could raise the money. And if the consumption didn't destroy him first.

Favian emerged from his musings to see Fulton staring at him intently. "I wonder, Captain Markham," he said, "if you would do me the favor of sitting for me, for a portrait. At no cost to yourself, of course," he added hastily. "I am interested, sir, in your physiognomy—may I handle your face?—you carry yourself in an interesting fashion, and you dress in style. I hope you will not wear a uniform; I like that open collar." His eyes clouded, he seemed now to speak more to himself than to anyone else in the room. "Such a deal of repressed power, strength, in the carriage of the shoulders. Truly a man of action, I should think, but a man firmly in control of himself the while. A fine contrast, but to bring it out? A challenge, truly."

Favian, taken aback entirely by Fulton's abrupt change of course, allowed the painter to touch his jaw, turning his head into the light. His portrait had been painted several times since the *Teaser* fight; he had commissioned a large portrait, full uniform and epaulets and a commanding expression, in the background *Teaser* heeling over with torn-open bulwarks while *Experiment* lay with fore topsail aback in the distance, flags flying. He had given the portrait to his father; it hung in the study next to the arranged trophies of the Revolution, all the swords captured in battle and tattered British ensigns. There had been a number of popular engravings, and of course Favian's profile was on the gold *Teaser* medal issued by Congress. Fulton seemed to have no interest in the martial side; that was a relief. Favian was heartily sick of his own celebrity, the constant insistence by the public that he should relive over and over his moments of triumph, as if there had not been months since the *Teaser* had slid beneath the waves.

"No one, Mr. Fulton," he said, "has ever complimented my appearance in such terms. I'm flattered, but I have no plans to stay in New York for very long . . ."

"How long?" Fulton asked, peering at him owlishly.

"I—I can't say for certain, sir. My plans are rather, ah—"

"Captain Stewart and I are leaving a week from tomorrow," Jones said. "We had hoped that Captain Markham would join us."

"Thank you, sir," Favian said. "That would fit in splendidly with my, ah, as-yet-unformed plans. But, Mr. Fulton, I can hardly expect you to rearrange your schedule to accommodate a series of portrait sittings in the next week. I'm much obliged to you, and I'm flattered, but—"

"Stuff!" Fulton said. "Can you come tomorrow? Perhaps in the evening—we can meet in my studio at home. You can meet my wife—perhaps you can come for supper, sir?"

Favian grimaced inwardly; this conversation was rapidly turning into a series of apologies. "Mr. Fulton, I regret to say that I am engaged for tomorrow evening. With my cousin and his family, whom I have been neglecting unforgivably."

"The night following?"

Favian saw Jones watching him with an amused smile. Favian bowed, at once to the inevitable, to his own mounting curiosity, and to Fulton. Perhaps the man would have some helpful suggestions for Markham's Recording Log: he seemed an expert on things mechanical.

"What, sir," he asked, turning to Fulton with a polite, acquiescent smile, "shall I wear?"

4

Fulton's house at One State Street had a solar loft where he did his drawing and his plans for war engines; for three successive afternoons Favian had stood below the skylights, sweating in spite of the paper fan Fulton had given him, while the artist worked with his pastels. An oil painting would come later, whenever there was time; for now Fulton was fixing Favian in his mind and on paper.

"I have fought the British, you know," Fulton said, his long-fingered hands darting over his pad, working swiftly—it was surprising how swiftly the man worked. The sound of a harp filtered up from below: Fulton's young wife Harriet, one of the great beauties of New York, a young blond girl with a laugh that tinkled like her harp; but her intellect, Favian thought, would not set the world afire. "I made two attempts to blow up blockading ships with my submarine boat *Nautilus*. That was in the month of Fructidor, the year nine. I suppose even in France nowadays they call it September of 1800. Would you turn your head a little to the left, please?"

Favian turned his head. "Was either attempt successful?" he asked.

A brief frown crossed Fulton's face. "Nay. They must have heard the *Nautilus* was in the area; they ran away while I was paddling toward them under the water. Later I had to take my boat apart to keep the French from stealing the idea. Bonaparte would not pay a man for an idea, but if he could steal an invention he would not mind having it."

The words, meant to be spoken pleasantly, had an edge of bitterness that Fulton could not entirely suppress. Favian knew he had been fighting for years to protect his patents and his steamboat monopolies on the rivers of New York state. It seemed that the steamboat had a great many fathers. Favian felt sweat dripping in his eyes and swiped it away.

"Not like you, of course. No real battles," Fulton said. He smiled lightly. "I never had a talent for subordination. Could never take orders from anybody." His arm moved with swift precision; it appeared to draw automatically, needing no conscious guidance from Fulton, who seemed entirely free to speak of whatever came to mind. He had spent the afternoons talking charmingly of his intentions, his wife, his friends, and his experiences among the great movers of Europe: Pitt, Bonaparte, Melville, the Duchesse de Gontaut-Biron. He had expressed an interest in Favian's recording log, but had not been able to offer much in the way of advice: metallurgy was not his field. On the financial side, though, he had counsel to give: "Don't put your own money into it if you can avoid it," he'd said. "Find subscribers; sell 'em shares. No reason to assume all the risk yourself."

"There are many men in the navy who do not take orders gladly," Favian said, sweating. The sound of the harp floated delicately in the air.

"Are you among them?" Fulton's curiosity seemed earnest; Favian wondered if his response would alter the shape of the forthcoming portrait. Was there an interpretation hanging in the balance here, staid senior officer or young flashing-eyed buccaneer?

"I am the navy's to command," Favian said. There was a little pause, filled only by Harriet Fulton's harp.

"Hm," said Fulton. He frowned over his pastels. "You are an uncompromising servant of the republic, I see."

"I am a navy man. The pursuit of glory is my avocation," said Favian.

Fulton frowned again. Favian fanned himself briskly, thankful he'd been allowed the open collar. *Glory*, he thought. A wispy concept, bearing images of banners blowing in the wind, the sound of trumpets, portraits of officers with their eyes flashing romantic ardor, arms pointed sternly toward the objective. He'd seen a copy of West's *Death of Wolfe*, that triumph of American painting, the mortally wounded general in his red coat lying back in the arms of his staff, officers flanking him in studied, composed groups. The apotheosis of the realistic school: the academicians had been scandalized that Wolfe was not in Roman dress.

Realistic, aye. Wolfe was shot three times; had West known it? Perhaps the general had puked all over his neat silk stockings; that sort of thing happened to bodies outraged by too many wounds. Or maybe his intestines were hanging out of his satin waistcoat. The great man's staff would not have so calmly watched, either: if they'd had any sense they would have been hugging the muddy ground while the French volleys twittered over their heads. It must have been a confused blundering muck of a battle, for both commanders died because they had to run forward to sort out their troops. Glorious deaths. Honored dead. *Glory*. A thing immortalized on canvas, in novels, in commemorative verse. "I seek glory": no one would think it an odd ambition.

Had he ever pursued glory, Favian wondered? When he was seventeen, leaping from boat to boat off Tripoli, slashing at the Moors? Once, in a rage because James Decatur had been killed treacherously, he had led eight men against thirty-five; he had killed thirty-three at the cost of three men wounded, and the enemy captain had been shot with muskets as he tried to swim to safety; the Tripolitan thwarts had been slippery with gore. That had been glory; he'd known it for certain, had exulted in it. Himself, Richard Somers, the two Decatur brothers: they had all gone for glory and won it, James by dying nobly of a bullet in the brain after hours of agony in *Constitution*'s orlop, Somers by blowing himself to smithereens on the *Intrepid*, Decatur with his string of victories, the *Philadelphia* capture, which even Nelson had called "the boldest act of the age," and the capture of the *Macedonian*, Favian with Markham's Raid and the *Teaser*. Decatur was a true believer still, seeking the bubble reputation in the cannon's mouth, but Favian knew he had fallen from grace. There were reasons he fought still, reasons he owed the navy his duty, reasons many and tangled, but glory was no longer among them.

Another triumph, he supposed, of the realist school.

He shied from admitting this to Fulton. Burrows he might have told, if his friend hadn't died on the *Enterprise;* but then Burrows was raised in the school of the navy, and would have understood. Fulton, despite his adventures with the *Nautilus,* was not among the band of brothers: he had not seen James Decatur lying pale in the *Constitution*'s orlop, or seen *Macedonian*'s well deck ankle deep in bloody brine with arms and legs and other parts of men rolling from one bulwark to the other with the motion of the sea. It was sights such as these that bound the navy men together, sights more compelling than anything painted on canvas.

"You may step down, Captain," Fulton said. "I have an appointment, and I think I've done studies enough to complete a canvas later. I thank you for your patience."

Favian stepped from his place, thankfully mopping his forehead with his handkerchief. "May I see?" he asked. Fulton looked down at his pad, pursing his lips doubtfully, then held it out.

It was a strange, saturnine Favian, scowling, the eyes glowering and yet somehow haunted: it was disturbingly eloquent, powerful but truly unpleasant. Favian felt his heart lurch. "Is that how I look?" he said.

Fulton cocked an eyebrow at his pad. "I didn't think you'd like that one," he said. "I think it's more of a caricature than anything drawn from life." He laughed. "Don't worry, I won't use it. I find you damnably hard to draw, sir—this was the last attempt. It expresses my own difficulty more than your character, I'm sure; I am not like my friend West, able to bring a man's personality to the fore with a few strokes. There is something contradictory in you, and I cannot resolve it. Damme, I wish I could!"

He turned to a folio and opened it, showing other sketches, the series he'd done of Favian. They were conventional renderings, differing in approach and in the use of lighting: there were several idealized Favians, romantic fervor glowing in his eyes, a nautical *beau sabreur;* there were realistic renderings of a tall, long-limbed gentleman, his collar open, twisting a riding crop in his hands, reflective, pensive, or impatient to go about his business. Conventional stuff, but nothing with the power of that last rendering, that strange feral expression, guilt and cunning and something of desperation, a man somehow cornered. It had come as Favian spoke of glory. Terrifying.

"Which do you prefer, Captain Markham?" Fulton asked, genial.

Favian hesitated, then pointed at one of the idealized portraits, this one a little more rugged than the others, a mature man of action rather than a dreamy glory-struck youth. "This, I think," he said. The navy would no doubt approve the choice, showing him as a respectable post captain and a leader of men.

Fulton nodded. "I like it myself. After I've completed the portrait I will send you these studies, if you wish."

"I will be happy to have them, sir."

Fulton held up the last rendering, and Favian received a glimpse of those corrupted, haunted features. "I will destroy this, of course," he said.

"Keep it, I beg you," Favian said impulsively. He laughed, carelessly, as Fulton watched him with acute artist's eyes. "It may help you with the portrait. Resolving, as you say, the contradictions." Why, he wondered, did he not have the thing destroyed? Horrible, yet there was truth in it. More truth than in the *Death of Wolfe* and all its ilk.

"Yes, if you like," Fulton said, thankful, perhaps, that his best work would be preserved. He slipped the sketch into his portfolio.

"I might beg an indulgence, Captain Markham," Fulton said, taking Favian's arm, leading him downstairs to a study. He smiled nervously. "You are a nautical gent; you know the worth of my designs. May I ask you to sign a paper testifying to the usefulness of *Demologos*? Commodore Decatur has already signed—so have Captains Jones, Perry, Warrington, and Biddle."

"I will be honored, sir, to set my name alongside theirs," Favian said. Fulton smiled as Favian picked up a pen and signed the paper.

"And if, sir, you have some prize money at hand, I can recommend no safer investment than my steamboats," Fulton said heartily. "We have built twenty-one steamboats in seven years—there are four on the Mississippi, seven on the Hudson, others in Jersey or used as ferries. We are returning eight percent per year on investments. Solid as the rock of Gibraltar, sir, solid as a rock."

Favian remembered what Fulton had said earlier: "Don't put your own money into it. Sell 'em shares." It was to the man's credit, Favian supposed, that he followed his own advice.

"I shall consider it, sir," Favian said. Fulton brightened, and escorted Favian to the door. "I shall see you, I hope, before you leave. We'll talk about the steamboat business—the way of the future, y'know."

Two days later Favian was dining with Charles Stewart near the navy yard, the both of them drying out by the fire after a short, drenching gale, when the alarm bells in the yard began to clatter, calling up the marines. It seemed Fulton's turtle boat, on its maiden voyage, had got in trouble with a British frigate.

Favian jumped for his horse and rode full-tilt for the Long Island shore, and from a nearby hill he saw the turtle boat beached on the sand—a victim of the gale, it appeared—with the frigate *Maidstone,* Captain Burdett, anchored in the offing. Redcoated marines were coming ashore in their boats; militia were forming up to meet them. Favian rode down to help the militia dress their lines, seeing the pale part-time soldiers, shopkeepers and wheelwrights and schoolteachers, clasping their muskets whiteknuckled and staring at the weapons as if they had never seen their like before. Fulton was there, his eyes savage. Favian wished for his pistols or at least a sword as he rode behind their line, back and forth, bawling hearty professional phrases: "I've fought these redcoats, and they're nothing much. Keep your ranks, and when you fire aim low."

The British boats struck the beach, rocking in the surf, their swivel guns and carronades banging out canister that wailed high overhead, not touching a man. The militia got out one rattling good volley as the British tumbled from their boats. Favian, still riding behind the lines brandishing his riding crop, smelled powder and heard the rattle of ramrods, seeing the redcoats forming on the beach, most of them sopped to the waist in brine. Most of the balls would go high, Favian knew, and it was foolish to stay on horseback; but he wanted the militia to see him. Foolish, to die in a fight for an iron rowboat. Not even his fight. The volley came, ragged and high, the bullets whistling about Favian's ears, and then the lobsterbacks lowered their bayonets and charged, coming on in ragged clumps, wailing like Irishmen. The militia paused for a paralyzed second and then turned.

Favian ran with them, galloping in the pack with his whip in his teeth, knowing there was no point in rallying them.

From his hill he watched as the turtle boat fell prize to the *Maidstone*. No one seemed to have been hurt. The Battle of the Rowboat, Favian thought, 25 June, 1814. British casualties: nought. American casualties: the rowboat. The turtle boat was set alight; in a few hours nothing was left of the world's first iron war vessel but scorched timbers and glowing iron plates. The lobsterback pickets chatted with some local men and a few bold ladies: not treasonous correspondence, Favian knew, just curiosity. The marines from the yard came up at a loping run, out of breath, Lieutenant Twiggs in front with his sword bared, Charles Stewart trotting among them on horseback. "Shall I attack, Captain?" Twiggs asked. "The boat is lost," Favian said. "Your men are tired. But do what you want." Twiggs waved his blade and led his leathernecks forward with a laughing smile, seizing his chance for glory. The militia, rallied now, came down behind them, brave enough with federal troops between them and the enemy. There was a little skirmish on the sand as the British scattered back to their boats, leaving a few redcoats lying like sacks on the beach: Twiggs had his glory and a few enemy dead. *Maidstone* had the turtle boat. Both had reason to be happy with the day.

Favian saw the inventor afterwards, staring pensively down at the ruin, his thoughts unguessable. Stern war, rather than art, Favian thought, had produced another triumph of the realist school.

5

The Elk Horn Tavern in Groton was full of sailors. There were a few of *Macedonian*'s men on liberty but the majority were from the *Tom Bowlin* privateer, newly fitted out with fourteen carriage guns, which would try to slip out past the British blockade during the first spell of bad weather, or during the next moonless night—plans at this point were being kept securely within the mind and heart of Captain Shelby Wohl, but it was assumed that the cunning old blue-light skipper had planned the escape with his usual ingenuity.

The floorboards of the Elk Horn were slippery as the result of a shortage of spittoons; but the beer and whiskey were cheap, if a little watery, and the worst class of those vultures who preyed on sailors were kept out, so the Elk Horn was a popular place. The fiddler Lazarus, a man reputed to be as mad as old Mocha Dick but filled with demonic talent and energy, had been playing reels, jigs, chanties, hornpipes, forebitters, old fo'c'sle songs, ballads; his bow flashed with dazzling speed on the fast songs, the notes flying with the racketing pace of hail in a November storm but yet as clear and distinct; the slow tunes were played with such clarity and sentiment that half the grizzled old shellbacks in the Elk Horn wept openly.

Vihtori Kuusikoski, able seaman, foretopman of the *Tom Bowlin*, felt the whiskey warming his insides, the fiddlestrings tugging at his heart. In this lachrymose and sodden company, beneath these smoke-stained low beams, Kuusikoski felt contentment rising in him. It was the first time he had felt so nearly at peace since the day, four years before, he'd fled Finland, refusing to live under the Russian conquerors.

> Rolling home, rolling home, rolling home across the sea,
> Rolling home to old New England,
> Rolling home, dear land, to thee . . .

That was perhaps the universal sailor's song, an international melody; Vihtori Kuusikoski had heard it sung in Finnish, Swedish, and Plattdeutsch aboard the Baltic merchantmen he'd sailed in, the name of the destination changed according to the nationality of the sailors, but always with the same sentiment, sung to the same tune. The droning of the assembled sailors, accompanied by Lazarus on his fiddle, filled the tavern, echoing from the low beams of the ceiling. It sounded as reverent as a hymn. Kuusikoski felt his eyes smart. He would never be rolling home to his own land again. Never to sail among those pine-crowned islands, seeing the little towns marked with their wooden slope-roofed churches . . .

"Have ye some more bob smith, Koozy," said the privateersman next to him, pouring whiskey. " 'Tis a good old song, this."

"Derry, you're a friend," Kuusikoski said. "I ain't got nothing but the ship now." He gestured vaguely at the men seated with him: Wilks, the muscled, white-bearded, scarred old patriarch of the *Tom Bowlin*'s fo'c'sle, known as "Majesty"; Feld, the grinning, gap-toothed Carolinian in his red knit cap; Derry, the Irish exile, with the scars of the Royal Navy's cat on his back. "You men is my family now," Kuusikoski said.

"You'll get back to, to wherever it is, never fear," Derry said. " 'Tis I that cannot return. 'Tis me head in a noose I'll be putting just by goin' to sea, what with the British just off Groton Point. But what can a man do? A man must work." He nodded profoundly. "A man must practice his craft."

"I'll protect you, Derry," Kuusikoski said. He threw an arm around Derry's shoulders. "I'll tell 'em you're from Turku, like me. You just act like you don't got no English."

"Aye," Derry said, cocking his head. He took a swallow of the whiskey, his adam's apple bobbing. "It might work," he considered. "I'll tell 'em I got my scars in the Suo—in your navy, whatever it's called."

"The Swedish navy," Kuusikoski said.

"Derry's look was puzzled. "Sweden? Is that the same as this Suo—Suomi—whatever—the same place as the one you come from?"

"Nay, but Suomi was a part of Sweden. Had the same navy." Kuusikoski blinked. The sailors had fallen silent, but Lazarus was continuing the chorus solo on his fiddle, playing simply without his usual flourishes. A moving melody played by a master.

"A part of Sweden?" Derry said. His brow furrowed as he tried, through the whiskey that slowed him, to concentrate on the mystery. "And you can't go back because the Russians took it? Like Finland?"

"Finland, Suomi. Same thing. Different lang—different tongues," Kuusikoski said.

"You mean you're a *Finn*?" Derry's voice was almost a shriek. Lazarus was playing a drawn-out concluding note, wrapped entirely in his own art, and the room had hushed to hear him; Derry's cry had been heard by everyone nearby.

Vihtori Kuusikoski saw the eyes of his friends turning toward him, solemn, withdrawn, suddenly the eyes of strangers. He felt a touch of fear without understanding why. "Is that true, Koozy?" asked Wilks, known as Majesty, the tattooed muscles on his arms knotting. "Are you a Finn?"

Applause filled the room as Lazarus stood and bowed, but the table where Kuusikoski sat was silent.

"*Jaa*. I'm a *Suomalainen*, a Finn," Kuusikoski said, bewildered. "What's wrong? I say something?"

He watched, baffled and somehow afraid, as Majesty, his blue eyes solemn, made a commanding gesture, and in obedience the others went into a sudden consultation at the other end of the table. Kuusikoski caught a few words, heard through the haze of drink and the sound of ringing coins as money was flung at the fiddler: "Witch . . . not his fault . . . can't have a witch aboard . . . Finnish witch . . . witch!"

"What are you saying?" Kuusikoski said, trying to hear. He leaned forward and knocked over a cup of whiskey; he tried clumsily to right the cup and mop up the mess.

The conference ended. His friends stood, solemn.

"You should have told us," Majesty said, frowning. "We've got to leave now."

Not comprehending, Kuusikoski allowed himself to be rushed outside, past the other tables where he saw the same baffling, hostile stares on other faces, even on the faces of strangers, past where the fiddler was bowing and scooping coins into his cap. He was unsteady on his feet but the others held him up as they pushed out through the door, down the street, into an alley. "What happened?" Kuusikoski pleaded. "What's happening?" The first blow caught him behind the ear and he staggered against the side of the building. "Hey!" he shouted, but the fists were coming very fast and all he could do was to try to protect himself, covering his face with his arms, curling down to protect his midsection. The blows were drunk and wild and many missed entirely, but trying to escape he fell to the mud in the alley and then kicks were added to the blows. One kick missed and Derry thudded to the ground himself. The Irishman tried to rise but fell again, and groaned as if it were he who had been beaten.

At last they left him alone, Majesty and Feld standing over him, breathing hard, their knuckles bloody. Derry cursed as he tired again to rise, and again failed. "Damned witch," muttered the Irishman. " 'Tis me legs he's cursed!"

"Shut up," Majesty growled, leaning against the building while he caught his breath. His stern look was fading, replaced by what might have been shame.

"Me legs!" Derry wailed, clutching at his knees. Feld bent to help him to his feet, the two of them groping and cursing in the dark, managing only to drop Feld as well into the mud. Kuusikoski looked up through bruised eyes and saw Majesty looking uncertain.

"I'm sorry, Koozy," Majesty said. "But you should have told us. We can't have a witch aboard, bringing bad luck on a voyage as dangerous as this."

"Me legs is cursed. I'll never walk again," came a sobbing voice. Majesty looked at Derry with regal disdain.

"Shut your potato trap, you puisne little hopping Gyles," he said. He bent over Kuusikoski, rocking unsteadily from drink. There was kindness in his face, but to Kuusikoski it looked only grotesque. "If I was you, Koozy, I'd leave town. You can collect your gear tomorrow, and then you'd better push off, see?"

Majesty helped a weeping Derry to his feet and the three lurched unsteadily into the darkness. Kuusikoski lay in the gutter, pain throbbing through him. He tried to move and then almost screamed as his back went into spasm, the muscles knotting rigidly as they refused to obey his orders. He gave up and lay on the wet earth, the shock of his beating wearing off, replaced by outraged pain. He could hear people leaving the tavern, stepping wide around him, seeing only another drunken sailor on a binge, collapsed into a gutter and bruised with falling.

The footsteps faded away. From a distance came the sound of someone vomiting in some gutter. Then there was a hushed sound near him, a scraping; Kuusikoski wondered dimly if it was a rat. Invisible fingers began plucking at his clothing, heading for his purse.

"Hey!" he shouted, rolling, swinging a fist blindly. There was a thud and a curse, but he felt the purse twitched from its pocket and then he heard the thief running. His back began to spasm again, telling him it was too torn to move, and Kuusikoski lay quietly in the alley, eyes shut, merely suffering. They had all been his friends, shipmates. Why did they think him a witch? What was wrong with being a Finn in this America?

There was another set of footsteps, a strange jingling noise, and then the footsteps and the jingling stopped. Kuusikoski tried to move an arm and succeeded through his agony; he wiped blood from his eyes and peered at the dark form standing in the street, recognizing something in the silhouette. "Help me," he croaked, his voice sounding strange, cracked. "I been robbed."

Lazarus, the mad fiddler, his brow shadowed by a battered leather cap, bent to examine the beaten form. Coins jingled heavily in his pockets as he moved. "I shall help thee," the fiddler said. His eyes gleamed strangely in the dark. "Canst thou stand?"

Kuusikoski groaned as Lazarus helped him to sit up. His head swam and his vitals seemed to turn inside out, but there were no spasms until suddenly he clutched his midsection and vomited into the street. Lazarus, seemingly ignoring the stench and the vomit that splashed him, held Kuusikoski up until the spasms ended with wrenching dry heaves.

"That's done," the fiddler said briskly. "The purge will do thee good, sailor. I have some lodgings near here. Thou canst sleep in my captain's bed; he won't be using it tonight."

The reputed madman helped Kuusikoski to his feet, dabbing at his cuts with a handkerchief. "Lean thou on me," he said, slinging his fiddle case over his shoulder on its strap. Kuusikoski obeyed, scarcely wondering through his shock and misery where he was being taken. Together, the madman and the reputed witch staggered into the cool evening.

6

Favian snapped awake at dawn, the sea-born reflex surviving even the months of duty ashore. His eyes traversed the ceiling of the rented cottage, recognizing it, hearing the steady ticking of the clock in the parlor. No, he was not at sea. His six feet, four inches were not crammed into some little box of a bed; a telltale compass did not wave overhead in its brass box; the cottage, despite a momentary illusion when he first opened his eyes, did not rock to the scend of the seas. He glanced next to him, seeing Caroline's hair spread on the pillow, comforting and familiar.

He closed his eyes, hearing through the window the distant bellow of a cow as it awaited the morning hands that would relieve it of its burden of milk. *Captain Favian Markham, USN, man of property!* Owner of a hundred and sixty acres of Manhattan Island, five hundred acres in New Hampshire, a tenanted house in Portland, and a mistress kept out of sight in a rented cottage outside Poquetanuck.

The final few days in New York, three months ago now, had been busy ones: he had invested much of his prize money, but not in Fulton's steamboats. His banker cousin Micah had handled all the financial details, and Favian had been compelled to spend many hours in that unhappy household. Micah was bearing his misfortunes well, at least in public, and if Favian hadn't been alerted by the sidewalk gossip he would have noticed nothing he could have put a name to; but as it was, a number of Micah's intemperate outbursts at Toryism, flung angrily when his wife was out of the room, seemed to confirm the worst. But Micah had mentioned nothing directly and so Favian had followed his cousin's lead, refraining from intruding in Micah's affairs when there was no hint of any intrusion being wanted or appreciated. They had remained friendly cousins and businessmen, not intimates; perhaps Micah had been relieved to deal with someone he thought had not known the gossip.

Micah obviously had a firm grip on his business. Approached with Favian's hesitant questions, Micah had discerned their object immediately and virtually ordered Favian to invest. In land, not steamboats; Micah explained that it would take only a single court case to end Fulton's monopoly and that would be the end of profits. The surveyors boarding with Frau Fux had suggested some land they knew to be for sale; Micah had approved of most of the suggestions, adding one or two of his own, places farther south where houses could be built immediately, generating immediate income in rents. Several days later, when Favian had ridden north on his mare, preceding the stage in which Captains Stewart and Jones were riding, it had been as the owner of eighty acres of farmland west of Broadway at Twelfth Street, another sixty acres off Bleecker Street just to the east of Frau Fux's place, and twenty acres—the acres on which rental buildings would be constructed that winter—just inside New York City proper near the intersection of Greenwich Road and Prince Street.

Favian was still not entirely easy about the land. Speculation was not his line, and it was all speculative; there was no absolute guarantee that New York City would continue to grow northward, but Micah assured him that much of the land would have been tenanted already had it not been for the combined misfortunes of the yellow fever epidemic of '01, the economic catastrophe of the embargoes, and the halt to commerce brought on by the war. Favian had invested, comforted somewhat by the awesome thought of *Demologos*, which might well break the blockade and bring about a resurgence of prosperity. It had seemed safer, at any rate, than keeping his money in the banks and watching its value fall.

The procedure—writing the bank drafts, signing the contracts with the banks and builders, acquiring the deeds to land that, for the most part, he had not seen, and paying for it with money in sums that, with the reflexes of a naval lieutenant earning fifty dollars per month, he was not able quite to comprehend—all had seemed slightly unreal. He was slowly unlearning poverty and trying to learn instead the habits of a moderately wealthy man.

Favian Markham, man of property! Perhaps the acquiring of a mistress, as much as the land speculation, had marked the transition. Favian's carnal habits had been formed early, during his year at Harvard, and strengthened during his years in the navy: long periods of enforced abstinence followed by a prolonged, covert plunge into high-class brothels. That had been the pattern generated by poverty: he had not been able to afford a relationship with a woman extending beyond a few hours, let alone a wife. Favian's first experience with a professional courtesan had been in Norway; it had been, initially, a delirious experience, far superior to the sort of thing he'd been used to; but complications had arisen and a duel had been fought, leaving the memory bitter.

Caroline Huxley was, she claimed, an actress. She spoke with a soft Maryland accent and was about twenty-five. Favian knew her to have formerly been the property of a dragoon lieutenant who had been called off to the Niagara frontier; Favian had met her at someone's lawn party, a week or so after his return from New York, walking on the arm of a local politician; she'd flirted expertly and invited him to call. The first visit had been proper,

Favian feeling the waters; the second, decidedly, had not. Caroline had blushed charmingly as he tugged at her clothing and then torn at his with an ardency that had amazed him. By the third visit he'd concluded arrangements for the cottage near Poquetanuck.

It was a convenient arrangement. Favian was getting too old, and far too well-known, to be leaping in and out of bordellos. This was New England, after all, and although sporting palaces existed they were under considerable harassment from the authorities. The spectacle of a national hero caught in a raid was not at all the image the navy preferred for its captains; a discreet cottage in the country was much better.

Favian stretched lazily and glanced to the window. Early September had been unusually cool; soon the maples would be turning. Autumn would soon be here. *Shark* was nearing completion; by November at the latest she'd be off the stocks and given her masts. The guns, the main broadside of thirty-two pound carronades and the long twelve-pound chasers, would leave Philadelphia any week now, if they hadn't already. Favian hoped they'd arrive before the roads turned to muck.

Caroline stirred on the bed next to him. Perhaps sensing his alertness through her sleep she turned to him with a lazy, unconscious moan, laid her head to rest on his shoulder, throwing her arm across his chest, and promptly fell again into deep slumber. Favian felt the warmth of her body lying beside him, smelling the comforting female scent of her massed auburn hair. What else did he need? Moderate wealth, property, the status of a hero, a desirable mistress—that was a lot, more than he had ever hoped for. But Emma Greenhow was lost to him, and William Burrows was dead; his only intimate friends were gone. Caroline, though he enjoyed her company, was not a substitute.

He heard Caroline's breathing grow shallow, then the little crystalline *tink* of her eyelids coming unglued. She stretched up lazily to kiss him good-morning; he felt his bristles scratching her lips. "I'll bring water for shaving," she said. "Would you like some coffee?"

"Yes. Thank you."

"You were far away, weren't you?" She had propped her chin up on her hand and was peering at him with amused curiosity from out of a shroud of unbound hair. "I can always tell when you're thinking deep," she said. "Were you at sea?"

Near enough; no point in going into it. "Yes," he said.

"Do you want to go to sea very badly?"

He hesitated before answering; the question touched him. He did not love the sea in itself, the way Burrows had, but he was, by training and occupation, a seaman. Watching the *Shark* building had been a considerable education; knowing he was to be her first commander he had been able to offer suggestions and make certain the dockyard made no mistakes. But the civilian shipbuilders knew their craft well, and were furthermore honest men; they wanted *Shark* to be a success, intending to make their reputations with her; in this rampant honesty they were radically unlike their English counterparts, and a good many American ones. In truth, aside from the testing and tinkering with Markham's Recording Log, Favian had little to do. The financial arrangements he'd made, the property he'd purchased, were not entirely real to him; the *Shark* and the sea were. He needed an occupation.

"I would like to be at sea, yes," he said.

Caroline shook her head. "I don't understand you sailors. Always rushing off to sea when there's so much more fun to be had here. Or do you like boys better, hey?" She jabbed him playfully in the ribs with a knuckle, grinning wickedly. "I hear there are men that do," she said. "Are you one of them?"

"Silly girl. You should know better than anyone what I like."

"I'll get your shaving water," she said. Her smile was irresistible, creating delicate little lines around her eyes and nose. With both women and ships Favian had always found something to love that was uniquely their own, something that existed in each that was superior to any other. With the frigate *United States* it had been the stolid way she shouldered through the water, making her a uniquely steady gun platform; with Caroline Huxley it was almost certainly her smile.

He crossed his arms behind his head, propping himself up so he could watch her leaving the room, her figure swaying inside its thin shift, female and therefore by definition wonderful—even after the best part of a year ashore he had not entirely lost a sense of wonder at a woman's walk, a sensation that could strike him like a hammer after months at sea with only men for company. Caroline was aware of his interest and moved with deliberate provocation, smiling over her shoulder as she disappeared into the kitchen.

Favian swung out of bed, pulling on his smallclothes and

stockings more because it was chilly than for reasons of modesty, dancing on the cold planks of the floor until he got his stockings on. Caroline brought in his shaving water and today's razor—he had seven of them, each marked with a day of the week—on a tray. She kissed him on the cheek, announced that coffee was on its way, and padded back into the kitchen on bare feet. He bent his considerable height over a table mirror, picked the razor up in his scarred hands—Caroline, thankfully, had not minded the touch of those torn fingers on her body—and scraped away the whiskers.

Domestic bliss, he thought. Was this something of what marriage was like? But no; with marriage there was not so much to be kept hidden, such a great deal of skulking and pretense. Caroline, as far as the deaf old woman who owned the cottage was concerned, was a female niece under his protection, engaged to be married to Favian's cousin Gideon, who was at sea in a privateer. That Gideon had been married for more than a year now was something Favian hoped had escaped the attention of the entire state of Connecticut; there was no reason why it shouldn't. As far as his landlady in New London knew, he was spending many of his nights sleeping at the shipyard, supervising the construction of the *Shark*.

Caroline, bound by the conventions of her existence no less than more respectable folk, spent a great deal of time alone. In a larger city, New York or Washington, where there was a demimonde existence that kept to its own circles independent of life elsewhere, she would have been less lonely, but here there was no place for her. It was fortunate that for the most part she was capable of amusing herself; she kept the cottage in immaculate order, well beyond the standards even of orderly sea officers; she had stitched Favian a number of shirts; and she read plays, poetry, and romantic novels. She claimed that she had committed great chunks of *Pamela* to memory. Why Caroline, something of a professional kept woman, should be so fond of Richardson, whom Favian considered a prating, moralistic prig, was something beyond Favian's comprehension, but he accepted the fact with amusement.

Favian scraped off the last bristles and cleaned the razor. The smell of coffee was beginning to infiltrate the bedroom. The coffee he'd bought had cost him dear, but it was one of those luxuries in which he indulged himself; brewed acorns and scraped burnt bread—"Scotch coffee"—which were offered as substitutes, did not at all suit his fastidious palate.

"Will you come tonight?" Caroline asked, bringing in the first cup.

"I'm sorry, no," he said. "There's a dinner tonight. The Sons of Saint Something-or-other, raising money for war orphans." What saint was it, anyway? Favian wondered, annoyed at his forgetfulness. Saint Tammany? No, that was Burr's old outfit in New York. Certain to be a bunch of whiskey-sodden Revolutionary veterans, anyway.

"You can come afterwards," Caroline said, resting her cheek on his shoulder.

"Staggering with drink and asleep from dull speeches. You wouldn't want me."

"I'd wake you up," she said with one of her smiles.

He put down the coffee cup and took her in his arms. She *was* alone too often; he wished he could find her a discreet companion, but discretion was not a New England quality—like any bluestocking society, it thrived on gossip. He kissed her, sensing her need for reassurance, feeling her arms going around him.

He held her next to him, feeling a sudden surge of desolation sweeping him. The need to be desired, to be *wanted*, was so plain in her; she knew as well as he that he would never marry her, that probably none of her lovers would, that she would most likely spend years in rented cottages and rented rooms, unable to appear in public. But still she longed for a place, for a happy ending in a prim Richardson universe. Was that what he, too, desired? A simple conventional life, free from the publicity of being a navy officer, *sans peur et sans reproche*, whose every breathing moment was presumably spent in scheming to increase the accumulated glory of the United States of America, and whose private vices had to be kept rigorously out of sight? Was that what he had sought with Emma Greenhow, a life like an epilogue to one of the Walter Scott romances Emma favored? "He lived long and happily with Rowena, for they were attached to each other by the bonds of early affection." Yes, he had wanted that, and yet he had been perfectly aware, all along, how foolish such desires were.

Caroline pressed herself tightly against him; he burrowed through her heavy mass of hair and kissed the soft flesh of her neck. This part at least was simple; he would make early morning love to Caroline and hope the memory would comfort her during her long day and night alone, and when he came in two nights he would try to bring her an expensive present.

She knew the rules; so did he. There was nothing, really, to be sad about.

7

Favian flung the door inward with a crash and stepped into the room. "Who in blazes is that man in my bed?" he roared, his sea officer's booming voice, used to hurl commands aloft during the teeth of a slashing gale, echoing from the low beams. He walked to the huddled figure on the bed and shook it, wincing from the scent of beer and onions rising from the pillow.

Lazarus turned over, his yellowed eyes opening, gazing up in dawning comprehension. "Who is that man in my bed?" Favian repeated. Understanding flooded into the fiddler's visage.

"Oh, aye, him. A young man set on by the crew of the *Tom Bowlin*. His name is Koozy Koskey, or something like that. A foreigner."

"And you took it upon yourself to put him in my bed? Mrs. George said she'd never seen him before."

"Thee were not using it," Lazarus said, all wide-eyed innocence. "It was Christian charity, sir."

Favian snorted. "You are not a Christian, as you've told me many a time!" he bellowed. "He could have bunked in here with you, or lay rough on the floor! I won't have some drunken shellback snoring in my bed and puking up his guts on my pillow! Good God! The recording log is in there—what if he'd stolen it!" Favian's quick temper had already begun to recede in dawning awareness of the absurdity of the situation. He suppressed a grin, maintaining with some effort his steely scowl. "What did they beat him up for?" he asked.

"Don't like foreigners, I guess," Lazarus shrugged, rubbing his whiskered face. "They threw him off their ship, too, told him not to come back. His pocket was picked in town and he's without money."

"Sounds like they caught a thief," Favian said. Theft was the one unforgivable crime among sailors; ships' officers rarely had a chance to inflict punishment in such cases because retribution was usually exacted informally below decks.

Lazarus shook his head. "I don't think he's a thief. He's a little odd—maybe it was just his strangeness."

Favian made no reply; he knew Lazarus's powers of judgment were acute, even if they were not, as he claimed, supernatural. Lazarus was something in the nature of a human piece of baggage Favian had involuntarily picked up in his wanderings of the last two years: Favian seemed to have acquired him without meaning to. They had first met at a New Year's debauch in honor of a just-launched 1813; Favian and his friend William Burrows had been disguised as common sailors, a thing Burrows did often and well; but Favian's disguise had been without practice or conviction and Lazarus had spotted the anomalies quickly. Lazarus had turned up again in Portsmouth months later, just after the *Teaser* fight, making a celebrity of himself with a fiddle tune called "*Experiment*'s Victory." At the height of his popularity Lazarus had vanished from the town, but had later reappeared in Maine when *Experiment* had been wrecked, leading the rescue party that plucked Favian and twenty-two others from the drink.

It was his powers, Lazarus claimed, that had enabled him to be in the right place at the right time, knowing the wreck would occur on that desolate spot on the Maine coast. No rational explanation had ever offered itself; why would Lazarus leave Portsmouth, where he had a living of sorts, for some isolated fishing village, if it were not at the behest of some supernatural agency? No explanation, that is, save madness, and madness was the explanation Favian had thought most likely. Lazarus's powers, he insisted, had been granted him on Nantucket, along with an unnaturally long life and his talent with the fiddle bow, by His Satanic Majesty during a dark ceremony in 1682, in return for which the devil had purchased his soul; the story confirmed an old sailors' superstition that fiddlers got their powers from Old Nick.

It was arrant foolishness, but Lazarus believed it; his intense, glowing-eyed conviction could be frightening. Whatever his real name was, wherever he was born—he looked about forty, gray beginning to shoot through his fair hair, worn long in an old-fashioned seaman's pigtail—he had lived the fantasy of satanic convert long enough for the fantasy to replace his real past. Favian tried to avoid the whole subject of Lazarus's cloven-hoofed master, and hoped that Lazarus would eventually turn into a more conventional sort of comic retainer.

The fiddler was not precisely in Favian's employ, although Favian paid him to run errands and had given him transport money to New London—Favian owed him that much, at least, for the rescue from that Maine mudbank—and Lazarus had told him that he would join *Shark*'s crew as a chantyman once the new sloop was put in commission. Warships normally did not carry chantymen; work was supposed to be accompanied only by bosuns' whistles, but Favian, like his longtime superior Stephen Decatur, knew how the morale of his crew would be improved by a musician of Lazarus's talent; the concerts would help to while away lazy afternoons near the Line, and work at the halyards and capstan would be quickened.

"Well," Favian said, scowling. "The man's in my bed. Koskey, you say his name is? What are we going to do with him?"

"He's a sailor without money and possessions," Lazarus said. He grinned, showing his stumpy, brown-stained teeth. "Sounds like navy material."

"*Macedonian* is signing crew. Take him to Adrian Stone and have him signed up."

"Thou knows they will not wish to sign up a man all bruised, Captain Markham," Lazarus said.

"Just tell Mr. Stone he's been robbed and beaten. You don't have to explain why or how."

Lazarus scratched his chin in thought and nodded.

"Aye. I'll do that."

"I'll be having luncheon with Captain Jones. When I return I'll expect the man to be out of my room. And mind he doesn't harm the recording log!"

Another nod. "Aye," Lazarus said. His strange blue eyes were dreamlike, as if focused on some internal conversation with his spirits or familiars or whatever Lucifer had given him. Favian, uneasy, said his farewells and stepped backward out of the room.

The walk to where *Macedonian* was moored alongside a New

London wharf was a short one. The frigate's tall masts, the standing rigging tarred a military black while the running rigging stood out in white manila, were immediately recognizable among the clutter of sticks crowding the New London and Groton banks of the river. Favian turned the corner around the Beach Tavern and saw the frigate's hull lying against the wharf. In spite of the collision matting deployed to protect her paint, in spite of the bustle and the untidy clutter of stores obscuring the view, it was obvious that *Macedonian* was a handsome vessel. Large for a British-built thirty-eight, made of good English oak instead of the fir the British had been substituting lately, she gave the impression of controlled power and grace from the white-trimmed banks of glazed windows on her transom to the glittering figurehead of Alexander the Great brandishing his sword beneath the bowsprit. Despite the ship's beauty, Favian's overwhelming memory was of a mastless, rolling hulk, the well deck knee deep in bloody water with a third of her crew butchered by Favian's twenty-four pounders: that was how he'd first seen *Macedonian* up close.

The Macedonians seemed to prefer knit caps to the usual glazed hats; knit caps were all over the wharf, in many colors but with blue predominating, most of the caps embroidered handsomely with miniature whales, ships under clouds of sail, mermaids. . . . Among them, his back to Favian, was a tall, broad figure, almost a giant, somehow familiar. Without a knit cap, without any head covering at all, but even with a cap he would have stood out—there weren't many men taller than Favian, and he had seen this one somewhere, but where? Favian slowed, narrowing his eyes.

"Captain Markham." It was Jones, emerging from behind a stack of about two hundred barrels of salt beef. The arms of his pea jacket were streaked with tar, which stained as well the toes of his unpolished boots. He looked like a middle-aged boatswain. In a moment he was asking Favian's advice about stowing *Macedonian*'s hold, and Favian had forgotten the long-armed giant on the wharf.

Jones, normally a talkative, social man, was distracted and fidgety during their meal at the Mermaid Inn. Favian understood well enough; orders had come, no less from President Madison himself, to make *Macedonian* ready for sea and leave port at the earliest opportunity. The order seemed to reflect a disagreement in Washington policy concerning the navy, and part of Jones's worries, Favian thought, might be that the orders would shortly be canceled as the wind from the Potomac shifted.

During the year 1814 the deep-sea navy had been neglected in favor of the squadrons on the Great Lakes, reflecting the policy of William Jones, secretary of the navy. The secretary's policy had paid off in a stunning victory, a few days ago, at Plattsburgh on Lake Champlain, where Favian's old *Constitution* messmate Thomas Macdonough had destroyed Commodore Downey's far superior British squadron. The battle had stopped a British invasion of New York dead in its tracks, the enemy army unable to move farther south with the American squadron preventing waterborne supply. The victory had been total and very much against the odds, and it had been the only good news in a long two months filled only with disaster.

Washington had been lost. Apparently the old Revolutionary privateer and elderly navy commodore Joshua Barney, with two guns and some marines, had done well, but the rest had been disgraceful: an entire American army, far superior in numbers to the British force, had fled at the first few shots and allowed the redcoats to march unmolested up the Washington avenues. The Capitol and the little Executive Mansion, where two years before Favian had bowed before Dolley Madison in her pink cloak and white plumed turban, had been gutted by fire, and Mrs. Madison had been forced to flee the city with the few possessions she could lay her hands on, leaving behind a banquet table with places already set for the victorious American officers who had expected to rout the British forces with a few hours' battle. Lost with the seat of government was the Washington Navy Yard with its priceless store of guns, the new sloop *Argus*, the frigate *Columbia*, which had been only a few days from completion, and the old frigates *Boston*, *New York*, and *General Greene*.

Elsewhere the news was scarcely better. General Brown's Niagara army, conspicuously without aid from the Lake Ontario squadron under Commodore Chauncey (which had once again let the summer pass without a battle), had apparently won a battle at Lundy's Lane, but then had retreated and been besieged at Fort Erie. The British General Drummond was bombarding the fort, repelling Brown's sorties, and plastering the frontier with broadsides denouncing the "damned Yankees."

Admiral Sir Thomas Masterman Hardy had been slowly advancing, with a naval and army column, down the coast of

Maine, capturing Bangor and Machias, and now controlled the entire coast from the Penobscot to the Passamaquoddy Bay. The crew of the American corvette *John Adams,* trapped in Hampden by the attack, had been forced to burn their ship and flee. The inhabitants of northern Maine had been given the choice of swearing allegiance to Britain or of being deported as prisoners to Halifax; most had taken the oath.

There was nothing, so far as Favian could tell, to keep the British from marching south to Portland and completing the conquest of upper Massachusetts, and then invade New Hampshire by taking Portsmouth. Certainly the political situation in New England was working to the British benefit: Nantucket, surrounded by British naval forces, had declared its "neutrality"; Massachusetts and Connecticut had refused to answer the last militia call; New Hampshire had forbidden Isaac Hull, the new commandant of the Portsmouth Navy Yard, from manning state batteries with federal troops in order to protect Portsmouth, the frigate *Congress,* and the unfinished ship of the line building there.

This last bit of news had come in a letter from Favian's brother Lafayette, who was preparing to help their father evacuate his estate near Portsmouth if the British attack came. "The political situation is at its worst since our grandfather's time," Lafayette had written. "The peace faction has allied with the old Tories throughout much of New England and are prepared to sell the nation to King George for a chance to loot the homes and reputation of their opponents.

"We can but thank our Author for Mr. Webster, who has kept New Hampshire from following in the treasonous footsteps of Massachusetts, Rhode Island, and Connecticut by sending representatives to that damned convention. Our Mr. Greenhow, his daughter, and his son-in-law will be attending as 'observers,' and will doubtless contribute their talents and venom to the cause of overthrowing the Constitution."

The convention mentioned by Lafayette would take place in Hartford in December; it had been called by Governor Strong of Massachusetts to discuss "public grievances and concerns" and to suggest amendments to the Constitution. Rhode Island and Connecticut would send delegates, but Vermont had refused and New Hampshire, thanks apparently to Daniel Webster, had declined to answer the invitation. The whole business had an unpleasant stench to it; the delegates and "observers" seemed not to know how far to go, or indeed how far they had already gone. Favian remembered his own cousin David, a few years ago, saying cheerfully that the "question of union ought to be reconsidered," and although it was more fashionable to say such things now, he knew that David had paid for his opinions—had, in fact, been hanged for treasonable correspondence with the British squadron off Boston. He hoped Emma would not suffer in the future for her husband's participation in this convention. But then, Favian reflected, that was now her husband's worry. And the convention seemed only too likely to succeed; if they had their way it might be the patriots hanging from the gallows, not the traitors.

All these disasters, and the threat of rebellion against the federal government, had probably spurred the change in naval policy. Naval resources were being shifted from the Great Lakes to the deep-sea navy; Favian knew that *Constitution* and *President*, as well as *Macedonian*, were under orders to sail as soon as possible, and President Madison had written a letter to Favian ordering *Shark* to sea as soon as she was armed and provisioned—an unusual order indeed, considering that *Shark* was not even off the ways yet, and had no crew other than a few warrant officers. Cynically Favian wondered if Madison was hoping to deflate the Hartford Convention with a few quick naval victories, fought (with any luck) off the New England coast.

There had been sobering news of a more personal nature as well. There had been a letter from Jehu, Favian's father, written in an unsteady hand, and announcing the death of Favian's uncle Josiah. The old, pious, fierce Revolutionary privateer had passed away quietly in his sleep, on the night of the eleventh of September, while visiting Jehu at his estate. Jehu seemed quite shaken; he was sixty-nine—four years older than his brother—and had probably expected to go first.

It was difficult for Favian to think of Portsmouth without Josiah Markham; the man had been such a fixture, white-haired, battle-scarred, unforgiving, quoting biblical texts and damning the British he had fought all his life. Half the population of Portsmouth had attended the funeral, and Congressman Webster had spoken the oration, giving Josiah's life and spirit as an example to every true-hearted Yankee. A newspaper text had been included with Jehu's letter, and Favian had been impressed by the man's cadence, by the latent power of the phrases that coiled like steel springs within the taut body of the text. Josiah's will had been a surprise; it left his house to Gideon, the middle son who was off with his privateer in the Gulf of Mexico, and the older sons were presumably vexed. Nor was Josiah's the only will scheduled to raise eyebrows.

Jehu's letter had informed Favian of the contents of his own will.

> Josiah's death, and the unsettled condition of the nation, have served as *memento mori;* they have set my thoughts toward meditations on mutability, and how swiftly the old world is fading. It may only be the vanity and sentiment of a disturbed old man, but I wish to know certain things are settled beyond question.
>
> Briefly, Favian, though all else will be divided evenly, the land is to come to you, subject only to the condition that your mother is to be allowed to live here as long as she wishes. The estate has been losing money for years, but I could afford the losses and shall be able to afford them for many years yet. Your brothers Lafayette and Benjamin are businessmen; I would not imagine they would suffer losses in the name of sentiment. Should the land come to them, it would be broken into parcels and sold; the timberland would be cut; the horses auctioned.
>
> Do not imagine me so foolish as to think that, when the estate is in your hands, you would choose to run it as I have, or to deliberately accept losses on the property. But I hope you will have some regard for the land itself, and for the life we have lived on it; I hope the changes you make will be made with care, not by the hand of an exploiter but by the hand of a lover of the good things the land has given us. Bless you.
>
> > Your loving, and affectionate,
> > Father

The letter, received just days ago, had taken Favian aback entirely. Jehu's estate was a thousand acres or more, mostly rolling pastureland but including a few tenant farms that generated a little income and several hundred acres of virgin timberland. It had been Jehu's conceit, having retired from business on New

Year's Day, 1800, that he should retire to his lands, act the country squire, and raise horses; this had he done. New Hampshire was scarcely the best land for horsebreeding, but he had done a remarkable job; he had concentrated not on raising racers, but rather horses for gentlemen and ladies: fast, well-trained, able to clear a hedge or gate when necessary, to perform the ancient cavalry maneuvers, levades and caprioles, that were part of the horseman's repertoire, hardy animals able to go long distances at a rapid pace, beating any racers over the long haul.

The breeding and training programs had been successful—Jehu Markham's horses were known as the best north of Maryland—but they had cost money. Jehu's baronial mode of life had been, if not extravagant, at least richly ornamented: there was the big, rambling mansion house full of the trophies collected by Markhams over the generations, swords captured from enemies, portraits, shot-torn ensigns, pikes, silver plate, and there had been the big carriage with its footmen—plus two annual balls and generous contributions to charities and to the radical political causes Jehu had always favored. Yes, a lot of money was lost, and everyone knew it; but they also knew Jehu was a wealthy man and could afford it.

Even with a share of the family money and whatever prize money he might earn with *Shark,* Favian knew he could not hope to continue in Jehu's footsteps; severe economies would have to be made. Some of the land would have to be leased or sold, at least part of the timber would have to be harvested. But yes, Favian thought, he would have a care; he did not want the homestead broken into parcels. Jehu's wishes would be respected.

If, of course, there remained an estate to inherit. With the British advancing southward through Maine, the stud and mares might be requisitioned for the officers, and the house and stables burned to ashes. . . .

"This should be an opportune time to break out of New London," said Captain Jones. Favian's wandering attention returned to the Mermaid Inn, and to his distracted conversation with the fretful captain of the *Macedonian*. "Admiral Hardy's preoccupied with his invasion of upper Massachusetts, and his strength in Long Island Sound is not as great." Jones scowled, rubbing absently at his long nose, then his receding chin. "But it's so hard to get a frigate ready for sea without everyone knowing about it. Liberties are canceled, water brought on board,

·buoys and marker boats are placed. . . . I'm afraid of those lights on Groton Long Point, Favian, and I don't mind admitting it." Jones's lips twitched as he wrung his hands around his mug of beer. "They've kept me in port this last year. Each time Stephen tried to ready the squadron to slip out past the British, the enemy gathered in strength right off the Thames and we had to warp upriver just to keep them from trying to cut us out. We've been told that each time we tried to escape, blue lights were seen burning on Groton Long Point—that means treachery, if it's true. I want badly to get out of this port. I feel too vulnerable here."

Favian nodded. He, of all people, should know how vulnerable New London was. In December of 1778 his father and uncles were blockaded here by a British squadron; the enemy had run in with fireships and devastated the port, blowing up his uncle Malachi's *Royal George* privateer, capturing Josiah's schooner with Jehu aboard. It had been a disaster of the first magnitude. And that was not all: in 1781 Benedict Arnold had landed with a force to attack Forts Trumbull and Griswold that defended the entrance to the Thames. There had been a gruesome massacre at Fort Griswold, the defenders bayoneted even after their surrender, and New London had been put to the torch. *Macedonian*, *Shark*, and *United States* were a temptation to the British to repeat Arnold's attack; it was best to reduce that temptation if possible.

"The Long Point can be patrolled by marines," Favian said. "That will keep the lights from being lit."

"Then the Tories will light them somewhere else," Jones said, sipping petulantly at his dish of coffee. "The British and Tories are very thorough about these things; you may be certain they will have an alternate plan. Besides, all they have to do is hire a pilot boat to run out to the *Ramillies* or *Superb* with a message."

Favian looked down at his pheasant pie. Jacob Jones was entirely preoccupied with the task of getting *Macedonian* to sea; it was unfair to expect him to worry about ferreting out traitors as well. He sipped his whiskey punch and considered the problem. Perhaps a covert patrol, lying hidden on Groton Long Point, might catch the spies red-handed . . . but then what? Not all of them would be hanging lanterns on the point; the rest would have to be dealt with somehow. If only the political climate, with the Federalists in revolt and the Hartford Convention looming on the winter horizon, were not so kind to treason . . .

Suddenly a tide of memory tugged at him, and he remembered where he'd seen that broad-shouldered figure on *Macedonian*'s wharf. "Gardell," he muttered. "Buck Johanan Gardell." He looked up at Jones's surprised face. "The man's in New London!" he said. "There's a warrant out for his arrest in Massachusetts—for treason, no less!"

"Who the devil are you talking about?" Jones demanded, and Favian told him the story. The year before, early on Markham's Raid, Favian's *Experiment* had come across an old merchant brig called the *Pride of Richmond* that carried a cargo of wheat from Virginia to Wellington's armies in Portugal; the brig had been equipped with a warrant from Admiral John Borlase Warren in Halifax permitting them to do business with the British Crown. *Pride of Richmond* had been captained by one Buck Johanan Gardell, a giant, ham-fisted man who had spewed defiance from his quarterdeck even as *Experiment*'s boarders had been rowing toward him. Favian put a prize crew aboard, and the brig had later been declared a fair prize and had created a scandal resulting in the arrest of the brig's owners and various others subsequently proven to have traded with the enemy, but Gardell and his officers had been released on bond and fled the state.

"He's a great bull of a man," Favian said. "Booming voice, long arms, big hands. Carries himself like a prizefighter. Surely you've seen him on the wharf, if that's where he's been working. He might even have signed aboard *Macedonian*!"

"No, he's not among our crew," Jones said. "I'd remember a man like that."

Favian gulped the remains of his whiskey punch and stood. "I want to have that man," he said, throwing money on the table and picking up the remains of his pheasant pie. "There are a good many questions the federal marshals need to ask of him."

Jones, looking resigned, nodded and stood. Gobbling his pie, Favian walked swiftly to the docks, craning his neck for the sight of Buck Gardell's massive arms and shoulders, Jones on his shorter legs half-running behind. "Can you bring out a file of marines, Jacob?" he asked as he turned onto the pier. "Gardell won't be easy, I'll reckon."

"Very well," Jones said, puffing; he accelerated and jogged toward *Macedonian*. Favian slowed, peering between the pyramids of salt beef and pork, the barrels of molasses, vinegar, and flour, the busy sailors and dockmen working in gangs under the supervision of dock foremen and the officers of the frigate. There was a sunburst of recognition, but no—It was Midshipman Phillip Stanhope, the *Experiment* survivor who had testified at Favian's trial, since assigned to *Macedonian* and commanding a gang of workmen. Favian hastened to where Stanhope was standing on a barrel and received the midshipman's surprised salute.

"Have you seen Captain Gardell—that's Buck Gardell of the *Pride of Richmond*?" Favian asked.

Stanhope registered complete surprise. "Gardell? He's here? I haven't seen him, but then I just came on watch—I had the anchor watch all last night and just got up."

"Damnation! I saw him here on the wharf not an hour ago. Help me look, will you?"

"Certainly, Captain. I won't forget that man, believe me."

They split up, weaving amid the piles of stores, out of sight of one another. Favian heard the rattle of muskets and equipment as a file of marines was double-timed down the gangplank to aid in the search. "You're looking for a big man, name of Gardell!" he heard Jones's voice shout. "Search everywhere. He's dangerous—go in pairs!"

Favian doubled around a pyramid of incredibly odorous molasses barrels—ships carrying molasses could always be distinguished far downwind—and came out into the open, seeing the marines splitting up under the direction of Jones and his first lieutenant, Adrian Stone, while the workers on the docks ceased their labors to watch. "Markham! There you are!" Jones said. "What d'you say the man looks like, now?"

"I think he's flown, blast him," Favian said. "We should talk to a federal marshal, if there is one here, or the town constable."

Jones's eyes left Favian's face and glanced in alarm at something behind him; Favian turned to see Midshipman Stanhope being half-carried toward them by a pair of marines. The right side of Stanhope's face was scratched and bleeding lightly; tomorrow it would be black and blue. Even damaged as he was, he had the presence of mind to uncover in salute to the two captains.

"I found him, damn it," he reported. "But he was ready for me. I had just enough time to tell him, 'Gardell, you're under arrest,' but he was on me before I could draw my dirk. Smashed my face against a barrel of pork and ran. I called these men and they came running, but he was long gone. He was over there"—

Stanhope pointed—"close to the street. He'll have got into town by now."

"Mr. Stone, take half the marines; I'll take the other half," Jones snapped. "We'll search the streets and the taverns. Captain Markham, get yourself to the marshal's office and swear out a warrant. Mr. Stanhope, cut along to the surgeon. And the rest of you," he said, his voice rising, "get back to your duties! Bosun, that laggard is trying to hide among those flour barrels—start him! Corporal, your men with me! Let's go."

Half an hour later, after visiting the marshal's office and the office of the town constable, Favian stepped into the street to see a file of marines standing outside a tavern, and concluded that Gardell had got away. The man would have been foolish indeed to have tried to stay in New London; he could easily enough have escaped on the Groton ferry or simply walked swiftly into the countryside on his long legs—a fugitive who had stayed at large so long would have half a dozen plans laid in advance. But still, either Favian or Jones should have thought to have closed off the ferry early.

"Cap'n Markham, sir," said a familiar voice. Favian turned to discover Lazarus, his leather cap pulled down over his eyes and his fiddle case under one arm. "Koskey has gone aboard the frigate," he said. "Late this morning, sir. Mr. Stone did not question his bruises."

"Very well," Favian said, walking toward where the marines were forming up outside of a tavern.

"Art thou looking for something, sir?" Lazarus asked. "A very tall man, perhaps?" Favian turned to him.

"Where did you hear of this? On the docks?"

Lazarus's answer was grave. "My powers, Cap'n Markham. A tall man, they tell me, a treacherous man. If I were thee I would beware of him—there is a shadow between thee and he, perhaps a death." His blue eyes flickered. "I think there is a danger, sir, from this man and his friends."

"Friends?" It was difficult, when Lazarus sprang one of his little surprises, for Favian to maintain skepticism. Deep inside the revelations stirred him—spoken as always with such conviction, Lazarus's words moved a primeval, superstitious part of Favian that responded with absolute belief, an internal reaction that greatly vexed Favian's more skeptical, conscious self. But then, Favian reflected, there was no great mystery here: the town being turned inside-out by marines, Jones bellowing Gardell's name on the docks, the work interrupted on the wharf . . . Lazarus could have picked up the news from any streetcorner gossip.

"Friends, aye," Lazarus said. "I do not see the man acting alone. They are devious—beware them, Cap'n."

"I thought I was to live to a ripe old age and turn schoolmaster?" Favian asked, trying to grin. It had been one of Lazarus's first predictions, and one of the most unbelievable, that Favian would be a schoolmaster at the end.

"That is thy most likely fate," Lazarus said. "There are many turnings in thy path, Favian Markham."

"Ah. We are speaking in terms of probabilities rather than certainties?" Favian asked lightly. Stone, commanding the marines ahead, saw him and raised his hat in salute. Favian acknowledged.

"If thee says so, sir," Lazarus said.

"Wouldst thou, ah, I mean, would you estimate the danger from Gardell at, say, ten percent?" Favian asked, unconsciously falling for a moment into Lazarus's antique speech pattern. "Or perhaps twenty-five percent? I have difficulty quantifying your remarks, Lazarus."

"I could not tell thee," Lazarus said, scowling. "I tell thee what I see. Beware him. The warning should be enough, by Lucifer!"

Lieutenant Stone, a serious, frowning young man of twenty-five or so, had been listening to this dialogue with a properly immobile face. When Favian smiled without making reply, he judged it a proper moment to speak. "Sir, we've found his room. He was staying at the Beach Tavern—his clothes are still there. I've put two marines in the place in case he returns for his belongings."

"Very good, Mr. Stone. Have you seen Captain Jones?"

"I'm afraid not, sir. We've been searching the waterfront, and he's farther back in town."

"Has anyone been guarding the ferry?"

Stone's expression of bleak chagrin answered Favian's question well before Stone could put it in words. "No, sir. We didn't think about it. I guess we're new to this manhunting business."

"We should all have thought of it, Mr. Stone," Favian frowned. There was no use worrying about might-have-beens. "I should have recognized the man when I first saw him; he'd be in irons by now."

"I can put a guard on the ferry now, of course," Stone offered.

"That seems sensible. If you'll give me the men I'll station 'em and leave you to your work here."

"Thank you, sir. Foster! Macdougal! Fall out!"

Favian found himself approving of the grim young Mr. Stone, a man who knew the names of the men he commanded, even those of the marines who were not normally the first lieutenant's department. It had always seemed to Favian that a commander should know his men's names, even if there were, as in this case, almost four hundred of them.

"Come with me," Favian said, making for the ferry, hearing the marines falling into step behind, Lazarus's unmilitary shuffle bringing up the rear. Although he hoped Gardell might yet be caught, Favian felt in his soul the certainty that the man had made his escape. Even if there was, as Lazarus had implied, a death between them, that death would have to wait for another day.

8

"So much tension here," Caroline said. Her nimble long fingers dug at the muscles in Favian's neck and shoulders. "Worse than it's been in a long time. Since the first week I've known you."

He was stretched out naked on her bed; Caroline, dressed only in her shift, straddled him as she probed the muscles of his back and shoulders. He could feel their resistance breaking down under the tireless kneading of her fingers; he was approaching a rare state of relaxation, breathing more easily, the knots in his musculature losing their stiffness. Lovely, to feel the urgency ebbing away . . .

It was a Sunday evening. That morning Favian had set out on a journey to his mistress. His had been the only horse on the road, and he'd caught glimpses of scowling faces through the window curtains—Sunday travel in puritan New England was no longer against the law, but it was very much disapproved of, and Favian had felt his neck prickle at the thought of all those disapproving stares from the windows of the town.

After he'd arrived the day had been good. He and Caroline had been able to spend the balance of the day together, talking, walking in the late September fields, enjoying one another's company. Caroline had given him an impromptu performance, declaiming from memory a scene from *Oroonoko,* and Favian had been surprised to find that she possessed considerable talent— she performed half a dozen parts, the princely slave Oroonoko, his lover Imoinda, the villainous Byam and Banister, each distinct and drawn to a T, her voice and inflection changing along with her gestures and carriage. Favian had never taken seriously her claim to be an actress; he saw now that it deserved respect.

"Much better now," she said, her hands warming his shoulders. "Turn over."

He rolled onto his back and watched her lazily as she began to work on his shoulders, her fingers digging expertly into the muscle beneath his left clavicle. Her eyes were narrowed, her brows contracted, as she concentrated on her work. Her ringlets shadowed her forehead; a little of her auburn hair had come undone from the knot at her nape, and she absently brushed it back into place with the back of her hand. He watched her pear-shaped breasts moving within her shift as she rocked back and forth, pressing down on his breastbone with both hands.

"All these scars," she said, her hands gently touching the old silvered wounds, the saber scar on his shoulder that Count Gram had given him in the duel in Norway, the scratches from Tripolitan scimitars, the long splinter wound he'd got along his ribs when Robert Spence's gunboat, nearly alongside his own, had been blown up by Moorish red-hot shot off Tripoli. "You're like an old tomcat, all scars and gristle," she said.

"Honorable wounds," he said. "All in front."

She leaned back, brushing back a strand of hair again; her eyes met his, and she smiled.

"You're not thinking of going straight to sleep, are you, tomcat?" she asked, teasing.

"No. I'm not."

"I didn't think so." She bent over him and kissed him gently, her lips brushing his. He could sense the nearness of her warmth, the presence of her scent. That strand of hair had fallen forward and was tickling his neck. Her feather kisses touched his neck, crossed his chest; he felt her warm tongue lapping at his little nipples. His hands, scarred in a battle with the sea, a battle his court-martial had happily declared honorable, reached to touch the thighs that straddled him, sliding up into the shift that had ridden high on her; he heard her sigh as he cupped her sturdy hips.

Caroline sat up abruptly, her face abstracted, dreamy; her arms crossed, she pulled the shift up and over her head. He saw her breasts rising high with the movement, the ineffectual tufts of hair beneath her arms, the way her belly flexed as she moved. . . . She looked down at him for a long moment, smiling as if to herself, and then bent to kiss him again, pressing her breasts into his chest.

The lovemaking was lazy, relaxed, prolonged, giving each partner the opportunity to explore the other's body, to change the mood and rhythm. It was, in a way, the purest form of self-indulgence, extending the pleasure as long as possible, luxuriating in it. They moved freely on the bed, changing positions, teasing, laughing, changing roles. He did not restrict himself; he knew she was protected, like Cleopatra, with a sponge soaked in vinegar.

Ultimately he rolled her onto her back and possessed her, his weight on his arms so he could watch her broad, intent face as he moved between her thighs. They were still a little apart; he was giving her room to move, experiencing the sensation of his being in her. Her breath was rushing in and out of her; he changed the rhythm and pattern of his movement and heard her gasp, her strong thighs gripping him. He quickened the pace, seeing her intensity build as he watched her; she seemed oblivious, now, of herself, of him, to all but the pattern of movement and texture. He moved boldly against her, the space between them vanishing, catching a last glimpse of her face, the eyes closed, the teeth resting on her upper lip, before he buried his own face in the pillow, hearing the breath rasping in his windpipe. Caroline's pelvis lunged upward, almost throwing him off, her sharp, staccato cries sounding in his ear. She clutched at him, holding him to her as her body arched; her cries were lower now, throatier, bearlike, or perhaps the cries were his own. The pleasure intensified, exploding in a series of—of what? The metaphors were military: crashing gunshots, thundering broadsides, thumping cannonades . . . no matter; Favian's perceptions were tangled now in the oblivion of release, and comparisons were scattered to the winds.

They fell easily into one another's arms, grinning, beyond speech. . . . She scratched his long sidewhiskers, playing tweakyfingers with the spit curls on his brow, and then her hands came to the muscles on his neck, prodding, feeling their ease, their lack of tension.

"Much better," she said. "Much more relaxed." He kissed the inside of her arm, the elbow joint; she laughed and hugged his head to her breast.

Amazing, he thought, that this loving should be so successful and yet there should be no real intimacy between them. Caroline knew very little about him, really; she seemed content with his physical presence, with his gifts and small kindnesses. She was satisfied to live without knowledge of the life he led outside the cottage; she never asked about the navy, about his family or friends, about why he came to her so often with his muscles knotted into ropes from the effort it took him to play the hero, to wear the uniform and the epaulets and the acclaim. He, in turn, knew very little about her; her past life was opaque—deliberately, he thought, for perhaps she assumed he might be jealous of past loves. Or possibly the profession of mistress simply accustomed one to living only with a fraction of a man, the fraction that could escape the duties owed to family, profession, honor, and wife.

And very shortly, Favian knew, she would be deprived even of that little she had of him. *Macedonian* was nearing the day when it would be ready for sea; Jacob Jones was growing more and more fretful about those treacherous blue lights on Groton Long Point. It was more of a burden than was fair, and Favian, as a captain free, for the moment, of most time-consuming duties, would have to deal with the problem of treachery himself.

It was not a decision he had made consciously, but some part of him had made it, perhaps the part most aware of what the navy would want. Favian decided he would begin spending his nights at Groton Point, hidden in a safe place, keeping watch. Lazarus had agreed to accompany him; the fiddler seemed happy with the thought of spending his time under the meteor-strewn night sky, communing with whatever dark spirits his fancy would provide. There would not be many of the British spies, Favian had thought; perhaps only one, possibly two or three. It did not take many personnel to hang lanterns. Well armed, Lazarus and Favian should be able to catch them unawares and bring them under military arrest to the town. Any of their friends not apprehended would probably flee, afraid of being denounced to the authorities by their captured comrades. Word might still get out in some way to the British, but even if *Macedonian* did not sail there would still be a spy ring smashed, a useful service in itself.

Favian had told Jones and no other; he knew how small the world of such towns as New London and Groton really were; he knew how easily information, gossip, and speculation could travel. If fewer people knew that Favian was spending his nights on the point, fewer were likely to pass on the information to those Favian was trying to apprehend.

But if Favian were spending his nights on the point, he would not be spending them with Caroline. Caroline would have to be told something, and Favian scarcely knew what to say. She deserved the truth, he thought, but the errand—and the navy's harsh code of duty—demanded secrecy.

"I can stay all day tomorrow," he said, kissing her breast, feeling the firm nipple against his cheek. Caroline pulled his head up to eye level, a dreamy half-smile on her face.

"It will be good to have you," she said. "You aren't going to be needed at the shipyard?"

"*Shark*'s well in hand," said Favian. "But I'll have to leave late in the afternoon—there will be navy business tomorrow night."

"Another banquet of veterans?"

"No," he smiled. "Real navy business this time, not social. I'll be able to spend a lot more of my days here." He saw pleasure reflected in her eyes at the news; she kissed him.

"I'm glad you'll be here more often," she said. "I'm so isolated, Favian. There's no one to talk to, not really. I walk into Poquetanuck every so often, but I don't know anyone there except the landlady, and she's deaf."

"I try to give you what I can," he said.

She smiled sadly. "I know, Favian." She was telling the truth, he knew; Caroline understood the situation very well, well enough to be saddened by her comprehension.

"If it weren't such a little place you'd have more to do," he said. "I wish it were New York or Philadelphia."

"So do I," she said. She put out a hand to touch his chest, running her fingers through the light coat of dark hair, and then leaned forward to kiss him. "It's all right. I understand."

"I can't come in the evenings anymore." He felt her stiffen, and he continued quickly. "Not until *Macedonian* sails. I'll be spending every evening on board, helping Captain Jones plan how to get the ship ready. He's asked me, and I can't turn him down."

"Can't you come afterward?"

"I can come in the mornings and stay all day. Most days, anyway."

"I see." Her eyes were cheerless. She sat up suddenly, reaching behind her head to unbind her hair, letting it fall down her back, then stood to walk to the table and pick up her hairbrush. She brushed it out, her face expressionless, seemingly concentrating entirely on the rhythm of the brushing. Favian wondered suddenly how her other lovers had said their farewells, and if he had unknowingly echoed the dragoon's excuses, or some other man's withdrawal from her life. Was that how it was done? Did the lovers come less often, spending their nights courting other mistresses, or perhaps women whom they could marry in respectable wedlock? How often had Caroline lived through such scenes?

Favian could tell her, of course, that there was no one else in his life; he could even tell her the truth, that he would be spending each night wrapped in a blanket on Groton Long Point. But she would be under no obligation to believe him; she had probably been lied to many times before. He would never be able to say that he would never leave her; as the days brought *Shark*'s completion nearer, they also brought nearer the end of their time together. Perhaps it was better that she become aware of how suddenly it could end; from the day *Shark* was completed he would have to be ready to sail at a moment's notice, his life more firmly the property of the navy; it would be better for Caroline to know this firmly. Favian decided to say nothing, but he wondered how much the decision was his own, and how much that of the navy, the navy that from the beginning would have disapproved of this relationship, of this relaxing of Favian's devotion by involvement with a woman.

She brushed her auburn hair with two hundred strokes, staring at herself in the table mirror: a young woman, lovely and with a certain talent, alone too often, perhaps a little too fragile for her profession. She put down the brush and sighed, looking into her reflected blue eyes, and then came back to bed.

Scars, Favian thought; they were not all on the body. His own were within; and now he had given a wound.

They kissed, conversed, made love. There was no outward sign that she was disappointed, or that she didn't believe him; she seemed as ardent in bed as she had been formerly, and laughed unself-consciously at his jokes. Yet in the next day he saw less of her smile and there was a new melancholy in her eyes. When she kissed him farewell he had the sense that perhaps she suspected it would be for the last time.

Yes, he thought, she had known the rules of their relationship, and she would live up to them. Yet there was a difference between knowing, intellectually, what would eventually happen, and hoping that it would be otherwise. Perhaps she had lost the hope she'd had for him, a hope she'd cherished even though she'd known it was irrational. Caroline would live up to the unstated contract between them, and so would he; yet perhaps with her illusion had gone more than a little joy. So Favian kissed her back, told her he would try to return tomorrow morning, and mounted his horse, hoping the while that it would all be for the best.

9

Favian rode through the country lanes at a gallop, enjoying the exhilaration of the ride, the perfect interaction of horse and rider, Favian clean of the saddle, his body perfectly still, not moving at all in the vertical plane, the roan responding to the merest suggestion of the check snaffle, Favian's knees and hips absorbing the shock of the ride, the mare's mane flicking his face as the animal raced down the narrow lanes. When the mare began to labor he slowed her to a walk to let her rest, then finished the ride at a canter. He stabled her at the inn and went in to seek Lazarus.

"Sir! Captain Markham!" He was hailed as he walked through the inn's common room, and turned to discover Midshipman Thomas Tolbert, USN, formerly of the *Experiment* brig, one of the survivors who had testified in Favian's behalf at the courtmartial. Tolbert, blond, just turned twenty, his natural pugnacious attitude modified by a kind of worshipful civility, was in a battered, faded everyday uniform, his boots scarred, his hat worn; but the uniform was clean, the cravat tied neatly, the dirk hilt and brass buttons polished—he had made an effort to look well through the rigors inposed by his poverty. Midshipmen, once ashore, did not even have the comforts of half pay to help them make their way.

"Mr. Tolbert. I am surprised," Favian said. Tolbert's very appearance—his home was Philadelphia—was enough for Favian to guess what was going to happen very shortly. He had no idea how he would respond to Tolbert's ultimate appeal; he decided to delay as long as possible. "Will you sup with me?" he asked. "I have no plans this evening."

"Yes, sir!" Tolbert's eager response was more than enough confirmation for Favian's suspicions. They found a table and ordered; Favian could see Tolbert mentally adding up the cost of his choice and deducting it from whatever he had with him: more confirmation.

"Tell me, Mr. Tolbert," Favian said, heading straight to the matter he knew would come up sooner or later. "How have you been faring these last months?"

Tolbert sighed: not well, it seemed, not well at all. His father, a wheelwright, was ill; Tolbert implied, without meaning to, that the illness was drink. His mother had all she could do to take care of her other eleven children; the uncle who had got him his midshipman's appointment had quarreled with his father and would no longer help. Since he had failed his lieutenant's examination, it was proving difficult to find a berth in the navy; he had hopes he would pass it on the next try, if only he could practice his navigation and spherical trigonometry, but how could he practice his navigation on land? Elsewhere there was no room for a seaman; the blockade was strangling trade. He had worked awhile at one of Philadelphia's ropewalks, but had quarreled with his employer and been dismissed.

Things had not worked out in Philadelphia. Tolbert knew *Shark* was signing crew; on the chance a place might be available Tolbert had taken the stage north. Unable to afford to sit inside, he had ridden the roof north, wrapped in a blanket at night. Or if *Shark* could not take another midshipman, perhaps there was room for a plain master's mate? Or a common seaman?

"I wish you had written, Mr. Tolbert," Favian said. Then he could have turned Thomas Tolbert down without a further thought. Tolbert had been one of Favian's greatest trials during Markham's Raid: not a good seaman, something of a bully, Tolbert had concluded that Favian was a coward and had not hesitated to proclaim his opinion; he had also, by way of showing himself not to be the coward he'd claimed his captain was, challenged one of the other midshipmen to a duel, a duel only aborted by the fact that the other midshipman had died in the *Teaser* fight before he and Tolbert could blow out one another's brains. Tolbert could not be trusted to stand a watch unsupervised by a superior; he could, on the other hand, certainly be trusted to throw himself headlong into any perilous situation without apprehending the consequences.

But then, here he was. He was loyal, at least now that Favian had convinced him he was not a coward; he was personally fearless; he probably deserved a chance at passing the lieutenant's examination again, and would not have a hope of doing so without some tutoring from a more knowledgeable superior. And he had testified in Favian's behalf at the court-martial; Favian felt he owed Tolbert something for that.

"I shall consider your application, Mr. Tolbert," Favian said. "In the meantime I can perhaps find some employment for you here. You haven't, I take it, been sleeping on many mattresses lately?" He saw Lazarus enter the inn, his fiddle case tucked under his arm and his pockets jingling with change, and Favian waved him over to their table.

"No, sir," Tolbert said, his eyes gleaming with eagerness to prove himself. "When I haven't been sleeping on stagecoach roofs I've been sleeping in fields."

"You're used to lying rough, I see. The job I have in mind will involve a great deal of roughing it. Lazarus, this is

Midshipman Tolbert from the *Experiment;* you may remember him. We shall be working together, I think."

As he walked aboard the Groton ferry, Favian cast a glance at the signal station Jones had established on Great Neck to keep track of British movements: simply a mast with flag halyards manned by a midshipman with a telescope and a pair of seamen. The signals were elementary, a white pennant for no British ships in sight, a red pennant if enemy were present, various other simple devices to report the identities and positions of the by now familiar blockaders—the signal hoists were easy enough to decipher, and by now half New London could tell by a glance at the signal station what British were in sight and where. Surely the British had also deciphered the code. A white flag was flying: no enemy in sight. A pity *Macedonian* wasn't ready for its run to the sea . . .

On the ferry Favian saw a local man walking ahead of him, a typical New England man of business: dark clawhammer coat, a pale, pinched face beneath a round beaver hat, a newspaper tucked under his arm. He leaned against the larboard rail, cut himself a plug of tobacco, took a pair of spectacles from his pocket, unfolded the newspaper, and held the spectacles about an inch above the paper, peering squint-eyed at the magnified letters.

"By Jupiter!" he muttered, plainly audible on the silent ferry, and then he hunched over the paper, hastily setting the spectacles on his nose. He looked up at Favian, open-mouthed. "By Jupiter, sir!" he said. "Baltimore's bombarded! Th' British may take th' city!"

"Let us hope they will not," Favian said. Bad news, but not surprising; after the burning of Washington, Baltimore was the logical target. Yet Baltimore had good men defending it: John Rodgers would be there, and David Porter with the surviving crew of the *Essex* . . . Porter was a tenacious battler, as he had proved with that last fight of the *Essex* after the British had run him to earth in Valparaiso.

"What date was the battle, sir?" Favian asked his informer. The man quickly scanned the newspaper report while the ferry lurched, beginning its journey across the Thames.

"The twelfth, sir," he said. "This correspondent says the issue remained in doubt as he wrote."

"Baltimore's taken by now, that's for certain," said a new

voice belonging to a youngish man. He was dressed fashionably, and stood next to a fine strong gelding. He sliced the air idly with his whip. "I wonder what Jimmie Madison will do now, poor lamb?"

The first man turned purple. He spat his tobacco overboard and advanced on the younger man, stuffing his spectacles in his breast pocket. "You wretched idle sniveling puppy!" he roared. "The burning of Washington by those red-coated barbarians was a national tragedy, not one belonging to Jimmie Madison alone! How dare you sneer!" He drew back his arm and let fly, his fist striking the young man squarely in the nose. The victim, entirely surprised, unbalanced and fell against the rail, the elderly man pummeling him left and right unmercifully.

"Take him, Joshua!" shouted a bystander. The crowd gathered quickly, enjoying the young man's embarrassment, calling advice. "Teach him about the flag, Josh! Beat him red and blue!"

Favian started forward after pushing the reins of his mare into the hands of the grinning Tolbert, intending to intervene as soon as the young man recovered himself and the elderly fellow began to get the worst of it, but the young man's gelding, unnerved, began to back away from the fisticuffs, jostling Favian, its left rear hoof rising as if uncertain whether to kick. . . . Favian jumped back out of the way, called to Tolbert to take the reins of the horse and gentle him, in the meantime working his way around his own animal, stroking it as he saw its own thoroughbred temperament aroused by the melee and proximity to the snorting gelding. The two horses would be kicking at each other in a very short moment.

Favian seized the bridle, then the reins, of his mare, seeing Tolbert clutching at the reins of the gelding, a man of the sea unused to horses, trying to hold its head down in imitation of someone he had seen once in a similar situation, his face expressing alternately bewilderment and stubbornness. . . . The young gentleman was trying to put the rail between himself and his attacker, apparently unaware that his Joshua seemed to be giving him active help, having grimly altered from pummeling to a determined shoving. . . . The gelding's head tossed, Tolbert stubbornly hanging on, its rear hoof lashing out. Favian lunged for the gelding's head, gathering the reins, speaking softly to it, finally calming it just as Joshua, his face radiating ferocious triumph, loosened the grip of his victim on the railing and watched with satisfaction as the young dandy, arms windmilling, went backward into the Thames.

"Crazy old man! Lunatic!" the young gentleman shouted, paddling in the water, trying to keep his top hat from floating away, his voice drowned by the passengers' laughter.

Favian, stroking the gelding's finely shaped head, watched as grinning passengers stepped forward to shake Joshua's hand. The little drama had seemed significant somehow, symptomatic of a sea change within the body of American opinion. Just a few weeks before the young man's ideas, or something very like them, could have been heard on any New England streetcorner; those who found them objectionable, like old Joshua here, would have been very much in the minority. The news that the British had burned Washington had changed everything, had infected the war with a new sort of grim purpose. Suddenly it was no longer fashionable to scorn Madison, to laugh at the war, to preach New England secession; suddenly an old patriot attacking some young idiot on a public ferryboat was finding himself cheered by an approving crowd, a crowd that, short weeks ago, would either have restrained him or taken the other side.

The British capture of Washington had altered the popular perception of the war. Formerly it had been considered the ill-shaped creation of a few ambitious political brains in Washington, to be opposed politically, as had the embargoes and so much else. The war had touched few directly except by way of the hardships imposed by the British blockade, which had been blamed on Madison rather than the British. Favian had always had to restrain his temper when he heard such attitudes expressed publicly; those, like Favian, who had seen men blown apart by canister at close range, knew the war was something more than a coffee house dispute. But now the war was being perceived, not as a political issue, but as a matter of national survival. The British would destroy the republic if they could, or render it impotent, and that threat took precedence over homely political squabbles.

Favian found himself wondering about the meeting of New England political brains that was about to convene in Hartford. They and that young gentleman splashing for shore shared a great many common assumptions about the present emergency; they, like that young man, believed that fighting Madison should take precedence over the cause of battling for liberty from the tyrannies of the Old World. Had the Hartford men and their allies, those like Nicholas Greenhow and Benjamin Stanhope, realized the change taking place in New England? Would the Hartford Convention, producing its resolutions and recommendations expected to alter the relationship between New England and the federal authority, find itself cut off from those citizens it professed to represent? Seeing the laughter and applause that greeted Joshua's ducking of the young dandy, Favian felt a rush of hope. The convention might not prove a menace at all. They might well meet, pass their resolutions, and in the end find that the attitudes they expressed had become obsolete almost overnight.

The ferry thudded against the Groton pier. Favian turned the gelding over to one of the ferrymen for transportation back to its spluttering owner, then took his roan's reins and led her on to the shore. He, Tolbert, and Lazarus would have a long wait tonight, and perhaps for many nights to come. They would be waiting for men who were truly dangerous, not for foolish braggart fops; it was best to concentrate on the job at hand. Preventing the Hartford Convention from doing harm was beyond his power; helping *Macedonian* to run the British blockade, perhaps, was not. He was navy, he reminded himself; he would concentrate on the navy's worries, and hope the rest would work out for the best.

The wait, that night, was fruitless. Groton Long Point, thrusting into Fishers Island Sound some five miles east of the Thames mouth, was fairly flat and mostly untimbered, but there were sheltered places where Favian's horse could be hidden and where a man could keep out of the wind, and there were vantage points where a lookout could keep most of the point under surveillance, and where anyone moving onto the point, particularly carrying lanterns, would easily be seen.

But no one had been seen. Even the British blockaders were absent; the sea had been empty of sail, and the only sight greeting Favian's telescope had been the gray waters breaking against the Cormaralit Rocks just north of Fishers Island. They spent the night standing two-hour watches, wrapped in blankets and juggling the telescope and night glass; there had been a cold sprinkling of rain in the early hours of the morning and everyone had stiffened with the cold and damp. After a dim sun had risen over the gray waters, Favian had called an end to their watch, packed his brace of dueling pistols and the cutlass he'd brought for Lazarus into his saddlebags—Tolbert, having come late into the scheme, had been armed only with his dirk—and led the weary party back to Groton, seeing the flags above the signal station on Great Neck confirming what they already knew, that no British sail was in sight.

And so it went for days. There would be a cold and sodden night on Groton Long Point, and then the men would rub their chilled and stiffened limbs and walk back to town, where Lazarus and Tolbert would stumble into their room and Favian would write a note to Jacob Jones reporting his lack of success and then ride to Poquetanuck to collapse into Caroline's bed. Caroline would bring him breakfast at noon along with a pot of coffee, and another day would commence.

His relationship with Caroline continued in its most recent course; they enjoyed one another's company, enjoyed one another's bodies, but there was a certain distancing that had not been present at first. Favian had a sense that each was preparing, when the time came, to say farewell.

Eight days after his lookout had begun at Groton Long Point, Favian felt uneasy as he rode into Groton, heading down Church Street to the ferry. The quality of the uneasiness was difficult to quantify . . . perhaps it had something to do with the distant ache in his stomach, just below his breastbone, that might be signifying an upcoming attack of his old enemy, dyspepsia, but he didn't think so; it was as if something, in his absence, had changed. Absently pressing a hand to the distant ache in his stomach—he hoped it was not the dyspepsia again—he slowed as he approached the ferry, looking closely at the people on the streets, his eyes searching the horizon—what the devil was it? Then his eyes caught the glimpse of red against the white of a cloud, and he knew.

There were several flags flying from the signal station on Great Neck, a red pennant atop the hoist: the British blockaders had returned to the Connecticut coast. Favian narrowed his eyes, trying to discern the flags. *Macedonian* had lost its chance to run the blockade unopposed. The blue-and-white checker, that was *Orpheus* of thirty-six guns, commanded by Captain Hugh Pigot—known as "Pigot the Third" to distinguish him from Admiral Pigot and the Hugh Pigot killed in the *Hermione* mutiny—and the white flag with the red saltire was for the *Tiber*, Captain Dacres, a new-built forty-four-gun frigate that, it was hoped, was the equal of the big American forty-fours. Dacres had been the loser in the *Constitution-Guerrière* fight, and would presumably be anticipating revenge with his new, big frigate. Dacres, Favian knew, was very young for such a major command; the Admiralty, therefore, considered him an able captain despite his loss to the *Constitution*.

Familiar names, familiar ships: they had lain off American shores for months, and no doubt Dacres and Pigot knew as many details of Favian's biography as Favian knew of theirs. There was a fourth flag below the others, one less familiar: Favian thought it might represent the *St. Lawrence* schooner, but couldn't be certain—the *St. Lawrence* had spent most of its career privateer hunting off the Canadian coasts, and its use as a blockade vessel was thus far unprecedented.

The British, no doubt, knew that the *United States* had been hauled far up the Thames and deprived of its crew—that meant that the *Orpheus* and *Tiber* were here for the *Macedonian* alone. It was a source of grim satisfaction, Favian supposed, that the British considered it necessary to use two frigates, one of the largest class, to keep Jones and his *Macedonian* in port. Possibly the British knew *Macedonian* was nearing readiness, possibly they were here as a matter of routine—they had been absent for some weeks, engaged in one of Admiral Hardy's operations in Maine or taking on water in Halifax, and had now returned, and that was all Favian knew. It was a shame Jones had not been ready earlier; he might have got clean away by now.

He crossed on the ferry, shading his brow as he gazed out to sea: aye, those were British topsails. He returned to his tavern, gave the horse to his groom, stepped into the common room for his dinner, pulling off his gloves, and then heard his name called by a familiar voice.

"Stephen, by God!" It was Decatur right enough, a clean-shaven, grinning Decatur in a black civilian coat, hurrying from his table. Favian shook his hand gladly, seeing smiles on the faces of several of the inn's customers—Decatur had been a popular figure when he had been blockaded here in the *United States:* New London would be happy to have him back.

"What brings you to Connecticut?" Favian asked. "I see the British have laid on a blockade to honor your arrival."

"I was called up to Lake Ontario to inspect our forces there," Decatur said. "I decided to visit New London on my return. I think the President will appreciate a report on how soon *United States* can be got ready for sea."

"Ontario," Favian repeated, surprised. Lake Ontario was Commodore Isaac Chauncey's territory; Chauncey would not at all have appreciated Decatur's showing up to report on his progress. But then great things had been expected from Chauncey, and his expected successes had never arrived, unlike the American victories on Erie and Champlain . . . Good God!

"Stephen," Favian said. "Will you be ordered to Ontario?"

Decatur pursed his lips, looking doubtful. "This is in confidence, Favian," he said, his black eyes grave. "I have been told to hold myself in readiness, but that will depend on what the President decides."

"It will be the largest American squadron in history," Favian said. "They're laying down three-decked sail of the line on Ontario." The greatest plum in the navy, transferred from Chauncey to Decatur—Chauncey must be half mad with anxiety.

"Hush, Favian," Decatur said. "I don't want any rumors getting out ahead of the fact—it would be most unwise to make Commodore Chauncey's job any more difficult than it already is."

Favian nodded. One did not criticize fellow navy men, even in confidence—aside from the discourtesy, men had been challenged to duels for less.

"Join me at my table, Favian," Decatur said. "I arrived late this morning and have been looking for you ever since. The innkeeper here said you haven't slept in for many nights now."

"Yes. There's a reason for it," Favian said. He lowered his voice as they sat down. "Those lights on Groton Long Point. You know the ones I mean."

Decatur's eyes flashed surprise, then alert interest. He had been blockaded here for over a year; he knew the rumors as well as anyone.

"We could have patrolled Groton Point with marines," Favian said, "but that would have given the game away. Instead I and a few friends—we've been keeping lookout on the point each night."

Decatur looked at him, absorbing the idea, then nodded.

"How many do you have with you?" he asked. "And what can you make of the other side?"

"I have Midshipman Tolbert—you may remember him from the trial, he was a witness—and the fiddler Lazarus."

"I remember him, I've seen him perform. Has he joined the navy now? He didn't seem the sort who would."

"He's—he seems to have joined *me*, at any rate," Favian stumbled. It was even more difficult to explain Lazarus's presence to others than to himself—in truth, he had no more notion of Lazarus's motives than those of a great ocean whale. "He says he'll join *Shark*'s crew when the time comes."

"Anyone else?"

"No. Just the three of us—Captain Jones knows, but of course he's too busy to be spending his evenings on Groton Point, and we decided to keep it between as few people as possible so as not to alert, ah, alert the—the enemy, I suppose we'd best call them."

"The enemy, yes," Decatur said. His fingers toyed with the mug of whiskey punch on the table before him. "I don't like calling our own countrymen the enemy, but enemies they are, however unpleasant the idea may be. Who are they, d'you think?"

Favian fell silent as the barman came up to take their order for supper; they ordered chowder, whiskey, and some of the coffee from Favian's private supply, and then after the barman's hunched shoulders retreated to the kitchen, Favian leaned over the table and answered in a low voice.

"I've no idea who they are, of course," Favian said. "There aren't any Tories left here, not considering the reception they'd get from New London for burning their town. The political men seem too intelligent to actively oppose their own countrymen in such a way. I'd guess that we're either dealing with spies the British have sent in—perhaps old Tories or their sons that are unknown to the people here—or perhaps native malcontents, those that might have a grudge against the federal government for some reason. There are, I suppose, those romantics who will take adventure where they can find it, thinking the additional danger of spying will add spice to their endeavors."

Decatur smiled wryly. "Thus far we have old Tories or their children, American malcontents, amoral adventurers—quite a list, don't'ee think? Is it possible to narrow it down a bit?"

Favian grinned. "There's only one major suspect—a man

named Gardell, and for him there's no proof, and we can't seem to find him." Favian quickly told Decatur about meeting Gardell while the man was carrying wheat to Wellington's armies, and how the man had oddly turned up in New London just a few weeks ago.

"It may be coincidence, of course," Favian said. He paused while the barman brought deep bowls of chowder and bread along with a pot of coffee and glasses of whiskey. "But still," he said after the man had left their table. "Why should he hide in New London? And hide at the Beach Tavern, where from his windows he could look down at the wharf where *Macedonian* was getting ready for sea?"

"Why *not* New London?" Decatur asked. "It's as good a place as any other—Connecticut will host the Hartford Convention, and the authorities here are presumably sympathetic to any poor man of business"—his voice took on heavy irony—"trying to make a traitorous living in the midst of this unjust war."

"But there are navy ships in New London," Favian said. "He must know the navy is looking for him, and there might be someone here who would recognize him. Why not some other place—New Haven or Bridgeport or Providence?"

"No doubt he's in one of those places now, congratulating himself on a successful escape," Decatur said. He began to spoon into his chowder. Favian looked down at his own bowl and felt a spasm of pain in his stomach. Not dyspepsia, he thought, not now.

"Here's our Mr. Tolbert," Favian said, seeing the midshipman enter, blinking while his eyes adjusted to the darkness of the common room. "Mr. Tolbert, will you join us? There is someone I wish you to meet."

Tolbert's jaw almost dropped to the ground as he recognized Stephen Decatur—the man's reputation was the envy of every ambitious junior, and to actually be within arm's reach of the most admired, most worshiped man in the navy almost stunned him into imbecility. Favian watched, amused, as Decatur effortlessly put the young man at his ease, drawing him out with a few questions, passing on some harmless service gossip to draw Tolbert into his confidence and create the impression of intimacy, made a few airy jokes . . . In his years of acting as Decatur's chief subordinate, Favian had watched the process many times; he had seen how Decatur could work his magic upon an entire ship's complement, convincing each shellback among them that he was Decatur's dear friend and confidant. The sorcery of his personal charm was astonishing, and wielded, Favian thought, without conscious art; Decatur could no more stop himself from being charming than Favian could halt the wind and tide. In another man Decatur's abilities might have been envied, but Decatur was unique; no one could possibly envy the sun or the stars, and Decatur's talents seemed as much a phenomenon of natural creation as anything in the heavens.

Lazarus appeared after supper, his fiddle case under his arm, cocking an eye at the newcomer; when Decatur informed him that he would go with them tonight—by then no one questioned the decision, or wondered when it had been made, even though the issue had never been discussed—Lazarus simply shrugged, grunted an assent, and informed them that he'd just had Favian's horse saddled and made ready. The pain in Favian's stomach had faded slightly, but remained there, a hovering reminder, warning that it might return at any moment.

It was near dark by the time the four men arrived on Groton Long Point. Decatur had his own hanger and pistols, as did Favian; Jacob Jones had contributed one of *Macedonian*'s cutlasses for Lazarus, and another to supplement Tolbert's dirk. Favian had considered asking for pistols for Lazarus and Tolbert, but he'd never seen Lazarus in a fight and he knew Tolbert's impetuosity and aggressiveness all too well, and in the end decided that the chance of his being shot by accident outweighed any possible benefits, and decided to reserve the pistols to himself.

The British blockaders rolled on the slate gray sea, under reduced sail as darkness approached: *Orpheus* and *Tiber* were well out, a safe distance from the rocks of Fishers Island and the Connecticut coast; the little schooner was in closer, tacking easily between the Thames mouth and Fishers Island. Favian wondered if the schooner was assigned to observe the signal from the spies on shore, or even if the schooner was riding so close to the shore in order that it could pick up a boat, receiving the spies' messages directly. In that case Favian and his cohorts should be rowing guard in a boat off the Thames mouth, not freezing themselves on the Long Point.

"You've been out here every night?" Decatur asked as Favian led the party to the depression that had been sheltering them from the westerly gales. "Even though there haven't been any blockading ships to signal to?"

"The spies might not know that," Favian said.

"They can see the flags on the signal station," Decatur reminded.

"They might not live in New London. If they live far out in the country to the east, they won't see the signal flags every day. Besides, they might be out here making preparations, or signaling to a ship popping above the horizon just at dawn. We've been standing two-hour watches. We've got a night glass in case we need it. Mr. Tolbert has been standing the first watch."

Decatur glanced up at the darkening sky. "Do you mind if I stand the first watch along with Mr. Tolbert? I'd like to get a look at the ground before it grows entirely black."

"If Mr. Tolbert has no objection," Favian said. It was curious, after those long years of subordination, to have Decatur deferring to him. Even though Decatur had many years over Favian in seniority, and seniority was everything to the navy, he recognized this little party as Favian's to command, and had given himself the role of observer. Not many officers would have done that, Favian knew—but of course relinquishing the command of a party of four men, one of whom was was not even a member of the navy, was no great sacrifice of honor. If it had been a question of commanding a squadron of navy ships, Favian knew, Decatur would not have been so magnanimous.

Tolbert, of course, had no objection to Decatur's company, and the two went off to the observation point. Favian unsaddled his horse and picketed the roan, putting on her blanket and nosebag, then opened the saddlebags to bring out blankets and a canvas groundcloth. Lazarus peered out to sea, catching the last fading light on the British schooner's topsails.

"The signs and powers proclaim the time is ripe," he said. "*Macedonian* can sail within the week. The British lie offshore, and the signal station at Great Neck gives the news free to anyone with eyes." He turned to Favian, his eyes burning. "The powers say: soon. The powers say: there will be blood spilled."

"Do the powers say whose?" Favian asked, staking out the groundcloth. Really, Lazarus was not performing up to his usual standard; all that his powers had told him were things available to anyone with a deductive mind.

"Thine, I think," Lazarus said. Favian straightened, surprised at Lazarus's boldness. "Thine," Lazarus repeated, his face solemn. "Thee are not protected against the powers of the night."

"And Captain Decatur, and Tolbert? They are protected?"

"Captain Decatur has another death reserved for him—I can see it in his face. Mr. Tolbert is as naked as thee."

A gust of wind whistled down the little depression, stirring the leaves strewn on the grass. Favian repressed a shiver, finding the need to shiver at all annoying. "You are protected yourself, as I take it?" Favian said. "Cannot you extend your protection to the rest of us?"

"It is not for me to offer protection. Thee must commend thy soul to the Master, whose powers they be."

The Master; that would be Satan. Favian felt a certain distaste; Lazarus was proselytizing for his faith after all.

"I'll take my chances," he said shortly.

"As thee wishes." Lazarus's voice was calm; he had spoken his piece. Favian turned up his collar and sat down on a blanket, opening his case of pistols, checking the priming, then returning the pistols to the case until such time as it was necessary to transfer them to his waistband. Overhead a shooting star tore flaming across the heavens.

"Captain Markham," came Lazarus's quiet voice.

"Yes."

"I may not—I think my own time may be near, Captain Markham." Favian looked at the old fiddler, startled.

"How do you mean, Lazarus?"

"My life has been long. Had the Master not given me protection, it would have ended long ago. The powers I deal with—they are not—they are not to be trusted completely. They always keep their word, thee understands, once they give it, but they do not always tell the truth if they are not pressed. They will not answer all my questions. I think they know my death, and that it will be soon."

Favian looked at Lazarus with surprised curiosity. Lazarus had never been this plain-spoken about his devils before; always he had spoken in ringing, bombastic tones, which Favian had thought were intended to impress the credulous. Now he was speaking as if they were old acquaintances, as familiar to him as Decatur and Jones were to Favian.

"You are not a young man," Favian said. "It is wartime, and

you intend to join the crew of a warship. I should think that the thought of death should not be far from you."

Lazarus shook his head impatiently. "That's not what I mean," he said. "My death will come when it wishes, and I will not resist. There is something concerning my death that I wish thee to understand. Wilt thou do me a favor, Favian Markham?"

"If I can."

"I wish to be buried at sea, Captain Markham. With a round shot at my head, not at my feet. And I wish no Christian burial read over me, dost thou understand?"

Inverted burial, matching his inverted faith. It seemed a small concession. "I will try to arrange it if I can," Favian said. He would not treat this lightly, as he usually did Lazarus's omens and portents; he knew this mood in seafaring men. He remembered the night before he left the *Constitution* to go into the *Intrepid* ketch to burn the *Philadelphia* in Tripoli harbor, when he and Decatur, Charles Morris and James Lawrence and the others who had volunteered for that mission had drunk a toast together to fortune and victory, and how the presence of death had seemed to hover there in the wardroom, and how despite the drink and comradeship the party had broken up early, each man going alone to write to his family, or make a will, or simply to face the specter of death alone. Favian remembered how his right arm had, in the middle of a letter to his parents, suddenly gone limp, utterly paralyzed, and his own horror at the discovery, mixed with a curious relief. If his arm were paralyzed, he would not have to board *Intrepid* on the morrow, and no one could blame him. Yet he knew that there would be suspicion, that even if his comrades accepted the paralysis as real—and it certainly was real; he remembered his own terror as the arm simply hung at the end of his shoulder, numb to the touch—he knew that he would himself always wonder.

He had lain awake all night, sweating in the Mediterranean heat, hugging the arm to him, praying that life would come back, yet also hoping it would not. In the morning, when the cabin steward knocked at his door, he dressed clumsily, put the hand in his jacket pocket, and stepped forth from the cabin pale as a sheet, determined to get aboard *Intrepid* if all the hosts of Islam stood in the way. He had clumsily swung down into the ketch, breathing hard, seeing *Constitution*'s shrouds crowded with men watching the doomed volunteers go forth on their hopeless mission, seeing the brig *Syren,* the warship that would escort them to the harbor mouth, rolling on the sea two cables away, its backed topsails white against the Mediterranean sky, seeing Preble on the quarterdeck with his hat raised in salute, feeling the manila line rough against his left palm as he lowered himself to the deck of the little ketch.

The paralysis left his arm slowly, as soon as *Constitution* began to slide below the horizon. If anyone else aboard thought it was odd that Midshipman Markham's hand should remain in his pocket all day, none were curious enough to mention it. The *Philadelphia* was taken and burned, Favian's arm functioning well enough as he slashed with his cutlass at the defenders, and the party of raiders and their ketch made their bloodless escape through the fire of two hundred guns, and throughout the long anxious hours Favian had felt only relief that none had discovered the stigma of his cowardice.

So Favian accepted Lazarus's odd request quietly and without comment, giving the man the privacy to live with his fears—if fears they were—and with his premonitions. He would talk if Lazarus seemed to want it, but Lazarus unrolled a blanket, wrapped himself in it, and stretched out on the ground, staring up at the waking stars. Favian shrugged deep into his collar and listened to the wind and the far-off sound of the sea, feeling the ache growing in his belly. It was, as he'd feared, dyspepsia; now it would be with him for days. He could dose himself with opiates, but he didn't want to be wandering about Groton Long Point in a drugged daze with spies, and possibly among them a monster like Gardell, in the offing. He had the sense that there would be dirty weather soon, that throughout Connecticut the barometers would be falling—there was no real basis for that intuition, but he knew it was true; perhaps, after all these years of living with the sea, there was some built-in response in his body to the change in pressure.

He turned at a sound, seeing Decatur and Tolbert walking toward him like shadows. He restrained an impulse to look at his watch; he knew they hadn't been out there for two hours yet.

"Men coming, Favian," Decatur said. "Three, I think, leading a horse."

Favian heard Lazarus stir beside him, and calmly leaned forward to his pistol case. He opened it, checked the priming again, stood, tucked the pistols into his waistband. *Thy blood, I think,*

Lazarus had said, in his growling voice, his antique dialect. He clipped his sword to his belt, seeing Lazarus adjusting his own cutlass-baldrick over his shoulder. Calmly. Surely. Both of them acting as if they'd done it a thousand times before.

Thy blood. Lazarus was expecting his own death; Favian had seen the truth of such premonitions too many times to take them lightly. Yet there was nothing else for either of them to do. Favian's life had been at hazard many times before; he knew well this dry-mouthed false calm that precedes action. One does the things that must be done, checking the pistols' priming, adjusting the sword belt, making sure the cloak is thrown back to allow access to the sword hilt, pulling the sword a little out of the scabbard to make certain it is loose—and all the while the heart is racing like a runaway four-in-hand, the brain is flailing, reaching for strategies, seeking alternatives . . .

But why now? Three men, Decatur had said, and a horse—traitors or spies, men terrified of discovery, looking over their shoulders every few seconds. Outnumbered, not expecting trouble, possibly not even armed, facing professional warriors who were prepared for them. There was no reason, save Lazarus's premonitions, that he should be any more concerned with this than with a stroll down Bank Street in New London.

"Are we ready, Favian?" Decatur asked. Favian saw Decatur's eyes glittering like gems in the starlight and felt a stab of empathy; Decatur, too, was feeling the mad rush of blood through his limbs, the strange coursing sensation, so like the first flushing intoxication of a good brandy, that preceded action. The galloping near-madness of fear held in control, like a tearing Thoroughbred held firmly between the knees of a master rider. Decatur lived for these moments, Favian knew, the moments when he was most certain of himself, of his place at the center of things—and many years ago Favian had lived for such times as well, back in the days when he'd been leading boarding parties onto Tripolitan gunboats, slashing madly with his sword at the Moors. Years ago, before he'd lost—lost what? Faith in himself, or in the navy? Or perhaps the navy's deadly training had simply taken hold, and he now performed his duty without question, killing when necessary, striking poses when the navy required it, hiding his mistress out in Poquetanuck because he knew the navy would not approve . . . whatever had happened, Favian seemed not to be a part of it, not really, not like Decatur, who was still *inside*.

"Let's go," Favian said. "Stephen?" He held out his hand; Decatur clasped it. Favian saw again the glittering eyes, the wild hair, the grin whitening the darkness, and then he turned and led them out of the hollow.

They knelt among the dead grass on the top of the rise; Decatur wordlessly pointed and handed Favian the night glass. Favian saw movement to the seaward of them—they must have passed below the rise while Decatur was dodging into the shelter to warn the party—and put the glass to his eye. The image in the night glass was inverted, and it took Favian a brief second to adjust to the image of men and a horse walking upside-down on the sky. Hunched figures, the nodding form of a horse: Favian counted. Three, yes. He saw no giant figure that could have been Gardell, and felt relief swarming into him. Buck Johanan Gardell could have made this expedition a dangerous one.

He handed the glass back to Decatur and said, "Follow me," in a low voice. Ridiculous; they were two or three hundred yards off and with the sound of the wind and sea they probably wouldn't have heard even a shout.

Once out of the shelter of the little hollow Favian felt a brisk wind plucking at his clothing. They came down onto the path the others were following and walked in their wake. Dead leaves scuttered in little whirlwinds ahead of them.

Occasionally Favian lost sight of his quarry among the trees, but there was no reason to worry; the three men went right to the stony tip of the point, just short of where it dropped into the foaming sea; there was a kind of ledge there, a little rise behind them where any light would be concealed from anyone looking from the land, a flat place where they stood, and then the sea.

Favian had seen the place in daylight and knew, once he saw the rise in front of him, where the quarry had to be. He halted a hundred yards short of the end of the point, knelt, and asked Decatur for the night glass. He carefully swept the arc of the rise, seeing nothing disturbing its silhouette except a gnarled little evergreen twisted and bent by the blustering New England winds. The spies had set no lookout: nothing could have so well proclaimed their status as amateurs.

He beckoned to Tolbert, who came up and went down to one knee beside him. "I want you to head up the path and block their escape," Favian said. "If they bolt, it'll be up to you to stop them. Don't try to close with them or they might get around you; just block them if they run." Favian saw Tolbert nod, his jaw set—he had exaggerated the importance of Tolbert's mission, and the prospects for excitement, in case Tolbert thought he was being slighted: evidently Tolbert had no such qualms. Favian turned to the others. "I would like to spread out and head up that rise. Stop just short of the crest and wait for my signal, then we'll all go over at once. Lazarus, go on my right; Stephen, I'd be obliged if you stay on my left."

Lazarus nodded. "Good," said Decatur.

"Let's go." They advanced in line abreast, Tolbert walking with drawn cutlass down the path, the others spreading out to his left. Favian put his right hand on the pistol in his waistband, his left hand holding his scabbard so it wouldn't rattle. The wind brought them a coherent slice of speech from beyond the rise: "Get the shovel, Bob. Damn it, I'm holding the light! Get it!" Favian felt a grin tugging at his lips. Amateurs.

Just short of the rise, the strange dwarfed tree on his left, Favian waved the party to a halt. He drew his pair of pistols from his waistband, holding one in each hand, clumsily snapping off the priming pan covers with his thumbs, then cocking each pistol with two heavy clicks that seemed infinitely loud in the night. He glanced to his left where Lazarus stood with his hand on his cutlass, then right where Decatur had his own pistols ready, Tolbert a shadowy form behind him. He waved to the left with a pistol, then waved to the right, catching nods in response. They began the walk over the rise.

"Hurry it up, Bob. I'm tired of holding this godforsaken tree." A different voice this time. There they were, clustered in a yellow spill of lantern light, the horse tethered behind them. One, a thin middle-aged man whose white hair blew in the wind, was holding a ten-foot pole with a crossbar that made a T, hooks for storm lanterns driven into the underside of the crossbar—the pole where the signal would hang, presumably carried in by the horse. And there was Bob with his shovel, widening the hole where the pole would sit—apparently it had fallen in a bit since the last time they'd used it. Bob was a small, weathered man, probably in his late thirties. Carrying the lantern was the third man, a skinny youth with a blotched face, shivering in the wind. Favian had time to study them all as he approached; they were all intent on the shovel work. He glanced left and right, making sure everyone was in position. Amateurs. Dead easy.

"Hands up! You're under arrest!" he barked. There was a shriek from the young one and the lantern fell, clattering on the dead grass, the light snuffing out. Favian blinked in the sudden blackness, seeing motion, the thin youth running for the path while the others stood frozen in surprise. Favian held out his right-handed pistol—a balanced thing of beauty, octagonal barrel to make it possible to snap-shot by sighting along the top of the pistol if there was no time to use the sights, fitting Favian like an extension of his arm; he sighted on the running figure, leading it, blinking again to help regain his night vision, the running youth and the pistol and Favian's eye connected invisibly by a line of Euclidean purity . . . Favian squeezed the trigger, feeling the snap of the priming followed, an instant later, by the crack of the main charge and the buzz of a receding, spinning bullet; some good, steady men never learned to lead a moving target in such a fashion as to account for that little delay between the explosion of priming and the main charge, or flinched when the priming went off so as to spoil their aim, but in this case the geometry was near-perfect and the bullet-Achilles caught the running man-turtle and the boy went down hard, the breath knocked out of him as he fell in an audible *whuff*. Favian had hit him in the thigh; he'd been aiming for the hip: close enough. There was motion in front of him; he dropped the smoking pistol in his right hand, shifted the left-hand pistol to his right, held it out aimed squarely at the chest of Bob, who was coming at him with the shovel cocked back ready to strike, drawing another line in the air, eye-pistol-chest, seeing Bob's eyes widening as the pistol came up.

"Don't do that," Favian said mildly.

Bob slowed as if he had run into a wall of molasses; the shovel came slowly down and thudded on the turf. Bob's hands came up reluctantly. There was a moan from the man on the ground.

"Stephen. Lazarus. Search them. Take any weapons."

Decatur and Lazarus approached from right and left, Decatur kneeling by the sprawled boy, inspecting the wound, patting his pockets. Lazarus came up behind Bob, his cutlass out and held ready. He seized Bob roughly and searched him, finding a long dirk in a coat pocket, throwing it to the ground a safe distance away. Bob glared at him in resentment of his rudeness. He turned to Favian.

"Lieutenant Robert Stackpole, Royal Marines," he said. "Might I be searched by a gentleman?"

Well. So Bob wasn't an amateur after all.

"Captain Favian Markham, United States Navy," Favian said. "I'm sorry if you object to our company; perhaps you ought not to have come. Lazarus, this man is dangerous: search his sleeves for knives, and his boots."

Lieutenant Robert Stackpole, Royal Marines, grimaced as Lazarus turned up a throwing knife in his right-hand boot; no doubt he'd hoped to make good use of it. If he hadn't identified himself as British, Favian might well have failed to have him searched thoroughly, and would have certainly regretted it.

Stackpole didn't look like an uppercrust officer, one who would object to being handled by the lower orders—Stackpole looked thoroughly dangerous, a small, lithe, weathered man, probably very fast. If he hadn't been caught by surprise he might well have done some damage with that shovel. Most likely, Favian thought, Stackpole's acting the gentleman was a ruse; he wanted to get Favian to search him, getting him near enough to be able to knock the pistol out of his hand with a sudden attack, then either seize the pistol or use one of his knives.

The ruse hadn't worked, and Favian and Stackpole both knew its failure doomed the Englishman; caught on an enemy shore in civilian rig, he was as good as dead. George Washington had set the iron precedent back in the Revolution when he'd insisted on Major André's execution, refusing to exchange or parole him: André's position as the adjutant-general of the British army had not inspired Washington to give him any special consideration. Spies were to be hanged, no matter how witty, well connected, or personable they might be. Stackpole might well be desperate; Favian would have to watch him closely.

Decatur turned up a pocket pistol on the youth, then patted the pockets of the white-haired man without finding anything other than a pocket knife and some loose change. "The boy is my son," the white-haired man said. Since his apprehension he had stood motionless, his hands in the air, his face fixed in an expression of bleak despair. "I'd like to see to his hurt."

Favian nodded, not quite daring to take his eyes off Stackpole. "Stephen, go with him," he said. "Let him bandage the boy, see if he can walk. Lazarus, take Lieutenant Stackpole's belt, and cut his waistband."

"Sir, I protest!" Stackpole said. It was an old press-gang trick; men have a hard time running when their chief concern is holding their trousers up.

"There will be a time to file protests later," Favian said. Out beyond Stackpole, on the dark waters, he could see the sails of the *St. Lawrence* schooner, awaiting a signal that would not come. Stackpole might be hanged, but Jacob Jones would have a fair run at breaking the blockade.

Stackpole's trousers fell to his knees, and Lazarus backed away to a safe distance, his cutlass still ready. The British spy looked at Favian in sullen humiliation. "You may hold up your trousers with one hand," Favian said. "Keep the other aloft, if you will."

Lieutenant Stackpole bent to retrieve his trousers, holding them up with his left hand, his right hand still in the air. The youth moaned as his father tore away the cloth over the wound. The grand romantic gestures always come to this in the end, Favian thought. The old man and his son, traitors by inheritance or greed or political conviction or simple hatred of their own kind, probably thinking of themselves as dashing, secret heroes, signaling from the dark cape in the dead of night . . . look at them now. A young man, his life barely started, groaning on the cold ground with a pistol ball in his thigh, the old man bent over him, helping to save him for the hangman. Lieutenant Stackpole, by his looks a competent, deadly man, volunteering for the unsavory mission, hoping, perhaps, for the promotion denied him because of his lack of influence, or simply because the dashing life of the spy appealed to him . . . and here he was, bereft not only of liberty and the chance to live out his life, but of dignity as well, standing here holding his trousers about his loins and hoping his captors would not mistake his shivering in the cold for tremors of fear.

There was a cry on his left, and Favian turned to face it, his pistol still on Stackpole. Tolbert, standing on the path blocking it, had turned around, his cutlass raised. Behind him there was a blackness moving within the night, a giant form with outstretched arms. Tolbert stepped forward, the cutlass whipping through the air; there were sparks, the clatter of steel on steel, and Tolbert with a despairing cry was overwhelmed by the blackness, crashing backwards into the ground, his hold on the cutlass broken, Buck Johanan Gardell bending over him to retrieve it.

"Run, ye men!" Gardell's voice bawled, and then Gardell came at Favian, trampling Tolbert, the cutlass raised high. Favian sensed Stackpole moving, readying himself, but made an instant decision that Gardell was the real danger and that Lazarus could handle Stackpole if necessary; he swung the pistol toward Gardell, centering it on the big man and squeezing the trigger in one easy gesture, the pistol barking. Gardell seemed to slow for an instant as he charged, as if he had lost a little of his velocity as he absorbed the lead, but the sensation might have been illusory. Favian backed, Gardell growing larger, throwing the pistol at him, hearing the thud as it struck; then Favian drew his hanger rasping from the scabbard and went on guard, ready to absorb that charging momentum on the tip of his sword. Gardell seemed to have a knife in his left hand as well as Tolbert's cutlass in his right; that might make things tricky—if necessary Favian would have to parry the knife with his arm. There was a shot from Decatur, the muzzle flash shooting across the grassy ridge. A grunt from Gardell signaled that the shot had hit, but it slowed him down no more than had the previous shot.

"Run, ye bastards!" Gardell howled.

Favian braced himself for the onslaught, in a moment of clarity seeing how his plans had gone astray. Gardell had been delayed—perhaps his horse had thrown a shoe, perhaps he'd been on lookout behind the others and seen Favian's party emerge from the hollow—and had arrived a few minutes late. Favian's first shot had alerted him; he'd scouted his enemies and come charging over the weakest, taking Tolbert's weapon. The cutlass came sweeping down.

Favian parried it, feeling the shock move up his arm as it absorbed Gardell's incredible weight and momentum, sensing movement to his right and hearing a cry from Lazarus that meant that Stackpole was moving. He turned aside another desperate cut from Gardell—the man was no fencer—and made his riposte—what was going on to his right? his mind demanded—the hanger tip slicing for Gardell's midsection, going between two of the ribs, another shock going up Favian's arm as Gardell's oncoming weight drove the sword into him. Then something crashed into Favian from the right, coming under the sword arm, and Favian saw the ground coming up at him. Stackpole had run, not at

Lazarus's cutlass—that would have been suicide—but away from
Lazarus, toward Favian, taking him from his blind side. Favian
felt the hilt of his sword jerked from his hand, then saw Gardell's
knife, used *à la main gauche*, coming down. There was a tearing
pain in his upper right arm and then he crashed to the ground, the
impact knocking the wind from him. There was the sound of a
shot, a cry, blood spattering Favian's face as he tried with his
wounded arm to reach up and grab that knife before it came
down again. He heard Stackpole's panting breath, the thud of
feet on the ground, and then Gardell's giant form came toppling
down, and the night and the sea and all were obliterated in a final
crash. . . .

10

Favian sat on the grassy bank, the smell of warm blood still
heavy in his nostrils. *Thy blood*, Lazarus had said, and there had
been more than enough of it spilled, but fortunately most of the
blood soaking into Favian's coat and trousers was not his own.
Favian let Lazarus slide the coat from his shoulders, then strip
the shirt from his wounded arm. There was the sound of tearing
as Lazarus began to make a bandage from Gardell's clothing.
The arm wound was not painful, at least not yet. Favian was
conscious chiefly of his own dyspepsia; his stomach felt as if he
had swallowed flaming brimstone.

Decatur's second shot had finally brought down Gardell. It
had been a twenty-foot shot at a moving target, fired in the dark,
while Gardell was standing over Favian with Favian's hanger in
his body, with Favian falling and Stackpole on top of him, a shot
that had hit Gardell in the temple and blown off the front of his
head. An incredible shot: anyone other than a master pistol shot
would have either missed altogether or hit Favian. Favian himself
would probably not have chanced it, and he considered himself a
good shot. But Decatur had not hesitated, and he'd put the pistol

ball within inches of where he'd intended—he'd said he was aiming for the place behind the ear.

Gardell had fallen on Favian and Stackpole, pinning Stackpole to the ground until Lazarus could reach him. With shots flying left and right, and without being able to be certain there were no more attackers to come howling out of the darkness, Lazarus had not taken chances: as soon as Stackpole began to rise Lazarus had felled him with a single cutlass blow to the neck. Lieutenant Robert Stackpole, Royal Marines, lay dead in a vast pool of his own blood, the grass slowly clotting under him. There would be a military funeral, Favian supposed, with *Macedonian*'s marines firing volleys over the grave. They'd have to procure a union jack from somewhere.

"You'll need a surgeon and a few stitches," Lazarus said. "This will bind the wound until you can see a doctor."

Stephen Decatur crossed the shelf of grass. The white-haired man and his son watched him with dull eyes. They hadn't moved throughout the entire incident; the man would not leave without his son, and the son was crippled. "Tolbert will be all right," he said. "That knife wound looks worse than it is, and I think his nose is broken, otherwise just bruises. I think he's more angry than anything else."

"It wasn't his fault. No one expected Gardell from that direction," Favian said. Decatur glanced down at the giant corpse spread-eagled on the brown grass. Favian's hanger had been wrenched out of the body and now was lying across it, its forward third stained with blood.

"He kept going with two pistol balls in him, and a sword thrust clean through the body," Decatur said. "An incredible man, traitor or not."

"Blackbeard was shot twenty-five times before he was killed," Favian said. "He must have been like Gardell—so muscular that the muscles stopped the pistol balls before they penetrated. If you hadn't hit him in the head—well, I thank you for it, Stephen."

"I thank God the ball flew straight and there was no misfire," said Decatur. Favian felt blood—or perhaps Gardell's brains— drying to a crust on his cheek; he swiped at it with his good hand and felt it crumble. Dyspepsia burned inside him. Lazarus tore his improvised bandage, doubled it, tied it off.

"That will suffice thee until we return to town," he said. He bent Favian's arm back, inserting it into the torn shirt-sleeve, the heavy punctured jacket. Favian stood, his head swimming.

They gathered their gear and began their march to Groton, leaving the bodies behind for the constable and his party to clean up. Tolbert, his side bandaged where Gardell's knife had slashed into it, his nose the center of a just-rising, unpleasant-looking set of swellings and bruises, rode on the spies' horse along with the youth Favian had shot, the white-haired man leading the horse, Decatur ahead, Favian bringing up the rear. When they reached Favian's hiding place, Favian saddled his roan and rode her to Groton; he would have offered the horse to Tolbert, but knew the midshipman could never handle her, let alone the check snaffle Favian used. It was near dawn by the time they entered the lanes of Groton and began their search for the town constable.

Behind them, forgotten, the *St. Lawrence* schooner tacked back and forth, the cold, spray-drenched men on its decks watching for blue lights on the shore.

11

It had started again. Vihtori Kuusikoski could sense it, sense the fear and distrust among the men with whom he now labored. It had been good at first; he had been a stranger among strangers, men who didn't think to question him about his past. He had told them he was Estonian, and they had shrugged, most of them not ever having heard of Estonia, not knowing the Estonians were bastard cousins to the Finns, who, for some reason, were so hated.

Macedonian's crew were almost entirely born Americans; the frigate's officers had been careful, hoping to enlist only those who had a native reason to want to fight the British. But they hadn't been entirely immune to the appeal of sentiment; the destitute, beaten foreign sailor, his money and belongings gone, had seemed a worthwhile object of charity.

But perhaps the time in the navy would not last very long. He'd seen the whispered conversations among the crew, the sidelong looks. Perhaps before *Tom Bowlin* had slipped out of the Thames mouth to commence its privateering raid, a few of its crew had encountered some of *Macedonian*'s liberty men in the Elk Horn Tavern and spoken about the Finnish witch they'd found among their crew, and the navy men had remembered the beaten foreigner who had come aboard a few weeks ago, and begun to wonder . . . or perhaps some of *Macedonian*'s people had been in the Elk Horn that night, and not known what the fight had been about until just recently.

However the news had traveled, it had certainly arrived. During the morning breakfast, the crew sitting crosslegged on the deck around their common pots, some of Kuusikoski's messmates had refused to eat with him, saying nothing but pointedly moving to other messes. The others had been distant, possibly a little ashamed of their own behavior but unable to reject entirely the burden of conduct the others had put upon them. After breakfast, after Commodore Decatur had come aboard and then left with Mr. Byrne and a file of marines for a forced march to Groton Long Point, one of Kuusikoski's friends had come up to him as they were swaying aboard the barrels of salt pork. He was an older man, a well-muscled little man named Tiffin, something of a fo'c'sle patriarch, a man who had been sailing before the mast for forty years or more, like Majesty of the *Tom Bowlin*, a man who calmly watched the world unfolding before him and judged it with quiet intelligence, and whose words were heeded in the world of the common navy sailor. Tiffin had not hesitated; he had watched Kuusikoski with an alert, measuring eye, then spoken right up.

"They say ye're a witch, Koozy."

Kuusikoski had half-expected it; he was ready this time, had been ready, really, for weeks.

"I ain't. I'm just a sailor."

Tiffin cut himself a chaw of tobacco, then offered some to Kuusikoski. The Finn took it.

"I know," Tiffin said. "Ye're a reg'lar jack, I think. But they won't believe it, them other fellas. They're scared."

"I ain't afraid of scared men."

"Not one scared man, maybe. A hundred scared men are different."

The men on the wharf signaled the casks were ready, and Mr. Stanhope, the quiet young midshipman, called the hands to man the halyards. They hauled together, little cracking sounds coming from the blocks as they took the weight, the brisk, sharp tugs bringing the casks swaying aloft to the end of the yardarm as the line *whooshed* through the sheaves. Then another gang of sailors on the well deck began to haul on another line, bringing the casks over the main hatch as Kuusikoski and his gang began to slack their own halyard. As the casks came down the hatchway and the strain came off, the yard groaned like a living thing.

Kuusikoski and Tiffin spat tobacco juice into the cold Thames water, waiting for the next load to be readied. Tiffin looked appraisingly at the suspected witch.

"If I was you, I'd leave," Tiffin said.

"They hang deserters, don't they? Besides, I ain't got no money. This ship is my home. I'm not afraid of those fellas. Let *them* run if they're so scared."

Tiffin rubbed his chin. "I hope what ye're doin' is wise, Koozey. I like you, but I can't stand in their way."

"I ain't askin'. And I ain't got anythin' to lose. I'll cut an ear off the first one to touch me. You tell 'em that." Kuusikoski put a hand on his knife, the long, heavy *puukko* that had followed him into exile. The single-edged, curved fighting blade was designed to be used point-down, its blunt upper edge laid along the forearm where it could slice to the bone with a single forearm smash; the heavy brassbound reindeer-bone butt alone made a dangerous bludgeon. He had been carrying the knife with him the night he was beaten, but he'd been so surprised he hadn't thought of using it. This next time, he swore, would be different.

"I'll tell 'em," Tiffin said dubiously. "But everyone's heard the stories. Everyone's heard how the Finns can call up winds and storms, and everyone knows someone who knows someone who's been on a ship becalmed in the horse latitudes, and seen a ship full of Finns, flyin' the Swedish flag, sailin' by with a ghost wind. Everyone knows the stories."

Kuusikoski snorted his contempt for such fantasies. "I been becalmed plenty of times, I tell you that," he said.

"I hope you know what you're doin'," Tiffin said.

Kuusikoski shrugged. "I ain't got any choice, th' way I see it," he said. He spat a neat stream of tobacco juice overboard. He tried to look confident, but inside he felt a growing weight of fear. He couldn't fight them all, not by himself, not if they were all determined to throw him off the ship. Not if he couldn't acquire allies somehow. And if even Tiffin, who knew the charge of witchcraft was nonsense—or said he did—would not interfere, then any resistance was ultimately hopeless. He felt his heart sink.

"Just watch yerself, Koozy," Tiffin said. He laid a fatherly hand on Kuusikoski's shoulder. "It won't be easy for you. But mebbe you can earn a place here. Just try to let 'em know you ain't afraid. That's half the fight."

"I'll do that," Kuusikoski said, trying to grin, hoping the grin was not as skeletal as he felt it to be.

Tiffin changed the subject after that, speculating about why the marines had been marched off just after breakfast, and after that Mr. Stanhope called the work detail to the halyards once again. During the break for dinner, and for the midday whiskey ration, Kuusikoski ate and drank alone. He felt the hostile eyes on him, and saw Tiffin talking to a few of the hands, hard men with hard eyes, the men that even many of the other hands avoided. Their stony eyes looked back at Kuusikoski, unforgiving, untempered, and Kuusikoski felt a chill of fear. He would have to work alongside these men, somehow, and there were so many situations on board a ship when it was dangerous to be without friends—moments aloft, furling canvas, when a man had to depend on the man next to him on the perilous footrope, or at night in a storm, when the sailors in oilskins clung to lifelines knowing that they could so easily be swept overboard without anyone even seeing them go. There were hundreds of situations that had their potential dangers, dangers that were hardly even to be considered so long as a man had his friends who would look after him. Situations where a man without friends was in danger.

Looking into the glittering, unforgiving eyes of those hard men, Kuusikoski thought that perhaps these men believed he was a witch, perhaps they didn't; they saw only a man alone, without friends, a born victim, and Kuusikoski understood that they knew as well as he the little dangers to which sailors exposed themselves, and that they knew very well how to take advantage of them . . .

That afternoon he was working by himself on the quarterdeck, overhauling the side tackles and breeching ropes of the starboard carronades. Mr. Stanhope had gone ashore on an errand; Tiffin was below with a gang that was restowing the casks of salt meat that had been brought aboard that morning. Their initial stowing had altered the ship's trim, and Captain Jones and Mr. Stone, the first lieutenant, had spent their dinner break working out a new way to lay the casks in the hold.

Kuusikoski doubled the side tackle back on itself, then reached down for his coil of small stuff with which to put a racking seizing on the tackle to keep it in place. His fingers encountered nothing, and then he remembered he'd left the coil of twine on the other side of the carronade, where he'd overhauled the larboard tackle first. He stood up and took a step, then jumped as something whanged from the carronade slide, leaving a white gouge on the red-painted wooden frame. Something metal rolled on the deck.

"What the hell was that?" roared the officer on watch, Third Lieutenant Eastlake.

"Don't know, sir," Kuusikoski answered. "Something fall from aloft, I think." But he knew; he'd caught a glimpse of the marlinespike before it rolled under the neighboring carronade. Falling from aloft like that, it could have split his skull wide open, or stabbed him fatally. If he hadn't moved . . .

He narrowed his eyes as he stared aloft, seeing a man straddling the mizzen topsail yard. He knew there was a party aloft overhauling the mizzen footropes and stirrups.

Eastlake bent to look under the carronades and swore. He walked to the carronade, reached under it, and brought out the marlinespike.

"Who the devil is that up there?" the third lieutenant demanded, squinting against the sun as he stared aloft.

"Richards, sir."

Richards. One of the hard men. Perhaps it had been a warning, perhaps it had been meant to kill, but in any case it had not been an accident.

"Richards! Damn it, be careful up there! Your carelessness could have hurt someone!"

"Sorry, sir."

Richards, Kuusikoski thought. He wouldn't dare drop something else, not after his first attempt had been noticed by an officer. The hard men would have to await another chance.

Unless, Kuusikoski thought, the hard men were shown that

Kuusikoski would not be a willing victim—that the witch could be a hard man as well, and would not submit himself to this terror so easily.

Picking up his coil of small stuff, Kuusikoski returned to work, working the twine around and between the thick rope of the side tackle, using the marlinespike that had fallen from aloft to help tighten the seizing. He worked slowly, meditatively, trying to avoid looking aloft lest Richards think he was afraid—but as he worked, his hand occasionally strayed to the reindeer-bone handle of his fighting knife, and his jaw muscles clenched.

It was time, he thought, to strike back.

12

"Your poor arm," Caroline said. "Here. Let me." Favian let her slide the silk shirt off his shoulders, exposing the bandage *Macedonian*'s surgeon had wrapped around the wound. The bandage was not to keep the wound from bleeding, but rather to guard it from further injury. There were twelve stitches altogether; Favian had winced with each knot as he watched the young Mr. Truscott ply his needle. Another scar for his mistress to wonder about. Favian had acquired some opiates for his dyspepsia, told Decatur that he would be asleep for the next twenty-four hours and would talk to him the next morning, then got on his horse and ridden to Caroline's cottage. It was not, perhaps, discreet, but Favian was finished with discretion for the day.

"Just lie back," Caroline said. Favian gratefully collapsed onto the pillow. Outside, rain spattered on the window; the dirty weather Favian had felt the night before had arrived.

"My horse," Favian said. "I didn't rub her down or feed her."

"I'll take care of that later." She brushed a palm over his forehead and kissed his cheek. "You're so pale. How could you have hurt yourself like this?"

"From a British marine," Favian mumbled. "He was running a gang of spies, signaling to the enemy. That's where I've been every night these past weeks. I couldn't tell you. I swore I wouldn't." He opened his eyes, looking into her concerned face. "It's not a secret anymore," he said, touching her cheek, wincing with the pain the movement brought him. "I wanted to tell you as soon as I could."

"Favian," she said. They kissed, Caroline not minding his bristles grating against her. She kicked off her slippers and slid into bed with him, her arm pillowing his head, her warmth lying against him.

"My horse," he said again.

"I won't forget. Go to sleep." He swallowed Mr. Truscott's prescription and sank gratefully into oblivion, trying to forget the burning fire of his dyspepsia, the little prickles of pain from his wound. Dimly, through his unconsciousness, he sensed her leaving to care for his horse. He didn't perceive her return, but when he awoke, hours later, it was to find her next to him, curled up like a child in the great bed, watching him with calm blue eyes.

The next few days were cold ones, the maples turning to fire, but inside the cottage it remained summer. It was, Favian thought, as if he and Caroline had begun their relationship anew; there was no more odd reserve, no more awkward silences, no more sense of an ending. Odd, he thought, because the inevitable end now seemed nearer in time.

Two days following the incident on Groton Long Point, the *Shark* was ready to be sent down the ways into the Thames. Great battleflags flying from its stubby lower masts—the topmasts were not yet set up—the open-mouthed, devouring figurehead glaring at the assembled dignitaries who huddled from the drizzly weather in their greatcoats, the new sloop of war's radical design was clear to see. The keel drew much more water aft than forward, and was cut at a tremendous run; she would, it was clear, be fast as a witch, and have few of *Macedonian*'s difficulties in running the blockade. Favian stood on the platform by the ways in his number one coat and cocked hat, slipping in and out of a light blue cloak as the rain came and went, listening to *Macedonian*'s band as it puffed its way through old marches and reels. The wound in his arm was a little stiff, but was healing well; his dyspepsia, though still painful, was fading under the assault of Mr. Truscott's opiates and Caroline's care. He could see Caroline in the crowd in a new bonnet he'd bought her, looking extraordinarily lovely as she watched the proceedings with flushed pleasure. He threw discretion to the winds and waved at her; the navy, he thought, owed him a little indiscretion. There had been cheers as Favian had ascended the platform, long, extended, howling cheers, the men waving their hats, women their handkerchiefs, and Favian had felt a joyful astonishment swelling in him—it had been a long while since a New England crowd had cheered a navy man so. He hoped the politicians present—most of them staunch antiwar Federalists—were taking proper notice of the change in popular attitudes.

The proceedings were delayed somewhat by the absence of Captains Decatur and Jones, who arrived together some forty minutes late, just a few moments after Favian had decided to go on without them. Favian watched them mount the platform with ill-concealed annoyance, wondering if this was one of Decatur's plans to attract attention to himself by building up suspense prior to his entrance, but a single look at Jones's glowering face convinced him otherwise. Jones was obviously upset about something, and Decatur himself seemed ill at ease. Favian crossed the platform to clasp their hands.

"What's the matter, Jacob?"

Jones's face was a picture of misery. "I've lost *Macedonian*, Favian," he said. "They're sending me to Sackett's Harbor to take command of the *Mohawk*."

"Good Lord." It was incredible; *Macedonian* was virtually ready for sea, and in a few days could have set out against the British. *Mohawk*, a forty-eight gun frigate being built on Lake Ontario for Isaac Chauncey's squadron, would be a good command, but it couldn't sail until the ice broke up the following spring. What were those idiots in Washington—or rather Fredericktown, Maryland, that being the current seat of the government—thinking about?

"Who is to have *Macedonian*?" Favian asked.

"God knows. My orders don't say."

"What an incredible situation! I'm sorry, Jacob."

Jones nodded, morose. Decatur bent close to Favian's ear and spoke in low tones. "I've been trying to convince Captain Jones to ignore the orders and sail anyway, or just pretend they didn't arrive until he's already left. But he's determined to obey them."

"They're proper orders," Jones said. "Signed by the secretary of the navy. What choice do I have?" His face showed utter misery.

"We'll have to talk of this later," Favian said, glancing at his watch. "We'll have to get through this launching, first."

"Aye, Favian," Decatur said. "Ceremony first, then talk of disobedience."

There were a number of tedious speeches, to which Favian listened with half an ear. Poor Jacob Jones, to lose his command in such a sudden, disappointing fashion. The man's naval career had been filled with such frustration, from the surrender of the *Philadelphia* to the victory over *Frolic* followed by capture in the same afternoon, to the repeated ill luck in trying to get *Macedonian* to sea, including the dispiriting experience of having most of his crew sent to Lake Ontario without him. Now he would be sent to Ontario without his crew. The poor man.

Yet the disobedience Decatur was suggesting might well prove Jones's salvation—but only if *Macedonian*'s cruise was a successful one. When Isaac Hull wanted to take the *Constitution* frigate to sea at the beginning of the war, he had done it against specific orders to stay in Boston—he had even borrowed money from a private citizen to help outfit his ship. But all had been forgiven when *Constitution* took the *Guerrière*, producing the first of the long string of American naval successes. Favian himself had disobeyed the letter of his orders the previous year, when he took the *Experiment* brig to Europe on a pillaging raid around the British isles, but no mention of the disobedience had ever been made after *Experiment* destroyed forty-odd enemy merchantmen and followed up its success by sinking the *Teaser*.

Disobedience was punishable by court-martial, at least in theory, but the American service had not yet court-martialed a man for a successful cruise. Yet there was no certain guarantee that the cruise of the *Macedonian* would be successful; the blockading squadron off New London was a powerful one, and *Macedonian* was not one of the powerful American spar-deck frigates, but rather a captured Britisher, much more vulnerable to enemy action than the likes of *Constitution* or *United States*. Jones, sunk in meditation as he sat on the platform, was no doubt considering this.

It was Favian's turn to speak. He had a speech prepared, a short address that concentrated chiefly on *Shark* as a commerce destroyer, a fast, powerful ship that could make the British suffer something of what had been suffered by the New London merchants as the enemy blockade wore on, but as soon as Favian stood up the crowd burst into roaring applause, an ovation that went on and on. Favian was overwhelmed by the enthusiasm, the stunning welcome; he saw Caroline in the crowd, leaping up and down, her gloved hands applauding wildly, and he gave in to impulse and turned to gesture at Decatur and Jones, asking them to join him, and the crowd went mad at the sight of the three navy heroes standing together, *Macedonian*'s band deciding this was an opportune moment to flail away at "Hail, Columbia." Favian determined to throw away his speech; his little appeal to the thrifty commercial instincts of New England seemed a little small, a little patronizing in the face of this welcome.

"Ladies and gentlemen, my comrades and I am stunned by your reception," he began, when there was a little space, and the audience began roaring again. They seemed resolved to applaud his every sentence. He let them continue, his mind searching for the proper response to such enthusiasm.

"I am gratified," he said at last, feeling a little breathless himself at this tribute, "to see so many people united in this place, and for such a purpose. If the British peace commissioners, Lord Gambier and Lord Bathurst, now meeting with our own ambassadors in Ghent, could see this crowd, and feel this enthusiasm, then I think they would make a just peace within twenty-four hours."

More cheers. Favian cleared his throat, feeling his dyspepsia rumble its discontent. "But they *cannot* see you," he shouted, his voice trumpeting over the last trickle of applause. "They believe that the United States of America is a weak, divided country, afraid to face them—they believe they can cut us up like a pie, and that there are many who will cheer at the sight, and cry out 'God save King George!' "

Jeers. Shouts of "No!" Favian held up his hand for silence, and received it.

"This is what the British believe," he repeated. "And how can I know this? Because *they act as if they believe it!* They strike at Washington City, because they believe that with its destruction the United States will break up into its constituent parts, and never reunite! They occupy the Penobscot, because they believe that New England men will never dare oppose them!

They strike down the length of Lake Champlain, because they believe that once they cut New England off from New York, they can make a colony of us once again! They send spies to our shores, because they believe they can find sympathizers here, who will fight against their own!

"People of New England, let the British be wrong!" Favian shouted. He could feel the crowd hanging on his words, absorbing them into the cyclone of their own massed emotions. They began to roar again, but he cut them short.

"Let them be wrong!" he repeated. "Let each British attack be met by men united against them—united in their wish to sail the free oceans without restraint, to move where they will within the boundaries of their own country without the fear of losing their scalps to hatchets bought and paid for in London. I plead with you, people of New England, to unite yourselves against your real enemies, and unite behind the determination *never again to be enslaved to the wishes of a European monarch!*"

He stepped back from the podium and felt the mad applause of the crowd wash over him, hearing the band striking up "Liberty Tree." He mopped his brow with his handkerchief—hard work, this rabble-rousing—and tried to catch his breath while the band thumped on, the crowd spent its enthusiasm, and the others on the platform rushed forward to congratulate him.

"Always said you had the makings of a demagogue, Favian," Decatur grinned, pumping his hand. Even Jacob Jones managed to work up a smile.

"That was what this crowd needed, by God," he said. "I hope they reprint that speech from Savannah to Machias Port!"

The actual launching of the *Shark* was anticlimactic. Favian, Decatur, Jones, and a Connecticut congressman who was supporting the Hartford Convention but seemed willing to climb aboard any movement that showed itself popular, mounted a ladder to the sloop's quarterdeck; the fifteen-year-old daughter of the ship's designer spoke a few breathless, barely audible words and smashed a bottle of brandy over the ferocious figurehead— champagne was apparently not available in the blockaded port— and sledgehammers echoed in the heavy air as the final supports were knocked away.

Shark lurched, then with a wooden shriek began its descent of the greased ways, friction smoke shooting from beneath its keel. Favian clung to his hat as the ship rocked beneath him. The keel sliced into the water and quite suddenly *Shark* was in her element, buoyed up by the Thames. Favian found himself laughing as the ship-sloop bobbed in the river, free for a few seconds until she was checked by the limits of her hawsers. He found in himself a yearning for the sea he had not known he'd possessed; he wanted badly for *Shark* to be completed, so that he could take the new, yare sloop of war past the enemy yonder and into the bright ocean. Where would he go, he wondered, once he had the chance? The Narrow Seas of England once more, the Pacific like David Porter, the Brazils, the West Indian hunting ground that had proved so fertile to the fortunes of his family?

The Indies, he decided, the Orient. The Indies that had been the focus of so many of Napoleon's efforts, where so much of Britain's wealth was concentrated. *Shark* would not be expected there; the British forces would be reduced. Since taking Mauritius years ago the British had faced no opposition in the Indian Ocean; they might have no warships on station at all, and certainly none that could catch a ship-sloop as fast as *Shark* would surely prove to be.

But that was as the fortunes of war and the secretary of the navy would decide. For the present he would simply prepare his ship for whatever orders came—but if those orders contained the least hint of discretion, he knew that within a few months he would be bound around the Cape of Good Hope to the Bay of Bengal.

Decatur seemed downcast as he entered the common room of the inn, sitting down for supper with Favian and Jacob Jones. He brandished a thick, official-looking document, and threw it down on the table before them.

"My own orders were waiting for me when I got back to the inn," he said. "They must have come in the same post as Jacob's."

"Yes?" Jones asked.

"I am to prepare the *President* for sea and seek to break the blockade. Signed by President Madison himself," Decatur said.

"Why so downcast, Stephen?" Jones wondered. "I'd give my captain's commission for orders like those."

Ah, Favian thought. Jones didn't know that Decatur had been preening himself for the Lake Ontario command. Apparently Isaac Chauncey was going to get another chance at bringing Commodore Yeo to bay, and Stephen Decatur would return to the port of New York and command of the *President*. Not that command of the navy's finest frigate was a little thing; it was a considerable honor, but perhaps compared to commanding the greatest fleet in America's history it seemed just a trifle small by comparison.

"I was—oh, nothing," Decatur said, waving his hand. "I was expecting something else, let us say. But your own orders, Jacob—what's to be done?"

"Obey, Stephen," Jones said. His expression was mild, matter-of-fact; the grim desperation that had been so obvious when he'd ascended the platform earlier that day was gone. He had obviously given the matter a great deal of thought. "The orders are legal, they are binding. The navy has my oath. I won't violate it."

"My dear sir," Decatur said. "The orders came from Fredericktown, from a little hotel that, due to the misfortune of war, is now the seat of the United States government. They are issued by Secretary William Jones, who is far removed from the ships and individuals he commands, and has lost all Navy Department records, which were burned by the British. He is isolated; the orders were sent weeks ago; he doesn't know that *Macedonian* is provisioned, fully crewed, and ready for sea. Perhaps countermanding orders are already on their way, prompted by your reporting your ship near-ready."

"If such orders arrive I will obey them," Jones said gruffly. "But until then, I can but obey these."

"Captain Jones," said Decatur, "the good of the service demands, not only that we be obedient, but that we exercise our own discretion when necessary. There are dozens of precedents; the secretary of the navy, when he issues his orders, surely must know that conditions may have changed by the time the orders are received. The fact that you have been promoted to post captain surely indicates that the Navy Department trusts you to act at your own discretion when the situation demands it. The hallmark of a *good* officer may be obedience, but the sure sign of an exceptional, audacious commander is a creative *disobedience*."

Jones, his brow wrinkling in annoyance, looked sourly at Decatur. "Sir," he said, "I appreciate your advice, but it is not in me to disobey a direct order from the secretary of the navy, nor do I find your definitions to my taste. That is the end of it, sir."

Decatur, beginning to recognize that Jones's mind was made up, grimaced and leaned back in his chair, then looked questioningly at Favian. "What can we do?" he asked. "Can you add anything to my appeal?"

"Stephen, I cannot counsel a man to disobey an order," Favian said. "I cannot presume to decide for another what course he must take." He glanced quickly at Jones, whose smile showed bitter vindication. "I can but say," Favian went on, "that were I in Captain Jones's place, I would choose to disobey and take *Macedonian* to sea." Jones scowled.

"You've both said your piece," Jones said. He smiled broadly, making an effort to be civil. "Let us leave the matter on the table, and call for supper."

Decatur shook his head, then threw out his hands, palms up, to indicate acquiescence. The barman brought drinks, chowder, a dinner of lobster.

"Your Mr. Tolbert," Jones asked. "What will you do with him?"

Favian thought of Tolbert, unwillingly confined by doctor's orders to his bed upstairs, his side bandaged where Gardell's knife had gone in and his nose protected by a metal splint and a web of bandages. Tolbert had volunteered for Favian's watch on Groton Long Point, and had performed bravely. He could not be sent back to Philadelphia, not with justice.

"I'll take him aboard *Shark* when the times comes," Favian said. "I can't send him back to Philadelphia, even if he came without invitation."

Jones nodded. "It's a pity there isn't some occupation for midshipmen when they've not been assigned to a ship. There's a great deal of their craft they can learn when they're not at sea."

"I've thought that myself," Favian said. "I'll go further, though—the environment aboard a warship, I think, contributes a negative influence to learning some aspects of the midshipmen's curriculum."

"Such as?"

"Mathematics. English grammar and polite conversation. French, and other languages. Quite possibly sketching and mapmaking, unless the student officer happens to be assigned to a hydrographic survey vessel and practices daily." Favian raised a hand as he saw Jones about to speak, anticipating Jones's objections. "The life aboard a man-o'-war will teach a boy the mechanics of sailing and something of navigation, and it will teach him the way shipboard society is structured, and that is all valuable. But the life is intense and absorbing, and it is not in many young men to be able to discipline themselves to the extent of learning French and spherical trigonometry when they'd much rather be in the fo's'cle yarning with the carpenter, or playing cards in the gunroom with their friends. Unless the captain and the officers take a special interest in the more rigorous aspects of a midshipman's education—and not all of them do—the boys will be left to their own devices, and that will be the ruin of three boys out of four."

Decatur smiled. "Was it our ruin, Favian? Come now, you exaggerate."

"I had my family, Stephen; I wrote French, Latin, and Greek before I was ten, and knew the rudiments of navigation by the time I was fourteen—my father, like yours, was a privateer, and you know what nautical families are like; we learn our craft from the cradle. Captain Jones came late into the navy after careers in medicine and law; he knew how to discipline himself and learn a new science.

"No, it's boys like our Mr. Tolbert I'm talking about. His family is poor, not like ours; when he's afloat he contributes most of his pay to their support, and when he's ashore he must labor for a living. He is not accustomed to discipline himself intellectually; mathematics and navigation do not come easily to him. If I hadn't taken a particular interest in the mids' education while captain of *Experiment*, he would have no more idea of French and spherical trigonometry than we have of the politics of the Chinese court. Even as it is, he's failed his exam for lieutenant. If he had been granted a place to study ashore, for perhaps six months or a year, I think he probably could have passed the exam. Not done well, perhaps, but at least passed."

Jones looked at him evenly. "You are suggesting the establishment of a naval academy?" he asked. "Like the British one at Portsmouth Dockyard?"

"No, not like the British one," Favian said quickly. "Not a nursery for the sons of the idle rich, where they can collect their pay while they pursue their carousing, whoring, and foxhunting ashore, without the bother and inconvenience of actually having to serve on shipboard—nay, not like the British academy. But yes, an American navel academy would be of value. An academy where the boys could retire, with full pay, to their studies in an atmosphere of strict discipline, without having to worry about whether they must starve in order to purchase navigational texts, or Truxtun's *Extracts from the Best Authors on Naval Tactics.*"

"A worthwhile dream, perhaps," Decatur said. "The idea has its value, yes—but not in our current democratic political climate."

"True," Favian said, nodding. "But the climate may change following the war, when the people realize what value we have been. It does not hurt to plan ahead." But he knew Decatur's objection was valid. The American public did not trust the motives of any elite, and the officer corps of the United States Navy was perhaps the greatest elite, not only in America, but in all Christendom. Disciplined, periodically purged by politicians and by duels and courts-martial, competitive, explosive, and talented beyond all expectation, the navy had demonstrated its competence and talents in three major wars within the period of twenty years, and in so doing had earned the distrust of many of the people it was alleged to protect. They had not trusted these quarrelsome, high-strung young men, and had not liked their necessary power and privilege: to interpret, far away and out of the sight of watchful politicians, major issues of national policy, and perhaps, with one zealous broadside too many, embroil the United States in a war it did not want to fight.

The current war with Britain, perhaps, had changed things; it had demonstrated the necessity of the existence of a navy—a necessity that had often been challenged in the past—and it had made heroes out of the new generation of navy men, who had seized incredible popularity by virtue of their lonely victories on the seas, and by contrast with the inept bungling of the army. Possibly with popularity would come power, a power to affect things for the better. To create an academy, for one thing, and perhaps to drive home a few lessons.

It was to be hoped that the politicians would accept the advice of navy men at least as regarded their own field, and never again declare war on a naval power without bringing the United States Navy to a state of readiness. The navy had done well with what it had, astonishingly well, but how much more could it have performed if those six new sloops of war, *Shark*'s sister ships, had been completed at the war's start, and able to raid enemy waters without having to cope with a hardened blockade? If the new seventy-four-gun liners had been ready, able with their massive guns to prevent the blockade from ever being formed? If the navy's ranks had held more than twelve captains, some of whom were too old to serve at sea?

The navy was popular now, but the months following the conclusion of peace would tell whether the new popularity would last. Would the navy once again be cut to the bone, the new ships going under the gavel or hauled up on some beach to rot, the list of officers, expanded now to a full wartime strength, once again cut back, good men being dismissed the service because they were no longer needed, as they'd been dismissed in 1801, and again in 1806? Or would the popularity last long enough to be able to affect some needed change in the way the services were run?

Time would tell. In the meantime, Favian would hope to be able to use his own personal popularity to achieve what good he might.

"The education of the young gentlemen is, to be sure, a problem," said Jacob Jones. "I'm not certain that an academy would be of use—Congress would not understand the problem, for one thing, and that would work against the idea, as would the bad example of the British academy. Perhaps installing a full-time schoolmaster on the larger vessels?"

"That would be of service, I'm sure," Favian said. "Better than the present system. But that will still leave the mids on the brigs, schooners, sloops, and gunboats uncared for, and that's where the majority of midshipmen do their service at present."

"We must simply take care to educate the young men properly," Decatur said, matter-of-fact. "Aboard *United States* it was my, and Favian's, particular care. We must educate them as we were educated, by Commodore Preble."

There was silence after that; the invocation of Preble's name and method had brought the debate to an end. It was Preble more than anyone else who had made the navy, who had imbued it with its principles of aggressive tactics, scientific practice of gunnery and sailing, humane, sensible concern for the health and well-being of the common sailor combined with a no-nonsense approach to ships' discipline, and a proper care for the education of the next generation of naval officers. The young men who had made their reputations during Preble's term off Tripoli, and won such surprising victories over the British in the current war, proudly called themselves "Preble's boys"; it was no coincidence, they felt, that every single victorious American captain, except for Perry on Lake Erie, had served his apprenticeship under Preble.

"Amen to that," said Jacob Jones, after the pause. "There is a lack in one particular area of education, you know, that none of us have ever addressed, not even the Commodore, God rest him. Our navy has never been big enough to concern ourselves with it up till now, but now that we're building sail of the line it will become important."

"Indeed?" Decatur said. "What is it? Maneuvering among the shoals of politicians, the Federalists on the right and the Democratic-Republicans on the left?"

"Nay, Stephen," Jones said with a smile. "The navy's always done that. I was referring to fleet maneuvers. None of us know how to sail in formation, how to dress a column of seventy-fours. And fleet tactics—that's something the British know far better than we. And it's important. Tactics for a large line of battle are much different from the sort of fighting we're used to, battling one-against-one in frigates and sloops."

"That can't be done until they sail together, surely," Decatur said.

"I've given it some thought, and I believe it can," Jones said. "You know I was second lieutenant on the *Philadelphia* when it was captured, and I spent most of the Tripolitan war in prison. Captain Bainbridge took special care that our education should not suffer due to our confinement, and David Porter made it his particular duty to see to the education of the young gentlemen. There were some books we'd salvaged from the *Philadelphia*, and the Danish consul provided others." Jones smiled. "Porter called his school the University of the Prison of Tripoli.

"I was acting as ship's doctor, and my duties concerning the health of the men were many, so I wasn't able to attend many of Porter's classes, but I remember that he did an interesting thing. He wanted to teach theory of seamanship, tactics, and practical navigation, but despaired of doing it without being aboard ship. So he had one of the hands make a few little ship models, and he taught using the models. The little masts were movable, and he could illustrate how to brace the yards when the wind was coming from different quarters. He'd set out navigational and tactical problems, with books or someone's jacket representing shoals or land, and let the midshipmen solve them."

"Interesting," Decatur said. "But scarcely a substitute for maneuvering a real ship."

"True," Jones admitted. "But it's more thrifty, I believe, to let a little wooden model go aground on a reef rather than to learn the same lesson by wrecking a frigate, don't'ee think?"

Decatur laughed. "I suppose so."

"Porter's lessons grew more elaborate," Jones said, "and in the end there were rules and diagrams written out on paper, and it had become a kind of game. There were fleet maneuvers in which the Emperor of Atlantis fought the Lord High Admiral of Utopia, that sort of thing. The midshipmen grew very excited about it, and I think they learned a great deal. When we were released from Tripoli everyone went their separate ways, and to my knowledge the game was never played again. Until just recently, when I've revived it aboard *Macedonian*."

"Have you really?" Decatur asked, obviously intrigued. Favian pushed aside the last of his lobster and signaled for coffee.

"I have a half-dozen mids aboard who have just got their appointments," said Jones. "Most have never been at sea, and none of them as officers. We've been unable to sail, and I can't give them that practical experience. In a way, we're in prison. With use of Porter's game we can at least give them a basic knowledge of seamanship, and of the vocabulary of their craft."

"You say *we*, Jacob," Favian said. "Is that an editorial we, or do you have assistance?"

"Mr. Stone, my first lieutenant, has greatly improved upon Porter's original concept," Jones said. "He's got the right sort of mind for it. Precise, analytical. Porter might not even recognize the game after Mr. Stone's revisions."

Favian, sipping his coffee, began to be interested in this "game," if game it was. He had always been a technical sailor, responding intellectually to the science of sailing rather than the rule-of-thumb precedents, so often proved wrong, handed down by previous generations of sailors. He had drawn a "naval square" on the deck of the *Experiment* during his term as captain, a handy device for judging the movements of his own vessel and that of the enemy, and the square had proved useful in spite of the skepticism of his officers. The precision of his naval gunnery was legendary in the service, as was the care he lavished on his ship's rigging and sails, which he was forever adjusting to make certain they were contributing to the ship's performance. His annoyance with the Navy Department's lack of interest in improved devices for navigation had resulted in his experiments with Markham's Recording Log. If Jones had come across a device for making the profession of sailor a more scientific one, Favian wanted to see it.

"There will be an exercise tomorrow," Jones said. "After dinner, Mr. Stone will be making a game of *Macedonian*'s attempt to break the blockade. In dubious taste, perhaps, but more useful than a fight between the forces of Atlantis and Utopia. You're welcome to attend. I, unfortunately, will probably be packing for Sackett's Harbor."

"I'll hope to dine with you before you go," Favian said. He finished his coffee and stood, pushing back his chair. "For now, I shall visit with our Mr. Tolbert for a few minutes, and then come down to say my farewells. It will be an early night, I think; today's festivities were exhausting, and if I'm ever to get rid of this cursed dyspepsia I should get my rest."

"I'm sorry you must leave," Jacob Jones said politely, rising. The three captains shook hands. Favian did not know if they suspected the existence of Caroline, and would probably never know unless he asked—his excuses had been fairly transparent, and then there had been that twenty-four hour absence following the fight on Groton Long Point, when half the magistrates in Connecticut were looking for him and he had, very obviously, not been in his bed at the inn. But Favian knew the matter would never come up; naval officers had a way of being discreet about one another. Part of it was natural courtesy; the other part was that indiscretion would so very often result in a duel.

The discretion could cut both ways; Favian did not know, and could not ask, whether these other two men, comrades in arms who, like Favian, made a profession out of putting their blood and fortune at risk for the navy, also led secret lives outside the view of the public that worshiped them. He did not wish to know; it was, possibly, dangerous to know. But still there was a part of Favian that wondered, when all was said and done, if the rest of his world was as duplicitous as he, hanging in the wind between duty and inclination.

13

Adrian Stone, Jones's polite, unsmiling first officer, had, in their brief acquaintance, struck Favian as a serious, intelligent man, dedicated to the service and his craft, disciplined and probably a taut officer, possibly one of those men who was devoted entirely to the service and had no life outside it. After watching Stone demonstrate his version of David Porter's old Tripoli training game, Favian was pleased to credit Stone with high imagination as well. Stone had been pleased to show his creation to Favian, as proud as a new father, and after Favian had observed for the balance of the afternoon he knew that Lieutenant Stone had a reason to be proud. What he had made out of Porter's game was astonishing.

The first thing that had surprised Favian was the scale of the exercise; the furniture had been cleared from *Macedonian*'s wardroom after dinner, the sailcloth carpeting rolled up, and the Connecticut coastline, copied neatly from charts, had been drawn in chalk on the planking. Favian could recognize Groton Long Point, Fishers Island, Homo Island, even the Cormaralit Rocks and the Latimore Rock Ledge near Fishers Island. Next to the chalk wharf in New London was a model *Macedonian*, executed in loving detail, even including the black gunports dotting the white hull stripe, with the red port lids picked out above them, tissue paper sails set on delicate masts; keeping station off the port were the "British," represented by a model that was recognizably the *Tiber*, another of the *Orpheus*, and a third, a two-masted schooner, the *St. Lawrence*.

"Mr. Stanhope is playing the part of Captain Dacres," Stone said, indicating Midshipman Phillip Stanhope. Stanhope grinned and saluted British style, hand to forehead. "As senior captain, he will be ordering the British dispositions," Stone said. "Mr. Lovette will command the *Orpheus*, Mr. Killick will take the *St.*

Lawrence. The role of the captain of the *Macedonian* will be taken by Mr. Portius Pratt. We will assume a westerly gale to drive the British off station and allow the frigate to escape; after that it will be a pursuit situation. If the British can close, engage, and damage or capture the *Macedonian*, they'll have won. The *Macedonian* can win either by capturing one of the enemy frigates, or by escaping into the Atlantic."

"Sir," Stanhope said to Stone. He was imitating, with a fair amount of success, the languid, gargling modern accent of upper-class Britain. The other "British," grinning, watched his performance. "We—that is, His Britannic Majesty's captains—would like to speak to you about one of our, ah, innovations."

"Yes, Mr. Stanhope?" Stone said.

"We propose to baffle the barbaric Yankees with signals. Is that permitted?"

"I don't understand, Mr. Stanhope. Please explain." Stanhope produced a sheet of paper and announced that he and the other "British" had prepared, in secret, a signal book. Rather than simply speaking to one another about their maneuvers, they were proposing to communicate in code, presumably to prevent Mr. Pratt, their opponent, from understanding their intentions.

"I protest!" Pratt said.

Stone turned to him quietly. "On what grounds?" he asked. Pratt grimaced, thinking desperately.

"Because it hasn't been done," he said finally. "It's unfair. We've always talked about our moves. It's—it's more educational that way."

Stone gave a taut smile. "I scarcely think that the *real* Captain Dacres will allow us to be privy to the conversations on his quarterdeck, or grant us admission to his counsels of war. Perhaps, Mr. Pratt, a little uncertainty in your knowledge of the enemy's intentions will serve to make you a better officer. Mr. Stanhope may use his signals."

Pratt frowned, then shrugged, accepting his loss. Papers and foot rules were distributed to each of the "captains." The exercise commenced.

Favian spent the afternoon with Stone, watching the exercise from chairs set in the corner of the room. The little models were moved with the foot rules, taking into account the ships' angle to the wind. Adrian Stone acted as umpire, resolving disagreements and also serving as the "gale," blowing the British vessels off station in accordance with Phillip Stanhope's plans for storm dispersal.

Stanhope's schemes proved effective. Even with the chaos wrought on his dispositions by the Stone-produced storm, he managed to cover enough water to sight *Macedonian* shortly after it slipped from the Thames, and to intercept it with Lovette's *Orpheus*.

"Now we'll have a little shooting," Stone said with a smile. "We 'shoot' by comparing the number of pounds of broadside guns with the tonnage of the vessels. So many broadsides knock away so many tons. When the target has half its tonnage knocked away, we assume it surrenders. And for every twenty-five percent of its tonnage knocked away, we assume it loses a mast. *Orpheus* and *Macedonian* are both British-built thirty-eight-gun frigates, with equal broadsides and tonnage, so they should knock each other about pretty evenly."

"Could you show me how it's done, Mr. Stone?" asked Favian.

"Certainly, Captain Markham."

They approached the upcoming combat, being careful not to tread on the models. Lovette, his concentration formidable, was writing on a pad with a stub of a pencil, glancing up from time to time to gaze at the position of the models. His mouth twitched in the beginnings of a smile, then he assumed a masklike expression and put his pencil in his pocket.

"We write our moves out in advance," Stone said. "Then we move the models, following the instructions on the pad. That way it's possible to achieve surprise."

Stone's prediction about the *Orpheus-Macedonian* fight did not come true. Lovette ordered his model frigate into a sudden turn, slipping across the stern of Pratt's model. "Damnation!" Pratt cursed, and Lovette smiled triumphantly.

"Watch your language, Mr. Pratt," Stone admonished, then turned to Favian. "Mr. Lovette has succeeded in raking Mr. Pratt by firing into his stern. This will do increased damage. Mr. Pratt is not able to fire, because *Orpheus* did not come within the arc of his broadside guns."

Midshipman Pratt's position worsened as the battle wore on. Lovette, grinning craftily, maneuvered his model like a miniature Nelson, and Pratt's expression began to take on a haunted, woebegone look. Stanhope, charging across the wardroom floor with his model of the *Tiber*, walked jauntily to and fro. Eight bells echoed down the frigate's companionway, and Favian looked up.

"I think Mr. Pratt has just been saved by the bell," he said. "You'll have to clear this away to make room for supper."

"I'm afraid not, sir," Pratt said, staring hopelessly at his pad and his pencil, as if wondering what to do with them. "This punishment will go on for at least another two hours."

"Captain Jones altered the system of watches," Stone said, as Favian looked to him for an explanation. "He was concerned about the hands' going sixteen hours without a meal, and decided to alter the situation."

"Indeed?" Favian said. It was something he had always wondered about himself. Ships traditionally stood four-hour watches, half the crew being available for duty during any given watch, with a full crew theoretically being available during the daylight hours. Watches were rotated during the period from four till eight in the evening, which was split into two "dog watches," making certain the crew did not stand the same watches two days in a row. The hands were fed three times each day, breakfast at eight in the morning, dinner at noon, and supper at four in the afternoon, dinner and supper being supplemented by the daily liquor ration. With all their meals crowded into an eight-hour period, the hands were truly hungry by breakfast, and there had even been instances of men fainting from hunger during the early hours of the morning. With the watches being altered every four hours, the system also meant that no seaman got more than four hours' sleep at a stretch. The officers' meals, of course, were at more reasonable hours, varying from ship to ship with the wishes of the captain, who was usually granted the privilege of eating last of all; Favian remembered his first captain, mad old Daniel McNeill, had eaten his noon meal after five in the afternoon. Many times, when standing watch at night, Favian had crept down to the wardroom pantry for a quick snack and a cup of coffee, and had wondered if there were some way of providing the same service for the crewmen.

Jacob Jones's innovation was so simple and effective that Favian found himself wondering why it had not been thought of before. The hands were given their breakfast at six in the morning, and then stood a six-hour watch until their noon meal. Following dinner there was another six-hour watch until supper, at which point the hands stood four-hour watches until time for breakfast again. The concept was brilliant. Not only did it shorten the time without meals to twelve hours, but the system of five watches to the day, two of them six hours long and three of them four hours long, resulted in the watches being rotated daily without the bother of dealing with two-hour dog watches. And the off-duty watches, during the daytime, got a full six hours to sleep in their hammocks.

"Mr. Stone, my compliments to Captain Jones," Favian said. "It's a remarkable idea." He frowned. "But seamen are traditionalists, of course; I would imagine they would not approve of losing their four-hour watches." Blind adherence to tradition was one of the nautical vices Favian had always opposed, both in the world of the sea officer and that of the humble sailor: one clung to flogging and rum as the antidote to all ills, scorning the finer points of scientific navigation while maintaining that firing overchoked broadsides in the general direction of the enemy was the best way to win sea battles; the other hung relentlessly onto his belief that manatees were mermaids, that a knife in the mainmast could witch up good winds, and that leaving port on a Friday would bring disaster.

"On the contrary, Captain Markham," Stone said. "The only complaints I have had are from the cooks, who have to get up two hours early to fix the men's breakfast."

While Stone was explaining the new watch system, Midshipman Pratt's toy frigate had been slowly being torn apart by Lovette's; the model *Macedonian* lost a mast, which made it less maneuverable. Lovette's frigate lost a mast itself shortly thereafter, but by that time Pratt was so torn up that when Stanhope's *Tiber* finally arrived, Stanhope had but to fire a single broadside to bring Pratt's flag down in surrender.

"A deserved comeuppance for our upstart Brother Jonathan," Stanhope said, still acting the Englishman. Pratt looked sourly on the scene of his defeat.

"Let us hope, Mr. Pratt, that this is not an omen of the future," Stone said. "Mr. Stanhope, I'll thank you not to act so smug—doubtless your own time will come. Bear a hand now, and let's have the wardroom made ready for supper." The midshipmen bent to the tasks of picking up the models, foot rules, and paper, and scrubbing the representation of the Connecticut coast from the wardroom floor.

Stanhope, it seemed, would make a promising commodore one day. Favian had suspected, from the youth's first week aboard *Experiment*, that he would have a successful career if he could avoid the perpetual midshipman's hazards of war, dueling, and drink; Stanhope was clearly very intelligent, though aboard *Experiment* he had also been a little aloof, serious and watchful, perhaps because he was a raw mid all too aware of his own ignorance of his craft-to-be. This afternoon he had been more relaxed in the other mids' society, smiling and joking; perhaps now that he was not so ignorant, and a veteran of the *Teaser* fight, he felt himself more a man among equals.

"It was quite interesting, sir," Favian said, as Stone escorted him to the deck. "Do you think I might send Mr. Tolbert to your next exercise?"

"Your wounded midshipman? Of course. I shall send a message to inform you of the time."

"Thank you, sir. I wonder if I might trouble you for a copy of the rules?"

"I shall have a copy made and sent to you, sir," Stone said. "Unfortunately, a great many of the 'rules,' such as they are, were not ever written down, and simply exist as an oral tradition. They evolve so quickly that to write them down in their entirety would be an exercise in frustration. Richards!" he barked at one of the hands, a muscled, sour-faced man with blackened eyes and a scabbed face. "Lend a hand there. You do not have a doctor's certificate, you have no excuse for your sloth. Smartly, there!"

At Favian's questioning gaze, Stone turned to Favian and lowered his voice. "Richards. A bad character, I think—sullen, uncooperative. He says he fell down a hatch during a night watch, but I'm certain he's been fighting. There's no one else with bruises, though, and Richards refuses to make an accusation, so unless I can ferret out who he was fighting with, there's no punishing them for it." He frowned. "Another case of ship's discipline subverted, I suppose."

"Yes. Inevitable, I should say, but it's a pity the men won't trust the officers more," Favian said. He had spent years as a first lieutenant, charged like Stone with the duty of maintaining order and justice, bringing breaches of discipline before Decatur, his captain, and he had faced the same sort of frustration. The forecastle had its own rude notions of justice, and quite often disputes were settled among the hands without recourse to Adams's *Regulations*.

Favian saluted the quarterdeck and Eastlake, the officer of the watch, and then descended to the wharf. He would be having supper with Decatur and Jones, but there was the space of an hour before their appointed meeting. He would visit Tolbert, and tell him of Stanhope, his old shipmate from the *Experiment*, and of his success as a British admiral.

Jones left early the next morning, taking the nine o'clock stage to Hartford en route to Albany and Sackett's Harbor. Favian spent the morning with Caroline and rode into town after noon, intending to spend the rest of the day supervising the riggers as they fitted *Shark* with her upper masts. He was expecting his officers to begin reporting any day, and then he would have to start recruiting new men to make up the crew. It should not be hard to find new men; with the British blockade choking off all merchant shipping, a lot of prime seamen were begging hat in hand for employment. Most preferred berths aboard privateers if they could get them, but once the privateers were full the navy would have the rest, and there were hundreds of good men that the privateers could not take.

> Oh, Sally Brown from New York City,
> *Way, hey, roll and go!*
> Oh, Sally Brown she is very pretty,
> *Spend my money on Sally Brown!*

The chantyman's baritone sailed out over the Thames as the work gang stamped at the capstan and sang out the choruses. Lines tautened, and *Shark*'s new foretopmast, lying across the fo'c'sle forward, lurched and began to rise. Favian, not yet in command but present because he wanted to know the new sloop forward and back, aloft and alow, before he took her to sea, watched from the quarterdeck as the dockyard foreman shouted out his commands and the chantyman stamped time on the deck with his booted foot.

> Oh, seven long years she would not marry,
> *Way, hey, roll and go!*
> Oh, seven long years I courted Sally,
> *Spend my money on Sally Brown!*

Capstan pawls clacked, and the mast climbed into the gray October sky. Favian could feel, somewhere in his seaman's intuition, that there would be dirty weather soon, much as he had felt it the night on Groton Long Point. This time worse, he thought, a full autumn gale.

Favian's eyes narrowed as he perceived something peculiar on the horizon, something different concerning the signal station on Great Neck. Cursing because he did not have a long glass, he shadowed his eyes with both hands and peered carefully at the flags. There seemed to be a different set of signals flying this time.

By God, Favian thought, *Tiber*'s no longer lying off the port! The big forty-four-gun frigate, the largest frigate in the Royal Navy, had left the Connecticut coast and gone elsewhere. It had waited for the signal on Groton Long Point, the signal that *Macedonian* was ready to run out of harbor, and when the signal had not come Captain Dacres had assumed *Macedonian* would not come and had gone about his business, presumably assisting Admiral Hardy's efforts in Maine, or helping to blockade Charles Stewart's *Constitution* in Boston. With the most dangerous of the two blockading frigates gone, and dirty weather in the offing, *Macedonian* would stand an excellent chance of getting out of harbor.

But of course, Favian thought bitterly, *Macedonian* was not going anywhere. Dacres had been perfectly right to leave; he would not be needed here. It appeared that Secretary of the Navy William Jones had won his administrative battle with President Madison; the Great Lakes would once again have priority in American strategy, and deep-sea cruises by American frigates would again be given low priority in officers, men, and equipment. He hoped that Decatur would bear that in mind when he set out for New York to get *President* ready for its own attempt to run the blockade.

> Now all my troubles now are over,
> *Way, hey, roll and go!*
> Oh, Sally's married to a sojer,
> *Spend my money on Sally Brown!*

" 'Vast swayin'!" The foreman's voice called a halt to the chorus, the foremast swaying majestically as it swung near-parallel to the lower mast. "Lash th' topmast to the lower mast," the foreman called. "Smartly, there! Jenkins, get the cap on th' lower masthead."

Favian remembered the last time he had seen a topmast rise aloft; it had been aboard *Macedonian* nearly two years ago, when he'd been given the task of repairing the torn ship and taking her to Newport. All three of her masts had been shot away, along with much of what had supported them, and the job had really required a dockyard overhaul. But he'd done it in just a few days, and when *Macedonian* had finally sailed into Rhode Island she'd looked as smart as the capturing frigate *United States*.

Macedonian had new masts and yards now, ones designed for her instead of spare spars borrowed from *United States* and hewn to fit. She would sail very well now, and it was a perfect shame that she would not get the chance.

"Permission to come aboard, Captain Markham?" It was Stephen Decatur, already coming up through the entry port without the permission that, technically, Favian could not give in any case, *Shark* still being officially in civilian hands.

"Greetings, Stephen," Favian said, startled. "I didn't see you ride up." He gestured to the activity. "I was thinking about the *Macedonian*. What a job it was to get her home!"

Decatur smiled. "Interesting you should say that," he said. "It was on a matter concerned with *Macedonian* that I came to speak with you."

"Shall we do our speaking over luncheon? I haven't eaten mine yet."

"Very good."

Decatur followed while Favian got his coat and hat from where he'd stowed them in the captain's cabin. As they returned to the spar deck, Decatur glanced up at the sky.

"Barometer's falling. It's coming on to blow."

"Yes. A good privateering wind, I'll wager. A pity Jones wouldn't wait a few days more—by tomorrow night there may be a good chance of getting *Macedonian* out past the blockade."

Decatur gave a faint smile. "Especially now that *Tiber* is gone. Have you seen the signal?"

"Yes."

"*Orpheus* keeping station in the race, *St. Lawrence* right off the Thames mouth. And neither of them able to maintain the blockade during a northwesterly blow."

Favian sighed. "Water under the bridge, I'm afraid."

"Perhaps not."

Favian stopped dead in his tracks, turning to face Decatur. Decatur's face still wore its faint smile, but Favian recognized the cunning in his black eyes.

"Stephen, what are you saying?"

There was a moment's dramatic pause as Decatur turned his head to look at *Macedonian,* tied up at the wharf in New London across the river, then returned his eyes to Favian.

"I want you to go aboard *Macedonian* this afternoon and assume command," Decatur said, speaking quickly, without inflection, as if afraid Favian might interrupt. "Then take her out of port at the first gale, tomorrow night or whenever. I'll support you. I'll even give you written orders, if you like."

"Stephen, are you mad?" Favian demanded. "You can't give those kind of orders—you're only the senior captain, not the secretary of the navy! If I assumed command it would be illegal, and everyone would know it!"

"It makes sense, Favian, even if it is a little irregular," Decatur said.

"A little irregular! Usurping the command of a United States man-of-war! For God's sake, Stephen, I could be court-martialed again."

"Listen carefully, Favian," Decatur said quietly, refusing to respond to Favian's outrage. "*Shark* won't be ready for some months yet. The secretary of the navy doesn't know the situation here—he's weeks away. His ordering Captain Jones to the Lakes shows that. Those months that it will take to equip *Shark* will be wasted. We could have had a cruiser at sea during all that time, attacking the enemy's commerce, forcing him to divert valuable forces. . . . The situation in the war now is critical. Any little delay thrown into our enemies' plans will win time for us—time to ready the *Demologos* and the new seventy-fours, time for the British public to grow weary of the war and urge their politicians to make peace, time for the Peace Commission in Ghent to win concessions."

Favian felt Decatur's persuasiveness eroding his position. This was utter madness, he reminded himself. All those years of subordination to Decatur had accustomed him to falling in line with Decatur's views; if ever there was a time to break the habit, it was now.

"If it's that damned important, Stephen, you take her out," he said. "Your position in the navy is unassailable; they'll never question anything you do."

"I can't," Decatur said grimly. "I'm to ready the *President*, and getting her to sea as soon as possible is at least as important as *Macedonian*'s getting out." He stepped nearer to Favian, lowering his voice. "I'll give you written orders, Favian. Once you get her clear into the Atlantic you can go anywhere—she's provisioned with food for twelve months and water for four. Head for the Pacific, like Porter, or the Brazils. You can be gone for months, blast it! By the time you come back, the fact you weren't ever legally put in command will be forgotten, but the success of the voyage won't be. They won't dare touch you, Favian. The war might even be over by then."

"Stephen, my God—" Favian began, then stopped, shaking his head, stepping back away from the power of Decatur's presence. He knew that a lot of what Decatur said was true. Once he was clear of the blockade, he *was* free; he could go anywhere. The British would have to send ships to find him, ships that otherwise would be applied to the blockade, or in harrying the New England coast. One frigate on the loose could tie up a dozen in searching for it. And once he got into the Indian Ocean he could start preying on East India Company ships, the giants that carried so much of England's wealth. He could survive for years if necessary on stores taken from his captures. And it would be months before the news of his presence could be carried around the Cape of Good Hope to London, and more months before a fleet could be assembled to hunt him down. He'd have six months in the Indian Ocean, minimum, before he would have to start worrying about his own safety.

But there were so many ifs, another part of his mind told him. *If* the *Macedonian* could be got out into the Atlantic. *If* it wasn't damaged in the storm and made vulnerable to an enemy cruiser. *If* it didn't encounter an overwhelming squadron during its cruise and get captured. *If*, once in the Indian Ocean, it wasn't hunted down and taken, and managed to get back to the United States through the blockade. *If* all these things happened, then he could expect a hero's welcome on his return, and not shackles and a corporal's guard.

"Stephen, if the voyage wasn't successful, they'd crucify me," Favian said. "Your letter wouldn't help; they'd hold me responsible for obeying an illegal order, not you for giving it."

He knew what Decatur's reply would be before the words had passed his lips. "Captain Markham," Decatur said, "do you anticipate failure?"

Favian fell silent, studying the ground at his feet. Hearing Decatur's reply, he suddenly felt a moment of release. He was free. Decatur was speaking, but Favian's mind floated independent of the other man's words. For a little space, all that had confined him was gone, and he knew that any decision he made would be made by Favian Markham, and no other.

All his life he had resented the navy, resented its intrusion into his life, the way it shackled his spirit and turned it to its own purposes. When he wore the uniform he was not his own creation; he was Captain Favian Markham, USN, Markham of Markham's Raid, the man who fought the victory over *Teaser* on August third, 1813, Markham the respectable man of property and owner of one hundred sixty acres of lower Manhattan. He had risked his life for the navy; he had once fought a duel because a man insulted the navy within his hearing, knowing that no navy man who wore the uniform could accept that insult. He had kept much of his life secret because he knew the navy would not accept untoward behavior from one of its officers; he had hidden Caroline in a cottage in Poquetanuck because he knew the navy would make him pay for the public acquisition of a mistress.

And now, Favian knew, the navy was holding its breath. The official navy prized obedience and discipline, and now two of its most famous officers were considering subverting that obedience. The navy would howl, Favian knew, if he took command of *Macedonian;* and even if the voyage were successful the navy would still howl, but behind clenched teeth.

For once, Favian thought, the navy would not own him. For once, let the navy howl. He looked up at Decatur and gave his reply.

And when he gave it, Stephen Decatur smiled.

14

Cold gusts whipped at Favian's face as he rode north to Poquetanuck, his cheeks and nose tingling with the chill. It was the cold beginnings of the winter weather he and Decatur had felt would be coming; the barometer had continued a downward slide all day. By the morning, Favian thought, the gusts would be stronger and longer, howling around the eaves of the cottage, and then before long rain and sleet would come. He would have to try to get on the road before the weather got too dirty.

The afternoon had been madness itself. First there was an interview with Lieutenant Stone, in which Decatur and Favian announced their intention of stealing *Macedonian*—both of them had been sensible enough to realize that the scheme was unworkable unless the first lieutenant, at least, proposed to accept Favian as his superior. Stone had scowled throughout the interview, looking blackly from one captain to the other, and Favian had felt his heart sink, certain Stone would still adhere to the letter of the regulations, but then as Decatur had finished his explanation Stone had smiled, offered to shake their hands, and offered them his wholehearted cooperation. Stone, Favian thought a bit cynically, had not entirely forgotten that the first lieutenant of a frigate moored semipermanently in a Connecticut river had little chance of a promotion, whereas the senior lieutenant of a frigate with a successful cruise behind it, and perhaps the capture of an enemy war vessel, was, in addition to being in the line for prize money, almost certainly guaranteed promotion to command rank.

After the interview with Stone had come another with *Macedonian*'s other lieutenants, with Stone, on this occasion, doing the explaining, and with Favian adding a postscript that, if any of the officers should object to the irregularity of the proceedings, they could leave the ship without any prejudice against them on the part of Captain Decatur or himself. None spoke against the proposal. There had been yet another interview with the frigate's midshipmen which had gone much the same way, Favian particularly remembering Phillip Stanhope's surprised smile as he realized he'd be sailing with Favian again.

There had been a hasty supper in which Favian and Decatur had written notes to the secretary of the navy explaining their reasons for their supercession of command, which Decatur agreed not to mail until *Macedonian* had left harbor. If the frigate failed to escape New London in the forthcoming storm, they both agreed, the situation would require a great deal more explanation; they agreed they'd deal with that when the time arose.

And then Favian had pleaded unfinished business outside of town—Decatur had been tactful enough not to inquire the nature of this business—and Favian had ordered his horse saddled. If the plans to run the blockade succeeded this would be his final night ashore, and even if he failed to get out of the Thames he would now be living on the frigate, and it would be much more difficult to escape to his mistress. Favian frowned as he rode up the dark country lanes. Caroline had been so cheerful lately, so happy with her life and her lover. This would not be easy.

He rode into the yard, glancing at the yellow lantern-lit windows, not seeing any sign of Caroline, who usually waited near a window for him. He dismounted, led the roan into the carriage house, rubbed the horse down, put her in the stable, and fed her. He washed the smell of horse from his hands by the well, scraped his boots on the scraper placed by the door, and then entered the cottage.

Caroline's smile, as always, was dazzling, the wrinkles around her eyes and nose accenting her delight; she was wearing a pale green, near-transparent gown, the sort she could never wear in public anywhere west of Ushant, one he had always thought complimented her wondrously. Her auburn hair was arranged in a *demi chignon,* caught and bound behind in a complicated knot—Favian had never been able to understand how she could arrange it by herself—little unbound ringlets fringing her forehead and ears. He felt his resolve fading as he kissed her hello, feeling her arms going around him. "Have you eaten?" she asked. "I can make a cold supper if you like."

"I've had supper with Captain Decatur," Favian said. "It's cold out—there'll be a storm tomorrow. I'd like a toddy."

"Hot. Buttered. Rum?" she asked, kissing him between each

word; he smiled and said yes. He got rid of his cloak, coat, and neckcloth, pulled his boots off, and sat down on the settee in front of the Franklin stove. Caroline brought his toddy and sat down next to him. He put his arm around her and she cuddled close on the couch, drawing her feet up, resting her head on his shoulder. He sipped the toddy, feeling the strong West Indian rum course its warming way through him.

"Favian?"

"Yes?"

Her fingers climbed his shirt front, crept into the open collar, and slid over the heavy pectoral, jabbing. Favian winced. "You're all tense again," she said. "I'll have to loosen you up." He offered her his toddy; she shook her head and rested on his shoulder again, her hand roving inside his shirt. He put the toddy down on the arm of the settee.

"Caroline," he said. "I'm taking command of the *Macedonian* tomorrow."

"Favian!" She sat up, delight plain on her face. "That's wonderful!"

He held up a hand, touched her cheek. "Caroline. I've got to get her to sea. Tomorrow, if I can."

He watched her face fall, the joy vanishing like a candle snuffed by an unthinking wind. He talked on, hoping to get the hurt out of the way all at once, the words that he had carefully arranged on his ride to Poquetanuck spilling out heedlessly, regardless of the finely reasoned order in which he'd originally constructed them.

"We knew I would have to leave. I don't want it to be this sudden, but we knew—we knew that's the way with navy men. Our time is not our own. I don't want you to feel entirely abandoned; my thoughts will be with you often; I've brought a draft for a thousand dollars on my Boston bank, enough so that you won't have to worry about money for two or three years. I hope you will go back on the stage, my dear; you're so talented and—"

And so the tears came, spilling from her blue eyes; he took her in his arms and let her sob against his shoulder. "I'm sorry, Caroline," he was reduced to saying, finally. "I wish it was possible not to leave you."

"Take me with you."

"In wartime? And in any case we're not married, it can't be done."

He knew the next question; it was "Why can't we be married?," but she did not ask it. He found himself admiring her; through her distress she had not forgotten the code which bound their relationship. He stroked her bound hair, her neck; he looked into her wide, hesitant eyes and kissed her. She groped for his coat, lying on an arm of the settee, and found his handkerchief. A moment later, the storm over, her eyes and nostrils rimmed with red but the color back in her cheeks, she reached across him to take a deep drink of his toddy, and then rested her head once more on his shoulder.

"I'm sorry I was so upset," she said with a sigh. "I should have known that you would have to leave."

"It was sudden. I'm sorry. I didn't know myself until this afternoon."

She reached for his toddy again, and he watched her as she drank. There was an abstracted quality in her eyes, and he thought it was because she was looking into a future that she had not expected to arrive for many weeks yet, forced once again to be mistress of her own fortunes. A future in which she was once again alone, a lovely, vulnerable girl, but not so vulnerable that she would, to appease her loneliness, compromise the understanding upon which their affair was based. Yes, there was steel in her.

"I should like to see you on the stage," he said. "I have never forgotten that scene from *Oroonoko*. You showed such talent. Passion."

She gave a wry smile. "Talent? Passion?" she asked. "That's not what our fine public wants on the stage, at least not in a woman. They would prefer to see a lovely little miniature on the stage, some kind of ivory statue that breathes, moves, and speaks noble sentiment." She kissed his cheek. "You are nice, Favian, but you have seen theater in this country, or what passes for it. The audience would be terrified by any real passion on the stage—it isn't ladylike, you know, it isn't exemplary. What the public wants, my dear, is Attitudes." She demonstrated what she meant, rapidly miming a series of affected poses: Devotion, Fear, Astonishment, Rapture, Repose, Delight, each distinct, unmistakable, and elevated, removed from the world of reality and genuine emotion by their total abstraction.

Caroline threw up her hands. "That's what they want, Favian," she said. "They don't want anything to touch them, not really. They want to be able to look at a thing onstage and be able to point at it and say, 'Thus-and-such is how things *ought* to be' instead of 'this is how things *are*.' To have to confine oneself to that, when it is possible to accomplish so much more!" She smiled sadly. "But I shouldn't go on this way—you can't understand it." But Favian did understand. The navy men were no different from actors; the public badly needed paragons of virtue, and the Navy Department was pleased to provide them. Noble, skilled, courageous, unbowed by defeat, generous in victory, passionate only in defense of their country—the navy men trod the stage daily, proclaiming their virtues, and by extension the virtues of the United States of America. As with actors, some, like Decatur, came naturally to the part; others, like Favian, had to work at it. But like an actor on a stage, a navy man dropped character only at his peril; the audience could well turn vicious if it sensed a bad performance. An actor faced only a barrage of rotten fruit; Favian would face a great deal worse, a total ostracism from the navy, from polite society, from the world he had known—possibly one or more duels as well.

"I think, Caro, I understand more than you know," Favian said, taking her hand and kissing it. "But you have a talent, and it would be a shame to waste it. You can afford to pick your moment—I'll see you won't lack means."

She looked at him dreamily, then shook her head. "I can't work on the stage again," she said. "There was a scandal—I ran out on a company during a tour, and there was no one to replace me. Ran with a lover." She looked at him to see if he was shocked; when he was not she went on. "The acting community in this country is small. The circumstances of my departure were not—not good, not at all. I was very young; I didn't have any following among the public; there will be no forgiveness. I couldn't find a place again."

"You could go abroad. You have the means. You speak French."

"Of a sort," she said with an indulgent smile.

"Of a sort," he said. "It could be improved. The world is gathering at Vienna—the two emperors, Blucher, Wellington, Metternich, Talleyrand . . . With your talent, you could make them notice. The theater abroad is not what it is here, Caro."

"And the blockade, sirrah?" she asked, mocking.

He grinned. "Leave the blockade to me," he said. "In any case there are cartels quite often. You're making excuses."

Caroline leaned forward, stroking his long sidewhiskers with her fingers. "You're a dear," she said, kissing his cheek. "I think I could learn to fancy you." Teasingly.

He put his arms around her. "You'll think about what I said?" he asked.

"I'll think about it," she said. There was a solemn melancholy in her eyes as she bent forward to kiss him lightly, and then again, and again, her lips tantalizing his, her warm breath on his cheek. They made love with slow deliberation, each making an effort to please the other, knowing all the favorite caresses were probably the last. He wondered why she had turned amorous when she did; was it that she wanted to end the debate on her future, refusing to give it further consideration? The wind increased as the night went on, howling around the cottage, bringing toward morning a drizzle of rain; there was a last, unhurried coupling in the deep bed, the lovers looking gravely into one another's eyes as they pleasured one another.

It was time. Favian rose and dressed, feeding his horse and packing his things; she gave him breakfast and watched him eat it. He kissed her farewell in the house, telling her there was no reason for her to go outside in the wet just to bid him adieu; they promised to write. Neither spoke of meeting again.

He had not seen her smile, he thought as he saddled his horse. The smile that he had loved most about her. Would the stage see that smile, he wondered; would Wellington and Talleyrand see it? Or would it be seen next in another rented cottage, with some other dragoon or state official? He hoped he knew the answer, but he suspected he did not.

15

" 'Tis yer last chance, witch," the man mumbled. He had brought the canvas hose of the channel pump to the water butts on the pier where Kuusikoski stood in his oilskins, and his message had been delivered in a low voice, out of the side of his mouth. Vihtori Kuusikoski froze for a moment in shock, then turned to contemptuously spit tobacco onto the pier. Talk was easy, action something else. Since he had caught Richards on a trip to the heads and pounded him half-senseless with the weighted butt of his fighting knife, there had been a few warnings, delivered like this one, sidelong, as if the messenger had been afraid of being attacked before the words were out of his mouth—but there had been no more marlinespikes falling from aloft, no mysterious accidents of any sort.

He was still treated as something of a leper. His messmates had returned to his company; they would eat with him, but few would exchange more than a few words: he clearly made them uncomfortable. Tiffin and a few others behaved to him normally; most were guarded like his messmates; many, including the hard men, avoided him entirely so long as their duties permitted. But since he had blacked both Richards's eyes, no one looked at him with scorn. He had the hands' respect, if not their friendship. He had earned a place, and for the moment was satisfied with it.

He maneuvered the heavy canvas hose into the water butt, and gave the signal to Midshipman Stanhope, who was standing on the horse block. "Man the channel pump!" he heard Stanhope shout. "Pump away!"

Kuusikoski watched the splashing of rain in the water butt as the level of water lowered with the pumping. *Macedonian* was taking on water; it was the last thing the frigate would do before heading out to sea. The two starboard channel pumps were both in operation; canvas windsails were also being used to catch the downpour and direct it into the frigate's water casks. Since the new captain had come aboard a few hours ago, *Macedonian* had become a beehive of swarming sailors; it was clear that Captain Markham intended to use the storm to run the blockade.

Once at sea, Kuusikoski thought, he was free. The crew would have no choice but to accept his presence once there was no way of his getting off the ship.

The water butt was dry, except for the splashing of rain in the bottom. Now he and his gang would have to haul away the water butt on its cart, and then haul another cart, with its two giant, full water butts, to *Macedonian*'s curved flank. Kuusikoski looked up and gave the signal to Stanhope.

" 'Vast pumping! Secure the channel pump!"

Kuusikoski jumped to the wharf from the bed of the cart, and with the other men in his gang tailed onto the towing line of the cart. This was draft animals' work normally, but the navy's teams of horses had been assigned to the other carts that were carrying empty butts inland to be filled.

"Heave, there! Move, you humps!" The coarse voice of the bosun's mate seemed oddly comforting. Within a few hours, Kuusikoski would have earned a permanent place aboard the *Macedonian*. Nothing could prevent it now. And with his place on the frigate, he would have a place in this America, the land, it was said, of freedom.

16

By midafternoon the sleet had coated *Macedonian*'s rigging and deck, and Favian walked carefully, wary of slipping in the half-frozen mush, every so often feeling a lump of sleet slide off his sou'wester onto his shoulders, then skid down his oilskins to the deck. Every so often Favian had been forced to send men aloft to knock the stuff from the running rigging in order to prevent the possibility of a line jamming in a block; if a brace seized up when they were trying to get *Macedonian* through Plum Gut or off the lee shore of Long Island the consequences were too horrible to be imagined.

It was almost as black as night. The storm wind howled through the rigging like a chorus of madmen, altering in pitch as the gusts plucked at the massed lines and shrouds.

A black oilskin-shrouded figure approached the quarterdeck, touched a hand to the brim of its sou'wester in salute: the regulations concerning the complete removal of the hat when faced with a superior officer were being sensibly ignored. "The hatches are battened down. It's high water now, Captain," the figure said.

"Thank you, Mr. Stone." A lump of sleet falling from the mizzen rigging above splashed down on Favian's sou'wester. He brushed frozen water from his eyes with the back of his hand.

"Barometer still falling," Stone continued. "Wind west nor'west, or thereabouts."

"Have you set one of your exercises in these conditions, Mr. Stone?" Favian asked. Stone flapped his arms to bring warmth into them. Favian realized that his own teeth were trying to chatter. If it was bad now, how bad would it be out in the race, with the frigate outside of the partial shelter offered by the Connecticut shore? And how bad was it aloft, where those poor sailors had to hang from footropes high aloft, knocking ice from the topsail sheet blocks and parrel tackles, their bodies leaning far out against the pressure of the wind?

"Not in these conditions, Captain," Stone said. He tried to grin, but the gesture had no conviction behind it. "I assumed it would be insane to bring *Macedonian* out in a storm like this. Sir."

Favian blinked more sleet from his eyes. "You were right, Mr. Stone," he said. It was only purest desperation that would force a frigate to leave port on a night like this, desperation occasioned by over a year of blockade with nothing but the fresh water of the Thames running under her keel.

The howl of the rigging went up a full octave as a gust swept down on the ship, rocking her on her moorings. At least they were tied to the wharf, Favian thought; there would be no necessity of sending men to the capstan to try to haul *Macedonian* to her anchor against this wind.

"Let's go below, Mr. Stone," Favian said. "I want to say

good-bye to Commodore Decatur without having to shout in his ear."

Macedonian was British-built; she did not, like the big American forty-fours Favian was used to, have a spar deck running flush fore and aft—instead she was built in the old-fashioned way, with the deck broken by a well running between the poop deck and the fo'c'sle, gangways running along either side to provide quick communication fore and aft. The ship's boats lay inverted over the gap, looking in their coats of sleet like misplaced whales cast up on some Arctic beach. Favian went down the poop ladder to the well deck, then made his way aft to his cabin.

Favian's quarters were warm only in the sense that they weren't as freezing as the quarterdeck had been, or as exposed to the weather. Favian nodded to Decatur as he walked in, sleet dripping off his oilskins onto the checked canvas "carpet," painted by the original British crew in black-and-white checks in imitation of Nelson's aboard the *Victory*. He walked straight to where a firebucket dangled from the deckhead: there an eighteen-pound solid shot, heated to an orange glow in the galley stove, had been placed in order to provide warmth for the cabin. Favian stripped off his gloves and rubbed his scarred hands over the cannon ball, flexing his fingers, bringing tingling life back into them.

Decatur was in damp oilskins; he'd been on deck from time to time, offering suggestions, taking command of a work party when there was need, running messages ashore and in general making himself useful. "The barometer is still falling," he said, duplicating Stone's message. He walked to where Favian was absorbing the steady heat of the cannon ball and held his own hands above the warm iron. He smiled. "*Orpheus* and *Rifleman* will have been driven off station, Favian," he said. "There's no way they could hold against that wind; they'll be far into the Atlantic by now. *Rifleman* will probably have to heave to under bare poles. If you so much as sight *Orpheus*'s topsails it will be a miracle."

Favian nodded. Visibility was so low that *Macedonian* might sail within two miles of the British frigate without being seen. "Mr. Stone," Favian said, turning to where the lieutenant was respectfully waiting his turn at the firebucket, "would you call for coffee?"

"Yes, sir."

Coffee had been one of the last-minute additions to the captain's stores; distracted with his other duties, Favian had forgotten about his private store of coffee, still at his inn in New London, until about an hour before, when a messenger had been sent into the storm to fetch it. The wardroom would probably make do with scraped, burnt bread, or brewed acorns, but the captain's table, at least, would serve real coffee.

There had been another last-minute article brought aboard: the day's post had brought a small package from Robert Fulton, and Favian had been surprised to discover a miniature portrait set in a locket, sent, the note said, in thanks for Favian's attempt to save the turtle boat. It was a version of the pastel sketch Favian had indicated as his favorite, the mature man of action, hair tousled as if by a breeze or a brisk action with the enemy, collar open, expression a little grim. An excellent piece of workmanship; Favian was touched by the thought. Favian wished it had arrived a day before so he could have given it to Caroline.

Besides the coffee, Favian had dealt with the ship's other stores; that morning he'd been through the paperwork certifying that supplies sufficient for twelve months' cruising were aboard, to wit: 64,000 "loaves" of bread—in this case hard biscuits, 60 barrels of flour, 1500 pounds of butter, 3800 pounds of cheese, 650 gallons of molasses, 250 barrels of beef, 219 barrels of pork, 650 gallons of vinegar, 163 bushels of beans and peas, and 4600 gallons of pure rye whiskey. In addition the warrant and petty officers heading the ship's departments, the master, bosun, gunner, carpenter, cooper, master at arms, cook, sailmaker, and surgeon, had all certified that their own supplies were sufficient for the frigate to proceed to sea. The only officer who had not reported was *Macedonian*'s chaplain, a cheerful young man with the auspicious-sounding name of the Reverend Doctor Solomon, but Favian presumed the Missionary Society had provided enough bibles for his purposes and had not bothered him. It was unusual for a ship of war to have a chaplain—as a species they were considered unlucky by the sailors—but Jacob Jones, a social man, belonging to a dozen organizations concerned with reforming the world, or at any rate talking about it, had encountered Talthibius Solomon just after the latter had obtained his degree from the College of New Jersey at Princeton, and so impressed him with his descriptions of life at sea that Solomon had promptly volunteered.

Jones was known for attempting to foster the moral development of his crews; Favian himself preferred to leave such matters alone and concentrated simply on trying to curb drunkenness when he could. His own religious thought lodged somewhere between skepticism and outright atheism and in the normal course of things he would not have brought a preacher aboard, but the Reverend Doctor Solomon had been inherited from the previous captain and Favian could not fling the man off. He would try simply to keep Doctor Solomon away from Lazarus.

For Lazarus had volunteered, as he had said he would; he had expressed no surprise at the sudden news of Favian's new captaincy and their sudden departure, but simply gone to his room to pack his seabag and fiddle. He had been given the rank of able seaman and the duty of ship's chantyman. Tolbert, Favian's other stray, had been likewise brought aboard the frigate and installed in the midshipmen's berth; with his stitched arm and splinted nose he'd been confined to light duties involving no tasks aloft.

Favian's cabin steward—a man named Crane, currently on trial along with the other servants, Jones having taken his own personal servants along with him to Sackett's Harbor—brought in a tray with coffee, and Favian and Decatur began to warm their hands on the cups instead of the firebucket. The stuff was ill-brewed; Favian suspected that Crane might not last long as steward.

"Have you given any thought to your destination?" Decatur asked in a low voice, first making certain Crane had left. "After you bring the frigate out of New London, I mean?"

Favian glanced behind him, seeing Stone watching him with guarded curiosity from the firebucket. "Yes, Commodore," he said, with a nod acknowledging Stone's interest. "We'll be heading first to the Caribbean and spend some weeks harassing the British islands, but that's only a red herring—after we've drawn the pursuit to the West Indies, we'll be setting course for the Indian Ocean. We'll live off our captures like Porter did in the Pacific, and any likely capture we make can be armed and sent out as an auxiliary cruiser. We'll survive a long time there; the British will take nine months to respond, at the very least."

Decatur whistled, impressed. "You do not lack ambition, Captain Markham," he said. " 'Tis a bold plan. I wish you all success."

"Thank you, Commodore," Favian said. He turned to Adrian Stone. "Mr. Stone, I'd be obliged if you mention none of this to the wardroom."

"I won't, Captain," Stone said, then added formally, "I am sensible of the honor you do me in taking me into your confidence, sir."

"It's nothing you don't deserve, Mr. Stone," Favian said, and saw, as he spoke, a knowing look in Decatur's eyes. Decatur knew, perhaps better than anyone in the world, how to inspire his subordinates with loyalty and devotion; it was one of his oldest and best stratagems to take his men into his confidence, sharing a secret with them with the intention of animating first a feeling of shared intimacy, then undying fealty. Favian had absorbed the tactic at his master's elbow, and now used it unconsciously as he had with Lieutenant Stone; no doubt Decatur, judging by his look, thought the gesture calculated. Favian, annoyed at his transparency, sipped his coffee.

Macedonian shuddered as it moved against the wharf, its timbers groaning, the collision mats cushioning the shock. The tide was beginning to ebb, coming down the Thames in a rush; Favian could take the frigate out at any time. He saw Decatur's eyes still on him and he drank his coffee deliberately, taking in its warmth, trying to seem nonchalant as his mind worked at problems of wind and tide, wondering how much sail he could set in this wind, attacking and rejecting plans for getting *Macedonian* to sea. And wondering, of course, whether he had forgotten anything important on the land.

He finished the coffee and returned it to the tray with a little porcelain *clink*. He looked up and saw Decatur's solemn gaze.

"Well, Stephen," he said. "It's time."

Decatur nodded. "Good luck, Favian," he said, and held out his hand. "Godspeed."

"Thank you, sir. Let's go, Mr. Stone." There was little left to say; in the rush of getting the frigate ready for sea there was little room for eloquent discourse. Favian clasped the hand, then put his sou'wester back on his head and walked with Decatur to the entry port.

"Pipe the side for Commodore Decatur," Stone ordered. Officers assembled in a dark rank, swords drawn in salute. The bosun's pipe was almost drowned by the shriek of the rigging.

Decatur, a black figure against the deeper blackness of the storm, saluted Favian and the quarterdeck, and then turned and was gone. Favian felt a striking moment of aloneness, there on the dark well deck—it seemed, with Decatur gone, as if he were alone on the great frigate, cast there into darkness with the wind howling about his ears and the endless sleet coming down—and then he made a conscious effort to shake off the sensation, turning and walking up the poop ladder to take his place on the weather quarterdeck.

The sleet drummed down on his head. He looked aloft; seeing the encrusted lines and shrouds outlined against the dimly sensed clouds. He called up the officers and hands to their stations and soon the decks were dark with men, standing in silent, sodden clumps, waiting for orders. They seemed ghosts in the darkness, possessed only of a scant reality, and Favian's eerie sense of being the only man aboard increased. He forced himself to consider the state of the vessel, feeling the tide tugging at its keel, and then picked up a speaking trumpet and urged the orders from his throat.

"Strike the gangway," he shouted, his own voice sounding distant as compared with the humming, crying shrouds. "Parties fore and aft to cast off mooring lines. Hands to the braces. Fore and main topmen lay aloft to loose fore and main tops'ls. Three reefs in the tops'ls, ready to sheet home. Ready on the jib halyards and sheets."

He stood in silence by the mizzenmast as the rest of the ship began to boil with action. Clinging forms swarmed up the starboard shrouds, their backs arching against the push of the wind, clumps of sleet kicked from the ratlines, spinning in the wind as they fell to the deck below. The voices of the mast captains came to him, sounding like the cries of distant spirits calling from the grave: "Man the tops'l reef tackles and buntlines! Man the weather tops'l and preventer braces! Let go and overhaul the tops'l halyards and lift jiggers! Brace in—settle away! Haul taut the reef tackles and clewlines! Sail loosers, lay out along the yards! Stand by all the watch, tops'l sheets and halyards! Stand by—*let fall!*"

The big sails fell, whole sheets of sodden snow cascading down to the deck. Favian felt the frigate lurch as the wind caught the loosened canvas, the half-deployed sails bellying out with a roar. As the frigate was taken by the wind the mooring lines went taut, rainwater being squeezed out of their tightening fibers in a fine spray, the frigate heeling at its mooring as the wind pushed it over. The frigate was alive now, alive but still leashed, and Favian's sense of isolation was lost in overwhelming awe. His previous command had been the *Experiment* brig of fourteen guns, and before that nothing larger than a gunboat. *Macedonian* carried more than three times the brig's number of guns, had over thrice as many crew, was so much more of a ship in so many ways. The brig had been a comfortable little command; Favian and the crew had been forced into such close proximity by the little vessel that he had known their mood almost before the hands themselves had.

Now it was so different—a half-dozen lieutenants where there had been only one; the crew a sea of unknowns, no faces familiar yet; the ship itself last seen as a battered prize of war, barely afloat. Everything was unfamiliar, the ship, the storm, the crew; the *alienness* of it all was overpowering. Favian could so easily make a mistake, and the results of a mistake could be terrifying: the ship torn open on a lee shore, going aground in the New London channel, losing her sticks in this wind and then running smack into a cruising British squadron . . .

Poor James Lawrence had taken *Chesapeake* to sea after being in command for only a few days; he hadn't known the ship or his crew, and he'd lost her to Broke's *Shannon* in less than twenty minutes. *Chesapeake* and *Macedonian* were almost identical in construction and armament; Favian had only been in command a few hours; he was even more ignorant than Lawrence had been. There were so many reasons to be afraid, to resent the impetuous Decatur who had talked him into this. "Are you anticipating failure, Captain Markham?" Decatur had asked. Such a thundering foolish question! There was no way of knowing, no way at all. Favian would have to anticipate every possibility, failure and success both, glory as well as the everlasting hell that would result from a disaster.

"Lay in! Lay down from aloft!" The dimly seen figures were coming down the starboard shrouds again. Lieutenant Stone turned to Favian.

"Fore and main tops'ls ready to sheet home, sir."

Favian shook himself out of his meditations and stepped across the sleet-drenched deck to the starboard bulwark. The loosed sails, not yet sheeted, roared like thunder in the wind. He reached out and put his hand on a main backstay, feeling it taut, hard as iron as it strained to keep the mast upright in the face of the wind's pressure. The topgallants had been sent down long ago, leaving *Macedonian* with a stubby, half-finished look, but even so the pressure on the backstay was formidable. Favian felt the vibration of the wind through the stay, feeling the ship responding to the forces that were being exerted on it. The ship was straining at its moorings, a thing half-alive, a masterful assembly of wood and hemp and canvas, nothing rigid in its makeup at all, every element in its construction responsive to the wind, sea, and to the human will. Favian's will. The ship was his, by God, and if he treated her with care, if he could work within the complex web of strengths and weaknesses implicit in her construction, she would take him anywhere in the world. He felt joy rising in him, banishing the hesitancy and fear as if he had somehow been infused with the strength of the backstay. Confidence filled him. The frigate, a living thing, would respond to his guidance; he would take *Macedonian* to sea through the teeth of a raging storm, and perform wonders to astonish the Admiralty.

For too long had he been a creature of his own celebrity. Captain Markham of Markham's Raid, to the victory over *Teaser*, man of property, man of the navy, secret lover—he had been responding to what others believed, to what others expected. The world expected him to be forever Markham of Markham's Raid, and he had been unable to tell them that he had never been that man in the first place. Now he was captain of the thirty-eight-gun frigate *Macedonian*, which he was stealing, with the complicity of its crew, from the navy's control; his loyalties were only to the ship and the men aboard; he was free of any land-based expectations. When he had taken command of the frigate he'd made hash out of the navy's discipline, and the rest would soon be left behind. He was free of the land for a year at least, and he would try to make the most of it.

He turned to where Stone and the others waited, hunched in the wind, their shoulders coated with sleet.

"Gentlemen, to sea," he said. "Cast off moorings fore and aft. Sheet home."

The deck sang with activity. Once again the voices of the officers rose above the din. "Cast off there, forrard. Cast off aft!" *Macedonian* lurched away from the dock, the big hawsers splashing into the black Thames. "Sheet home and hoist away the fore tops'l! Sheet home and hoist away the main tops'l!" Showers of sleet cascaded to the deck as the lines roared through the sheaves. Favian felt a thrill of purest joy as the ship responded, the billowing, thundering sails tautening, flat as boards, *Macedonian* heeling far over as the topsails caught the wind. Favian turned to where Isaac Seward, the sailing master, stood on the starboard horse block, elevated above the deck with one hand clinging to the main topmast stay, ready to give commands to the helm through his speaking trumpet.

"Keep her in midchannel, Mr. Seward," Favian called. He saw the master's terse nod.

"Lay out and clear away the jib! Hoist away the jib halyard!" The officers' voices droned on. "Belay the fore tops'l halyards! Belay the main tops'l halyards! Take off the lift jiggers! Throw the tops'l lifts forrard of the yard!"

"Port yer helm!" Seward's voice was loud and grating, carrying clearly above the shriek of the wind. "There . . . amidships. Keep her so."

Favian peered into the dark. The Connecticut shore on either side was barely visible through the whirling storm; the surface of the water was choppy even here. He realized that once out to sea there would be a following wind, each rising wave smashing against the rudder from behind, making it hard on the helmsmen, very hard.

"Mr. Stone, send a party of men below to man the relieving tackles and take some pressure off the helmsmen. Relieve the men at the helm every half hour."

"Aye aye, sir." The sound of the ship's bell striking eight came clearly from forward. Favian looked up at the sky and frowned. Only four in the afternoon, and black as midnight.

He had worked out a number of stratagems for getting to sea. *Macedonian* could creep to the eastward through Fishers Island Sound, hiding from the British behind Fishers Island, but that would put the Cormaralit Rocks and Latimore Rock Ledge on a lee shore—too dangerous in this darkness. Favian had decided to take *Macedonian* straight out, heading a little west of south to clear Fishers Island, then once in The Race altering course to the east to avoid the Great Gull Islands. It was the most direct way out, the way the British would be almost certain to try to block if they could, but Favian trusted that the darkness and storm would get him past the British unseen.

"Mind yer helm," Seward called. "Mind it, damn'ee!"

"Sorry, sir," came the muffled voice of a helmsman from below the break in the quarterdeck. Ahead Favian could hear the sound of breakers. *Macedonian* was moving at incredible speed, especially considering there were only the topsails and a storm jib deployed, but of course the racing tide helped—how fast would she move when she took to the ocean?

"Mr. Stone, pass the word for Mr. Stanhope and Mr. Pratt. Tell them to bring the recording log."

"Aye aye, sir."

The white lines of breakers were dimly visible on either bow. Seward took the frigate directly between them, and as soon as the hull began pitching to the rougher water of the Atlantic the sound of the wind shrieked up half an octave and *Macedonian* slid over even farther. Favian cursed as he slid on the steep, sleet-covered deck; his boots scrabbled for traction. He fetched up against the mizzen monkey rail, gasping for breath, his mind whirling. Heeled over this far, the frigate's keel would lose much of its grip on the water; she would be making a lot more leeway than he had first calculated. He turned to Seward. Sleet stung his cheek as he turned partway into the wind.

"Make your course sou'west by south," he shouted.

"Sou'west by sou', aye aye. Sou'west by sou', there! Hands to the braces!"

On her new course the frigate took the wind just aft of the beam; her heel increased even more, and Seward clung for dear life to the main shrouds to keep from being flung off the horse block with every ocean wave. Favian half-walked, half-slid to the larboard rail, peering out into the darkness, hoping for a glimpse of Fishers Island. He saw nothing but the black ocean, spray curling from the top of every wave. Visibility was almost nil. He groped within his oilskins for his pocket watch, holding it almost to his nose before he could read it.

They were making five or six knots, he estimated. The tide would add another five knots to that; The Race did not get its name without good reason. As soon as Stanhope got on deck with Markham's Recording Log they'd try to confirm that. At five knots they'd clear Race Point in perhaps twenty-five minutes, and then he could alter course to the southeast and run for the open sea. Hold the present course much longer and he could run right onto the Great Gull Islands. It was all so risky. Getting a glimpse of Fishers Island would make things much easier.

He looked up, seeing the ice caking the running rigging. He'd have to keep it clear; if he miscalculated only quick work with the sails could preserve them from disaster. "Mr. Stone," he bellowed into the wind. "Men aloft to clear the ice from the running rigging!"

Stone's assent was lost in the wind, but Favian saw him going forward, stooping against the force of the gale, and then give his orders with much waving of arms, perhaps for emphasis, perhaps for warmth. Huddled figures ran for the shrouds. Favian's own legs and arms were almost numb; he knew that anyone going aloft in this wind would find his clothing no protection; the freezing gale would cut through it like a knife. Simply to cling motionless to the lines would be agony enough; to have to work aloft would be torture. The surgeon would have a dozen cases of frostbite to deal with tomorrow, Favian thought.

Two oilskin-clad figures began sliding toward him on the deck: Stanhope and Pratt, the former carrying the heavy case with the latest prototype of Markham's Recording Log. "Barometer's rising, sir," Stanhope reported, his tone hopeful.

"First rise after very low, indicates a stronger blow," Favian thought, recalling the old bit of seaman's doggerel; Stanhope's news brought little cheer.

"Prepare to trail the recording log, Mr. Stanhope," he said. It was imperative to get a solid idea of the ship's speed through the water; if he stayed on the present course too long there was danger of running aground.

He helped the two midshipmen to get the piece of machinery attached to its line, setting its gauges at the starting points and then heaving it over the taffrail. It was trailed far enough astern to be out of the turbulence of the frigate's wake, then hauled in hand over hand so the gauges could be read. The spray from the towing line soaked them, sopping through their mittens, the cold cutting into their fingers with razor sharpness. Favian peered at the gauges, his mind, familiar with the calculations from long practice, working out the speed of the ship.

Seven and one half knots! His own senses indicated they could not be traveling that fast. Was it possible? Were they running onto the Great Gull Island at such speed?

"Cast the log again," he said. "I want to make sure."

Again the log's gauges were set to zero, again the gleaming apparatus went splashing into the icy water. Favian's mind worked frantically at the problem. If they were moving so quickly he would have to alter course much sooner than he'd planned, but was the log giving him a true reading? He'd never tested it in these conditions; there might be some defect that was causing it to give false readings.

The second reading confirmed the first, and anxiety began to gnaw at Favian as he began to walk up and down the deck, trying to generate warmth within himself. The helmsmen were relieved and sent below, but there was no relief for the captain or the two midshipmen condemned to share his misery.

Markham's Recording Log was his own development; he had designed it carefully, observed as the clockmaker, assisted by a jeweler, had cast its components. He knew the device perfectly; he was confident in the science behind it; he knew of no reason why it should not work. Yet to trust the recording log in defiance of his own senses was a step he was not willing to take.

He began to glance anxiously to leeward, hoping for a glimpse of land in the murk, but he received no such consolation. The storm howled around the ship, the sleet turning to a driving snow that shrouded them from the world, turning the ship into an isolated, embryo universe of its own, alone on the friendless sea. Favian found himself staring forward into the whiteness, waiting for the sight of the rocks onto which the frigate would smash itself. Nightmarish memories of the *Experiment* wreck came to haunt him, the little brig canted on its side as it smashed up against a mudbank, the seas breaking over it, sweeping away the crew, breaking loose the guns that tore like iron beasts through the fragile planking.

The log was cast twice more; the average speed remained seven and one half knots.

In the end, in clean defiance of his own protesting, shrieking intuitions, Favian made the decision to trust his equipment. Twenty minutes after leaving the sheltering Thames he ordered the change in course that, if his calculations were correct, should bring them unscathed into the open Atlantic. If he was wrong, the consequences would be horrifying: *Macedonian* driving at a run onto Race Point, breaking up in minutes and casting its crew into the frozen, storm-lashed water. Favian strained his eyes peering forward, expecting at any instant the sight of the breakers that would signal his doom.

No such apparition came. Alone on its portion of the ocean, the frigate drove on into the Atlantic at a dead run, and after another hour of anxious waiting Favian knew the danger had passed. His mind bellowing relief, he dismissed Stanhope and Pratt and stumbled below to warm himself with a pot of coffee and a hot meal.

The frigate and its crew were free on the waves that England claimed proudly to rule.

17

"The man's a witch!"

Favian turned toward Lazarus in surprise. *Macedonian*'s long quarterdeck, lined with thirty-two pound carronades and their crews that were bustling to their battle stations, echoed to the activity around them. The trumpeter was still calling out the staccato call to arms. It was a daily gunnery drill, the first to be performed under Favian's scientific standards.

"What did you say, Lazarus?" Favian asked. The fiddler's face was unshaven—Lazarus and the other lower-deck men shaved only twice each week, to save water; even so the frigate had a full-time barber who did little but shave the men for the entire length of his watch, the barber being necessary because straight razors made such fine weapons and could prove too handy in case of a fight among the crew—and the dark beard around Lazarus's chin made his scowling, lined face seem like a caricature of resentment and anger.

"That man Koskey. He is a Finnish witch, Cap'n. He should be flung alive into the sea!"

Favian looked at Lazarus in bafflement. He had made Lazarus his messenger at quarters, which would allow him to speak with the fiddler during the daily gunnery drills. He had intended it as a way of establishing a conduit to the lower deck—normally the captain of such a large frigate as *Macedonian* would be completely remote from the ship's people, insulated from the hands by the massive, unbreakable chain of command, the petty officers and warrant officers, midshipmen and lieutenants, through which any communication between captain and seamen would have to be directed. Contact with the hands was limited to official and semiofficial inspections, when the people were expected to conform to fairly rigid roles, dressed in their best clothes, speaking only when spoken to, and probably responding to questions not with what they really thought, but with what they thought the captain would want to hear. The only other glimpse of their captain the hands received was during the hours when malefactors came before him to receive their punishment— extra duty, stoppage of grog, flogging, or worse—scarcely a time when a captain was regarded with sympathy.

Yet so much depended on the people. They outnumbered the officers nine to one; their attitude to those placed above them was crucial. What did they think of their officers? Were they too harsh? Too lax? Too ignorant of the gunnery or seamanship to be able to teach these concepts to the men? Did they resent the extra, newfangled drills Favian had introduced, or would they perform them willingly, realizing that during an emergency their own lives, no less than their officers', depended on the ship's efficiency? Lives might well depend on the answers, yet the captain had no regular way of obtaining them.

Thus Lazarus. In Lazarus, Favian flattered himself that he had a spy below decks, able to report on the people's attitudes and opinions. Favian was perfectly willing to accept the idea that the seamen might well think Lazarus was the people's spy on the quarterdeck; he hoped the conduit would work both ways. And today it had worked in a way that could only be considered unexpected.

"The man's a witch!" It was a strange response to that morning's incident.

After breakfast that morning, Favian had been about to go on deck when Lieutenant Stone and *Macedonian*'s portly little master-at-arms, Herzog, had knocked on his cabin door to report a breach of ship's discipline. It seemed that one of the hands, a naturalized Estonian with the odd name of Koozey Koskey, had been attacked in the night by at least three of the other crewmen.

He had been sleeping in his hammock when the line supporting his head had been cut. He had crashed to the deck, falling on his head, avoiding by a miracle the eighteen-pound roundshot placed there to crack his skull, and half-stunned with the fall had been unable to resist his attackers when they'd tangled him in his hammock and beat him senseless. He was now under the surgeon's care in the sick bay.

"It seems to have been a conspiracy, sir," Stone said grimly.

"It certainly was, sir," Herzog added. He tugged on the lapels of his civilian suit—no uniforms were prescribed for the master-at-arms, so most wore civilian rig; Herzog's was quite dandified, and contrasted oddly with his portly figure. "Koskey says he don't know who it was, an' maybe we can believe him, but he also says he don't know why they attacked him, and there he's lyin'. It's crowded down on the gun deck where the incident took place, and though it's dark at night there are a few battle lanterns lit. They couldn't have been entirely silent when they beat him, but the people all say they didn't hear it, and don't know who did it.

"They've taken against this Koskey, sir," Herzog concluded. "They're all protectin' the men who beat him."

"Could he be a thief?" Favian had asked. It was the most logical explanation. Thieves were the most hated of lower-deck criminals; frequently the crew didn't bother to report a thief, but handled the matter themselves.

Herzog pursed his lips. "Don't know, sir," he said. "I don't think he's the type. But they have somethin' against him." He straightened, his face taking on a determined expression. "I'll get to the bottom of it, don't 'ee fear, sir." As master-at-arms, Herzog was head of the ship's police, the center of a complicated web of relationships that included his deputies, the ship's corporals, as well as crewmen who for one reason or another informed on their shipmates. He was feared and resented by the hands, and for good reason: masters-at-arms had in the past been known to abuse their positions, protecting known evildoers in return for bribes or information, and sometimes deliberately accusing innocent men of crimes committed by others under their protection. Some were even criminals themselves. So far as Favian could determine Herzog was guilty of none of these things; the gross abuse of privilege accepted in the Royal Navy were not tolerated in the United States forces, and in many ships, Favian's old

United States among them, the trust between officers and men had been so fruitful that a ship's police was not needed and the rank of master-at-arms had ceased to exist, his duties being absorbed by the lieutenants and petty officers. But here Herzog, like the chaplain Solomon, was an officer that Favian had inherited from Jacob Jones, and could not remove from the ship without good reason and without insult to the former captain.

"I'll visit the sick bay and interview him," Favian said.

Koskey was a tall, broad-shouldered man, with a square face, pale blond hair, and remote, pale blue eyes. Both eyes were blackened, the lip was split, the nose swollen, and the rest of the body covered with bruises. Two of his fingers had been broken in the attack, and Truscott had splinted them; he had also given Koskey opiates to help relieve his considerable discomfort.

"I don't know how much help he'll be, considering I've given him the drugs," Truscott had said, and proved to be a good prophet. Koskey seemed clear-headed enough, and asked to be put back on duty as soon as possible, but insisted that he had no idea why he should be attacked, or who the attackers were. "Maybe they don't like foreigners, sir," he'd said, a frown on his face. That had been the only suggestion he'd offered.

And now, some hours later, Lazarus stood on the quarterdeck claiming the Estonian was a witch. Favian absorbed the information while he turned up the collar of his pea jacket against the brisk November breeze. They had been free in the Atlantic for three days now, with Markham's Recording Log registering well over a hundred miles of southing each day. The British Bermudas were somewhere out of sight over the port bow—a major British base, which Favian intended to avoid—and though the wind was a good deal warmer than the frozen gale that had blown them out of New London, it was still brisk and Favian was thankful for his jacket.

"Is that why Koskey was beaten?" Favian asked. "Because the men think he's a witch?"

"Aye," Lazarus said, as if he were speaking to a child. "He's a Finnish witch. The men want him off the ship before he turns into a Jonah. He was beaten and thrown off the *Tom Bowlin* privateer for the same reason."

"How do they know he's a witch?" Favian asked. It seemed a reasonable question to ask, yet for some reason Lazarus turned angry, his fury apparent in every word.

"Thou knowest he's a Finn!" he spat. "Finns are witches, are they not? Any fool knows it! Knowest thou that I have seen Finnish ships under the Swedish flag, sailing with a fine quartering breeze, when my own vessel was becalmed. The man is bad luck."

Well. This was a kind of contact with the lower deck that Favian had not at all anticipated when he'd made Lazarus his spy.

"But, Lazarus," Favian said, "you are something of a witch yourself, as you tell it. The people accept your presence. Why should it be different with Koskey? And if he can call up winds, why should he not call favorable ones? He's on our ship, not a Swedish one."

"I have powers, aye," Lazarus said. His eyes blazed with anger. "They come to me because I have opened my soul to the Dark Master, and do his bidding on earth. But Koskey is controlled by no dark powers; the witchery comes to him as his right of birth as a Finn, and he will bring bad luck to the ship whether he want it or no." Lazarus paced briefly on the deck, then swiveled back to face Favian. "I trusted the man—I brought him aboard after he was beaten! I could not see his nature, his powers protected him! I was a fool." He looked at Favian grimly, his hands clasped behind his back.

"There is a preacher on board—bad luck!" he snapped. "There is a Finnish Jonah on board—bad luck! Thou has brought evil fortune to the *Macedonian* by allowing these forces on board. The oceans of the earth belong to the Dark Master and his spirit Davey Jones, and thou offendest him when thee brings these people on his waters." He stepped close to Favian, his unshaven face taking on an urgent ferocity. "Let me deal with him!" he said, his fervor plain. "The preacher can stay—he's a fool, anyway. But the other shall go—thee shall never have to soil thy hands with him. The witch shall pollute the ship only a few hours after he's released from sick bay—Davey Jones shall have him!"

Favian took an involuntary step backwards, away from the violence of Lazarus's madness. The man was surely more insane than Favian had ever given him credit for—here he was proposing murder on the captain's own quarterdeck, with the captain as a silent accomplice!

"I do not, Lazarus," Favian said icily, "propose to involve myself in a doctrinal dispute among witches! I want you to know—and you may pass this among the hands—that this Koskey is under my protection. If he's hurt again, I will seek out the perpetrator and flog him until I see his backbone! And if he should disappear, I'll hang the man responsible, and I'll have a good idea where to start looking—so, Lazarus, I submit that it is in your interest to see the man comes to no harm."

Lazarus's face colored with rage and frustration. "Thou art a fool. Canst thee not see it? What a Jonah will bring to this ship?"

"Enough, Lazarus!" It was a mad conversation, speaking of witchery and murder on the quarterdeck of a United States man-of-war, speaking in whispers that the men might not overhear.

"My powers speak to me," Lazarus said. "If this matter is not dealt with, we shall meet an enemy ship soon. It will not be a happy meeting—we shall be cursed in that fight! I warn thee!"

This was too much. Favian found his temper boiling up, snapping his control like a strong man tearing a handful of straw—before he knew it he was roaring in his three-reef voice, his famous anger exploding. "Tell your blasted powers it is I who am captain of this ship, not some spook!" he shouted. "Get out of my sight, blast you! Get below and let me not see you until tomorrow!" The crewmen turned to stare as Lazarus retreated hastily before the captain's fury, forgetting to salute as he scuttled away, his bent figure disappearing down the quarterdeck ladder. Favian looked up, his rage still boiling, seeing the men standing in shock at their places, the officers at their stations but motionless, arrested at their duties by their spitting volcano of a captain.

"Back to your duties, the lot of ye!" Favian roared, and suddenly they were busy again, the sound of their labors seeming subdued against the violence of Favian's explosion. Favian turned abruptly and walked to the taffrail, staring out at the ship's wake, gripping the rail, wrestling the anger down. He heard a step behind him, and then the respectful voice of Lieutenant Stone.

"Captain Markham, the men are at battle stations. Six and one half minutes, sir."

He took a breath and turned. Stone stood with his usual serious expression, his hat off his head in proper salute. Favian uncovered in reply and walked forward. "The men will mock-load and practice firing in sections," he said. "Larboard sections against starboard. Commence when you think proper, Mr. Stone."

"Aye aye, Captain." Stone's voice raised in volume as he

roared through his speaking trumpet. "Out tampions! All sections load! Each gun captain to raise a fist when ready!"

The gun drill commenced, and Favian found his anger fading as the technicalities of the drill began to absorb him. He was determined to teach *Macedonian*'s gunners the system of firing by sections, rather than by whole broadside or at will, the system that he had developed aboard the *United States* and used to such success in *Macedonian*'s initial capture over two years before. Due to the scientific deadliness of Favian's techniques, coupled with two years of incessant practice on the part of *United States*'s gun crews, *Macedonian* had ended that fight as a dismasted hulk, rolling her gunports under with every wave, over a third of her crew dead or wounded and the well deck ankle deep in bloody seawater. He intended to bring that brand of gunnery practice to *Macedonian*, and if he was to respond to wartime pressures by bringing the frigate up to the standards of the *United States* in less than the two years it had first taken him with the other ship, it would require endless hours of persistent drill.

Nor was firing by three- or four-gun section the only advanced technique Favian intended to introduce to his new command. The previous year the British frigate *Shannon*, Captain Philip Bowes Vere Broke, had captured the American *Chesapeake*, Captain James Lawrence, in twenty minutes' equal fight off the port of Boston. The victory had heartened British naval partisans and astonished the American public, who had begun to think of nautical victories as their natural right. There were a good many reasons why Broke had triumphed over Lawrence, but certainly the greatest was the fact that Broke's interest in scientific gunnery bordered on the obsessive. Broke's innovations had been widely trumpeted in the British press, and Favian saw no reason why he should not borrow a successful tactic from an enemy.

During the last twenty-four hours *Macedonian*'s officers had been busy on the gun deck, spar deck, and quarterdeck, working with compasses, straightedges, and the yardsticks that the frigate's midshipmen had been using to play Porter's naval game in the wardroom. Behind each of *Macedonian*'s guns and carronades a series of short laths of wood was tacked to the deck, looking like a decorative sunburst behind each gun. These were actually geometric aiming devices, coordinated carefully with one another so that, if a line were drawn from, for example, the second lath aft, all the lines would converge at a single spot in the ocean a given distance from the frigate.

This greatly simplified the procedure of aiming the guns, particularly for those guns below on the gun deck, where the gunners would normally have to squint through a small gunport obscured by powder smoke to find their target. Now all that was necessary was for an officer on the quarterdeck, in the sunlight and with a better view of the enemy, to estimate the range to the target and relay his estimation to all the guns. If the officer called out "two hundred yards," all the gunners would know to lay their gun parallel with the third lath aft, the lath adjusted for two hundred yards' range, adjust the quoins to the proper elevation, also determined ahead of time, and fire. All of *Macedonian*'s twenty-six broadside guns would converge on the same space two hundred yards from the frigate—any enemy would find that one section of his ship was being torn apart by superbly accurate broadsides, and as the battling ships altered position the enemy would find the American frigate's point of aim shifting, making hash out of one section of his ship after another.

Things had changed a great deal since the days of Favian's father, when the standard tactic of successful naval gunners was to get within point-blank range—"biscuit's throw," as it was called, so close that the guns could not miss—and start firing the guns as fast as they could be loaded and run out, assuming that if a large number of the shot missed it was only to be expected. The guns themselves had not changed—*Macedonian*'s main battery of eighteen-pounder long guns was substantially the same as the eighteen-gun battery on any frigate in 1776, but the tactics for using the weapons had altered radically. In the Revolution gunners could be assured of accuracy only by closing with the enemy, getting inside a hundred yards; aboard *United States* Favian had been able to fire perfectly accurate broadsides out to six or seven hundred yards. *Macedonian*'s lighter main battery would not strike accurately quite as far, but perhaps using Broke's aiming system would do nearly as well.

The Revolutionary methods, however, had their advantages. The drill was simple: the gunners practiced loading and running out as swiftly as they could, and once they had achieved celerity could congratulate themselves on being able to do as well as any enemy they were likely to encounter. Since they rarely fired in practice, expenditures in powder and shot were kept to a minimum.

The three Revolutionary Markham privateers, Favian's father Jehu and his uncles Josiah and Malachi, had been rare among their contemporaries in insisting on live-powder exercise, giving their crews experience in actually firing off their ordnance, but it had not occurred to them to question the basic gunnery practices of their day, or to apply the new-burgeoning technology, beginning to make its appearance elsewhere in their world, to the practice of gunnery.

Favian's gunners would have to learn a great deal more about their weapons than in Jehu's day. They would have to learn to fire by section; they would have to learn the proper elevation for their guns at a given range; they would have to learn to coordinate their fire with the ranging laths tacked to the deck; twice a week, at least, Favian would insist on their actually firing their guns at a floating target; they would, in short, have to *learn* a great deal about their guns and capabilities. The aristocratic assumptions of the eighteenth century, in which the common run of seaman was assumed to be incapable or unwilling to learn anything of science or technology, were giving way to the egalitarian notions that had swept the world since the revolutions in America and France—that the common man was capable of learning, of betterment, of adapting to the new scientific world that was emerging.

And now, Favian realized as the gun drill progressed, his progressive notions had been given a jolt by the appearance of something as unexpected as witchcraft on the quarterdeck. The scientific paradise of the early nineteenth century had suddenly been startled by the appearance of a stark medieval anachronism, crawling out of the past to bring with it a cargo of madness, curses, Jonahs, witch burnings, and charges of heresy—for what complaint did Lazarus have against the Finn if it was not practicing witchcraft as prescribed by Lazarus's dark gods? Favian had always been aware of certain sailors' superstitions—they were dead set against leaving port on Fridays, for example, saying it was bad luck—and Favian's friend William Burrows had often disguised himself as a common seaman and gone among them, learning their ways and beliefs, occasionally transmitting to a surprised Favian the conviction that bosun's mates could never be summoned to hell, or that possession of the feather of a wren could guard against drowning for a year. Favian had not taken any of these ideas seriously, assuming that sooner or later education would eradicate the most obnoxious of them, and that in the meantime they could be tolerated, but Burrows had always insisted that the beliefs had to be respected, if for no other reason than that the sailors themselves believed them, and that it was the duty of a good officer to know what motivated his men.

It had been Burrows who had introduced Lazarus to Favian, and from that time Favian had begun to accept Burrows's opinions. Whatever might occur in the future, the sailors at present *were* uneducated, very often illiterate even in the American service, and believed heart and soul in a vast number of absurd superstitions. Favian, a skeptic even as regards conventional religion, was forced to accept that the beliefs had reality for the men themselves—Lazarus had assisted in that acceptance—and he had made allowances for them. He was heartily glad, for instance, that *Macedonian* had not departed New London on a Friday.

But no allowances could be made for the projected assassination of an accused witch. No compromise could be made here; the cold rationality of the scientific nineteenth century would come down hard on this madness, backed by the nigh-absolute authority of the captain and officers of a United States man-of-war.

The gun drill was a success; the hands seemed to understand what was expected of them and tried their best to perform it. They were not yet as fast as they would be with practice, but, considering many were new not only to Favian's system but the routines of a warship, they were far better than Favian had any right to expect. Jacob Jones and Adrian Stone had picked their men with care, and Favian was benefiting considerably from their diligence. Favian concluded that after another week of this, including some live-firing exercises, he could introduce another drill: the daily rotation "with the sun" of the men at the guns, so that each crewman could step into the role of another if the latter was wounded. In any combat the gun crews could be expected to take casualties; if the men were skilled at the duties of their neighbors the crews could continue firing efficiently even after their mates had been taken below to the surgeon.

The drill over, Favian congratulated the hands on their aptitude, seeing their pleased grins, and then called for Lieutenant Stone and the master-at-arms to report to him in his cabin.

"Lazarus has provided the solution to our mystery of this morning, gentlemen," Favian informed them. "It seems that our Able Seaman Koskey has been accused of being a witch."

Stone's normally stern face took on a look of surprise. "Witchcraft, sir?" he asked, scarcely believing, but Herzog accepted the information without a blink.

"That makes sense, Captain," Herzog said. "No one wants a Jonah on the ship. The preacher was bad enough, but a witch!" Favian looked at Herzog carefully. The portly master-at-arms had risen from the ranks, and could be expected to be more familiar than the first lieutenant with the beliefs of the lower deck—if, that is, Herzog did not actually share them.

"Witchcraft on *my* lower deck," Stone fumed, his features hardening. "I'll put a stop to it, sir."

"It seems that Koskey's life may be in danger," Favian said. "I don't know if word of Lazarus's beliefs has reached you, but the man is a hardened devil worshiper. He considers Koskey a rival and may well be the center of any conspiracy against him."

Stone looked astounded. Murder on a United States vessel was almost as rare as a trial for witchcraft. His jaw tightened grimly. "Sir," he said, "if there's actually murder in the air, we'll have to move fast. Round up the ringleaders and make an example of them. Before it spreads. But Lazarus, he's been treated differently, ah—" Stone hesitated, searching for words.

Favian knew what Stone was trying to say. Lazarus was probably regarded as something of the captain's protégé, and to act against him might be thought of as an attack on the captain by way of one of his favorites. "Mr. Stone, I know that I brought Lazarus aboard," Favian said. "Ashore he's acted as something of a servant, but now that he's aboard *Macedonian* he's just an able seaman deputed to act as chantyman. If proof can be brought against him, I'll treat him no differently from any other man in the crew."

Stone seemed much relieved. Herzog pursed his lips, his eyes abstracted, and then he looked up. "Captain, I don't see how I'm goin' to be able to protect this man Koskey," he said. "He's got his duties aloft like anyone else; he sleeps among the men. If he's hurt I may be able to find out who did it afterwards, but that won't stop any attack from happenin'."

"Put the word out among the men," Stone said. "Tell them that Koskey is being looked out for. Tell them that I'll see that any man who does murder is hanged."

"I'll do it, sir," Herzog said, clearly ill at ease. "But, beggin' your pardon, the best way to handle this is to get the Jonah off the ship. It won't be a happy ship until Koskey leaves. An' that's my opinion, sir."

The last words were spoken in a defiant tone, his eyes leveled at Favian as if daring the captain to contradict his words. Instead Favian turned away, staring out the great curving stern windows at the ship's wake. Even Herzog believed in the existence of a Jonah, it seemed. When the chief enforcer of ship's discipline half-believed in witches himself, it would be that much harder to protect Koskey and punish any attackers. He turned back.

"We're on a long voyage," he said. "We have no plans to touch port for months. The ship will have to learn to live with Koskey, and Koskey with the ship." The master-at-arms shrugged.

"I've spoke my piece, sir," he said.

"I see your point, but it's impossible to put Koskey ashore," Favian said. "As for the moment, I think it's time to interview Koskey himself. He may be able to give us some assistance."

Entering the sick bay forward, Favian was surprised to find the Reverend Doctor Solomon, *Macedonian*'s chaplain, sitting at his ease in the next bunk to the reputed witch. "Greetings, Captain Markham, Mr. Stone, Mr. Herzog," Solomon said cheerfully, saluting. "I was talking with Koskey here about the Baltic. Comfort to the sick, y'know. Fascinating, the customs of these foreign lands."

"Yes," Favian said. "It's just some of those customs I've come to ask about. Koskey, are you aware that the men on board accuse you of being a witch?"

Koskey's eyes widened, darting about the room as if seeking escape. Finally the eyes returned to Favian, and he nodded.

"A witch? Truly?" Solomon asked, delighted.

"Koskey," Favian asked. "Is it true? Are you a witch?"

Koskey, obviously terrified, shook his head. "Nay!" he shouted. "I ain't no witch. Anybody who says I'm a witch is crazy!"

"You've never cast any spells, or done anything to make them suspect you?" Favian asked.

"Nay. Nothin' like that. They think that because I'm a Finn, I got to be a witch. They got some dumb ideas."

"A witch!" Solomon marveled. "How delightful! I think perhaps I might be able to pen a monograph on the subject—*Quaint Superstitions on Board United States Vessels of War*, something like that. With a plea to the Missionary Society to furnish educational materials for the crewmen who wish to rise above their low state." He rubbed his hands. "Quite an undertaking, but I think I'm up to it."

"Doctor Solomon, your pardon, but this is serious business," Favian interrupted. He turned to Koskey.

"Koskey, if you knew they thought you were a witch, why didn't you tell us this morning?" he asked. "You could have helped your case if you had told the truth."

Koskey shrugged. "I thought if you knew I was a Finn you might give me a flogging," he said. "Americans hate Finns, I guess. Don't know why."

Favian looked down at the bruised man in his swaying sickbed, certain the man was telling the truth. He didn't know how Finns had got the reputation for being sorcerers—the belief was probably as old as the Dark Ages—but he'd heard of the superstition before, and lying here before him was one of its victims.

"Koskey," he asked, "can you cook?"

Koskey's bruised face registered surprise. "Cook, sir?" he said. "I can boil salt beef, but that's all. Not cook for a gentleman, if that's what you mean."

"I see." Favian had had a thought that if Koskey could cook, he could replace Crane, his current steward, who had still not learned to make good coffee. That would allow him to sleep aft with the officers, and give him some measure of protection from the others aboard the frigate.

"You can hand, reef, and steer?" Favian asked.

"Oh, aye," Koskey said. "As good as any sailor on the ship, sir."

"And can you handle a small boat?"

Koskey nodded. "Aye, sir. I sailed a lot of little boats when I was a boy in Finland."

"Very well, Koskey," Favian said. "If the officers in your division think you'd be suitable, I'll make you my cox'n. That'll give you command of my pinnace in port, and allow you some special duties. You'll share a cabin aft with my clerk, and that should prevent any more attacks."

Koskey's bruised lips widened in a smile. "I won't give you no trouble, Captain," he said, blazing with pride, and Favian nodded. He turned to the first lieutenant.

"Mr. Stone, I'll ask you to interview Mr. Koskey's officers, and if their reports are favorable see that the appointment is entered officially on the rolls."

"That would be Mr. Eastlake and Mr. Midshipman Stanhope," Stone said, displaying his encyclopedic knowledge of the ship's crew. "I'll check with them directly. Oh, Koskey—your first name is Koozey, is it not? I'll need to know how to spell it."

"No, sir," Koskey said. "My first name is Vihtori—in English that would be Victor."

"Victor?" Stone asked. "I thought you were enrolled as Koozey Koskey?"

"That's my last name, sir. My name is Vihtori Kuusikoski. I don't know how they wrote it down when I joined, Mr. Stone."

"Can you write? Is your hand able to hold a pencil?" Stone asked. The Finnish sailor nodded. "You'd better spell it."

Kuusikoski took a pencil and notebook from Dr. Solomon and wrote carefully. Favian watched him painfully composing the letters in Gothic script—apparently Finland used the German alphabet—and then glanced at the odd name as he passed the notebook from Kuusikoski to Lieutenant Stone. *Kuusikoski*. Such a strange spelling. At least "Koozey Koskey" was a fairly successful way to pronounce it.

"Very well," he said, as Stone carefully tore the sheet of paper from the notebook and handed it back to Dr. Solomon. "I think we all have duties elsewhere. Dr. Solomon. Dr. Truscott."

"Delighted, sir," Solomon said. "I shall continue my discussion with our patient, if I may. I am fascinated by this witchcraft business. Perhaps it will furnish the material for a sermon against superstition."

"I wish you success, Doctor Solomon," Favian said, and stepped out of the sick bay. He heard Truscott, the surgeon, call out softly behind him.

"Captain Markham. A word with you, if I may." Favian turned to the surgeon.

"Yes, Dr. Truscott?"

"This witchcraft business may prove difficult to deal with," Truscott said. "I'm not sure you and Lieutenant Stone know just how deep the currents of superstition run in these people."

Favian frowned. "They've been stirred up by some unscrupulous men, no doubt. Lazarus among them. But I hope our measures may prove effective."

"Yes. Our colorful fiddling madman has not helped," Truscott said. "But hatred of witches runs deep in the seamen, and in the New England seamen particularly."

"Dr. Truscott," Favian said. "The witches at Salem were hanged well over a hundred years ago. We have come a long way since then."

"I hope we have," Truscott said. "But there is much that remains. Have you ever looked at the hinges on the cabinets in your cabin?"

Favian remembered the ornate iron hinges on his cabin furniture; they were common in New England, known as H and L hinges from the extra spur on each that helped to fix it to the door. They were a graceful, ornamented design, and Favian had grown up with many such.

"Yes, I've noticed them," Favian said. "They're a standard design. What of them?"

"It may interest you to know," Truscott said, "that the design of those hinges was originally a charm." He looked up at Favian, his face solemn. "A charm against witches, and the works of the devil. They're on half the cabinets in New England."

18

The thumping rhythm of the marine drummers echoed through the ship, a steady baritone drumming to which the staccato call of the trumpet and the whistle of bosuns' pipes sounded in soprano contrast. On the berth deck, half-awake men groped blindly to roll their hammocks and run to their stations; on the gun deck men began to fumble with the lashings of the guns; on the quarterdeck, where Favian stood wrapped in his heaviest cloak, surrounded by his heavy-lidded officers keeping one eye on their stopwatches, the stars were still out.

It would be dawn in less than half an hour, and as long as there was a chance of the rising sun revealing an enemy force nearby, Favian intended that *Macedonian* meet each dawn standing at quarters. He stood on the weather quarterdeck, out of the way of the sailors stumbling up to man the quarterdeck carronades.

Below he heard miscellaneous crashes and bumps, indicating that the light wooden screens forming his cabin were being taken apart and whisked to the hold, lest they form a splinter hazard during battle. Lazarus, huddled into his pea jacket, his eyes wary under his leather cap, climbed cautiously onto the poop and stood with folded arms by the barricade.

Division by division, the hands were reported at their stations. "Eight minutes, thirty seconds, Captain," Adrian Stone reported, saluting; Favian uncovered in reply and said, "Very well."

They waited while the eastern sky lightened, then turned a blazing red, casting an orange reflection on the bottoms of the light, trailing clouds. The lookouts, normally on deck during the night, went aloft as the day approached, the better to take advantage of the increased visibility. The wind that had blown them into the Atlantic was still behind them, northwesterly now; its force had blown them across the Gulf Stream and into the colder southward currents on its Atlantic side; the wind had lightened greatly, but it was still cold. The cold wind and the mix of cold and warm currents tended to produce mists, squalls, and unpredictable weather. Sail had been much reduced at night for safety's sake, since approaching storms could not have been seen; now that the horizon was extended and seen to be clear, topgallants and courses were set and *Macedonian* began to rush through the water, a fine bone in its teeth, its sails, reflecting the dawn, a breathtaking, translucent brick red.

"A beautiful sunrise, sir," Stone offered, and Favian nodded. Four bells was struck: six o'clock in the morning, the time when, following Jacob Jones's revised shipboard schedule, the men should be fed. Favian had decided to continue with Jones's schedule, a useful reform; but as long as dawn continued about this hour the hands' breakfast would continue to be delayed.

At last the sun rose, banishing the red dawn and bringing blue to the sky. The men, standing at quarters, began to cast surreptitious glances at their captain, wondering when he would give the order to stand down. Favian was aware of the glances and the impatience of the men, but waited until the sun had cleared the horizon and the lookouts proclaimed the ocean clear for at least fifteen miles around before he gave orders to dismiss from quarters, and afterwards pipe the hands to breakfast.

Amid the relieved bustle Favian headed for the poop ladder, intending to get his own breakfast. He passed by Lazarus, still standing at his station forward of the mizzen, and saw the madman's cunning, insolent glance; Lazarus seemed to have regained a great deal of his confidence since he'd been sent scampering from the poop the day before. Lazarus saluted, doffing his leather cap; Favian ignored him, his face impassive as he headed below. The witchcraft business was not over, he knew. If anything went amiss Lazarus would seize on the incident to proclaim his theory of the frigate's carrying a Jonah, and that would lead to more trouble, perhaps even tragedy.

The only way to prevent it, Favian thought, was to prevent anything from going wrong. Quite a task, on a large frigate on its first voyage with nearly four hundred men aboard, officers and men both unused to the ship and to each other, the frigate with hundreds of untried working parts all subject to chafe, stress, or fatigue. Favian could only hope that any trouble would be minor, and that once any minor trouble started he would be alert and active enough to keep it that way.

He was halfway through his breakfast when there was a knock on his cabin door. "Mr. Stone sends his respects, and wishes to report a sail to the east'ard, Captain," Midshipman Killick reported, saluting; Favian acknowledged, sent his respects to Stone, and said he would be on deck shortly.

Favian bolted the rest of his breakfast and half a cup of coffee in thirty seconds, then drew on his cloak and made a run for the poop ladder. Calling the hands from breakfast, he altered *Macedonian*'s course from south southeast to east by north, set two topmast staysails and the royals to help accelerate the frigate on its new course, and sent the men back to their meals. Then he rummaged in the binnacle box for a long glass, slung it over his shoulder by its strap, and made his way forward to the foremast shrouds.

He hadn't been aloft in months, though he'd been planning to go up and inspect *Macedonian*'s masts, yards, and rigging in minute detail as soon as he could. Now, he supposed, was as good an opportunity as any.

Favian was pleased to discover that he hadn't lost his reflexes; he mounted steadily and surely, dangling inverted from the futtock shrouds when mounting to the fighting top, then made his way to the crosstrees at the base of the topgallant mast. Here the lookout saluted and pointed to the distant chaff on the eastern horizon; Favian braced the glass against the sturdiness of the topgallant mast, compensated, with a little difficulty, for the roll of the ship and its exaggerated whipping of the mast, and brought the distant ship leaping into focus.

The fleck of white was hull-down perhaps twelve miles distant, royals set, close-hauled a little north of west; the lack of perspective made it difficult to determine anything else, but Favian received an impression of massiveness, heaviness, and ultimately familiarity. Could it, he wondered, be a large transport? Perhaps an Indiaman that had lost its convoy? Or a British ship of the line, with a broadside throwing double *Macedonian*'s weight of metal?

He watched as the ship came closer, persistently nagged by the thought that he'd seen this particular set of sails before. It was just after an unexpected roll had jogged the telescope, and Favian saw to his surprise another set of sails some miles astern of the first, that he felt the indistinct memory slide into place, and with a jolt he recognized the first ship as the British *Majestic*, Captain John Hayes, the large razee frigate he'd seen, day after day, tacking back and forth off Sandy Hook as it blockaded New York. And was the ship behind *Majestic* another of Hayes's squadron, perhaps the frigate *Endymion*?

No matter. *Macedonian* was a typical thirty-eight gun frigate, mounting eighteen-pound long guns on the gun deck with thirty-two-pound carronades above, while *Majestic* was a razee—a sail of the line with the top deck "razored" off—created for the purpose, English newspapers had proudly proclaimed, of fighting the big American spar-decked frigates, carrying twenty-four pounders on the gun deck and forty-two-pound carronades. *Macedonian* couldn't possibly face her in open combat, let alone her possible consort; it was high time to assume the better part of valor.

Macedonian would not be sailing at her best in this light wind, Favian knew, but even so there was no ponderous, overgunned razee she couldn't outrun under any conditions. Favian, not wanting to waste the few minutes it would take him to reach the deck, cupped his hands and bellowed his orders down to his officers; by the time he got down to the foretop the frigate was already commencing its turn to the southwest, downwind and away from the enemy; when he planted his feet on the deck the topmen were already springing for the shrouds to get the studding sails set.

It was not long before the British responded: *Majestic* turned ponderously in chase, guns booming to call attention to its signals, and its consort turned within minutes and began spreading canvas aloft. Favian set a flying jib, topgallant staysails, and debated getting up the hope-in-heavens, moonrakers, or trust-in-gods— the little scraplike sails set above the royals, and used so rarely they had no set name. He decided against it for the present; the sails were so small they would contribute only negligibly to the frigate's progress.

Markham's Recording Log was cast, and the speed found to be gratifying: Midshipman Stanhope, sent aloft with the long glass, reported that *Majestic* was falling behind, but that her consort seemed to be overhauling, and that—even more alarming—a third ship had made its appearance at the tail of the British column. Favian scowled, feeling a petulant annoyance; it seemed unfair that Captain Hayes should bring three-fifths of his regular squadron away from their duty, and be so rewarded for their neglect as to find an American frigate at liberty in the great space of the Atlantic. Perhaps they'd been blown out by the storm; perhaps they'd gone to Bermuda for victuals and water, perhaps Lazarus had caused Davey Jones to fetch them here—but here they were, and *Macedonian* could not hope to fight them all.

"Man the fire engine, and wet the lower sails," Favian ordered. "Hand butts and fire buckets to stays." There were two schools of thought about wetting sails: one said that a wet sail held more air and would propel the ship faster, but another thought a wet sail would grow too heavy and lose its shape. Favian had investigated over the years, and had wet sails aboard *Experiment* once to outrun a British frigate; he knew the tactic had worth. He'd set the hope-in-heavens as well. It was time to set every scrap of canvas the frigate possessed.

The fire hose gushed onto the courses while bucket brigades wet the topsails and topgallants, droplets spattering down onto Favian's shoulders and round undress hat; the sails did not lose their shape, and Markham's Recording Log registered a slight increase in speed. By now Favian was beginning to worry about the ship's trim; with so much sail set *Macedonian* was heeling heavily. Favian had read Mark Beaufoy's calculations on the resistance of solids moving through a liquid medium, and though he didn't agree entirely with their conclusions—Beaufoy's conclusions tended to support the notion of a great long hull combined with an absurdly narrow beam, like an exaggerated Mediterranean galley, which was plain foolishness—Favian understood that to increase *Macedonian*'s speed he needed to reduce the proportion of wetted surface. A large degree of heel meant that the hull was not meeting the water at an efficient angle, because too much was submerged—in effect, speed gained by increasing sail would be lost because of increased water resistance, one of the unpleasant compromises scientific sailors were always forced to cope with.

"Pipe the hammocks down," Favian said. "Each man place two shot in each."

Not counting the men detailed to handle the sails, that left three hundred men each carrying two eighteen-pound shot. If each man averaged 150 pounds barefoot, then each carrying thirty-six pounds of iron meant over 55,000 pounds of movable ballast Favian could use to trim the ship. He would probably need every pound.

"Beg pardon, Captain." It was the ship's chaplain, the Reverend Doctor Solomon.

"Doctor?" Favian asked, puzzled. He had not dealt with chaplains previously; he was not entirely certain of the precedents. Solomon's place during action was below, in the orlop deck, where he could assist the surgeon and comfort the wounded and dying; but the ship was not yet at quarters and, Favian realized, the chaplain had no other station.

"I was w-wondering, Captain Markham," Solomon said, a bit nervously—if he had any idea of how dangerous it was for a staff officer to address his captain during a perilous situation, he would have probably been a good deal more nervous—"if I might be of some service? Anything at all, sir."

Favian's first impulse was to tell Solomon to get to the orlop and not come out till Sunday, but he bit it back; relations between staff and line officers were rarely good, and he would not make them worse. "Indeed, yes, Doctor," he said, as civilly as he could. "Go below and fetch a blanket from your bunk. Put two roundshot in it and stand over there." Favian pointed. "Stay there until directed somewhere else."

"Of course, Captain," Solomon said cheerfully. "Most happy. Your servant, sir."

"Cut along, Doctor Solomon," Favian said, his temper putting an edge into his words; Solomon choked down his next sentence, bowed—he had not yet picked up the habit of saluting—and went for his blanket.

Markham's Recording Log verified that keeping most of the crewmen on the weather side increased *Macedonian*'s speed, as Favian expected, by half a knot; for a full hour he juggled groups of men, sending them forward or aft, in the end trimming the frigate slightly by the stern, a configuration that seemed to relieve the tendency of all the canvas she carried to press her bow down into each wave rather than lifting to meet it.

He could see the glances of the men, follow their eyes over *Macedonian*'s larboard quarter; he caught himself imitating their gaze more than once, looking over his shoulder to see the three scraps of flax on the horizon, all visible now from the deck. One sailor only did not glance nervously at the enemy: Favian, whenever he looked forward, saw the baleful eyes of Lazarus looking into his own, a solemn reproach, or assignment of guilt. Another of Lazarus's little predictions fulfilled, Favian thought; what would the man suggest now? Flinging Kuusikoski overboard in chopped-up pieces, as the Argonauts did with poor Apsyrtus, to delay the pursuit? Or a solemn invocation of Satan, like the old pirate Lewis, who would tear the hair from his own scalp and fling it into the breeze, saying "Good Devil take this till I come!"?

Blast Lazarus, Favian thought violently, and blast his damned superstitions. He could hope for miracles, but until a miracle came he would have to work with craft and science. He strapped on another long glass and walked to the mizzen shrouds, feeling Lazarus's silent, eloquent eyes on him, and mounted slowly to the mizzen top. The mizzen topmen, congregated like a social club here on the broad platform, fell silent as he made his appearance on the futtock shrouds; he gave them a curt nod as he swung inboard and adjusted the telescope.

Favian studied the three pursuers carefully for fully half an hour. The massive but clumsy *Majestic*, as Favian knew it would, was falling behind, and might well be out of sight by nightfall. The next astern—Favian was fairly certain it was *Endymion*, Captain Henry Hope—had overhauled *Majestic*, but if it was overhauling *Macedonian* as well it was doing so very slowly, and if nothing else intervened probably would not catch up by nightfall. That was a relief, for although *Endymion* was rated at forty guns, only a pair more than *Macedonian*, Favian knew her lower battery were twenty-four-pounders, guns that could tear *Macedonian* apart at long range without the possibility of effective reply, just as the twenty-four-pounders of the *United States,* under Favian's direction, had ripped apart *Macedonian* two years before.

No, it was the third British ship that worried Favian. He recognized her as *Tenedos,* Captain Hyde Parker—a man whose name in the British news sheets was followed by the curious parenthetical 3, meaning presumably that he was a grandson of the Sir Hyde Parker who had fought his way out of St. Lucia in the American Revolution, and son of the Hyde Parker who had ordered Nelson to retire at Copenhagen—a thirty-eight-gun frigate, as near *Macedonian*'s equal in broadside weight as no matter, but swifter. Much swifter, in fact—Favian saw that at present rates of sailing she would be up with *Macedonian* by midafternoon.

That would mean a fight on even terms—better than if it were *Majestic* that was catching up, or *Endymion,* but bad enough. Favian had been in command of *Macedonian* for four days; his crews had exercised at the great guns only once under his supervision. He remembered all too well what happened to his old Tripoli acquaintance Captain James Lawrence when he took *Chesapeake,* which he had commanded only a few days, out of Boston after the *Shannon.* That, too, had been an even fight, at least as far as the ships were concerned, but *Chesapeake* had been captured by Captain Broke in twenty minutes' fighting.

Captain Hyde Parker (3) was, Favian hoped, no Captain Broke, but he'd been commanding *Tenedos* for at least a year and had a far better notion of the capacities of his crew than Favian did of the *Macedonian*'s. And he did not have to fight a decisive combat; Favian, heart sinking, knew that all Parker had to do was skirmish at medium gunshot, forcing Favian to turn and fight him until *Endymion* caught up and put its twenty-four-pounders to work.

That would be the end of *Macedonian*'s raid on the Indian Ocean, and quite possibly the end of Captain Favian Markham, USN. He was aboard a ship that he had stolen, coming aboard and abducting her from the Thames: after a successful cruise Washington would have no option but to clench its teeth and join in the public ovation; but after a disastrous failure that included the loss of the United States' only prize frigate Favian could expect no mercy from the secretary of the navy.

Well, he would do what he could. At least it would not be said that he had not made a gallant defense; the inevitable court-martial would find that he had fought on until half his crew were disabled and the scuppers ran with blood. Hard on the crew, but the honor of the navy would be satisfied. Besides, he might get lucky and knock away a few of *Tenedos*'s spars and be able to make his escape.

He came down to the deck, determined to try at least one more trick. "Knock out the wedges," he ordered. "Give the masts full play." That would put a lot more stress on the shrouds and stays, but might produce half a knot or so, and a little more time for bad luck to strike the British. He'd wait another few hours and then start making signals, as if to a ship over the horizon; if Hayes was a dunderhead and thought an American squadron was just ahead he might recall the *Tenedos*. Probably Hayes was not a dunderhead, but the signals would look pretty and would give the signal midshipman something to do. Favian glanced aloft, making certain the sails were all drawing well, seeing the little hope-in-heavens set above the royals. Their name, he thought, was growing more appropriate with each passing minute.

At noon he sent the hands to their dinner; a little way was lost when the 55,000 pounds of movable ballast dispersed to its messes, but the navy's position was that if one was going to fight a hopeless battle it was best to die with a full stomach, and Favian agreed. When "up spirits" was piped Favian noticed that the men drank their rye and water quickly, as if they wanted to get drunk; he remembered the way *Experiment*'s men had thrown theirs contemptuously into the scuppers, claiming they didn't need Dutch courage, and wished he had at least a few of *Experiment*'s old hands here. The signal trick was tried and failed utterly: Hayes's squadron above others should know there was no American fleet on the loose. Favian, knowing battle would come sooner or later, went to his cabin to clip on his sword, load his pistols, and don his heavy boarding helmet. A resignation to the inevitable, to the unwished for, accepting a fight forced on him by circumstance.

Once his movable ballast had their meal, and he was able to adjust the ship's trim to make up for the heavy weights he would be shifting, he set carpenter's gangs to work below in his cabin and on the taffrail. Space was cleared for two stern chasers poking aft out of Favian's quarters, and another two jutting out through the taffrail; the twelve-pounder chase guns were shifted aft from the fo'c'sle, and two eighteen-pounders from the broadside were trundled into the cabin. Stone picked four gun crews from among those who had demonstrated ability in drills, and these were assigned to the new battery. *Tenedos* would soon be in gunshot.

There were other things Favian could have done to increase speed, but he had decided against them for the present: all would have hampered *Macedonian*'s ability to accomplish its mission. He could have sent axmen below to smash the water casks, and then pumped out the water—but that would have left the frigate dangerously low on water in the middle of a hostile ocean. He could have started heaving his guns overboard, but a warship without guns was worse than useless. He could have disposed of other dead weight: ship's boats, spare spars, the livestock quartered forward, some of the anchors—but these, likewise, would render a successful cruise less possible. Even so he might have tried such tricks if *Tenedos* had not been overhauling so damned quickly, but as matters stood lightening *Macedonian* would probably have only delayed the inevitable for an hour or so. His only hope, Favian thought, was to somehow disable Parker's frigate, or capture it—a faint hope indeed, that last.

There was a thump from astern: Favian looked up to see the gunshot strike the water four hundred yards astern. Parker (3) was showing his impatience; he should have known he was not yet in range. Favian craned his neck to view the other frigates: *Majestic* had almost fallen out of view, and *Endymion* seemed, if anything, to be falling behind. He rubbed his gloved hands together briskly; perhaps he would have time enough to deal with Parker.

"Let's get our flags aloft," he said. "It's obvious enough by now who we are."

The big battleflag went up at the peak, with another at the mizzen; the jack, fifteen stars on a blue field, went up at the fore and the jackstaff; at the main went the Markham pennant, the personal badge of his clan, a perquisite Favian was granting himself as captain, the golden snake rippling on its scarlet background. Favian looked balefully at the serpent and wondered if this afternoon would see its first defeat.

"Choose the roundest shot you can, lads, so it will fly true," he said. "We must cripple her aloft if we can; aim for the tops'l tie." That was a command of wildest optimism; they would be lucky to hit anything at all the way the stern was pitching up and down in the swells. "Wait until she's on a rise," he said, repeating old Preble's drill for accurate fire, "and wait until the instant before she begins to drop. *Then* you've got a stable platform: not before. Mr. Stone, take charge of this battery. I'll be going below to the eighteen-pounders."

There was another thump from *Tenedos*'s chaser as Favian went down the poop ladder; he did not have to see the splash to know it had fallen far astern. Not only were they eager, it seemed as if their officers did not know their weapons. It was the one encouraging piece of news in many hours.

His cabin was in a shambles: the thwartships settee had been torn out from below the bank of stern windows, while the glass from the windows had been ripped out and sent below along with the furniture; the windows had been widened with axes and then filled with the black eighteen-pounders, their iron muzzles pointing aft into the heaving sea, the rest of the room filled with the guns' crews, the sponges and rammers necessary for loading the guns, and a pair of shot garlands each filled with choice iron. The room smelled of gunpowder and fresh sawdust. Jasper Hourigan, the second lieutenant, gave a salute, and Favian returned it.

"You may load, Mr. Hourigan," Favian said. "Your roundest shot."

Three more splashes came from *Tenedos*—only one was in line with *Macedonian*—before Favian fired a gun, following his own advice of waiting for the following sea to lift the frigate's stern, incidentally giving him a clear view of *Tenedos*. It came lunging back into the great cabin until it stopped short at the limits of its tackles, the gushing smoke blown into the faces of the men straining for sign of a hit. There was none that they could see, not a pockmarked sail or a splash. After that frustrating opening the stern chasers began firing rapidly, the great cabin filling with smoke and crashing sound, the guns' roar huge in this confined space, the rumble of the guns running in and out of the port echoing from the beams. *Macedonian* had a total of four guns in action, and *Tenedos* had, it appeared, only two, the starboard fo'c'sle chaser and the number one gun on the gun deck; the American frigate seemed to Favian to be firing faster as well— the sheet-lead cartridges were an improvement over the old flannel ones the British were still using, a fortune of war Favian was happy to accept—but there was no major damage done.

Once Favian heard a crash above as an enemy shot lodged home, and for one paralyzing instant he saw a ball come skittering over the wavetops aimed directly for him, foreshortening as if it were headed directly between his eyes, before it seemed to dip at the last instant and slammed into the hull below his feet. Favian calmed his hammering heart and sent a runner below to see if the sternpost had been injured; the runner reported a twelve-pound solid had fetched up in the wardroom, where it had squashed the coffeepot flat, but no structural damage short of a new, rudely fashioned porthole in Lieutenant Chapelle's cabin, which the carpenter would attend to directly.

In return *Macedonian* seemed to be hitting *Tenedos* fairly regularly; Favian could see pockmarks in the sails, but *Macedonian* seemed to be displaying an infuriating inability to hit any of the damned spars. Once a fore topgallant studding sail was hit and carried away, but Captain Parker's men replaced that swiftly enough. And eventually *Tenedos*, its masts apparently as sound as the day they were stepped, took up a position off *Macedonian*'s larboard quarter where the chasers couldn't train to reach her, and Favian ordered his men to secure the guns, and at last ordered his unemployed crewmen to drop their weighed hammocks and stand at quarters. Quite soon the real fight would begin.

19

Vihtori Kuusikoski sat on his pallet on the orlop deck in the dim light of candles, his arms around his knees. He knew the enemy were near; it was obvious from the urgency with which he'd been taken below that the danger was serious. The foolish, friendly chaplain had been in and out, popping up on deck every so often to report the news as seen through one of the gun deck ports, and though his reports were difficult to understand—Doctor Solomon was no seaman—it was clear enough that there was more than one enemy. Doctor Seward bustled in the dim light, setting up his operating table on the chests of the midshipmen, his assistants setting out the tools of his trade, the saws that would grind through bone, the probes that would search for splinters and musket balls, the little sharp knives to part flesh and slice muscle away. When the guns began going off it was right over his head; even through the two decks between him and the eighteen-pounders he could hear the growling cannon recoiling back on their carriages.

Kuusikoski clenched his good hand. Once again he was an exile on this ship, banished below from the sick bay, useless to his mates. He did not long for danger or war; his thoughts were not of glory. But he did want to be a part of the life of the ship, a man among other men, a sailor among sailors. It was unfair that he should not be a part of this attempt to defend their mutual home. It would, he knew, be another barrier between himself and them, that he had not stood with them at this time. And if the battle were lost they would hold him responsible; he knew that as a certainty.

When the crash came, the splintering sound of a ball striking home, he lurched to his feet, pain shrieking through his muscles. He would not spend his time in this pit, soon to be filled with bloody men and the smell of death. He stumbled for the companionway, moving painfully.

"Where do you think you're going, Koskey?" Doctor Truscott stared at him commandingly with his deep-sunk eyes.

"To quarters. To my place," Kuusikoski said, heading for the companion.

"You can't haul a tackle in your condition! Get back to your place."

"I can carry a cartridge," Kuusikoski said desperately. "I can do something."

Truscott laid a hand on his arm. The man was stripped to the waist and wearing a leather apron that would soon be dripping blood. His face in the dim light was a death's head.

"Back to your place, Koskey! I can't let you go in your state."

Koskey looked at the loblolly boys, Truscott's assistants, and knew it was hopeless. Defeated, he shrunk back to his pallet.

The guns roared above him, their wheels grinding into the deck. They would blame him for a defeat, he knew, the Finnish witch. Foolish, to think that just because he was a *Suomalainen* he had such power. Fools and madmen, these Americans.

He visualized the fight above him, the stern chasers barking out at the pursuing enemy; he saw the balls curving through the air to strike the enemy or splash harmlessly into the sea. Let our cannon strike, he thought. Let the iron come to the enemy. Futilely, not believing in the power with which the other sailors credited him, he began to try to use it. If the others thought him a witch, he would act as a witch. Let the winds be fair, he thought. Let our guns strike home. Let confusion come to the enemy.

Dimly, without believing it, he repeated the phrases, knowing it was all he could do.

20

When Favian regained the poop he saw the powder-marked faces of the men, one white-faced bosun's mate, a bloody handkerchief tied around his upper arm, refusing to go below to have his splinter wound treated. "No other injuries, sir," Stone said, indicating the scarred white wood that marked *Tenedos*'s hit. Favian glanced aloft and saw the pockmarked sails that, fortunately, were all drawing quite well. There was a bang from *Tenedos*, followed by the hollow, shrieking wail of a shot passing overhead; Favian, caught by surprise, jumped nervously at the sound, then stiffened to his interior discipline. Dodging was useless at times like this; the navy held it a bad example.

Favian turned to look at the *Tenedos*, judging the situation. *Macedonian*'s chase guns no longer bore, but Hyde Parker's did. The two ships were sailing parallel courses with the wind from their starboard quarters, *Tenedos* to larboard and seven hundred yards astern, overhauling rapidly. Sooner or later Parker would overhaul *Macedonian*, and then both ships could commence regular broadsides at perhaps three hundred yards' range, unless one side or the other tried to close the distance.

Three hundred yards: that was extreme range for the thirty-two pound carronades both ships carried on their upper decks, a difficult sort of in-between range, a teasing range really—as if Parker wanted to tempt Favian with the possibility of fighting at decisive range, but intended to hold back, sparring, until *Endymion* made its appearance, or until *Macedonian* was forced to turn toward him—and *Endymion*—to narrow the range and finish the contest. Parker was playing his hand very well.

Favian remembered the exercise Stone had conducted on the wardroom deck, the way the little model ships had maneuvered with geometrical precision on the mock Connecticut coastline. He remembered how Lovette's *Orpheus* had maneuvered nimbly to put broadside after broadside into the model *Macedonian*, until Stanhope's *Tiber* had arrived with its heavier broadside to finish off the American frigate and win the day for Britain. The situation here was remarkably similar, with *Tenedos* standing in for *Orpheus* and *Endymion* for *Tiber*, except, of course, that no model ships were being knocked about; these were real frigates, with real broadsides and real crews who would risk dismemberment and death, paying forfeit with their bodies and lives for the decisions of their superiors.

Tenedos's chasers fired again, the shot wailing overhead, puncturing *Macedonian*'s spanker; Favian watched the flame blossom from the British frigate's bows, saw the dark blur of the shot, and heard the shriek and the smack of the ball puncturing the flax, the rattle of the spanker gear and the sudden, grinning exhalations of the quarterdeck hands who had been holding their breath, waiting for the iron—he saw it and scowled, too lost in his own abstractions to react to danger.

There was a value to thinking of this in terms of a game, the frigates as nothing but little scrap-wood models with tissue-paper sails; that was the way the navy had taught him to think. Hull, sails, wind, guns, crew, ocean: all abstracts, all counters to be maneuvered on a board, units subjected to their commander's will, to be moved along strictest Euclidean lines, the gunshot creating lovely arcs as they flew in obedience to the rules of velocity, acceleration, gravity, until they plunged into their targets or skipped along the sea like stones.

Aye, that was how the navy man had been taught to think, but there was more to his grim thoughts than that. He had taken the frigate to sea in a spirit of rebellion, clean against orders: did the navy not punish rebellion? In this battle he was facing not only the end of *Macedonian*'s adventures but the end of his career—and however much he might resent it, whatever in life he was, whatever in life he had, was the navy's, and the court-martial that ended his career would end all he had become since his sixteenth year.

Rash, they would say. Markham's Raid through the Narrow Seas was the epitome of rashness, bold but uncalculated, succeeding by luck; taking *Macedonian* to sea was more rashness, met this time with ill fortune. They would consider him another James Lawrence, a brave, likable man who, when things turned against him, had nothing but bravery to fall back on, and when bravery did not prove enough could do nothing but die gallantly in the aftermath of the greatest defeat the United States Navy had yet suffered. And he was not Lawrence, Favian knew; all the risks he had taken in this war had been calculated ones, the result of careful thought and science—he had been friends with Lawrence, but his mentors had been Preble and Burrows, men who were cunning as well as brave.

But Favian would be pegged with rashness, dismissed the service for it, and that would be that. Personally, aside from everything else, all the usual reasons, he could not afford to lose *Macedonian*.

Wild plans flickered through his mind. Run aboard the *Tenedos*, take her by boarding, abandon the *Macedonian*, and sail the faster *Tenedos* to safety. No; boarding was a medieval maneuver, conjuring up pictures of armored knights battling on narrow gangplanks while arrows whizzed overhead. It was difficult to accomplish against an enemy who was not either surprised or beaten into submission by gunnery. Besides, there was no guarantee that Captain Hyde Parker would be so foolish as to allow *Macedonian* to run alongside; his tactics thus far showed more caution than that.

Boarding was out. Perhaps he could succeed by the use of dismantling shot. Dismantling shot—an all-inclusive term embracing chain shot, bar shot, grapnel shot, spider shot, all the diabolical though dubious contrivances used to cut up rigging and tear sails asunder—might be able to strip Parker's sails from his yards, or if lucky cut enough shrouds and stays to bring a mast down.

But it would require luck. Dismantling shot were so oddly shaped that they would not fly straight; there was no possible way of accurate fire, and the only way to be certain of its effectiveness was to keep flinging the stuff into the air as fast as possible. The shot—lots of it—would have to hit in order to have an effect.

The worst of it was that while *Macedonian* was blasting all these odd contrivances at enemy masts in the hope of getting a lucky hit, *Tenedos* would be firing broadside after broadside into *Macedonian*'s hull, killing men and doing serious damage. Dismantling shot was too unpredictable—too *unscientific*.

Dismantling shot, like boarding, was put aside, although the idea of getting a lucky hit on the enemy masts was not. Both frigates were carrying a lot of sail, and Favian, for one, had no intention of shortening sail down to battle canvas before opening fire. The masts and yards were strained to the utmost; any hits on them with roundshot, fired low into the hull, might eat into a mast below decks and bring it crashing down. If it happened to *Tenedos*, Favian could make his escape. If it happened to *Macedonian*, then Favian would have no choice but to try a desperate tactic—the boarding plan, probably—before hauling down his colors.

He saw *Tenedos* coming nearer, feeling the weight of the boarding helmet on his head, hearing the battleflag snapping on its halyard. Four hundred yards between them, he thought; the British captain was overtaking swiftly. There would be battle soon; and now that he knew what he was going to do, he found himself mentally urging Parker's ship forward. Get it over with, he thought, one way or the other.

Then he saw the enemy frigate's yellow stripe widening, the ports becoming distinct as *Tenedos* yawed to larboard, presenting its broadside. There was an instant in which Favian saw his enemy's strategy in all its cunning, cautious glory, and then he was turning forward and barking at the top of his lungs "Everyone lie down! Pass the word to lie right down on the deck!"

He heard the subdued rumble of nearly four hundred men obeying; he himself turned with disdainful pride—there was nothing left, really, but to become a Lawrence—facing what was to come. He saw the enemy guns in their ports, the white faces of gun captains peering over their pieces, and he began to count the enemy guns because, for the moment, there was no other occupation for his mind.

Parker was not bringing *Tenedos* into a fight. He was going to stay right where he was, off *Macedonian*'s larboard quarter where not a single American gun would reach him; *Tenedos* could stay there forever, yawing every so often to fire crippling broadsides. If Favian turned to fight him, he would no longer be running: *Endymion* would soon arrive, and that would be the end.

Tenedos's broadside exploded into smoke, flame, and iron; the shot came screaming overhead like a thousand bloodthirsty demons, the frigate quaking as its timbers absorbed the iron, shot striking the hammock nettings, spilling hammocks out onto the deck, hitting the bulwark to create waves of humming splinters, or shrieking high aloft to punch through canvas. Favian, in despairing, officerlike detachment, could tell that it was not, for all its effect, a well-delivered broadside: *Tenedos* had too much canvas aloft and was moving too fast for proper delivery.

Unless *Macedonian* began losing spars or *Tenedos*'s gunnery began to improve, Favian calculated, the American could probably take this for another hour or more; every time Parker yawed his ship he lost way and *Macedonian* forged ahead; Parker would have to yaw back to starboard and regain the ground he'd lost before he could fire again. Having the crew lie down would minimize their casualties, but still every broadside would weaken *Macedonian* until, eventually, she was helpless. If Favian was going to fight, he had better do it soon.

Favian saw the British frigate begin to swing back on its track, ready to take up the chase; he turned forward, glancing aloft to see a few new punctures in the sails, then looked down to see his crew stretched out on the deck, officers lying promiscuously amid the private sailors, their heads raised curiously to look at Favian. There were no casualties that he could see. "On your feet," Favian said gruffly, his head buzzing with plans.

"Next time she yaws," he said, as Stone rose by him, picking tar from the knees of his trousers, "we'll yaw with her and open fire with the larboard battery. I'll ask you and Mr. Seward to handle the helm—when you see the enemy begin their move, gybe and then luff her. You'll have to be careful gybing the spanker. I'll have those stuns'ls brought in, too, but I'll want 'em ready to set later. I'll be going below to the gun deck—the gunners will have three or four minutes to get ready, and I want to make the most of it. Understand?"

"Aye, sir."

Favian seized a speaking trumpet and dashed down the poop ladder, his sword clattering on the steps as he ran. He heard Stone's voice calling out to the sail trimmers to man the studding sail tripping lines, tacks, halyards, sheets, and downhauls, ready to bring the big, clumsy wings in as soon as *Macedonian* began its turn.

Favian was on the gun deck, seeing the long eighteen-pounders in their rows, their crews half standing by passively, half still lying on the deck, all regarding Favian with sober attention. Favian glanced fore and aft—no casualties here, either, though the bulwarks were scarred with hits; *Macedonian* had been lucky—and then raised the speaking trumpet to his lips.

"We'll be gybing in a few minutes, men," he said. "We're going to fight 'em gun for gun, with you men of the larboard battery." He paced as he walked, gesturing vigorously with his free hand. "Now we're still carrying a lot of canvas," he said, "and we're going to have a devil of a heel, which will try to make you fire high. Don't let it. We've got to give the enemy a hulling, and that means fire *aimed at the hull. Aimed,*" he repeated, "not just shot off in the general direction of the enemy. I don't want any of the gun captains to fire their pieces unless they know they'll hit—there's no point to fast fire if it doesn't hit the enemy."

He paused, seeing the hands exchanging glances. He had told them this before during the few gunnery drills he'd conducted, and they knew it in theory. But he hadn't yet conducted any live-firing exercises to show them his principles; he'd have to simply enunciate them and hope that they would remember.

"Aim for the hull," he repeated. "We'll be opening at three hundred yards' range. Now, Commodore Preble taught his men the best time to fire—I've told you this before, but now I'm going to repeat it to make sure you understand. It's just after a wave has lifted the ship, and just before the ship falls into the next trough. There's a moment of hesitation there, and you must seize it."

"Captain Markham!" It was Stone, bawling down from the poop barricade. "They're yawing, sir!"

"Commence your turn, Mr. Seward! Larboard broadside, run

out! Starboard broadside, I want you lying down unless you're replacing a wounded man, or carrying wounded below."

Favian, after he'd bellowed out his orders, ran back up to the poop, hearing the rumbling of the larboard broadside as the guns were hauled out of the ports, the cadence of orders from the mast captains to get in the studding sails, which had only been set on the weather side: "Tend the outer halyards and the outhaul . . . lower away, haul down . . . rig in . . ."

"Handsomely, handsomely . . ." Another set of orders was heard on the poop as the spanker sheet was eased under Stone's supervision. *Tenedos*'s turn was well advanced, her wake foaming, her weather studding sails flapping with a sound like distant gunshots as they were deprived of their wind. *Macedonian*'s spanker crashed over to leeward; sails began lifting as they came edge-on into the wind. Favian had left it too late; he should have turned first, without waiting for *Tenedos*. It would have avoided this hurry, the hurry in which something was almost guaranteed to go wrong.

"Braces, thar!" Seward's voice sang over the deck; there were only a limited number of sail handlers and most were aloft getting in the studding sails. Favian pointed to the unengaged starboard carronade crews, gestured them to the braces. Too late, the thought repeating itself, too late, never sacrifice the initiative again.

Tenedos's broadside came tearing at them before their turn was completed; all at once the enemy frigate's broadside gushed smoke and the air was full of screaming. *Macedonian* shuddered as the broadside—delivered more slowly this time, with greater precision, at a broader target—lodged home. Favian glanced uneasily forward, seeing someone down on the quarterdeck, his mates bent over him, wondering how many lives his blunder had cost. "Overhaul the lifts forrard of the yards." The mast captains were still going about the business of bringing in the studding sails, as if nothing had happened. "Trice up the gear."

Macedonian was slowing, wallowing, its sails not yet trimmed to the new course; but *Tenedos* appeared caught by surprise, uncertain whether or not to resume its old heading. Parker had put his helm amidships while he made up his mind, and the British frigate now was on a converging course with *Macedonian*, moving into the arc of its guns. The American frigate's loss of speed had lowered her maneuverability, but had greatly increased her steadiness as a gun platform. "Ready, larboard guns!" Favian roared into his speaking trumpet. "Fire as you bear! Make certain of every shot!"

He could hear the officers repeating his orders on the gun deck, and then a brass-lunged bellow that could only have come from Midshipman Thomas Tolbert, commanding the quarterdeck guns below. "We'll give it to 'em like we gave it to the *Teaser!* Hurrah for Yankee Doodle! *Fire, number twelve!*"

Tolbert, Favian observed, had moderated his usual impulsiveness; the order was well timed. His aftmost eighteen-pounder went off with a crack, followed shortly by the quarterdeck carronades and the other guns in the broadside, the ship's side suddenly gushing smoke. Favian saw punctures appearing in *Tenedos*'s sails, white feathers leaping up from her waterline. A good first broadside.

"Independent fire!" Favian shouted. "Two hundred fifty yards!" His preferred system of firing by sections required a crew more highly trained than the one he had available: independent fire would assure that the faster gun crews would not be held back by the slower. If only, he thought, he could have his old gun crews from *United States;* he had trained them for two years, and during the original fight with *Macedonian* he'd been able to order them to fire at the number two or three gunport, or to shoot away the mainmast, and they'd complied with ease. Not with these men; they were too new. He'd hoped that by the time the frigate got to the Indian Ocean he would have trained them thoroughly; now he'd have to trust to less scientific methods and hope for the best.

Tenedos swung to larboard, Parker having finally made up his mind, British sail trimmers going aloft to take in the studding sails. The two frigates were now on parallel courses, perpendicular to their original track. Seward's men got *Macedonian*'s yards braced round, and the sails filled, the ship heeling.

Macedonian and *Tenedos* raced along parallel to each other, guns firing as fast as they could be loaded and run out the ports, each ship still carrying far too much canvas aloft for safety or accurate fire. Favian went below to the gun deck, pointing and aiming the guns, giving quiet instruction to the gun captains when it was necessary, giving cheerful advice to the officers, many of whom were new to the work and needed it. "Wait, now, wait," he said over and over, crouching to look over a long iron barrel. "Feel that wave coming? Here's your time—*fire!*" Midshipman Tolbert, he noticed, was strutting jut-jawed behind his gun section with a drawn cutlass, presumably with the intent of running anyone through who tried to run; but Tolbert's guns were well served, and knew their drill—apparently Tolbert had learned something on the *Experiment* cruise after all.

Macedonian's fire, so far as Favian could tell, was faster than that of the enemy; the superior sheet-lead cartridges were helping there. He thought, though, that both ships were firing high; most of *Tenedos*'s fire wailed high overhead, though iron still came crashing into *Macedonian*'s timbers regularly, killing a few men outright, sheafs of splinters bringing down others. *Macedonian* was heeling and probably for that reason, as well as her inexpert gunners, her fire was pitched high.

Favian returned to the poop. Once out of the black, smoke-shrouded gun deck, he could see that *Tenedos* had her helm down slightly, increasing the range. Favian swore under his breath; Parker was toying with him, keeping out of decisive range until *Endymion*, sailing toward them at three hundred yards per minute, could arrive to finish the contest. Parker was not a glory-struck captain, risking defeat for the honor of defeating the *Macedonian* alone; he was an intelligent man. Damn him.

"Starboard your helm," Favian ordered. Perhaps it was a mistake—he would actually be sailing a little toward *Endymion* now—but he wanted to get *Tenedos* out of the fight if he could.

The air filled with wailing; the quarterdeck shuddered as a thirty-two pound solid plunged down from the sky to crash onto the planking, throwing up splinters as it rebounded to carom off one of the unused starboard carronades before spinning to a halt. The enemy's carronades were no longer at effective range, Favian realized; the ball did not penetrate. His own carronades would be as useless; it was the long guns below that were doing the work that needed doing.

"Carronades to load dismantling shot," Favian decided. Dismantling shot could be no more useless than solids at this range.

The dismantling shot added a new sound to the cacophony of battle, an eery banshee shrieking that brought erect the small hairs at the back of Favian's neck. *Tenedos* was edging away again, drawing *Macedonian* toward her consort. Favian glanced uneasily at the sight of *Endymion*—hull-up now, near enough for her form to fill with imminent menace. The solid anvil on which Parker would pound him flat.

He heard the boom across three hundred yards of water, the distinct sound—awesome close up, unmistakable at a distance—of tons of flax tearing itself to shreds; and suddenly his heart lifted as he looked at *Tenedos* and saw her main topsail flogging itself to bits, asunder. "Helm up, Mr. Seward!" he shouted, glee filling him—he was going to get away; he'd have the heels of all of them! *Macedonian* curled away from the battle, a turn to starboard as neat as a compass, *Tenedos* firing a few last shots that whimpered high and eventually missed entirely, whipping up white feathers off *Macedonian*'s larboard beam.

"Get those stuns'ls aloft," Favian said, seeing British crewmen swarming up the main shrouds to secure the tearing canvas, *Tenedos* commencing a belated swing to starboard. A sunny happiness filled his soul. "Man the stern chasers. After we have the stuns'ls set, I'll want our sheet anchors hove overboard—then pipe down hammocks again and fill 'em with roundshot. Sail trimmers to knot and splice." *Endymion*, and her twenty-four-pound long guns, was dangerously close; if he had to lose the sheet anchors to put the forty-gun frigate out of reach he'd do it.

Was it the dismantling shot that did it? he wondered. He didn't think so; scarcely two rounds would have been fired by each carronade before the enemy's main topsail went. The single largest sail on the ship tearing itself apart—a sight of beauty. Probably it had been weakened by all the preceding fire, by the chaser combat and roundshot fired high; perhaps the dismantling shot had been just enough to finish the already-weakened sail.

Macedonian gybed neatly, Seward bracing the yards around progressively as crewmen ran aft to man the chasers. Soon there was another chaser combat, *Macedonian*'s Parthian shots tearing away, as a final insult, a forecourse sheet that left the big sail flapping madly with British crewmen scampering to secure it before it, like the topsail, streamed shreds of tattered flax in the wind.

Tenedos fell behind, and the guns fell silent and were housed. "Two dead, six wounded seriously enough to be taken from duty," Favian was told; Surgeon Truscott's messenger was the chaplain, who looked over the scene of the battle with his usual bubbling interest. *Macedonian* had got away with little significant damage; the holes in the sails would be patched; most of the wounded would be returned to duty. Only two dead outright:

lovely. He was willing to swear *Tenedos* would have lost more. The navy would be pleased.

"Deck there!" It was the voice of Midshipman Stanhope, sent aloft again with his telescope. "She's bending a new topsail!" Stanhope shouted, and Favian felt his heart sink.

It was a repetition, with variations, of the morning's comedy. *Tenedos* had fallen behind *Endymion* while bending her new sail and repairing other damage, but once her new, undamaged sail was aloft she began to overtake her consort just as she had that morning. Favian, watching with rising despair the British frigate speeding toward them, began to feel Lazarus's eyes boring into the back of his head. *We shall be cursed in that fight,* Lazarus had said; and it seemed the prophecy was coming true.

"Damned if it will," Favian thought. "Damned if I'll let them take us." He realized from the surprised expressions on the quarterdeck that he'd just spoken aloud. He cocked his arms on his hips and forced a bloodless smile onto his lips. "If they didn't learn their lesson the first time, we'll just have to teach them again," he said. "Send the chaser crews back to their guns."

As he stalked down the poop ladder, avoiding Lazarus's gaze, he felt his neck hairs prickle; there was a change in the wind coming. He paused on the ladder, alert, and the change came, a blustering gust, then another, then a steady, fresher wind, still from the northwest. He turned and came back to the poop, peering at the pursuit. It was as he feared.

Endymion was a heavier ship, with bigger masts and spars; the day's light winds had not helped her, and the smaller *Macedonian* and *Tenedos* had been able to outpace her. The wind's increase in velocity had benefited her; she was clearly riding more easily on the water, a broader bone of foam at her bows, although *Tenedos* was still overhauling, and *Macedonian*, Favian thought, was still pulling away, but not as swiftly. *Macedonian* would not, in the upcoming combat, have as much time to fight with *Tenedos* before the bigger frigate was down on her. *Cursed.* He would not believe it. He went below to the chase guns, seeing a smear of blood on the deck that someone had made a half-hearted attempt to clean up with a swab.

The men knew their tasks by now; as soon as *Tenedos* was within range the chase guns began firing, as accurately as anything on the pitching extremity of a ship was likely to be, putting new shot holes in the British frigate's sails. Her own chaser came back, most of it splashing wide, not as accurate as before. Perhaps, Favian thought, they have lost a good gunlayer.

And then *Tenedos* sailed out of the arc of fire of the chase guns, and Favian called his men to quarters. He knew the pattern by now, the British frigate yawing to present her broadside, firing into the helpless *Macedonian* until the quarry was forced to turn, and he thought perhaps he had an answer.

Tenedos seemed huge as she hovered off *Macedonian*'s larboard quarter, her pockmarked sails clear against the blue sky. *Board her,* Favian thought. *Board her and sail away.* If necessary he would.

"Mr. Stone. Mr. Seward," he said. "I'll want those stuns'ls in again, and in quickly. We'll be turning at the same time and I'll need the yards braced around as that happens—it'll have to be neater than last time. Detail your men now—take men from the starboard battery if you need it."

The sailing master and first lieutenant went bustling away, pointing, detailing men to the braces. Favian turned aft again, watching his enemy, seeing the white foam contrasting with the deep green sea and the strip of copper flashing above the waterline as the frigate heeled. He felt a nervous exultation, a savage eagerness to come to grips with *Tenedos*. Perhaps it was delusion, perhaps the desperate feral energy of a trapped animal readying himself for a last lunge for the throat of his foe; at this point he didn't care. He would fight *Macedonian* till she sank; he would be firing his guns at the enemy until the green sea rose up to the portsills—see if he didn't. He felt the morbid gaze of Lazarus on the back of his head and grinned, baring his teeth. Let the madman's dark gods come; he would fight them, too. He turned abruptly and snatched up a speaking trumpet.

"They're coming for another beating," he bellowed, his ruthless intensity blaring from the trumpet. "Are we going to give it to them?" The frigate rocked with cheers; he knew the men were as desperate as he. "I'm going to try to get right alongside," he said. "We'll fight yardarm-to-yardarm until they strike, or we disable them. If necessary we'll go after 'em with cold steel. When I call for independent fire, I want you to shoot as fast as you can; you'll be so close you can't miss. For God's sake fire low. Now, three cheers for the old *Macedonian!*"

There was another burst of cheering, and Favian put his trumpet away. Was this what Lawrence felt at the end, being carried to the cockpit of his stricken *Chesapeake*, crying out his hopeless "Don't give up the ship!" while his men broke and ran before the British boarders? Was the reckless bravado a result of his own helplessness? He put the thought out of his mind and stalked to the maimed taffrail, his hand on the warm barrel of one of the twelve-pounder chasers.

Tenedos was closer, its battleflags clear spots of color against the sky. There was a distant figure on the poop, a plump man in a round hat shouting through a speaking trumpet—Parker? Favian looked at the little figure in its blue coat and thought, *Parker, you have lost. You just don't know it yet.*

And then *Tenedos*'s turn commenced, and Favian spun about to shout that every man should lie down. He caught the startled look of Stone and Seward—they thought he would be turning with *Tenedos*, like last time—before they got clumsily to hands and knees. Favian joined them, stretched out full length—no false bravado this time, he hoped, merely the real thing.

Macedonian shivered as the broadside came in, delivered well, smashing into the defenseless hull. Favian looked anxiously aloft, pushing back the visor of his boarding helmet with his hand, terrified of mast damage, but short of some new pockmarks in the canvas there was none. He jumped to his feet, feeling the tacky deck seaming sticking to his clothing, seeing *Tenedos*'s masts and yards standing clear above a pall of gray gunsmoke, watching anxiously for the beginnings of Parker's turn. He saw it, *Tenedos* beginning its curve toward *Macedonian*, as it had before, making up for ground lost during its yaw to larboard. "Parker, old son," he said with a bubbling laugh that he found impossible to repress, "you should have tried something different." He turned forward, brisk. "On your feet, everyone! Mr. Seward—in with the stuns'ls! Have your men at the braces ready."

Ignoring the sudden burst of orders from the mast captains Favian watched as *Tenedos* curved in toward him, its clean wake forming an S in the water. Not yet, Favian thought, let Parker come a little nearer. Not yet. His pulse was racing; he tried to calm it. Now.

"Hard a-larboard!" he barked. "Helm hard over! Larboard broadside, run out and fire on my signal!" Suddenly Stone and Seward were shouting orders; Favian felt the rudder bite as *Macedonian* began its swing toward the British frigate.

Geometry again: the wakes formed two curves on the ocean surface, the British frigate curving inward, to its right, toward its quarry, while *Macedonian* was suddenly making a tight arc to the left, directly in *Tenedos*'s path. If the arcs continued *Macedonian* would be able to fire a broadside directly into the British frigate's bows, raking fire that would send every ball that hit the length of the British frigate, doing appalling damage. Raking fire: with the cliffs of a lee shore, the nightmare of every man-of-war's man.

Macedonian's turn was performed smoothly, far better than last time: weather studding sails doused, the yards progressively braced as the frigate spun round, the spanker crashing to leeward as they gybed, *Macedonian* suddenly heeling over to starboard instead of larboard as the wind crept around to the starboard quarter. It was some time before Parker reacted to his danger, and then there was a hurried reaction, *Tenedos* rocking as it swung to larboard in sudden haste, studding sails flapping as they lost wind . . .

"Ready, larboard guns!" Favian shouted, triumph rushing through him. "Two hundred yards' range! Wait for my signal!"

It would not be a clear rake—he could see that now; it would not be fired right at *Tenedos*'s bows, but over the starboard bow—it would be bad enough, though, at this range. There was chaos among the British frigate's sail trimmers; the yards were swinging wildly as some got ahead of the others, straining the sails. Any second now. The number three gun fired prematurely: Favian saw splinters flying, a hit, but it was sheer luck. "I want that man's name," he said. There were a few rifle shots from the tops: marines trying their luck. He could feel the wave lifting *Macedonian*, feel the hesitation as it slid from the crest . . .

"Larboard guns, fire!" he roared. The frigate shuddered as the guns went off nearly together, flinging five hundred pounds of iron across the enemy's bows. Favian could see splinters flying from enemy bulwarks, white scars appearing in the paint. "Grape on top of roundshot!" he ordered. "Independent fire!"

Tenedos swung uncertainly onto her new course, a few guns poking out of her ports; Favian heard a shouted order and the guns went off. Overhasty: most of the roundshot shrieked high between the masts, but there was one solid crash forward. A musket round twittered into the spanker boom overhead, proving a Royal Marine had the range. Favian began pacing, giving the sharpshooter a more difficult target.

Guns began going off on both sides, the frigates on parallel courses a hundred fifty yards apart. Favian kept his helm down, hoping to get closer, but Parker wouldn't allow it and kept his distance; eventually both frigates had rounded up until they were close-hauled, near to the wind. *Endymion* loomed off their larboard bows, a reminder to Favian that things must be concluded quickly. The feral restlessness possessing Favian made this mere pacing intolerable; he itched to get closer, to come to grips with his pursuer and finish him. In the end he could wait no longer, and with a muttered statement of his intentions to Stone, he dashed below to direct the gun deck battery.

The gun deck was smoky chaos, lit by uncertain light from the ports and flashes from the bellowing guns, populated by hunched figures bending over their ordnance, stripped to the waist, kerchiefs wrapped around their ears to prevent their being accidentally deafened. Favian unstrapped his boarding helmet and threw it on the deck; he ran to the center gun section of four guns and announced his intention of assuming command.

"I'll show you some practice, boys!" he shouted, seeing the whites of their eyes staring surprised out of powder-streaked faces. "We're going to bring their mainmast down!"

The range was under two hundred yards, theoretically point-blank for these eighteen-pounders. Point-blank meant the shot, between the time it was fired and the time it struck its target, would fall toward the earth less than its own diameter, meaning that, assuming the murk, heel, ship's rolling, and windage could be accounted for, the shot would go where Favian put it.

Favian began aiming each gun as it was loaded and made ready, running from one to the other as they were rolled up to the ports. Sometimes the guns were loaded quickly, one or two waiting while Favian was dealing with another; he gave these permission to fire without him while he dealt with the first. He would crouch down behind the gun as it was run out, signaling with his hands to the men at the handspikes, training the gun left and right, aiming always for the mainmast, the lanyard wrapped around his fist while he stood, legs apart, on the rocking deck, waiting for the moment to jerk the lanyard and fire. The other gun sections fired on without him, hammering at the enemy, the frigate occasionally rocking as a British shot went home in her timbers.

Eventually, through the murk, he was pleased to see the

enemy's number six and seven gunports beaten into one—he was striking her in the right place. But the thought of *Endymion* nagged him. How much time did he have? One last round with each gun, he thought, and he'd run up to the poop to check.

"Train her left, there . . . now right, just a bit. Belay. Stand clear the tackles," he chanted, bent over his gun, seeing the enemy frigate through the port, the pockmarked sails and scarred hull. "There she is . . . fire." He jerked the lanyard and the gun lunged back at him, stopped short by its training tackles, its touch hole spurting a jet of flame that blackened the beam over his head. He stood, seeing the gun captain on his right with his fist held high, showing his gun was loaded and ready. He moved on to the next gun, seeing the trainers with their handspikes ready to heave it left or right at his instruction, and then a shout went up.

"She's lost her mainmast! Her mainmast's gone!" A savage laugh bursting from his lips, Favian leaped forward, thrusting his head from the port: through the drifting smoke he saw *Tenedos* awry, her entire mainmast, lower mast, top, and topgallant, leaning forward at a bizarre angle, the topgallant pitched up into the fore topgallant, fouling the foremast.

"Keep firing, lads!" he laughed, and ran like a madman to the poop as the Macedonians burst into a cheer that rang like a carillon in the closed space of the gun deck. On the poop he burst into sunlight and small-arms fire; he glanced to larboard to confirm what he'd seen, seeing the British frigate in trouble, her crew frantically trying to fly the sails on the mainyards, relieving the pressure on the mast. Another twenty minutes, Favian thought, and Parker would strike; he'd have no choice.

A look at *Endymion* showed he would not have those twenty minutes. Nor, if he had them, could he get *Tenedos* away. Raging frustration gnawed at him; he had earned a prize, and now he was cheated of it. He smashed a gloved fist down on the rail; he *wanted* that frigate. *Tenedos* was falling behind; the gunfire was dying. It was time, once again, to run.

Standing at his station by the poop barricade was Lazarus, watching the enemy frigate keenly. Favian leered at him. "I thought you said this meeting was cursed?" he demanded.

"Nay, not this meeting. I did not see these ships. I mean another time," Lazarus said, his unsettling eyes turning to Favian.

"Ha! Hypocrite!" Favian exulted. "Hands to wear ship! Larboard battery, house your guns. Starboard battery, load and run out!"

Seward called the trimmers away from their mad cheering and *Macedonian* spun on its heel, firing a parting broadside at *Tenedos* from extended range as they swept past the crippled British frigate. Favian thought, as they left *Tenedos* in their wake, that he saw a portly figure in a blue coat standing at the enemy rail, lifting his round hat in courteous farewell, and Favian raised his hand, his mind clearing as he received the tribute. Parker had handled his ship well; but Favian had been transported by a despairing rage, made desperate enough to start pointing his guns himself. Perhaps that had made the difference.

Favian received the salute of the carpenter, come up from his station on the orlop. "We were hit four times twixt wind an' water, sir," the man said. "Now we're on t'other tack the shot holes are under water. Better man the pumps, sir, till I can get the patches on 'er."

"Very well." Favian turned to Stone. "Secure the guns, and secure from general quarters. Man the pumps. All hands to knot and splice torn rigging."

"Aye aye, sir."

The carpenter ran below to commence his patchwork, and shortly after the trumpeter began to call the hands from quarters Favian saw the chaplain ascending the poop ladder. "Six men dead, sir, and fourteen wounded," Solomon reported. "That's for all the day, not just this last fight." Solomon craned his neck, seeing *Endymion* and *Tenedos* fading in *Macedonian*'s wake.

Six dead, fourteen wounded, Favian thought. And a ship unscathed and still able to run from its enemies. It had been a miraculous day.

"It's getting a little wet down on the orlop—there are some shot holes down there," the chaplain said. "Dr. Truscott would like to move the wounded up to the berth deck, if it will be safe for them. Oh, look, a strange bird! What is it, an albatross?"

"Mother Carey's chicken," Favian said. "Tell Mr. Truscott he may move the wounded to the berth deck if he wishes."

"He shall be delighted—I will tell him immediately," the chaplain said, remembering for once to salute. "Mother Carey's chicken! I declare—what a strange name, eh?"

"Save us," thought Favian, and turned to his work.

Endymion, flying signals, passed *Tenedos* and continued in pursuit of Favian, presumably leaving *Majestic* to offer the injured frigate assistance. There were a few anxious moments when the wind increased and veered a point; the British frigate's speed increased, but not enough to overtake. After nightfall Favian altered course, which should have resulted in the British being out of sight by morning, but luck was still not with them: at first light, with the men standing by their guns, *Endymion*'s topsails were seen to the northwest, and turned instantly in pursuit.

It wasn't until after the noon meal that the pursuit ended. "Up spirits" had just been piped when a black squall was seen tearing up from the south, moving like a giant *Demologos* steam battery; Favian put down the helm at once and steered to avoid it. It was fully ten miles across, traveling with incredible speed, a wall of white water in front where the wind had blown the sea flat. Favian had never seen its like, but the sailing master Seward, who had served in the tropics during the quasi war with France, said he had once been struck by one, and that it had blown out every sail in the old *Ganges* while dumping half a ton of warm water on her deck.

The storm passed between *Macedonian* and *Endymion*—perhaps it struck the British frigate and carried it north, perhaps not. But when the storm had passed, the sea was empty, and *Macedonian* was free to head for enemy waters. The blockade had been broken.

21

"Mind your helm there, Mr. Seward," Favian said. "The wind is going to be squirrelly, coming through that slot in the mountain."

"Aye aye, sir."

The bright Caribbean sun shone down through flat, low clouds onto the British West Indian island of Montserrat, lying, its green tropical vegetation slightly blued by distance, dead ahead of the frigate at a distance of perhaps two miles. The town and fort of

Plymouth, the union flag flying conspicuously from several flagpoles, lay beneath the low, bifurcated volcanic peak of Soufrière, extending left and right on the gloomy-looking black sand beaches. Two coasting schooners, *Macedonian*'s immediate prey, lay between the fort and the frigate. Favian, standing just aft of the mainmast, considered the position of the three vessels and the island with a careful eye. It was an interesting tactical problem.

Overhead, from the mainpeak, flew a white pendant with a red St. George's cross, the standard British commission pendant; the union jack flew from the jackstaff forward; and at the gaff peak flew the red ensign, the flag that would have been flown by any of the ships commanded by Rear-Admiral of the Red George Cockburn, KCB, the British admiral who had led most of the successful raids in the Chesapeake earlier that year, and who had provided naval support for the army under General Ross that had taken and burned Washington. Favian hoped that any lookouts in the fort would believe *Macedonian* to be a British vessel from the Chesapeake, perhaps come with dispatches.

It was not an unreasonable hope. *Macedonian* was British-built and the hull, from the gilded figurehead of Alexander the Great to the curved row of stern windows, was clearly of British construction. A week before, Favian had sent men dangling over the side to alter the standard American pattern of a black hull with a white stripe over the gunports to the "Nelson chequer," the pattern favored by the British since Trafalgar, consisting of a black hull with a yellow ochre stripe. As far as the hull was concerned, *Macedonian* seemed unmistakably British.

But the part of the frigate most visible to anyone in the fort, the masts and sails, would have looked decidedly odd. *Macedonian* had lost her original masts in the battle in which she'd been taken, and since had been rerigged in the American pattern, with spars larger and heavier than the British norm and a greater spread of canvas. The "cut of her jib" was definitely American, and the odd juxtaposition of a British hull with an American rig might set someone in the fort wondering. It might alarm the coasting schooners as well.

Thus far, fortunately, there seemed no sign of alarm. Why should there be? The United States Navy, except for a few sloops of war, had been mewed up in port by the British blockade, and no American warship, saving the occasional privateer, had been in the Caribbean in at least a year. At present the Caribbean was a lake controlled by the Royal Navy.

Favian intended to alter that situation. He did not expect to be in the Caribbean for long, but while he was there he intended to create a lasting impression.

Three days before, *Macedonian* had appeared in the British Virgin Islands, spending two days harrying the coastal commerce there, burning a brig, two schooners, and numerous small craft. Favian had then vanished out to sea on a long sweep west of the Leeward Islands, presumably shaking any pursuit. While out of sight of land *Macedonian* had run down a big West India merchantman loaded with coffee and tobacco, which had provided, after it was emptied of its crew, excellent live-ammunition target practice for the frigate's gunners. Favian had riddled the merchant ship until she was in a sinking condition, then burned her for good measure.

Now he was reappearing in the Leeward Islands chain. After taking the two schooners off Montserrat he intended to pass south of the island, then reach up northward after nightfall, appearing at dawn off Antigua, home of the Leeward Islands station of the Royal Navy. He would avoid Falmouth and English Harbor, the actual naval bases on the southern coast of the big island, but he did intend to head into St. John's, the commercial harbor on the northern coast, to seize what he could of British goods.

Afterwards *Macedonian* would head out to sea once more, probably to the eastward, leaving behind the hornets buzzing futilely in their Leeward Islands nest. He would appear once or twice more, off Dominica and perhaps the Grenadines, before vanishing again out to sea. He knew that certain of the French and Dutch islands, taken by the British during the course of the Napoleonic Wars, were being returned to their original masters, so he would avoid them altogether and concentrate on islands that had been British for thirty years or more.

And while the British frantically searched the Caribbean for *Macedonian*, diverting ships best employed elsewhere, the frigate would head into the Atlantic on the first leg of a months-long voyage, rounding the Cape of Good Hope to next appear in a totally unexpected place: the British East Indies, where the proceeds of a few months' uninterrupted hunting could easily run into millions of pounds' loss for British insurance underwriters.

It would be a bold strike, and Favian knew that the chances of success were good. It would prove to the British public, and more importantly the peace commission meeting at Ghent, that although the United States had lost its capital and the greater part of its commerce, Brother Jonathan still had a long reach.

A strong gust rocked *Macedonian,* the canvas roaring as it was caught aback, and with practiced ease Favian compensated for the swaying deck of the suddenly heeling frigate. "Port your helm!" he shouted, hard on the heels of the master's own orders, and *Macedonian* slid to starboard with what remained of its momentum, the new, brisk wind filling its sails again and speeding the frigate through the water at a faster pace, the sea hissing as it sped beneath the keel. "Amidships."

"Full an' bye, sir."

"Keep her so."

As Favian had predicted, the trade wind had funneled through the slot on the volcano, and almost had the frigate in irons. The altered course had changed the frigate's situation vis-à-vis the coasting schooners: though the wind shift meant she was no longer able to point as high as Favian wished, she was also moving faster through the water. Favian revised his calculations, and decided that at least one of the schooners would be intercepted before reaching the anchorage beneath the guns of the fort.

Favian looked at the men around him on the quarterdeck, and from their smiles saw that they had reached the same conclusion. *Macedonian,* it seemed, was on its way to becoming a happy ship.

There had been no more outbreaks of violence. Though Lazarus was sulking—he no longer offered to speak to Favian when they were together on the quarterdeck on drills, although he answered when spoken to—and though Favian had been told by Herzog that the fiddler was still predicting doom and despair, for the most part it seemed as if he was being paid little attention. After five days in sick bay Kuusikoski had been returned to light duties, his splinted fingers making it difficult for him to do else, and although the crew seemed wary they treated him with the respect due the captain's coxswain.

The eight days since the frigate had escaped Hayes's squadron had been full of drills, drills cheerfully performed after the running fight with *Tenedos* had proved their worth; there had been not only regularly scheduled gunnery drills in the afternoon, but gunnery alternating with sail drills in the morning, and surprise drills in the dead of night, in which the people were expected to clear the ship for action in the dark. The hands' performance had steadily improved, though it would probably be months before they reached the standard to which Favian aspired.

Favian had not watched the drills with the aloof eye of the quarterdeck tyrant, but had taken active part. There were captains enough, Favian knew, who left the technical running of the ship to the ships' specialists—the sailing master, the bosun, the gunner, and others who ran the ships' departments—and who rarely allowed themselves to give anything but vague orders on the quarterdeck, orders which the sailing master, or one of the lieutenants who had an understanding of the ship, would then interpret so that the sailors would know what to do. The ancient distinction between "the officers who ran a ship, and the gentlemen who commanded her," a truism in the Royal Navy, where promotion often depended as much on patronage and political leverage as on skill or knowledge of seamanship, still existed, though with increasing rarity, even in the United States Navy, though it was for the most part confined to the older generation. Preble's boys had not been raised to take their place among those genteel, old-fashioned, unseamanlike captains, more concerned with having the buttons of their uniforms properly polished, the canvas covers on the gun breechings blindingly whitened, and a proper store of Madras in their spirit lockers, than with running an efficient man-of-war.

Favian had set out to prove it to them. He had shown himself a fighter, and he knew himself a thorough seaman; he intended to demonstrate the latter fact to the crew. One morning he had appeared on deck in a tar-specked old shirt and a ragged pair of trousers, and had gone aloft with some of the officers and the mast captains of every mast, going out along the footropes, hanging with one hand a hundred feet up while examining the running rigging, suggesting which blocks needed to be greased with more slush from the galley, ordering some of the standing rigging retarred, ordering some of the blocks shifted so as to increase their purchase.

He had been fortunate in his officers. They had thrown themselves willingly into the merciless system of drills, and quite often had volunteered sensible suggestions. Adrian Stone, despite his serious manner and his formal demeanor, had in particular been a steady, intelligent, reliable support, often offering imaginative advice—Favian was used to thinking of imaginative men as being more effusive, more effervescent, but Stone belied his preconceptions: it was rare even to see the man smile, and only then when standing on the quarterdeck, his hands clasped behind his back as he gazed aloft at the drawing sails, *Macedonian* speeding gracefully through the blue tropical sea.

The other five lieutenants were less surprising, but no less supportive. Like Stone, none thus far in the war had seen real action at sea, and until the breakout from New London had been in danger of missing entirely on the chances for distinction, promotion, and prize money offered by a battle. Some, however, had war experience short of actual battle: Eastlake, the third, had been fourth lieutenant with Charles Morris in the *Adams* corvette, and had thus participated in several successful raids and the unsuccessful defense of the *Adams* against the overwhelming ground force that had burned it in Maine last August. The fourth, Chapelle, had been with Commodore Lewis's gunboat squadron in Long Island Sound, and had skirmished several times with the blockading enemy. Henry Swink, the sixth lieutenant, had been a midshipman aboard the little fourteen-gun brig *Nautilus* when she'd been run down and captured by an entire British squadron in 1812, at odds so hopeless she hadn't fired a shot.

All the lieutenants were alike in their eagerness for battle, and the readiness with which they accepted Favian's ideas. Their inexperience was balanced by the long service of the warrant officers: Seward, the master, had served in the wars against France and Tripoli, and Bosun Tucker had been in Spence's gunboat when it had been blown up off the Moorish harbor. In his officers Jones had chosen well, and Favian mentally thanked him for acute perception in picking his subordinates.

Except for the two from his old command, Favian had thus far had little contact with the midshipmen except for once observing some of them at Porter's naval game. They all had participated willingly in the drills, which was not unusual: midshipmen had no regular assigned tasks and were usually happy to be relieved from their daily monotony of spherical trigonometry and swaggering about trying to look important. Twice each week he intended to invite two of the mids to dine with him, conversing with them in French to improve their knowledge of the language and acquaint them with the terminology of the many French writers on naval tactics, but the program had barely got started. Tolbert was now one of the senior midshipmen, a fact Favian suspected he would one day regret—Tolbert could swagger, curse, and chew tobacco as well as any midshipman alive, and he was brave as a lion, but his mathematics and French were abominable, and he could scarcely put pen to paper without inflicting gratuitous acts of violence upon the English language.

Favian hoped that Tolbert's influence would be mitigated by that of Lovette and Stanhope, who—judging at least by the example of Porter's game he'd seen in the frigate's wardroom, and from his personal knowledge of Stanhope as an exceptionally promising young officer—seemed intelligent and sensible. Favian was not naïve enough to suppose that the general tone of the midshipmen's berth would be much affected by Lovette and Stanhope—he remembered all too well the competitive, ambitious, honor-mad atmosphere of his own days as a midshipman—but he hoped the more sensible among the midshipmen would at least serve to moderate it, and to do so without offending anyone. He would not at all enjoy having to deal with one of his mids challenging another to a duel, as Tolbert had on his previous cruise.

Macedonian slowed perceptibly as it passed out of the range of the williwaw caused by the slot in Soufrière. Favian glanced up at the masthead pendant and at the dogvanes on the backstays. "I think you can pinch her up a bit, Mr. Seward," he said.

"Aye aye, sir."

"Keep her full."

"Aye, sir."

Favian looked down at his feet, where a week before some puzzled hands, working under the direction of Stanhope, had laid out a naval square aft of the mainmast. A device recommended by an obscure French seventeenth-century naval theorist named Paul Hoste, the *carré naval*, or naval square, made it much easier to pursue to windward, its beam and keel lines marking out the frigate's current course, its course after tacking, and the beam line to the new course. There had been a naval square on Favian's first command, *Experiment*, and it had proven useful in spite of the skepticism of most of the brig's officers; Favian hoped it would show itself as helpful on *Macedonian*. Favian adjusted his position on the naval square, peering through the frigate's tangle of rigging at the masts of the two schooners. He would have to go about soon.

"Ready about!" he said. "Stations for stays!" He heard Seward, standing on the horse block, repeating his order, and then the stampede of bare feet heading for the braces.

It was nearing time to tack. He looked up to make certain that the hands were at their stations, seeing the grins on their sunburned faces. Yes, *Macedonian* was standing fair to becoming a happy ship, in spite of Lazarus and his predictions of gloom, in spite of the talk of witchery and violence. Lazarus and his talk of Jonahs aboard had been discredited entirely by the escape from the British squadron, and escaping from the misery of a New England winter into the sun of the tropics had brought the hands' spirits yet higher. Favian, despite his years of service, had never served in the tropics before, having joined in '01 after the quasi war with the French had been concluded; he was pleased at the effects the southerly latitudes were having on his men and self. The sun had baked the frigate, relaxed it, and officers as well as hands had come to their labors with a song on their lips. Sunburn had been a problem, many of the hands having gone pale during their long spell ashore and ended up in sick bay with flesh peeling from their shoulders and arms. Even Favian, who had a private supply of bear grease with which to coat his face, neck, and ears, was peeling from his ears and long nose, but even so he considered that the benefits of the Caribbean far outweighed the nuisance of the burning sun.

Favian saw the farthest schooner moving into line with the naval square's larboard forward beam line. Time to go about.

"Ease down the helm, Mr. Seward."

"Aye aye, sir. A spoke at a time, thar. Haul the spanker boom amidships. Overhaul th' weather jib sheets. Helm's hard down, sir."

Favian looked up just as the topgallants began to lift, a lazy wave rolling through the canvas in the instant before they began to thunder, turned edge-on to the wind. "Helm's alee!" he shouted.

"Keep fast the fore tack! Rise main tacks and sheets!" Seward said, his words following fast on Favian's. The mast captains rapped out a series of swift orders and the big maincourse went swiftly, evenly up to the yard, the sound of the sail's rumbling punctuated by the swift roar of the lines through the sheaves. The staysails set like gull's wings between the masts slatted back and forth, gangs of crewmen tending the sheets carefully, until, with some difficulty, they were doused by men tugging at the downhauls. The forecourse, which normally would have been clewed up to the yard, was allowed to remain set so that, in these light airs, the extra surface of the big sail would help the ship come round on its other tack.

"Let go the t'gallant bowlines! Let go and overhaul the weather lifts! Shorten in the lee main tack and maintop bowline!" Seward's orders followed one another in quick succession, each sending an obedient party of men to the pin rails, each party manipulating a part of the giant, complicated machine that was *Macedonian*, helping her get across the eye of the wind.

"Haul well taut the mainbrace, thar. Ready all. . . . *Mains'l haul!*"

Macedonian hesitated in the eye of the wind, its sails roaring, the men at the braces digging their bare feet into the deck for traction as they bent almost horizontal to bring the great main and mizzen yards around. The yards went around properly, but the ship continued to hesitate in the wind's eye, refusing to fall off. *Macedonian* shuddered, rocking listlessly on the sea, her forward momentum gone. In a few seconds she'd be gaining sternway, sailing rudder-first through the water. *Damn this wind,* Favian thought. Favian cupped his hands to his mouth and bellowed an order.

"Set the heads'ls flat aback! Shift the helm, there!"

"Damned old hog-in-the-wallow," came Isaac Seward's voice, in normal, conversational tones he hadn't bothered to amplify with the speaking trumpet. Favian spared him a glance; the sailing master was standing on the horse block, one hand on a backstay, the other, holding the speaking trumpet, propped disgustedly on one hip. If he was this annoyed with *Macedonian*'s missing stays in a light wind like this, Favian wondered, how angry would he be if he were sailing master on *United States*, which was so sluggish she was fully capable of going in irons in a brisk Atlantic breeze, and where the occurrence was so common that the crew were utterly practiced at turning the ship around on her heel after missing stays, a thing most ships' companies rarely did smoothly because of its rarity?

The frigate was gaining sternway, the rudder hard over to help her pay off, and slowly the frigate's head slid to leeward, a breath of wind beginning to lift the main topgallant. Favian, familiar with the commands from long practice as first lieutenant on *United States*, gave the necessary orders with practiced rapidity.

"Helm amidships! Head braces! Rise fore tack and sheets! Haul well taut, there . . ." Favian cast an anxious eye aloft, aware that the frigate was traveling smartly back through the water, her motion altered from a pitch to an uneasy combination of pitch and roll as the waves began to take her from the starboard bow. The main topsail began to fill, the canvas rolling lazily as the wind shifted aft. Now.

"Let go and haul! Smartly, there!" The men on the fore braces threw themselves into hauling the yards around, the canvas booming. "'Vast bracing! Flow the head sheets! Aft the spanker sheets!" *Macedonian*'s sternway began to slow as the sheets filled, the yards groaning as they took the strain; she stopped dead in the water, rocking as if undecided which way to go. Then, very slowly, she began to push forward through the water, the sea gurgling as it swept around her tumblehome. Favian heard a faint cheer from the fo'c'sle.

"Silence, there! Brace up—gather aft! Ease off the spanker sheet!" The frigate was gaining way on her new tack, a bow wave forming beneath her stem. Favian glanced anxiously at the schooners he was pursuing; he had lost time, and he was fairly certain he had lost the lead schooner as well.

"Helmsman, give her a good full. Haul taut the weather lifts—steady out the bowlines! Trim the windsails."

Out of the corner of his eye he saw Seward looking at him with admiration, but he felt little but a prickly annoyance at losing that other schooner. Even the near schooner might prove a doubtful prize.

"Mr. Stone," he said. "Clear away the starboard chaser, forrard. Clear the rest of the ship for action, but do it quietly—no trumpets, if you please."

Without the sound of the trumpet to lend it urgency the clearing of the frigate for action seemed haphazard, a chaos of hurrying figures performing a great many seemingly random actions: breaking down the partitions in Favian's cabin and bustling his furniture below, preparing the guns for firing and overhauling their tackles, the gun captains coming up from the magazine with their cartouche boxes and priming irons, rigging chain slings on the yards, powder monkeys running up with fresh cartridges, filling the fire buckets with water, sanding the decks to provide traction in case they were made slippery by blood. However haphazard the actions seemed, they had purpose and were performed efficiently; the frigate was cleared in less than six minutes, and the crews stood silently by their guns, awaiting orders to load and run the iron weapons out of their ports.

But Favian had been watching the schooners carefully, and concluded that all the preparations would probably go for naught. They had been forging steadily ahead; since *Macedonian* had lost so much time in irons it looked doubtful that even the near schooner could be caught. The near schooner was well within effective range of the guns, however; if Favian opened fire now there was a good chance of wrecking her, but that would mean abandoning all hope of catching her consort. He was about to conclude that the time had come to end the deception, hoist the American flag, and attempt to destroy the near schooner by gunfire, conceding the loss of the other, when suddenly the near schooner's square topsail began to belly out, spilling wind, the vessel's speed slowing considerably.

"What the devil . . .?" he heard Stone mutter, and then as a tattered British ensign began to rise aloft on the schooner's halyards, Favian realized like a thunderclap what was happening. The schooner was rendering a salute, thinking *Macedonian* a British frigate! Lowering the topsail yard was a submission the British demanded not only of their own merchantmen, but of the ships of other nations as well, a recognition of England's dominance at sea. Favian's realization was confirmed when he saw the schooner's ensign dip in salute.

"By God, they're saluting us!" Stone exclaimed, and then Favian turned to him.

"Acknowledge, Mr. Stone. Dip our ensign, if you please."

"Aye aye, sir!" Stone said, flashing one of his rare grins, and walked aft to the flag halyards.

The red ensign was dipped in response and *Macedonian* hurtled ahead, winning the race easily. The frigate would forge ahead of the schooner and put her under her lee, where she would never escape. Favian's attention shifted to the lead schooner, where the main topsail yard was just coming down, the big square sail spilling wind, the ensign rising to the top of the ensign gaff.

"Prepare to dip our ensign again, Mr. Stone," Favian said.

"Aye aye, sir."

"Mr. Seward, take up your speaking trumpet. As we pass the first schooner, hail them and instruct them to heave to and receive a search party."

"Aye, Cap'n."

"On second thought," Favian said, reaching for the speaking trumpet, "I'll do it. You sound too New England, Mr. Seward."

"As ye wish, sir."

They swept up within a hundred yards of the schooner, affording Favian a clear glimpse of her master, a young towheaded man in his twenties, and her mostly black crew. He raised the speaking trumpet. "What schooner is that?" he demanded, trying to talk with his tongue far back in his mouth, affecting the accents of the original officers of the *Macedonian*, whose acquaintance he'd made when he'd taken them prisoner.

"*Annie Graves*, out of Grenada," the master responded, cupping his hands to shout across the intervening distance.

"Heave to, *Annie Graves!*" Favian shouted. "Prepare to receive a boarding party. I'll see your manifests in order, sir!"

He saw the young master frame a response, then shrug—no doubt fully aware of the savage temper of many a Royal Navy captain when his hawse was crossed by a merchant captain—and give a few brief orders, probably resigned to the frigate pressing a few of his crew. *Annie Graves,* her crew obviously an efficient one and familiar with the ship, swung into the wind, her sails roaring from luff to leach, her crew jumping to clew up the square sails. *Macedonian* passed swiftly by, heading for the lead schooner.

No sooner had Favian returned his speaking trumpet to the rack than the frigate suddenly heeled over to a freshening gust, the same williwaw funneled down the slot of Soufrière that had taken them last time. With the fresher wind Favian was able to point the frigate nearer the wind and decrease the distance to his next target, but even so he saw he would lose the race.

"Mr. Chapelle!" he called out to the fourth lieutenant. "Load the starboard chaser, and fire a shot across that schooner's bow!"

"Aye aye, Captain," the fourth lieutenant responded, and jumped up to the fo'c'sle to supervise the loading of the gun.

The nine-pounder was loaded and trained forward, the dark-haired, portly young lieutenant bending over the gun, peering along its barrel to make certain of its aim. He raised his hand, then dropped it.

The gun went off with a bang, the twelve-pound shot buzzing as it receded, then skipping with three visible splashes not fifty feet from the schooner's bow. Chapelle straightened, a satisfied smile on his face, a smile that turned to a frown as the schooner's main topsail yard was hastily hauled up, the sail going flat as it filled, and the schooner altered course nearer the wind, clearly prepared to run.

"She smells a rat, sir!" Seward snapped, and Favian's reaction was instant.

"Out tompions! Load the starboard broadside and run out! Seven hundred yards' range! Helmsmen, stand by! Mr. Stone, stand by the flag halyards to douse the British ensign and raise our colors. Forrard, there! Ready to raise our colors!"

Stone stepped aft to fix the stars and stripes to the flag halyards, ready to raise the American ensign. *Macedonian* growled like a bear with the sound of the gun trucks rumbling to the ports, the gun barrels protruding from the ship's side like a row of blackened teeth, the ship's motion altering as the weight shifted.

"Raise our colors! Helmsman, let her fall off handsomely. Main battery, fire as you bear!"

The frigate slid slowly, carefully from the wind, the waves beginning to roll her as they took her broadside, the bright gridiron flag rising to her peak, snapping out in the wind, the long Markham pennant rising crimson at the fore. The guns, trained on their prearranged aiming point, went off almost together, the ship lurching, the sun momentarily obscured by clouds of smoke. White feathers leaped skyward around the schooner. Favian felt his heart race at the crash of the guns, the smell of the powder, and wondered why. This was no battle; this was little short of a gunnery exercise with an unwilling target.

"Load and run out!" Favian called, leaping to the weather side, jumping out into the mizzen rigging to improve his vision as the gunsmoke drifted back into his face. His first glimpse of the schooner was heartening; there were pockmarks in her mainsail, and figures were scrambling on her quarterdeck as if in panic. Just a few hits from *Macedonian*'s main battery of eighteen-pounders should be enough to smash the schooner's fragile hull; she was not built to take pounding.

Favian glanced to leeward at the *Annie Graves*, seeing her still hove to, bobbing on the waves. He could imagine the horror of her young master, seeing a frigate that had just taken the weather gage from her suddenly raising an enemy ensign and opening fire on her consort. He wondered if the man would bother to try to run.

The guns went off again, raising another series of splashes around the target schooner, and then Favian heard a drum rattling from the fort on the island. There would be incoming roundshot soon, he knew; he could only hope that the soldiers were typical of provincial garrisons everywhere, and unpracticed with their weapons.

After a third broadside the target schooner was a wreck, its maintopmast dangling over the side, its hull listing at an ever-increasing angle as water poured in through the shattered bulwark. She was obviously finished. Favian ordered the guns secured and wore the frigate sharply around, returning to finish his business with the *Annie Graves*.

The young master had decided to take his chances; he'd filled his sails again and was reaching downwind with every spar straining its utmost, a flight that he probably, and Favian certainly, knew was hopeless. *Macedonian* was at its fastest running before the wind, and the schooner, its square topsails notwithstanding, was not at its best point of sailing. Favian had just got his yards braced around on the new tack when the sky was suddenly torn apart by the buzzing wail of roundshot. Favian, whose automatic, involuntary response to the noise was to duck inside his collar like a turtle retreating into his shell, saw a hundred nervous faces turned involuntarily upwards at the sound of the sudden, tearing noise that marked the shots' passage; the iron solids passed far overhead and splashed into the sea half a mile downwind, and the nervous faces relaxed into easy grins, a scornful muttering at the fort's abominable gunnery breaking forth. After chastising himself for his own nervous reaction, for his ducking and the sudden pounding of his heart, Favian smiled, but for his own reasons: there was nothing like being shot at, and being missed, to hearten a ship's crew.

Annie Graves was a smart enough ship, and after it was obvious she was losing the race increased her speed by starting to heave overboard her cargo, so the chase went on for almost ten miles. Favian, who wanted the chase to last long enough to take the frigate out of range of the fort, refrained from setting his studding sails and settled back to enjoying the fine weather.

The fort's gunnery practice grew gradually more effective: roundshot began to splash around the frigate; one ball severed a fore topgallant backstay; another crashed into the larboard side, tearing off a few yards of paint before dropping, spent, into the sea, but no real harm was done.

In the end he used the chase as another gunnery drill; after the schooner got into extreme range he called the gun crews one by one to the bow chasers, giving each crew two shots at the quarry. Most missed: the art of aiming a chase gun from the fo'c'sle, where the pitch of the ship was most felt, was a new one to most of the hands. Favian found himself smiling to himself as the afternoon wore on; a successful chase, the smell of powder, gunnery and sail practice on a summery tropical afternoon: it had been a lovely day all told.

Eventually the range closed, a few twelve-pound shot went home into *Annie Graves*, and the schooner gave up and rounded to, waiting for boarders; through his glass Favian could see the towheaded master standing sullen on the quarterdeck, his arms crossed, while his men stood forward, huddled around one of their number who had been killed.

After Favian congratulated the schooner's captain on a chase well run, the crew of the *Annie Graves* and the crew from *Macedonian*'s earlier prize, the West India merchant they'd taken the day before, were put into the schooner's boats, and the schooner burned. The frigate, a pillar of smoke signaling the fate of its victim to the watchers ashore, shaped its course for the southeast. It would pass to the south of Montserrat, then after dark tack to the northward and shape its course for Antigua, destroying any ship found en route. Thus far Favian was happy with the day; the losses inflicted on Britain had been insignificant, but *Macedonian* had gained a great deal.

At eleven o'clock that evening he was on deck, enjoying the air after dining in the wardroom at the invitation of the lieutenants. There had been entertainment: Jasper Hourigan, the second lieutenant, was a fine hand with a German flute; sixth lieutenant Henry Swink proved adept at the clarinet, and both Eastlake and Chapelle strummed a guitar and sang, but perhaps the success of the evening had more to do with Mr. Eastlake's store of madeira—

prewar stuff, shipped north in straw-cushioned wagons from the cellars of his father, a wealthy Virginia burgess—and Swink's whiskey punch, which struck with the power of a thunderbolt and as mercilessly as an Algerine corsair.

In any case Favian found himself in need of a stroll in the open air, and so climbed the poop ladder, received the salute of fifth officer Ford, the officer of the deck, and took the captain's privilege of pacing up and down the weather quarterdeck in magnificent solitude. The trade wind cooled him and cleared his head, and he found himself stopping his pacing to look aloft at the figures cut by the sails against the starry heavens, patterning the Milky Way with the silhouette of man's nautical achievement. A shooting star pulsed across the heavens, breaking into several glowing fragments that rained down like a howitzer burst, and he held out his hand to measure the fading length of the meteorite's tail. "Sixty degrees of arc, at least," he concluded.

"Haul aboard the main sheet, there!" Lieutenant Ford's voice piped up. "Smartly, you wretched lubbers!"

Favian glanced at Ford, amused, realizing that the lieutenant must have thought that every time his captain halted his pacing and looked aloft, he was mentally criticizing Ford's set of the frigate's sails. Favian had stopped his pacing quite often; Ford must have been growing increasingly anxious. Favian was relieved, therefore, to see the frigate's chaplain walking up the poop ladder.

"Doctor Solomon," he called out, "will you join me?"

"With all my heart, Captain," said the young preacher with a smile. Favian snatched a glance at Ford; the lieutenant's relief was visible even across the dark quarterdeck.

"It was a most stimulating supper, sir," Doctor Solomon offered. "No doubt the success of the day's action had a good deal to do with the high spirits displayed."

"I hope, sir, the conversation was not too bawdy," Favian said as the chaplain fell in step with him.

"Nay," said Solomon, "hearty animal spirits only. To be expected in young men. I am not your New England puritan, sir; I am an Episcopalian of good family and see no reason to grow choleric over a little table talk."

"I am glad to know it. You will not hear the bosun curbing his oaths in respect of your collar, Doctor."

"Nor should he, if the Lord's name serves to send the people about their work with all appropriate speed. The Lord no doubt finds his name used with much less effect in other circumstances, and will not grudge a few oaths, particularly if they substitute for the blows the bosun would otherwise deliver." The chaplain ceased his pacing, looking up at the sky. "Two shooting stars, by thunder! Prodigious fine ones, too."

"Aye. One of the finer sights of the night watch, Doctor."

Solomon fell again into step with Favian, looking at him with ingenuous curiosity. "I was wondering, Captain," he asked, "if I might solicit your views on the smoking of Indian hemp?"

"It is a common practice down south, I believe, where it is grown on their plantations," Favian said. "No doubt that is where Mr. Eastlake acquired the habit."

"I was surprised to see him lighting up his pipe at the table—the smell was unmistakable. He seems to think it a social act, offering us all puffs from his 'pipe of peace,' as he called it—I accepted, of course, out of politeness. I had forgotten entirely the pleasant intoxication, so much less violent than that induced by alcoholic spirits."

"You are familiar with the practice?" asked Favian in surprise.

"Nay, not as a social thing, but as a medical one. I began at Princeton with the intention of becoming a physician, but grew enamored of philosophy instead. Indian hemp is often prescribed for women suffering from, ah, female maladies."

"I was not aware of that."

"I was wondering if hemp might be used medicinally on board ship, to woo the people from drunkenness?"

Favian considered the matter. "I think, Doctor, that in order to woo a sailor away from drink, the sailor must in the first place wish to be wooed," he said. "I did not notice that our Mr. Eastlake was any less abusive of the madeira following his indulgence in hemp. Adding one intoxicant to another seems a dubious course, to me, if abstention is what one is after—speaking entirely as a layman, of course, but as one with some experience of sailors."

"I thank you for your opinion, sir," Solomon said. "Doctor Truscott was of much the same opinion."

"Strike her, Jim." The voice came from forward, beneath the break in the poop where the half-hour glass had just been turned. A dimly seen figure stepped forward to the belfry, where he rang seven bells of the first night watch: eleven thirty. Lieutenant Ford seemed cheered: in another half-hour he might go to bed, and be rid of the intolerable burden of his captain looking over his shoulder for half the watch.

Favian looked carefully at the cheerful, indulgent preacher, wondering if he might breach the matter of the man's sermons. He had listened to two sermons thus far, and found them remarkably tolerant, quite well developed and organized, highly informed, and so damnably abstruse that he doubted that half a dozen men on the ship understood what they were about. When the business about Kuusikoski had arisen, for example, Doctor Solomon had announced his intention of preaching a sermon on the subject of superstition, and labored two solid days on it, finally preaching it the day after *Endymion* had finally been outrun. Proceeding from a biblical text on false idols, he had progressed to quaint and absurd superstitions of the ancient Greeks and Romans via a long digression about the Manichaean heresy; he had sprinkled his remarks with references to Descartes's deductive systems and quotations from Hegel and Kant in the original German, which he had translated himself while adding amusing verbal footnotes on the subject of comparative grammar and the problems posed by irregular verbs. It had been a well-informed, amusing chat, and would have made delightful dinnertable conversation, but there was no possibility of forcing the hands to listen to its like again, and when Doctor Solomon had proceeded the next Sunday to a lengthy examination, with amusing flings in every possible direction, concerning whether Christ's remark about the camel passing through the needle's eye was based on a misprint on the part of the original scribes, or possibly a mistranslation, Favian had looked forward at the restless sailors sitting discontented on their capstan-bar pews and scented mutiny on the wind.

"I was delighted, Doctor," he began, as easily as possible, "by the comprehensiveness of your sermon yesterday, by the very encyclopedic scope of it."

"Thank you, Captain Markham."

"It was, truly, unlike any sermon I have ever heard preached at sea before," Favian continued truthfully, wishing there was some way of heaving a deep-sea lead into this conversation, to help him to find his way. There were times when he wished he had Commodore Rodgers's bluntness, able to fix Solomon with a gimlet eye and growl "I don't want any more of these fucking philosophical sermons, Doctor! And don't'ee write that down!"

"I am happy my efforts were appreciated; I labored for days on it, sir, with scarcely an uninterrupted moment," the chaplain said, delighted. "It seems that every time I set down with my sermon and my books the trumpet would call the men to quarters, and I would find my cabin walls being broken down, my books flung willy-nilly into my trunk and carried down to the hold, and myself hustled down to the orlop in the company of the surgeon, to minister to the afflicted. Not that I am complaining, Captain; they were most stimulating drills, all of them, and the battle was very nice, a masterpiece truly. I am becoming quite enamored of the smell of powder."

"I am glad you are becoming acclimated. There was no trouble finding your sea legs?"

"Nay, Captain. I have a stomach of cast iron, sir, ate like a horse throughout that remarkable gale." The chaplain's smile was visible even in the faint light of the quarterdeck. "I very much enjoyed the action this afternoon. I watched it from the gun deck—remarkable, seeing that long row of guns in action! I've never seen the like."

"Your place, surely, is in the orlop with the surgeon."

"Oh, but there were no wounded to give comfort to," Solomon said. "I thought I might be permitted to witness the battle until I was needed. The thundering roars! The smoke! I felt quite at home."

Favian paused, reflected for a long moment on the navy's unofficial motto *Toujours l'audace,* and then spoke up.

"I wonder, Doctor, delightful and ingenious as your sermons are, if they might be somewhat over the heads of your audience?"

"Indeed?" Solomon said, his brow furrowing as he paced. "Efforts in a similar style have been received well at Princeton."

"I might beg to observe, Doctor, that man-of-war's men are rarely of the sophistication of graduates from the College of New Jersey. Not the wardroom, of course; they are all educated men there," Favian said, the falsehood springing readily to his lips. He rushed on, heedless of the consequences. "But the lower-deck men are different; they do not know your Hegel or Kant; they are not interested in your copyists' mistakes; they do not even know well the New Testament, ships' chaplains being more interested in the Old. Enlighten them, by all means, but keep close to your subject matter lest it be lost. A Princeton graduate may be able to keep your theme in mind while you track down a fascinating bit of etymology, but a man-of-war's man likes his preaching uncluttered, straight as the track of a ship so that he can follow it."

The chaplain seemed troubled. "Is that so? I am dismayed." He pursed his lips. "To what sort of thing are they used? I have not seen sea chaplains preach—pray tell me their usual subject matter."

Favian's brow furrowed as he considered the problem of how to tell this pleasant, sophisticated young man that all the hands expected from a preacher was the constant reiteration of the theme that, if they did not cease at once their drinking, swearing, chewing of tobacco, and the resentment of the officers whom God had seen fit to place over them, they would assuredly go to Hell. It was a message that, almost as a body, they would of course ignore, but it seemed to comfort them that the fundamentals of religion, as they saw religion, were being observed.

"They are more at home, I think, with a prescriptive preacher," Favian said. "It is what most of them remember from their Sunday schools, I suppose. They want to be told the difference between good and wickedness; they want to have a solid idea of sin."

Dr. Solomon gave a heavy sigh. "I have never liked those sort of pastors, Captain Markham. Those predestinarian sorts have such a Manichaean sense to their preaching: God on this side of the gulf, Satan on the other, and humanity all lined up for one or the other. All black and white, no gray at all." He looked out at the ship's glowing wake, his face faintly reflecting starlight and the light of the just-rising moon, and said firmly, "There is a great deal of gray in *my* character, Captain Markham, and I don't mind admitting it. I'm just not the prescriptive sort."

He turned away from the ship's wake, his hands clasped behind his back, and began to pace again. "That is the point I was trying to make about our witches. Kuusikoski is a sailor much like any other, it seems to me, an open, honest man, no sophistic falsehood in him, and half the crew has decided he's a villain and must be exorcised. Just because he's a foreigner and seems a little odd to them, suddenly he's on the wicked side of the gulf and ought to be got rid of." His voice grew stronger, his stance more upright. "Intolerance is the major villain I see, Captain Markham," he said heatedly. "Intolerance and unholy ignorance!"

"I venture to speculate," Favian said, "that you may have hit upon the subject of your next sermon."

Solomon stopped his pacing, looking up in surprise. "So I have, by God!" he said. He grinned, pleased with himself. "I'll give it to 'em!" he said, apparently unmindful of his own impulsive oath. "I'll give it to 'em double-shotted!" He looked at Favian, hesitating. "I *did* use that expression correctly, did I not?" he asked. "I *am* trying very hard to be seamanlike."

"You used it very well, Doctor." He felt a grin tugging at his lips. He did not have much use for religion personally; but as a navy man he appreciated its value in helping to preserve order in the face of man's natural anarchy. Anything Solomon could do in contributing to the orderly running of the ship would be appreciated.

"D'ye know," the chaplain said, lowering his voice. "I had a sailor approach me the other day—an old, steady hand, he seemed, old enough to know better—wondering if I could, as he put it, 'bless us up some holy water and let fly at the witch.' " Solomon laughed. "What a notion!"

Favian looked at him soberly. "Why not do as he suggests?" he said. "Throw in a few spells in Latin for good measure."

Solomon stopped dead in his tracks, a disbelieving smile on his face. "Surely you can't be serious!"

"If the men believe it will work," Favian said, "it may end the problem."

"But giving in so to superstition!" Solomon seemed appalled. "Next we'll be burning sheep on an altar!"

"Saaaail hooo!" cried a lookout from the forechains. From the tone it was Rees, from a Welsh colony in New York, a man who took seriously the notion of "singing out"—the words were delivered in a powerful tenor and sung to a solemn improvised melody. "Off the starboard bow! Right in the face of the moooon!"

Favian had snatched the night glass and had it trained in the right direction long before Rees finished his solo. The other ship was very close, perhaps only three miles to weather, its hull well above the horizon and slipping, as Favian adjusted his perception to the inverted image in the night glass, out of the disk of the moon. Now that he knew where to look he saw her clearly; he received the impression of a smaller vessel than his own, ship-rigged, traveling under topsails only and heading northwesterly, probably to clear the northern tip of Montserrat.

Macedonian was downwind of her, bound due north for Antigua on a converging course; if things stayed as they were the frigate would probably pass half a mile astern.

"Strike her, Jim." Favian heard the quartermaster walking forward to strike eight bells.

Suddenly Favian was shouting out orders, orders not formed consciously but rising rather from instinct, leaping fully formed from his mind once he'd seen the enemy ship and apprehended its position, the long years of experience at sea bringing the only sensible decisions to his mind and uttering them without thought. "Belay striking the bell! Call up the watch quietly! Main topmast stays'l and mizzen t'gallant stays'l! See to it, Mr. Ford!"

The wisdom of his first order was made apparent in the next few seconds when the clear sound of eight bells was heard from upwind. The frigate was only under topsails and forecourse, with the topgallants clewed up, ready to sheet home within minutes; Favian felt an impulse to clap on all sail to close the distance, but it was canceled by another instinct that didn't want to enlarge the frigate's silhouette; the staysails would have to suffice for the present until he got a better idea of the enemy ship.

The watch was turned up buzzing with speculation, in spite of Ford's repeated calls for silence; at least some of them had heard the lookout's sibilant cry and necks began craning to starboard as soon as they came out of the hatches. The remains of the wardroom party were on deck in minutes, all of them apparently steady on their feet, their familiar forms altered strangely by their boarding helmets with their hairy bearskin plumes; Hourigan relieved Ford formally of the deck, but Ford was no longer eager to go below. The staysails were set and Markham's Recording Log was hove to determine the new rate of speed; while the calculations were being made Favian saw through his glass that the angle was not good enough and ordered a change in course to the west, the ship heeling as it took the wind more abeam; the lines were still converging, but both ships would sail a longer distance before their paths crossed.

Favian glanced behind him, knowing there would be a half-hour at least before the ships came together in the night. *Macedonian* was near-invisible against the bulk of Montserrat behind them, and unless the other ship caught the gleam of moonlight on topsails it would go on being invisible for quite a while. He straightened, lowering the night glass. "Pass the word for the trumpeter," he said.

The trumpeter reported, his instrument gleaming in his left hand as he doffed his cap with his right. "I will clear for action shortly," Favian said, "and I *don't* want you blowing any calls! Not till I give the word—understand?"

"Aye aye, sir."

"Very well. Stay by my side until I need a call blown. Mr. Stone, clear the ship for action—very quietly, if you please."

There were the usual number of bangs and curses, but the ship's people understood the situation well enough, had done the job before in the dark, and kept the noise to a minimum. Favian kept his eye on the other ship—it was easy enough to see even without a telescope once he knew where to look—and was pleased enough when Stone reported the ship cleared in under nine minutes. The moon had cleared the horizon and hung yellow-red in the sky, gibbous; he could see its light gleaming off the ardent faces of the officers on the poop, eager as young hounds for the hunt, their brows and cheeks shaded by the shadows cast by the plumed iron-and-leather boarding helmets that looked in the dark like the helms of Arthurian legend. There could be promotion to weather, there, distinction and glory; the danger was, at this point, scarcely a consideration.

Favian saw the keen faces, the strong-willed and impetuous desire for honor, and, his professional instincts still commanding him, knew well how it could be used. He beckoned to Stone, who approached and saluted.

"Mr. Stone, I will try to run aboard her from leeward," he said. "I then propose to let you board her with a party of men. You can have all the larboard gun crews standing by; I'll release the rest as soon as you're securely aboard."

Stone's impassive face showed little, but his gleaming eyes betrayed him: should the mysterious sail turn out to be a warship, leading a party of boarders would be the making of him—he would be mentioned in Favian's report, and in any case were not the first officers of successful captains always promoted to command rank? Had not Favian, two years before, risen from Stephen Decatur's lieutenant to command of the *Experiment* brig and to the subsequent glory of Markham's Raid?

"Thank you, Captain Markham," said Lieutenant Stone, while Favian mentally added another item to his increasing mental file on his first lieutenant. Stone was not immune to the call of glory; his behavior, within certain limits, could be controlled by appealing to his desire for honor and advancement. A captain, Favian knew, needed such knowledge; his job involved manipulating not only his ship, working it in relation to the tides and wind, but manipulating the human cargo as well. He had just shown Stone and the others that he cared enough about their careers to offer them the chance for distinction; even if the black ship to windward turned out to be a Dutch neutral, Favian's offer would not be forgotten by the wardroom mess.

Favian took up his night glass and studied the apparition. There was something about that dark silhouette—perhaps the set of the sails was too precise; perhaps the fragment of hull visible above the horizon seemed too lean, too functional—but the sight aroused in Favian the suspicion that the mystery ship would not turn out to be a Dutch neutral, and would in fact prove to be a man-of-war. The suspicion grew as he looked through his glass; although he could not explain why he thought the ship an enemy, the conviction grew, and he returned the night glass to the rack and went below for his sword and pistols, telling Hourigan to call him if the other ship altered its course or showed sign of suspicion.

The pistols were those he had carried on Groton Long Point, the beautifully functional, well-balanced, gleaming weapons which his father had given him on the occasion of his promotion to lieutenant. They were a matched set of dueling pistols but had arrived too late for Favian's only duel with pistols, the duel that had provided his baptism of fire when he was seventeen, in which he and a Spanish *guardiamarina*, no older than Favian and probably as terrified, exchanged futile volleys at the drop of a handkerchief. He chose to wear his trustworthy Portsmouth hanger, the sword with which he'd run Gardell through on the Long Point, another professional memento of the Mediterranean, inscribed with the date of the raid on Tripoli harbor and the burning of the *Philadelphia*.

He put the pistols in his waistband and clipped the sword to his belt. He had performed the gestures often enough to be comfortable with them; without thinking he adjusted the pistols so that he would not be injured in the event of an accidental discharge; he took the boarding helmet from his wardrobe, heavy with the weight of the iron frame that supported the leather cap, and put it on his head, tying the hairy bearskin cheek pieces under his chin with their leather thongs.

The preparations were finished; they had been done purely by reflex, much as the orders on the poop a short while ago had been given solely on instinct, without conscious thought. He had slipped so easily into a specific persona, a grim automaton whose function in life was to maneuver a ship against an enemy and then to kill efficiently and swiftly, a mannequin consisting chiefly of professional reflexes built up over the years, reflexes that coldly assessed the situation, made decisions based on the assessments, and then acted to clear the frigate quietly for action, to silence a bell, to order a change in course in order to intercept a ship, to manipulate a subordinate by offering him the glory that he desired, to run alongside an unknown vessel and fire a broadside into its unresisting hull . . .

And so, he thought bitterly, the navy has won after all. He had spent his life resenting the navy's authority over his life, resenting the impulse to live his life to suit the navy's convenience, just as he had resented the deadly mannequin inside that was the navy's creation and servant. When he had taken *Macedonian* out to sea he'd fancied it a grand act of rebellion, an act at which the navy would recoil, appalled at the effrontery of it. He remembered his feeling of savage glee that first night on the *Macedonian*, his hand on the backstay feeling through its taut length the heartbeat of the living ship, knowing he had stolen the ship and it was *his*. But now the navy's creature had risen in him, and he knew that the act of rebellion had been foredoomed to failure. *Macedonian*'s cruise would be turned to the navy's account, after all, and he was himself back in the fold, a dutiful servant.

He returned to the poop, seeing a shadow by the ladder suddenly turn into Lazarus in a boarding helmet, his supposed messenger whose battle station was the quarterdeck. "Thou hast not forgot, Captain?" he asked in a harsh whisper. There was urgency in his lined face.

"Forgot? Forgot what, Lazarus?" Favian said, his annoyance at the interruption breaking into his voice.

"No Christian burial. A roundshot at my head," Lazarus said. Favian stood hesitating on the ladder, wondering what the lunatic was talking about, and then remembered the conversation on Groton Long Point, Lazarus foreseeing his own death. Was the fiddler still expecting to die? Apparently so.

"I remember," Favian said curtly, and came up the poop ladder. Lazarus seemed slumped, defeated somehow as he stood at the barricade; there was a sadness in his tone as he spoke.

"I warned thee of this. I warned thee no good would come of it."

Of this? An encounter with an enemy weaker and unsuspecting? The man was grasping at straws to maintain his own credibility. Favian made no reply but walked past Lazarus without breaking stride. He saw the officers standing on the poop, their plumed helmets heightening their silhouettes, and then saw a man bareheaded: Solomon, the chaplain.

"Doctor Solomon, I am surprised to see you here," Favian said. "Your place is in the orlop."

"There are no wounded there at present, Captain," Solomon said. "I hoped I might be allowed to remain."

Favian shrugged. "If you wish," he said. The position of the chaplain in combat was not one of the things he proposed to worry about.

"The other ship has shown no sign of observing us, Captain," Hourigan reported. His voice was hushed, as if he expected the other ship to overhear. Favian nodded, then turned to the weather rail and peered out.

He was surprised at how near the other ship had come during his moments below; there was no longer any need to use the long glass. He looked carefully at the darkened vessel: her spars seemed light, her hull gave an impression of grace and agility rather than strength. She was almost certainly smaller than *Macedonian*, but by what factor was difficult to determine; she could have been anything from an eighteen-gun ship-sloop to a thirty-two-gun frigate.

There was a clumping ascent of the poop ladder; Lieutenant Stone offered a salute. "Boarding party's ready, Captain."

"Very well, Mr. Stone."

The ships came closer: Favian could see individual stays and shrouds on the other vessel and still there was no sign that she had sensed *Macedonian*'s presence. The relative positions of the ships now clearer, Favian called minute corrections to the helm, making certain the frigate and the mystery ship would come gracefully together on the same spot of the ocean. Favian had the distinct impression that everyone aboard the frigate was holding his breath: except for the hissing of the sea beneath the hull, the gentle creaks of the ship's hull and masts, and the tapping of the reef points on the spanker overhead, Favian could hear nothing that indicated human presence.

"Pleasant night, Geoffrey," an English voice said. Favian saw the nervous grins on the faces of his officers as they realized where the voice had come from: it had traveled from the other ship, carried plainly on the wind.

"Yes," came the answer. "You startled me. I think I might have dozed off for a few seconds. Come up for a smoke?"

"Couldn't sleep. It's so blasted hot in my cabin. The windsail ain't drawing. Good God! What the hell is *that?*"

The last words were in abrupt contrast to the composed opening sentences, delivered almost in a hysterical scream. Favian smiled grimly; whatever the ship was, its revelation had come too late: *Macedonian* was three hundred yards to leeward and probably looked as big as Gibraltar to anyone on the smaller vessel. Anticipating events, Favian took a speaking trumpet from its rack.

"Ahoy there!" The voice had lost its hysterical edge, but was not entirely composed. "What ship is that?"

Favian had his answer ready. "HMS *Tiber*, Captain Dacres!" he roared back, trying to sound exceptionally British. "What ship are you?"

The *Tiber* was rated as a forty-four-gun ship, *Macedonian* as a thirty-eight; Favian had no objection to seeming larger than he was. He took his mouth away from the speaking trumpet and barked out an order to Seward, the sailing master. "I want the fore and main tops'ls set and drawing! We'll need some speed in a moment. Pass the signal for the larboard broadside to load and run out."

"Aye aye, Captain," Seward said, and sent the waisters to the halyards and braces.

"We are HMS *Carnation*, Captain Buckley," the voice, sounding ghostly with the distortion of the speaking trumpet, came back across the waters. "Why have you not made the private signal?"

"We just saw you, blast it!" Favian retorted. "Why haven't *you* signaled?"

There was the sudden rattle of a drum from the enemy ship, beating to the rhythm of "Heart of Oak"—more confirmation, if any were needed, that the mysterious ship was British. Favian heard the creaks of hinges as *Macedonian*'s port lids began to raise, revealing her long broadside; he tried to think what size a ship named *Carnation* would be. It didn't seem the sort of name to give a warship at all.

There was a heavy flapping aloft as the main topgallant was loosed, echoed instantly by the sound of the guns as they were run out the ports. Favian decided to end the pretense: with *Carnation* demanding the private signal there was no possibility of continuing the deception much longer.

"Two hundred yards' range!" he shouted. "All guns aim!"

He saw the captains of the quarterdeck carronades busily referring to the aiming slats on the deck as they wedged the squat guns around with their handspikes. Reports came back swiftly to the quarterdeck.

"Fo'c'sle battery aimed and ready, sir!"

"Quarterdeck battery aimed and ready, sir!"

"Main deck battery aimed and ready, sir!"

Favian glanced again at the enemy, hearing their rattling drum, the sound of feet racing to quarters, looking aloft just as his own main topgallant was sheeted home, feeling the increase in *Macedonian*'s speed. He judged the roll of the frigate, waiting for *Macedonian* to rise to a wave, hesitating before it slid into the trough, Preble's drill to create a stable gun platform. Now.

"All guns fire!" Favian roared into his speaking trumpet.

The result was blinding, great yellow flashes gushing from the guns, lapping the surface of the waves as they bellowed shot at the enemy. The quarterdeck carronades came leaping in to the limits of their tackles, hurling their heavy iron; Favian could hear the crashes aboard the *Carnation* as the shot struck her. For a moment the British drum stopped, awed into silence, and then continued to gamely rattle away, drowned, however, by the staccato shrieks of an injured man.

He could no longer hear individual voices on the enemy quarterdeck; everything was in chaos there. His own gun crews were busy reloading; Favian coughed gunsmoke from his lungs and peered through the smoke at the enemy. "Put down the helm, Mr. Seward," he called. "Let's get nearer." He shouted out orders for the guns to aim using the hundred yards' mark, and to add grape on top of the roundshot; the fore topgallant was sheeted home and *Macedonian* began its turn toward the enemy.

"All guns fire!" The flashes spilled out again, reaching like talons for the *Carnation*'s bulwark. This time the drum was silenced; Favian could hear the thudding of feet on *Carnation*'s deck and wondered if their crew were stampeding for the hatches.

Macedonian surged nearer, and Favian began plotting his approach; he didn't want to get his jibboom caught in the enemy rigging and broken off. There was the sound of a musket shot; the enemy had finally replied, a pathetic answer to the overwhelming American cannonade. The *Carnation*'s sails were stealing *Macedonian*'s wind and that complicated the equation.

"Commence firing by section!" Favian ordered; that would end the distraction caused by firing regular broadsides. "Helm up a spoke, there—very good. Hold her . . . hold her . . ." Two carronade sections fired out almost as one, followed by a section in the main battery. "Helm up! Hands to the grapples!" Another main deck section cracked out; he could hear the grapeshot whizzing over the enemy's decks. *Carnation* looked a very small ship indeed with *Macedonian* right alongside, her spar deck much lower than the frigate's. There was a shock as the hulls grated together, rebounding until Favian put his helm down again and brought them firmly together.

"Grapples away! Mr. Stone, assemble your party—good luck, there," Favian said, his eyes meeting his lieutenant's, sparing time for a curt nod, knowing that, too, would not be forgotten. The fo'c'sle guns fired, lapping at *Carnation*'s foremast rigging.

"Cease fire!" Favian bellowed. "Where's the trumpeter?"

"Here, sir." The man stepped out from the lee side, where he'd been keeping out of the way. A musket shot banged out from enemy decks.

"Sound 'boarders away'!" Favian said, and saw the man's answering smile.

"Aye aye, sir." The staccato trumpet call sounded high and clear above the sound of the two locked ships, and was soon answered from below decks by "battle rattles," simple wooden noisemakers calling the hands to the weapons tubs to seize cutlasses and pikes, and then away. A roar began down on the gun deck as the men took their weapons and began to pour up out of the well; Favian caught a glimpse of Stone straddling the hammock nettings, waving his sword, and then a dark wave of American seamen swarmed over the bulwarks into the enemy.

Boarding was a doubtful tactic if resorted to in normal battle; the enemy was almost certain to be able to seize their close-quarters weapons and repel the boarders as they struggled from one ship to another. This was different: *Carnation* was totally surprised; her boarding nets had not been rigged; her men had not cleared her for action. Favian suspected the boarding might not even be resisted.

Resisted it was: Favian heard the clash of steel on steel, but it soon faded and there was nothing but the sound of American voices bellowing in triumph. Favian walked across the quarterdeck—he was almost alone, save for the shadow by the mizzenmast that was Lazarus and a few other figures: Stanhope his signal midshipman and Crane his steward, Seward the master and the tall figure of his coxswain, the Finn Kuusikoski, who stood on the bulwark, one hand on a mizzen backstay, peering down at the fight below.

There were three cheers from the captured ship, and Favian came to the rail and waved his boarding helmet in acknowledgment, shouting down, "Three cheers for Mr. Stone!" The cheers came floating up from below, and when Stone came aboard the frigate, carrying a bundle in one hand and smiling a buoyant, entirely uncharacteristic smile, Favian stepped forward to shake his hand in congratulations. "You have captured yourself a warship, sir!" Favian said. "I trust you will have no objection to acting as her captain?"

No, Stone decidedly did not; his smile actually broadened. Favian saw a bare-headed figure behind the first lieutenant, a man carrying a cutlass and wearing a devil-may-care grin, and he felt surprise enter.

"Doctor Solomon?" he asked. "Is that you?"

"Indeed it is, sir!" Solomon answered, the words bubbling from him as he waved his bloody cutlass. "I've made surgeon's meat of two of them! I carved them like mutton!"

"Indeed? I am surprised," Favian said. He looked at his first lieutenant for an explanation. "Mr. Stone?"

"Doctor Solomon could not be restrained," Stone said, looking back at the chaplain. "He was first on the enemy decks. I couldn't hold him back."

"I am pleased to find a staff officer so zealous," Favian said, "but we are certain to have a few wounded. I hope, Doctor Solomon, you will tend to your more eleemosynary duties as well."

Solomon's smile faded; he lowered his cutlass. "Aye, Captain," he said. "I will do that." He turned to go below.

Stone leaned closer, speaking in a low voice. "Sir," he said. "I have some important news. They didn't have time to throw their secret papers overboard. I've got the lot, here in my arms," he said, indicating his bundle. Favian recognized the heavy volumes with their weighted lead covers, covers that were supposed to carry the secret books to the ocean's bottom in the event of capture. "Logbook, secret orders, signals. Everything, sir. We've got it all."

22

The *Carnation* was a corvette rated at twenty-four guns but carrying twenty-eight—most warships, including *Macedonian,* carried more guns than their official rate—bringing dispatches and mail from Fayal, in the Azores, to Negril Bay in Jamaica. Favian had spent the entire night with the lead-cased books and the thick dispatches, heavy with Admiralty seals, that had been found in sacks weighted with lead bars for disposal.

It was entirely due to Lieutenant Adrian Stone that the documents had been preserved. The British Captain Buckley had been wounded in the leg by a splinter at the second broadside; he'd had the bleeding stopped and remained on the quarterdeck until it was overrun, when he'd surrendered, but he had not been able to see personally to the secret papers, as he was supposed to. When Lieutenant Stone had gone over the rail at the head of his boarding party he'd gone straight for the corvette's aft scuttle, securing the surrender of Captain Buckley on the way; he'd charged down the scuttle at the head of a gang of men, shot with his pistol the marine guard at the captain's door, and pushed through it. His sword had cut to the brain the captain's clerk as he was in the very act of opening a window to toss the dispatches out. Stone had placed a guard over the secret papers, then returned to the deck to complete the corvette's capture.

The result had been not only the capture of the documents, but their *secret* capture. Captain Buckley had been wounded, but could assume that his clerk had disposed of the documents, and the only persons who knew otherwise, the marine guard and the captain's clerk, were dead. When Stone had brought the secret papers back, he'd made certain all the surviving British had been battened below, so no one could see the transfer of the documents to *Macedonian*.

Adrian Stone well deserved any mention that Favian could give him in dispatches, and deserved truly any promotion that came from that mention. For not only had he uncovered the signal books, which in themselves could prove of enormous value, but as Favian read the other documents he began, with increasing astonishment, to piece their story together, and discovered that when assembled they detailed nothing less than the latest attempt by the British to achieve domination of the North American continent. An attempt which, Favian realized as he read, seemed almost guaranteed to succeed, unless Favian and the crew of the *Macedonian* could somehow intervene . . .

At six o'clock in the morning Favian threw down the letter he was reading—without any hesitation he'd broken into the private mailbags as well—sent for another pot of coffee, and requested Mr. Stone's attendance as soon as it was convenient. He would have breakfast with Captain Buckley in two hours—the courtesy was customary—and he wanted to have his officers working at the new tasks he wanted to assign as soon as possible. He rubbed his temples, feeling a new urgency warring with his weariness. Not a moment could be lost.

There was a knock on the door; Stone and the coffee came at the same instant. Favian's greeting was in keeping with the sense of terse exigency that he'd felt rising in him as he'd read the British dispatches.

"Sit down, Mr. Stone. Crane, pour coffee for two and go about your other business."

The coffee's warmth brought with it an urge to lie down and snatch some sleep, an urge Favian fought. A leisurely night cruise between two British Caribbean islands had, in the space of a few short hours, turned into an occasion that would shortly send two ships piling on every sail and carrying urgent news to two different American coasts. *Macedonian*'s original mission, the cruise to the Indian Ocean, would have to be postponed at least for two months, possibly forever. Crane handed Stone his cup of coffee and left the cabin.

"Mr. Stone," Favian said, "I intend to give you *Carnation* and orders to take her to the United States with all possible speed. You can have thirty men—I can't spare any more, for reasons that will become apparent—you can have the midshipman of your choice, a master's mate, and a bosun's mate. I have every confidence that even with such a reduced crew you can make a safe landfall. You will be carrying dispatches of the utmost urgency, along with a copy my clerk is making of the British signals. The signals are good for another two months— they should allow you to enter the port of your choice, and when distributed among American ships may allow many of them to make their escape."

"Thank you, sir. I am gratified for your confidence," Stone said, as composed as usual. "There were twelve Americans on board *Carnation*—at least they claim they're Americans—and they've volunteered for the navy. That will help make up our losses. As to my officers, I will take Mr. Pratt, if I may, and Connor and Dutilleul."

"We'll be paroling the British later this morning, and putting them ashore on the windward side of Montserrat, where we'll be able to work in close without being shot by the fort. I hope to have the business concluded and get *Carnation* and *Macedonian* under way by afternoon."

"It will mean a lot of work, sir. The men haven't had much sleep."

"It will be necessary. The dispatches you rescued from the drink will make it imperative." Favian took another drink of coffee and rubbed his forehead, trying to penetrate the fog of sleep that was trying to overcome him. He looked up at Stone's determined face.

"My clerk is writing your orders, and transcribing two reports," he said. "Your orders are simple: you are to take *Carnation* to the most convenient American port and get to land with your dispatches. Charleston, Wilmington, Savannah if necessary . . . Norfolk if you have to, though you'll probably never get out again.

"Once in an American port, you will hire a horse and ride

flat-out for Fredericktown, or Philadelphia, or Blodget's Hotel in Washington, or wherever the government is now. If you're not a good horseman, hire a post-chaise and ride day and night—I'll give you the money if you need it."

"Not necessary, sir," Stone murmured.

"Once you've found the seat of the government, you will seek out Mr. William Jones, the secretary of the navy, and give him two dispatches, in addition to the British signal book," Favian continued wearily. "The signal book can be copied during your voyage to the States, and a copy delivered to the naval authorities in port. The first dispatch is a brief note detailing *Carnation*'s capture, suitable for publication, as is the custom, in the newspapers. The other details the information we received thanks to your prompt action earlier this morning, and is to be given only to Mr. Jones personally. If Mr. Jones is not in residence, you will attempt to deliver it to the President, or if necessary Mr. Monroe, the secretary of war."

"Yes, sir." Lieutenant Stone hesitated for a moment, then spoke up. "May I be informed as to its contents, sir?"

"Aye," Favian said. "It may help you to make any difficult decisions that may fall to you." He leaned back into his chair, feeling suddenly invigorated, entirely awake now, the coffee having at last had its required effect. He clasped his hands over his head and stretched, forcing blood into his long limbs.

"*Carnation* formed part of a squadron that left Plymouth a month ago," he said. "The other ships were the *Plantagenet* seventy-four under Captain Robert Lloyd, and the *Rota* thirty-eight, Captain Philip Somerville. Three weeks ago they put into Fayal for water, and encountered an American privateer there, the *General Armstrong*."

"The *General Armstrong* that took the *Queen* last year?" Stone asked. "That would be Captain Champlin, would it not?"

"The same ship, I'm sure," Favian said. The *General Armstrong* was a well-known American privateer; it had taken at least forty enemy during its long career and was the envy of many a navy man, even those who affected to despise privateers as mercenary irregulars. "But these dispatches indicate the captain was Samuel Reid."

"That would be Captain Reid of New York," Stone said, demonstrating again his lightning memory for names. "A good man."

"Despite the neutrality of Fayal, Captain Lloyd decided to attack the *Armstrong*," Favian continued. "He made three boat attacks in one day, employing the hundreds of men he had available. All three attacks failed. In his dispatch Captain Lloyd admits to sixty-three dead and a hundred ten wounded. The dead include *Roca*'s first and third lieutenants, and the second lieutenant and purser of the *Roca* were wounded. *Plantagenet* also lost three of her lieutenants killed or wounded."

"Good God," said Stone, awed. There was a moment of silence as they envisioned the action implied by the statistics: the embattled privateer surrounded by a swarm of boats, her crew, outnumbered perhaps ten to one, striking out with pike and cutlass at the men swarming up her rails. *Sixty-three dead!* That was more than Favian, with the full broadside of the *United States* in action, had inflicted on the *Macedonian* during her capture. And commanders tended to be less than candid when reporting their casualties: it was possible that Captain Lloyd had lost more men than he'd indicated.

"The next day *Carnation* warped in close to destroy the *Armstrong* with gunfire, but was shot up and had to retire. She came in later in the day, after repairing her damage and supported by *Plantagenet*, and succeeded in forcing Reid to abandon ship with his men and scuttle the privateer. Lloyd put men ashore to try to arrest Reid's men, but they fortified themselves in an old castle in the interior and hauled up the drawbridge, and Captain Lloyd admits he can't get at them without artillery."

He felt a grin tugging at his lips at the absurdity of it, at the sheer Gothic imagery of Captain Reid shouting defiance at a British commodore from the barbican of an ancient Portuguese castle. It had been, all along, more of a siege than a naval action, the privateers and British boarders hacking at each other with modern versions of chivalric weapons, with cutlasses and pikes—but even with its medieval flavor, the privateer from New York had inflicted more casualties on the Royal Navy than any other action during the entire conflict. It was, perhaps, the Bunker Hill of Mr. Madison's War.

"At any rate, Captain Lloyd can't move *Plantagenet* and *Roca* from Fayal until he buries his men, makes up some of his losses in officers, and somehow captures Captain Reid," Favian said. "So he took away half *Carnation*'s crew and all of her lieutenants, then sent her with his apologies to his squadron's destination, Negril Bay in Jamaica. She was severely understrength, and her men had been making repairs all the way across the Atlantic—no wonder they were so tired they fell asleep on watch last night. And now, thanks to Captain Samuel Reid of New York and the crew of the *General Armstrong* privateer, the plans for British action in the Gulf of Mexico have fallen into our hands. More coffee, Mr. Stone?"

"Thank you, sir."

He could feel Stone's eyes on him as he poured, fully aware of the suspense he was creating. He ended it as quickly as he could.

"It's New Orleans, Mr. Stone," he said flatly. "Cochrane's fleet from the Chesapeake is waiting at Negril Bay, along with General Ross's army that burned Washington. They're waiting for reinforcements from the British forces in France, and for the new commander they'll need now that Ross has been killed at Baltimore. Five thousand troops under Sir Edward Packenham, who I gather is one of Wellington's protégés. The soldiers are all Wellington's best, veterans of the Peninsula—there's a list somewhere here," he said, rummaging through the papers on his desk. "Here it is. See for yourself—the 95th Rifles, the 93rd Highlanders, the 85th, the 7th, and 43rd Foot. Ross's army already had the 21st, 4th, and 44th—and they'll have the West Indian Corps as well. They'll draw marines from Cochrane's fleet. An overwhelming force. There's no possibility of New Orleans being prepared for this."

Favian could see Stone's stunned surprise. "Good heavens, sir," he said, and fell silent. Stone took a hasty sip of his coffee, and then looked up, the alarm plain on his face.

"What can we do, Captain?" he asked.

"You can take *Carnation* to Secretary Jones as quickly as you can," Favian said. "And I'll sail *Macedonian* to New Orleans with every stitch of sail I can raise aloft. Every minute counts. If New Orleans is warned they may be able to raise a force in their defense, and if Packenham and Cochrane can be delayed a force may be able to get downriver in time. That's why the Cabinet has to be informed."

"Yes, sir," Stone said. He leaned back in his chair, all sign of weariness gone, his expression grimmer than usual. "Pray God it will be enough."

Favian made no reply. He knew what the loss of the Mississippi's mouth would mean to the United States. All the land west of the Appalachians, all the land that men had died for at Tippecanoe, Fort Dearborn, and the Thames, was rich, some of it incredibly so—but the riches were useless without the control of the Mississippi. The goods produced in the American interior could only with difficulty be sent in wagons over the passes of the Appalachians; the easiest route to market was down the Ohio and Mississippi in flatboats to the wharves of the Crescent City, New Orleans. The value of the Ohio and Mississippi was obvious; that was why Robert Fulton had been building steamboats at Pittsburgh almost immediately after he'd first put them on the Hudson.

Since the days when old Benjamin Franklin held the post of American minister in Paris, American diplomacy had aimed at securing New Orleans, either getting the city outright or acquiring the assurances of Spain that American commerce would be welcomed. Even back in Franklin's day, it was realized that the future growth of the United States of America was dependent upon the use of the Mississippi.

British policy during the war had consisted of attempts to encircle the United States, hemming in the northwest with an Indian empire under Tecumseh, restricting American growth in the Gulf of Mexico by encouraging the Creek rising, and blockading the entire eastern seaboard. Tecumseh was dead and the Creeks had been crushed at Horseshoe Bend, but now Whitehall was aiming at New Orleans and would probably succeed. It was easy enough to see what would happen once the British had possession of the Mississippi's mouth. American commerce from the interior could be crushed simply by raising the tariffs, making it unprofitable to trade at all. The entire economy of the American interior would collapse like a punctured kite. The western expansion of the United States would end, hemmed in by Canada to the north and New Orleans to the south, and whatever profit was offered by the American west would be gained by the British.

The United States of America would be confined to the eastern seaboard, and its commerce would remain a coastal one, easily blockaded by the British in pursuit of their own ends. The rest of North America would belong to a corrupt, cynical Old World empire, run for the benefit of its own privileged upper class, and whatever hope the new American republic held out to the rest of the world would be gone forever.

There had been, fortunately, a few hitches in the British plan. General Ross had been unexpectedly killed by an American sharpshooter at Baltimore, which delayed the British for the length of time it took to find a replacement. Another delay had been created, quite inadvertently, by Captain Samuel Reid of the *General Armstrong*, in combination with the belligerent stupidity of Captain Lloyd. If another few delays could be created, the British schedule of conquest might be thrown into severe dislocation.

Macedonian could make the difference. With New Orleans alerted to the danger, perhaps enough troops could be concentrated in the area to repel Packenham. It would be a race, whether *Macedonian* could carry news of the danger to New Orleans in order for an American army to be assembled. If the American army could not be assembled in time, *Macedonian*'s own strength would simply have to try to delay the British assault if it could.

If it couldn't, the result would be the loss of New Orleans, the *Macedonian,* and whatever hope the United States had for coming out of the war with its promise intact. The stakes were enormous, but the few cards held by the young republic were poor. They would have to be played with skill. Favian, a skilled player, knew the awesome weight of the enemy's cards, and he knew where they would be played. He would have to hope that the knowledge would be enough to forestall disaster.

23

"Give way, there! Smartly!" Vihtori Kuusikoski leaned on the tiller of the big thirty-six-foot pinnace, bringing it away from *Carnation*'s rolling side. His heart leaped as he looked back to see the two warships, hove to, their black hulls with their yellow ochre stripes contrasting with the translucent blue of the sea, surrounded by the little boats that were taking the British prisoners to safety on Montserrat's dark volcanic sands. *Home,* Kuusikoski thought. *Macedonian* was his home; he knew now that he'd earned his place.

As coxswain of *Macedonian*'s largest and steadiest boat, he had been assigned to bring the British wounded to shore: they lay on the thwarts, pale and bloodless, men with their limbs bandaged or ending in swaddled, red-stained cloths, one redcoated marine sitting listlessly on his thwart, still wearing the battered remnants of a shako that had been torn in half by grapeshot, his right hand and both legs bandaged. They would have to be got to shore somehow; they could not be expected to swim or wade through the surf, so Kuusikoski would have to bring the pinnace right up to the sand, through the waves that could so easily capsize her and pitch her living cargo into the deadly foam. It would not be easy, but Kuusikoski knew he could do it. Boats were easy for him.

He had served his gun well the night before; his quarterdeck carronade had fired more shots into the enemy than any other, and done it right under the nose of the captain. When the order to secure the guns had been given, Kuusikoski's gun captain had clapped him on the shoulder and roared his laughing congratulations.

He was a part of *Macedonian*'s crew now. The running fight with the British squadron had changed the spirit of the frigate, and the notion that Kuusikoski had been some sort of Jonah had been banished. The surgeon's assistants had brought word to the men that he had tried to make his way on deck to help them fight, even after the others had allowed him to be beaten; the story had helped. The men in his mess ate with him now, and men smiled greetings as he met them below decks. There were those he would have to avoid, Richards and Lazarus and a few others, but their menace was reduced, and they knew it; the other hands would protect him now, and his enemies dared do nothing but mutter. Besides, any sailor on a ship with nearly four hundred other men would be bound to make a few enemies. It was nothing he couldn't live with.

He steered the pinnace toward the roaring surf, seeing the British that had been landed earlier grouping on the beach, ready to help the wounded out of the boat and to the sand. It was a day, it seemed, of reconciliation. The British and Americans working together to bring the wounded to safety, Kuusikoski and the men who had distrusted him working together as if nothing had happened. It was a splendid thing.

"Stroke! Stroke! Fast now!" Kuusikoski called to the oarsmen. He stood up in the sternsheets, hearing the surf roaring about him, flecks of foam sprinkling his face and hands. His eyes danced as the pinnace lurched in the waves; he heard the grating roar of sand as the wave ebbed away. Behind, he knew, the *Macedonian* rode on the waves, his ship. After five years of wandering, Vihtori Kuusikoski had found a place he belonged, a home with bulwarks of wood.

UNHOLY MOURNING
DAVID LIPPINCOTT

All her life, Angie Psalter felt she was buried alive in the sleepy town tucked obscurely into a corner of Northern Michigan. Nothing ever happens—until Angie meets handsome, brilliant Jorbie Tenniel. His love, so overwhelming that it exceeds her wildest dreams, ignites her life with passion and excitement.

And then, one by one, people begin dying, mourning for their lost loved ones. Angie's dreams change to nightmares as she is led to the abyss of unnameable terror. The agonizing horror begins!

A DELL BOOK   19224-2 $3.50

At your local bookstore or use this handy coupon for ordering:

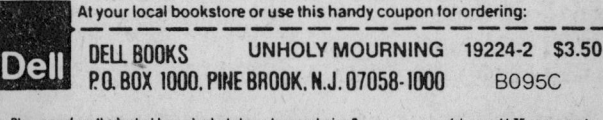

Dell	DELL BOOKS	UNHOLY MOURNING 19224-2 $3.50
	P.O. BOX 1000, PINE BROOK, N.J. 07058-1000	B095C

Please send me the books I have checked above. I am enclosing $ _____ (please add 75c per copy to cover postage and handling). Send check or money order—no cash or C.O.D.'s. Please allow up to 8 weeks for shipment.

Name _____

Address _____

City _____ State/Zip _____

By the bestselling author of the *Wagons West series*

YANKEE

by Dana Fuller Ross

A rich and historical saga that will carry you back to Revolutionary America. From the shores of a young nation to the fabled Ottoman empire, a young man sailed in search of honor, adventure and love.

A Dell Book $3.50   **19841-0-20**

At your local bookstore or use this handy coupon for ordering:

Dell DELL BOOKS   YANKEE $3.50   19841-0-20
P.O. BOX 1000, PINE BROOK, N.J. 07058-1000   B095A

Please send me the above title. I am enclosing $ _____ (please add 75c per copy to cover postage and handling). Send check or money order—no cash or C.O.D.'s. Please allow up to 8 weeks for shipment.

Mr./Mrs./Miss _____

Address _____

City _____ State Zip _____